The Little Fox & Tanuki

KORISENMAN

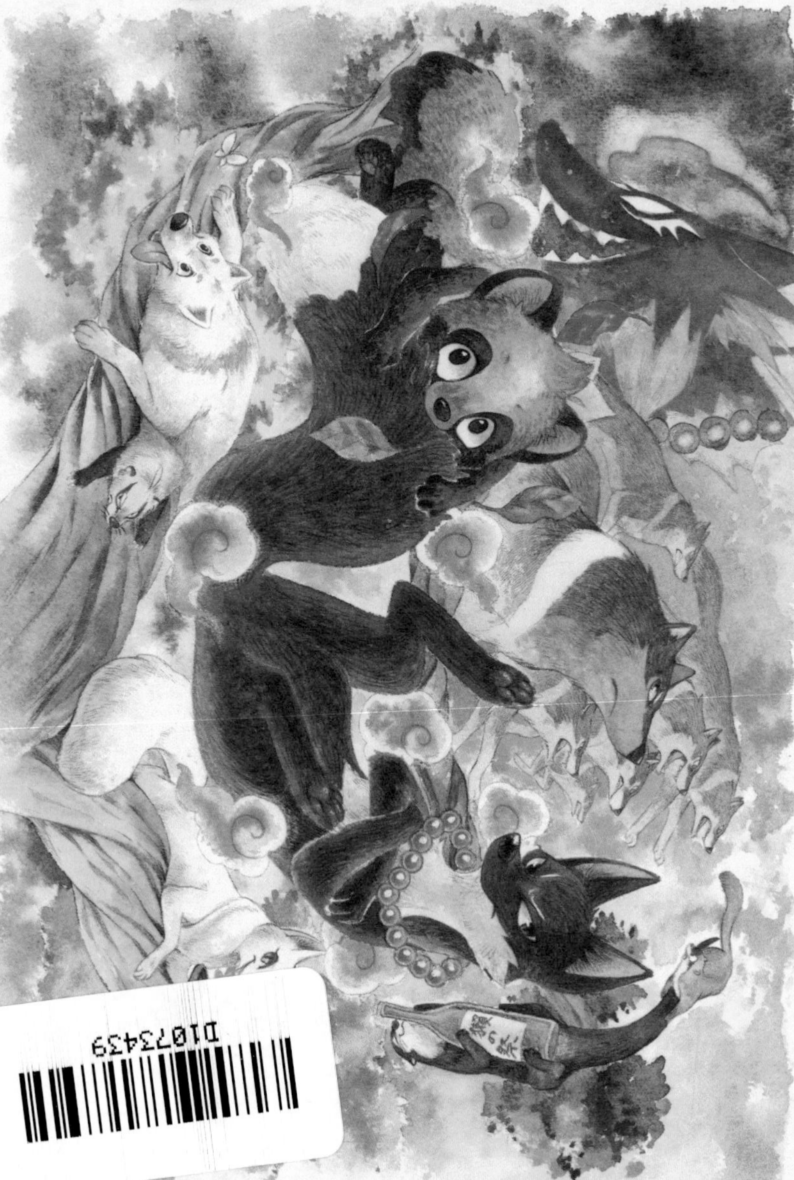

The Little Fox & Tanuki

KORISENMAN

Mi Tagawa

Table of Contents

The Little Fox & Tanuki
KORISENNAN

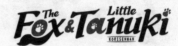

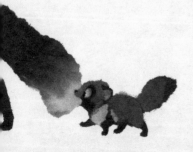

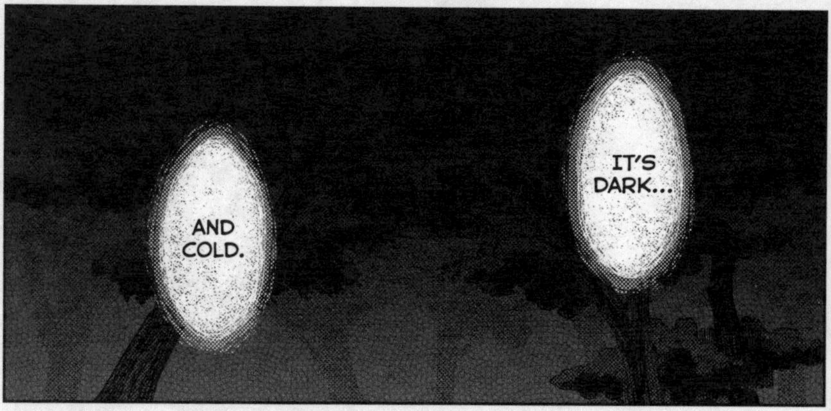
IT'S DARK...
AND COLD.

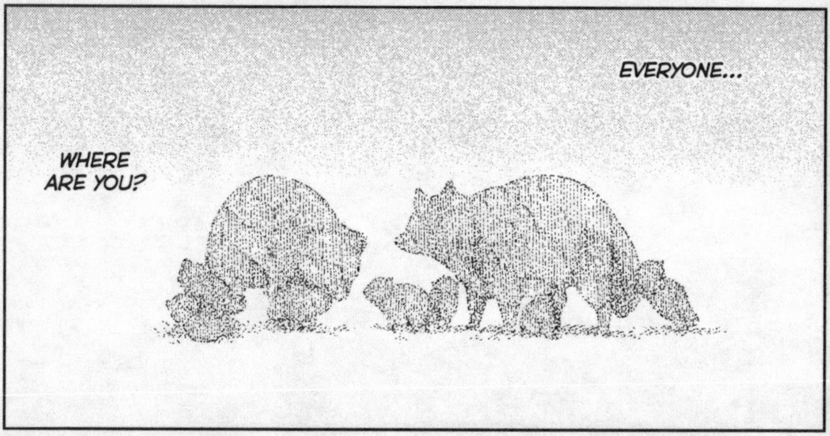
EVERYONE...
WHERE ARE YOU?

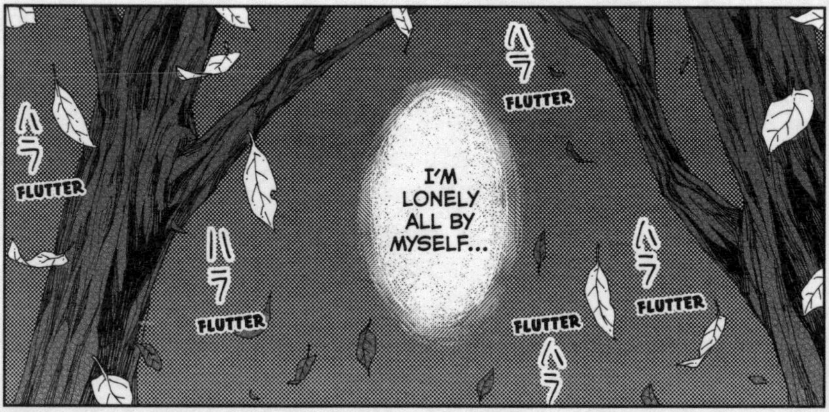
ハラ FLUTTER
ハラ FLUTTER
I'M LONELY ALL BY MYSELF...
FLUTTER ハラ
ハラ FLUTTER
ハラ FLUTTER
ハラ FLUTTER

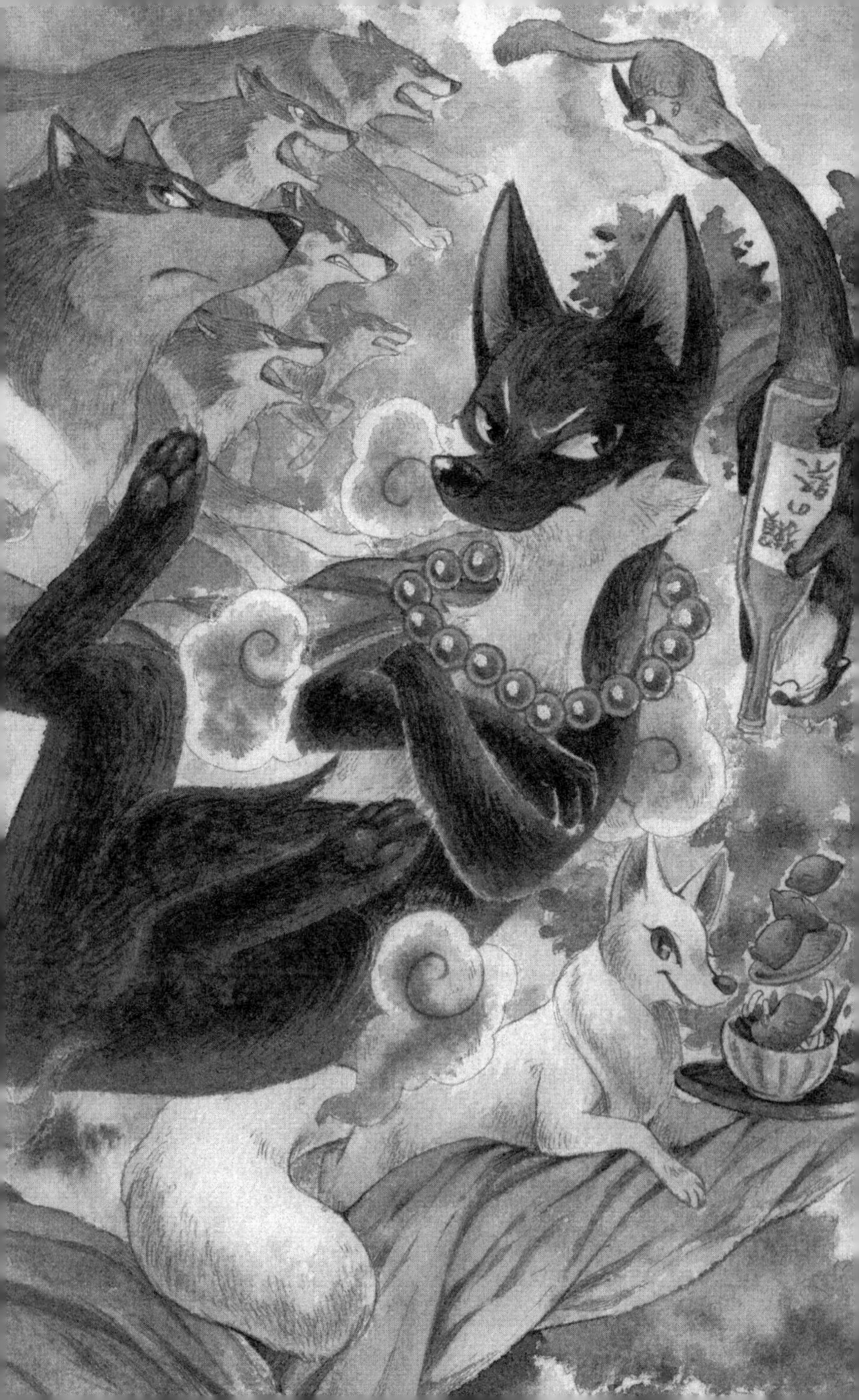

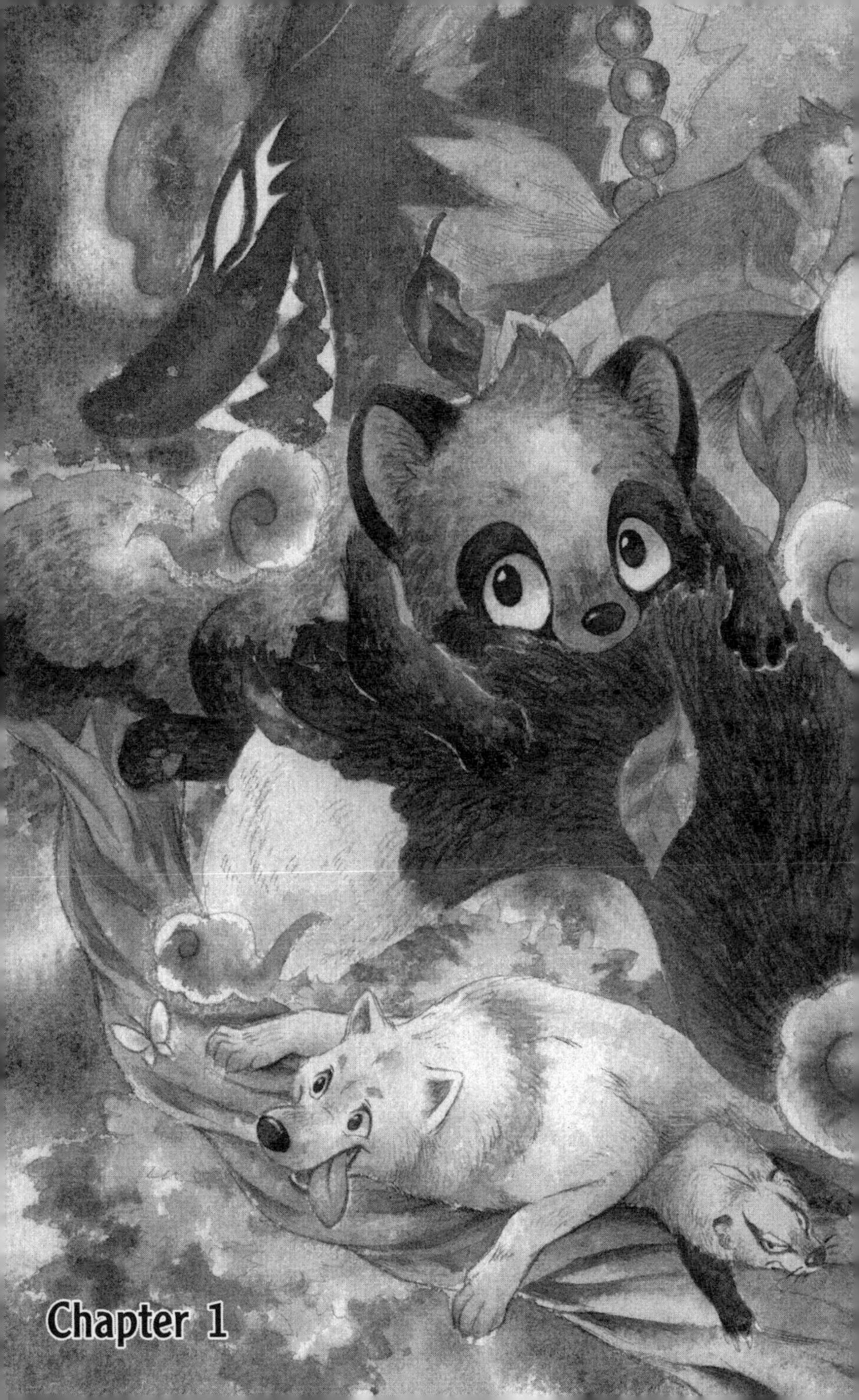
Chapter 1

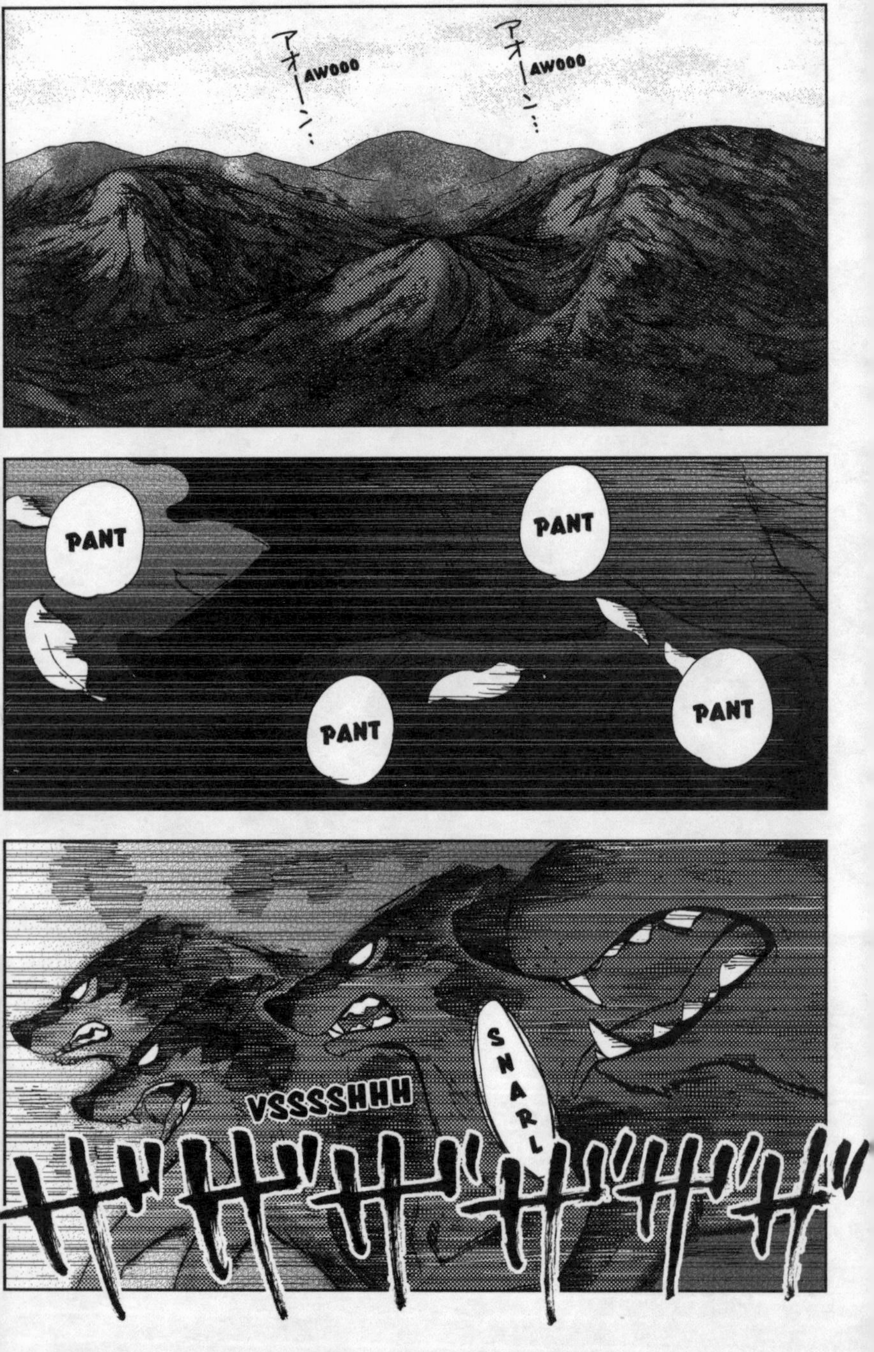
アオーン…
AWOOO
アオーン…
AWOOO
PANT
PANT
PANT
PANT
SNARL
VSSSSHHH
ザザザザザザ

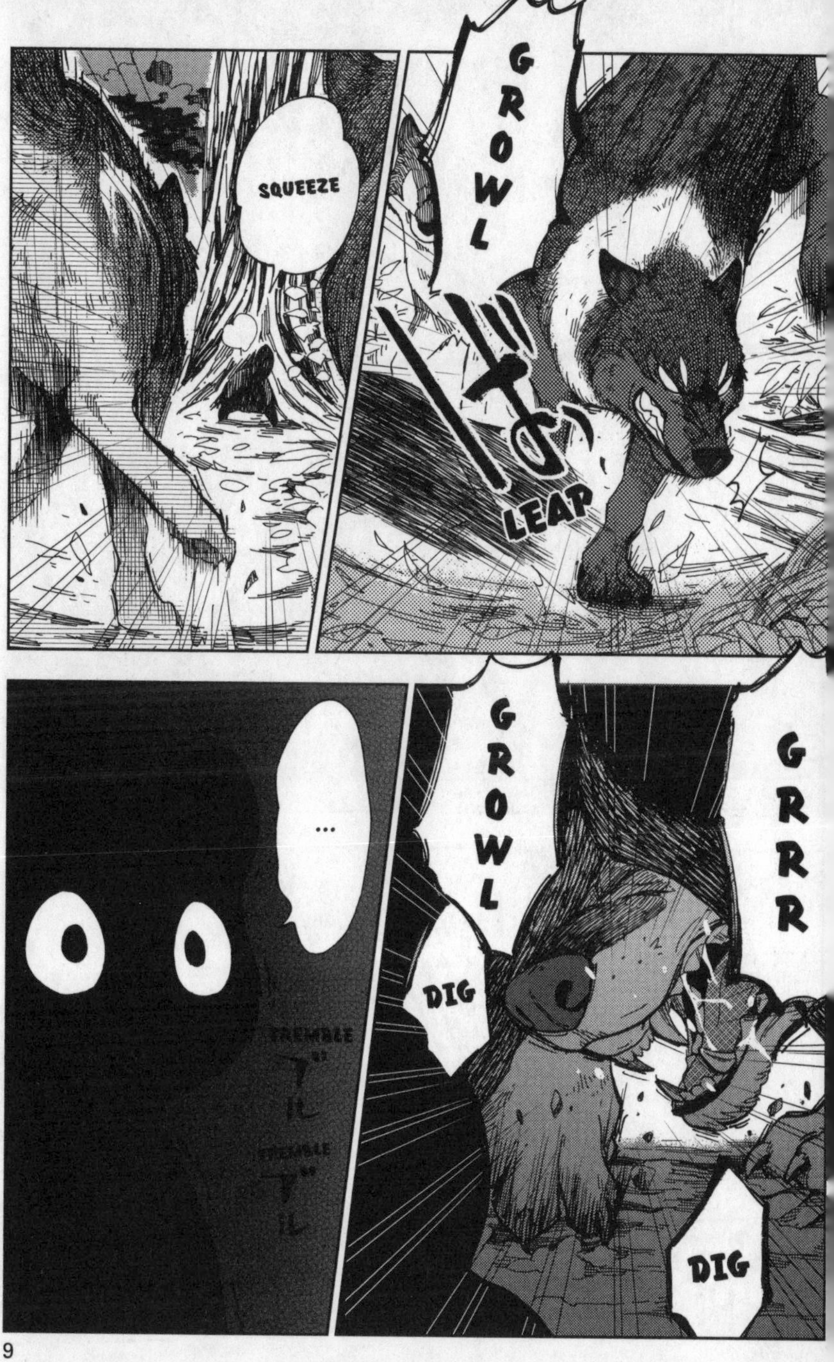
GROWL
LEAP
SQUEEZE
GROWL
GRRR
DIG
DIG
...
TREMBLE
TREMBLE

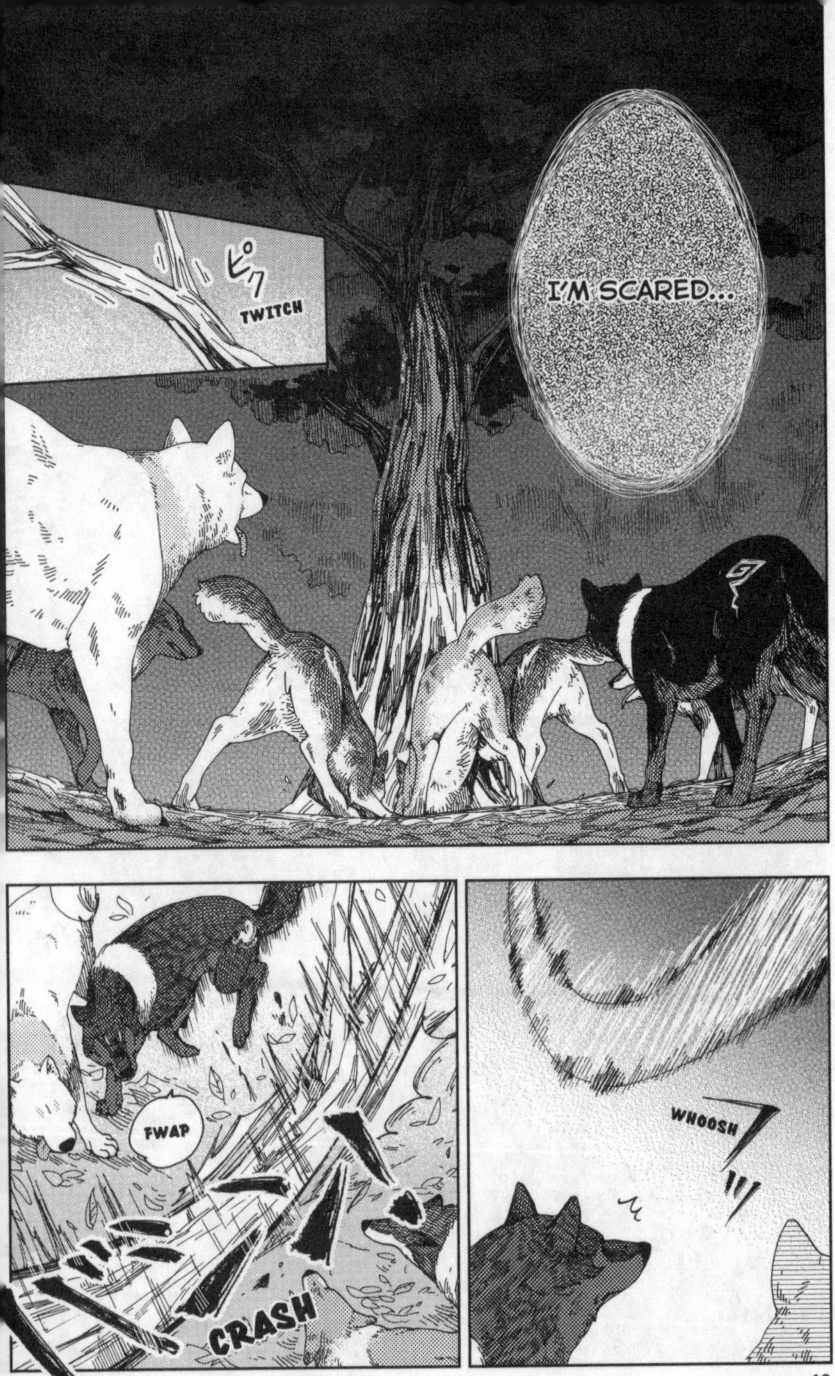
I'M SCARED...
ピク
TWITCH
WHOOSH
FWAP
CRASH

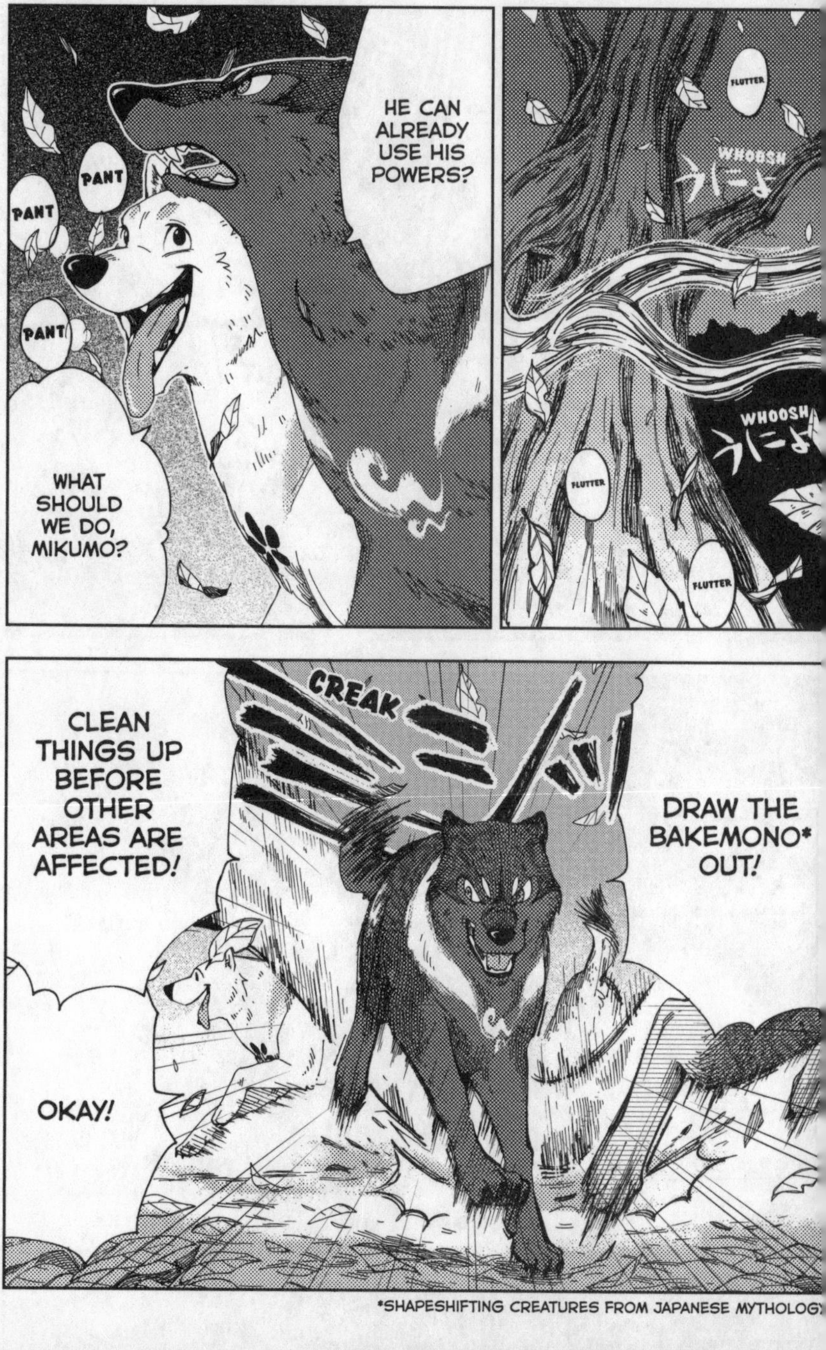
FLUTTER
WHOOSH
WHOOSH
FLUTTER
FLUTTER
HE CAN ALREADY USE HIS POWERS?
PANT
PANT
PANT
WHAT SHOULD WE DO, MIKUMO?
DRAW THE BAKEMONO* OUT!
CREAK
CLEAN THINGS UP BEFORE OTHER AREAS ARE AFFECTED!
OKAY!

*SHAPESHIFTING CREATURES FROM JAPANESE MYTHOLOGY

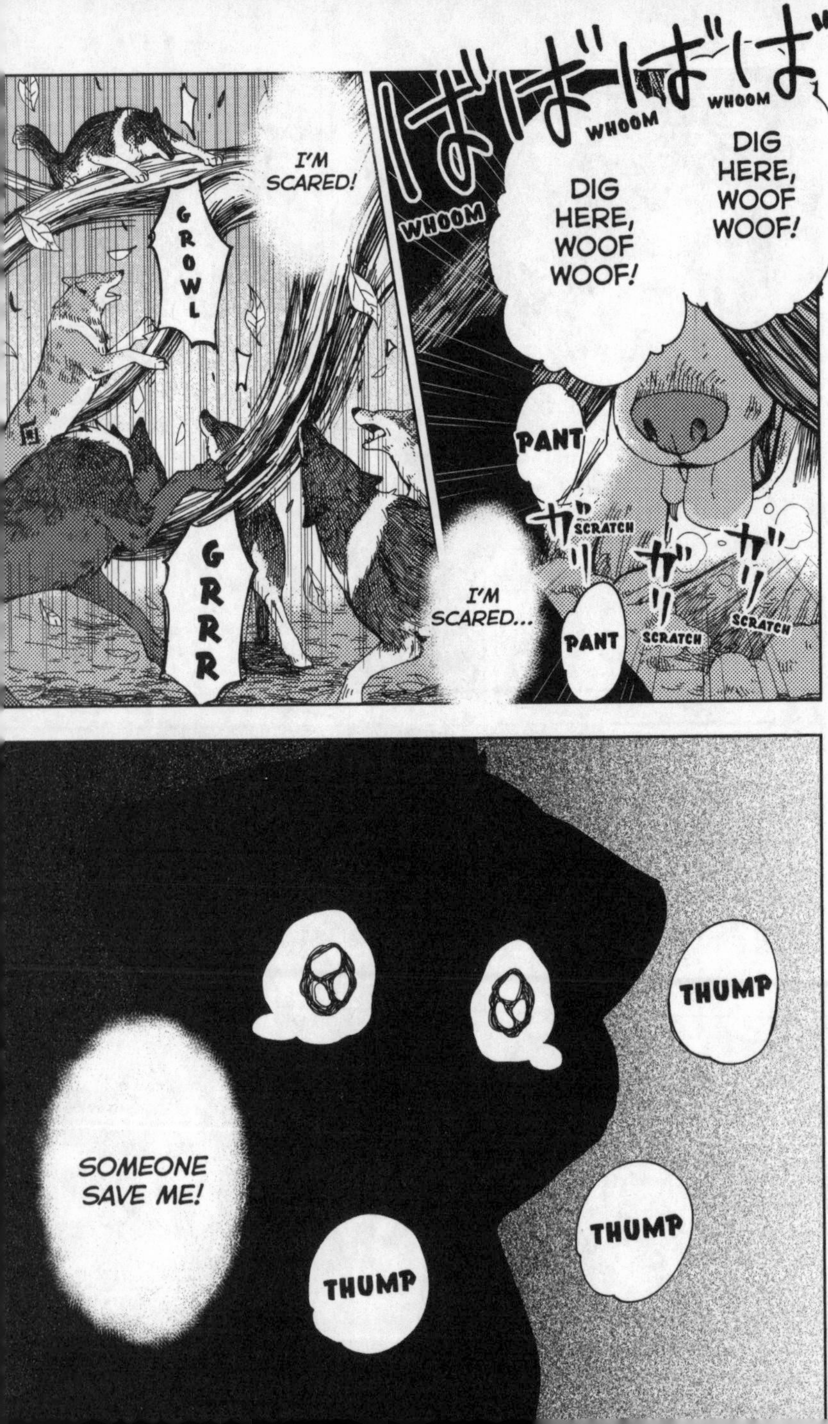

ばばばば
WHOOM
WHOOM
WHOOM
DIG HERE, WOOF WOOF!
DIG HERE, WOOF WOOF!
PANT
ガリ
SCRATCH
ガリ
SCRATCH
ガリ
SCRATCH
PANT
I'M SCARED!
GROWL
GRRR
I'M SCARED...
THUMP
THUMP
THUMP
SOMEONE SAVE ME!

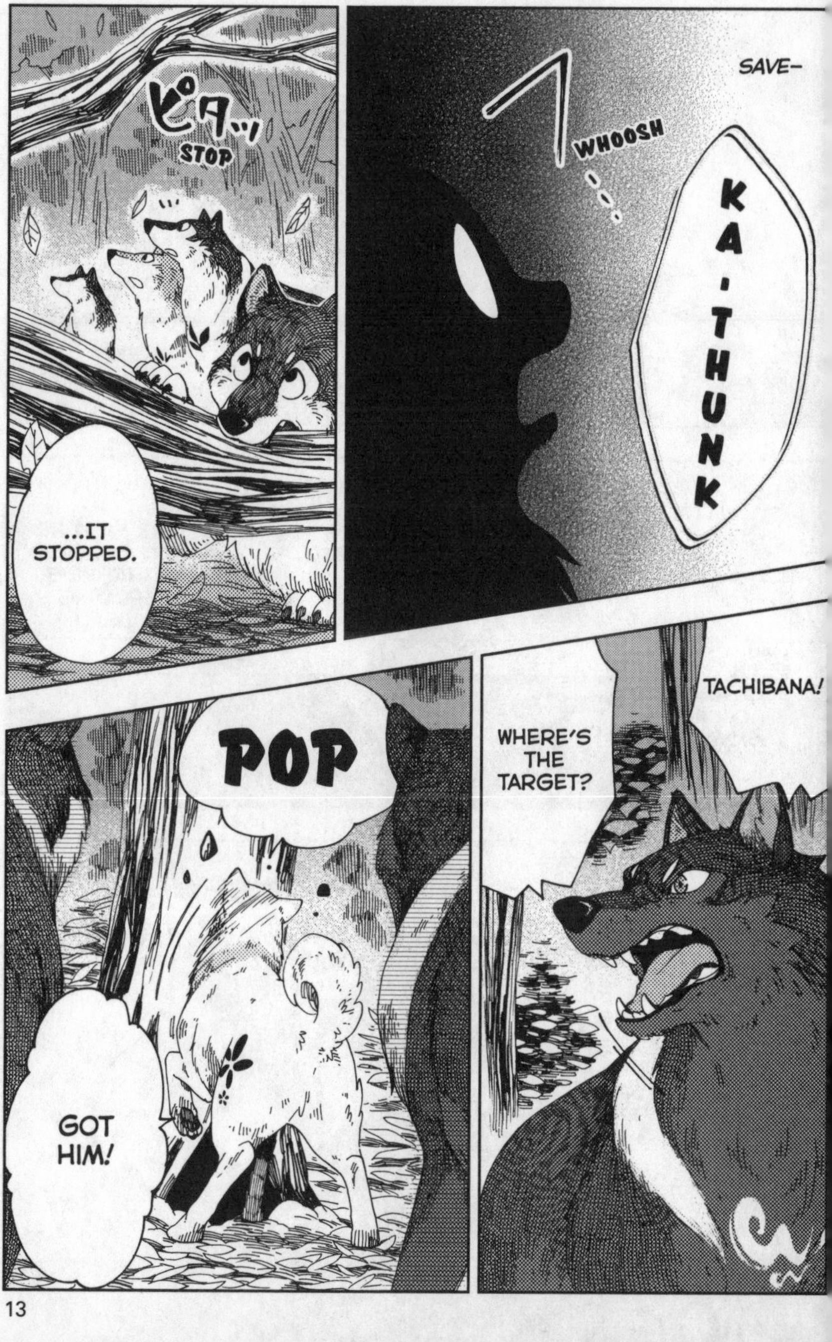
SAVE–
WHOOSH
KA-THUNK
ピタッ
STOP
...IT STOPPED.
TACHIBANA!
WHERE'S THE TARGET?
POP
GOT HIM!

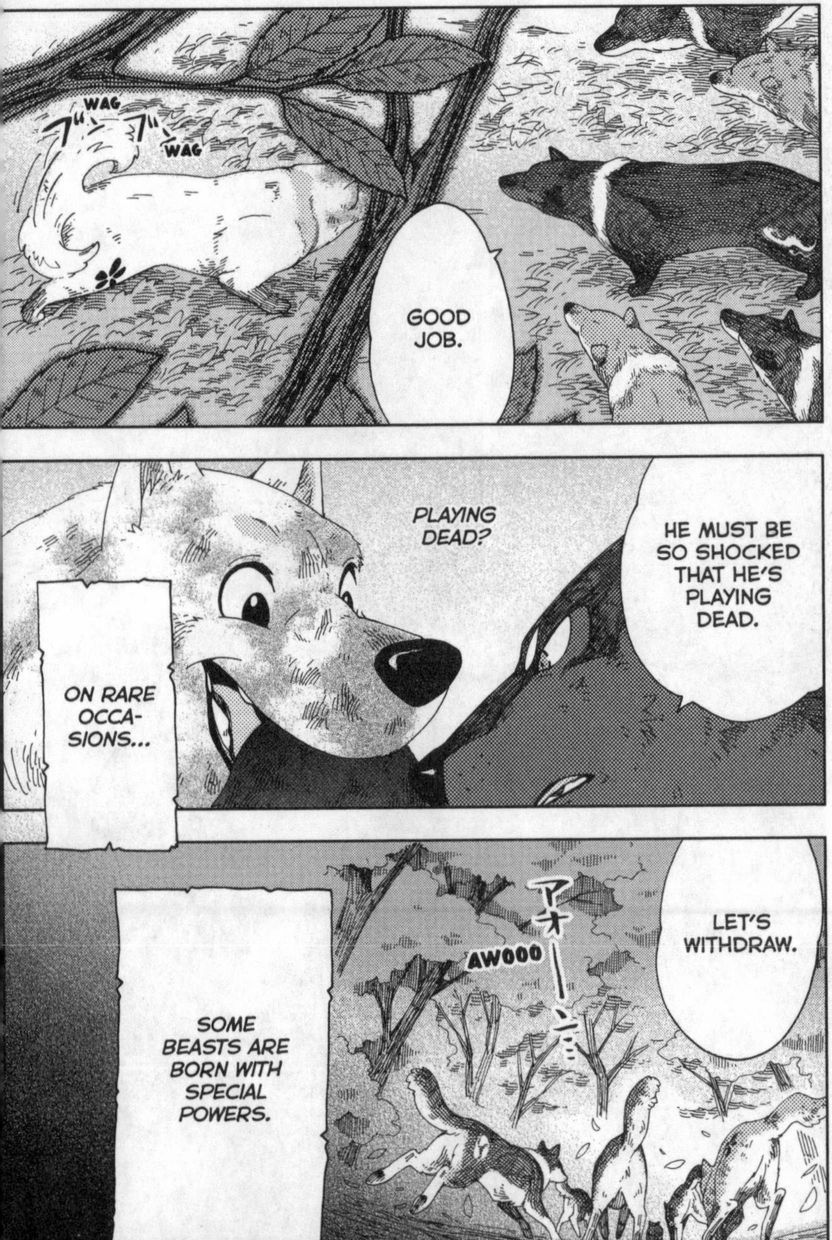
GOOD JOB.
WAG
WAG
HE MUST BE SO SHOCKED THAT HE'S PLAYING DEAD.
PLAYING DEAD?
ON RARE OCCASIONS...
LET'S WITHDRAW.
AWOOO
SOME BEASTS ARE BORN WITH SPECIAL POWERS.

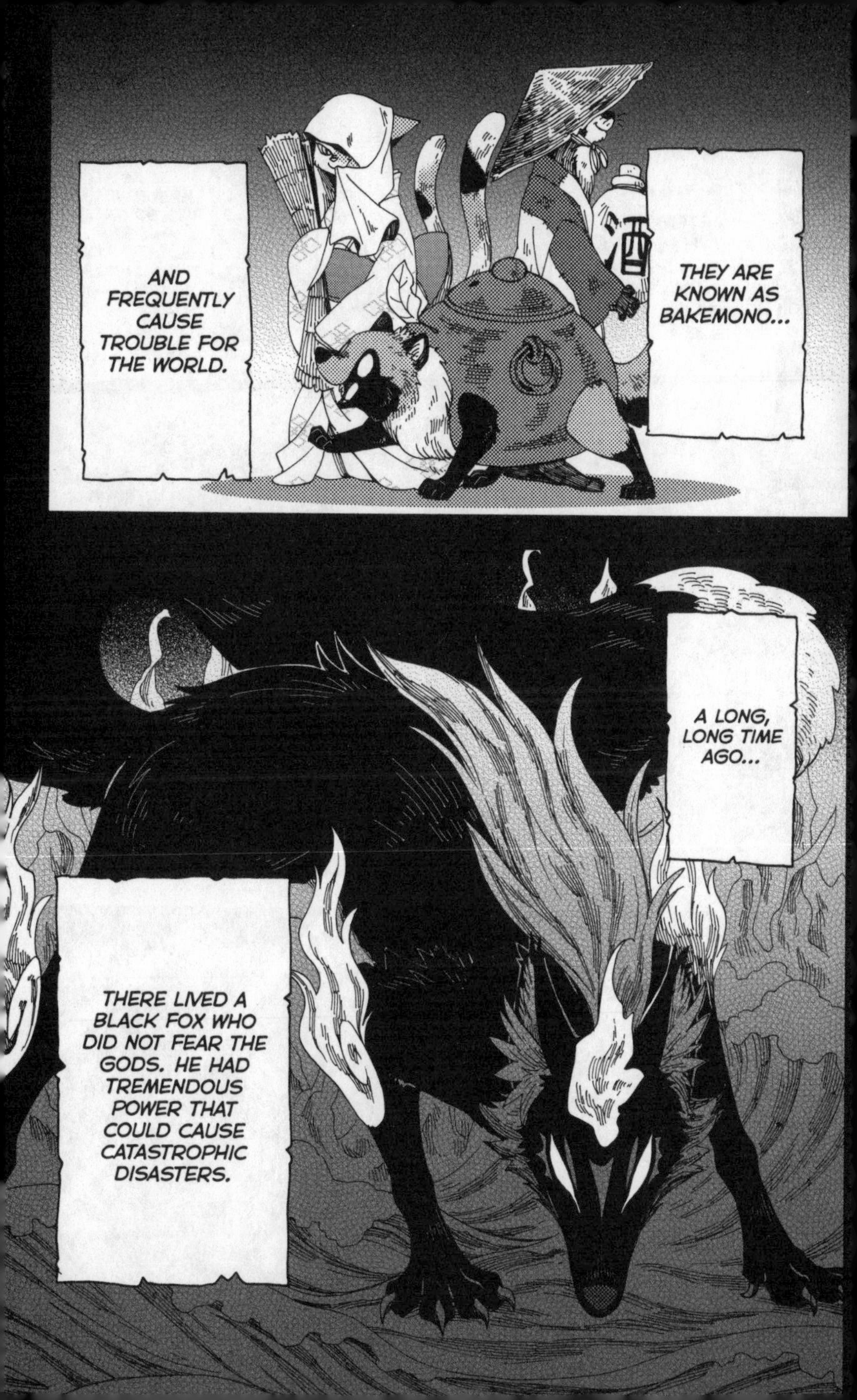
THEY ARE KNOWN AS BAKEMONO...
AND FREQUENTLY CAUSE TROUBLE FOR THE WORLD.
A LONG, LONG TIME AGO...
THERE LIVED A BLACK FOX WHO DID NOT FEAR THE GODS. HE HAD TREMENDOUS POWER THAT COULD CAUSE CATASTROPHIC DISASTERS.

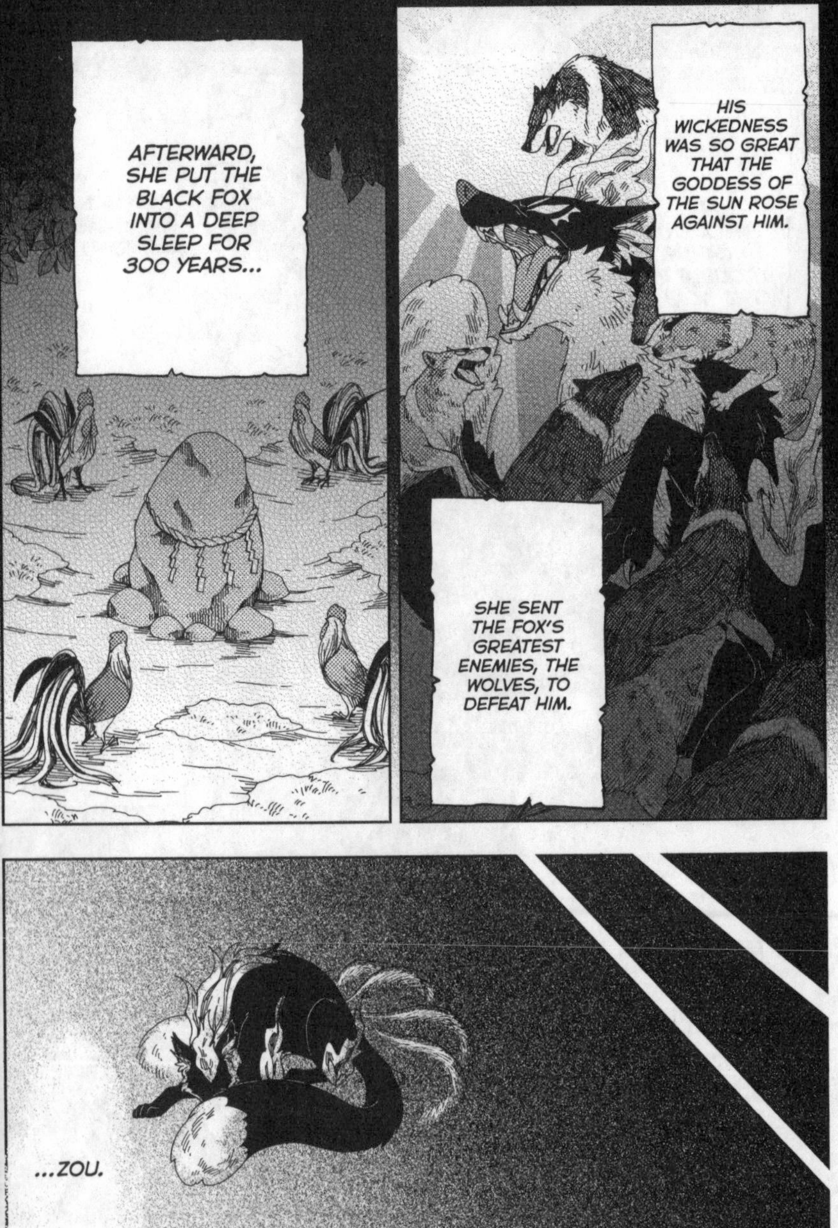
HIS WICKEDNESS WAS SO GREAT THAT THE GODDESS OF THE SUN ROSE AGAINST HIM.
SHE SENT THE FOX'S GREATEST ENEMIES, THE WOLVES, TO DEFEAT HIM.
AFTERWARD, SHE PUT THE BLACK FOX INTO A DEEP SLEEP FOR 300 YEARS...
...ZOU.

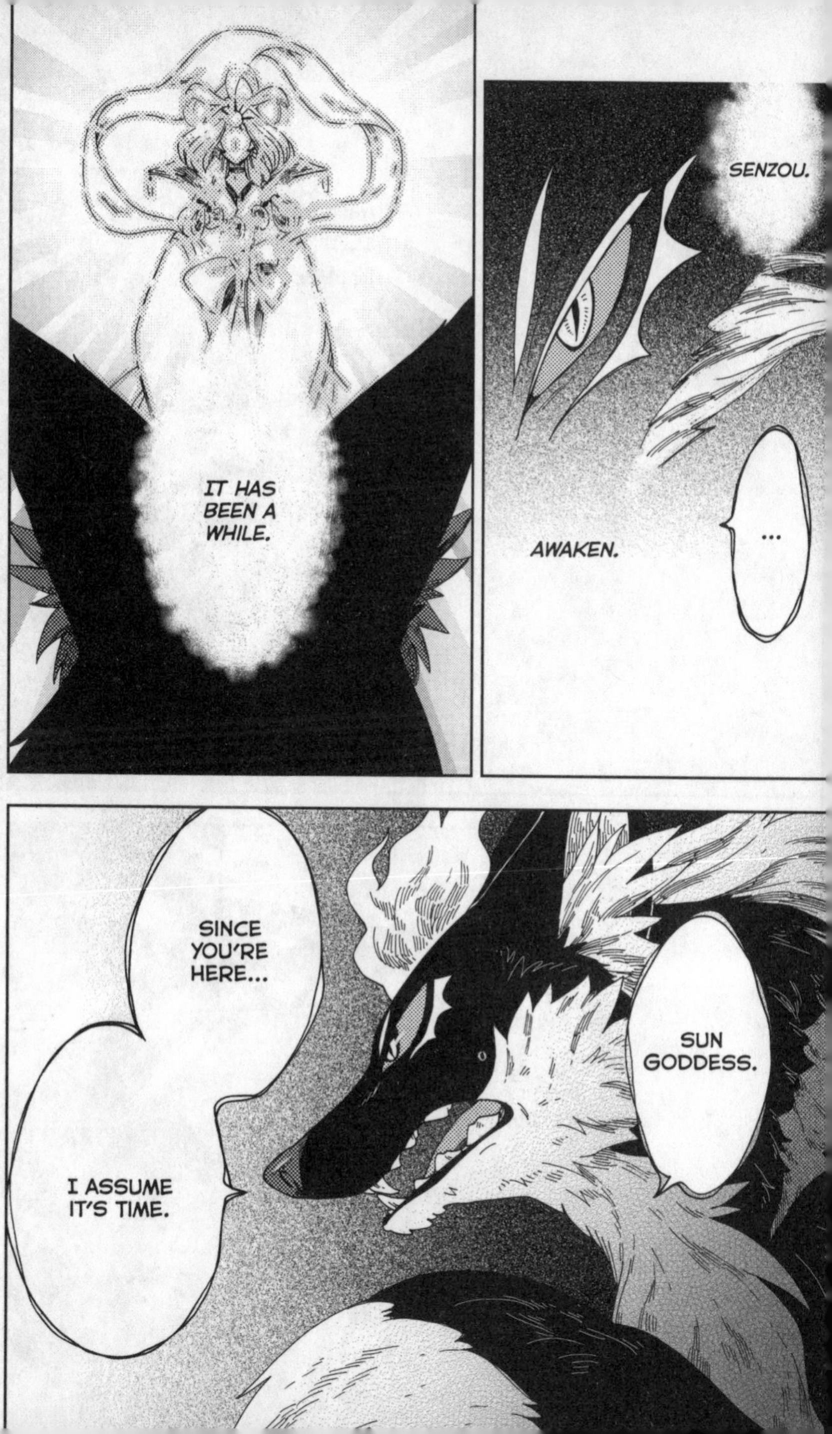
SENZOU.
...
AWAKEN.
IT HAS BEEN A WHILE.
SUN GODDESS.
SINCE YOU'RE HERE...
I ASSUME IT'S TIME.

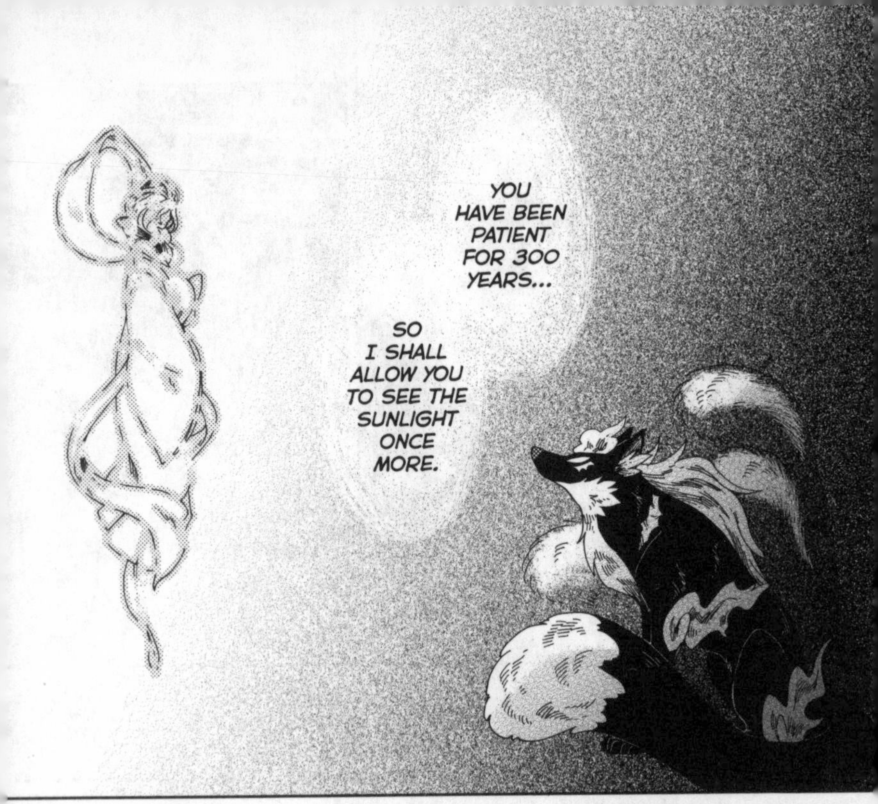
YOU HAVE BEEN PATIENT FOR 300 YEARS...
SO I SHALL ALLOW YOU TO SEE THE SUNLIGHT ONCE MORE.

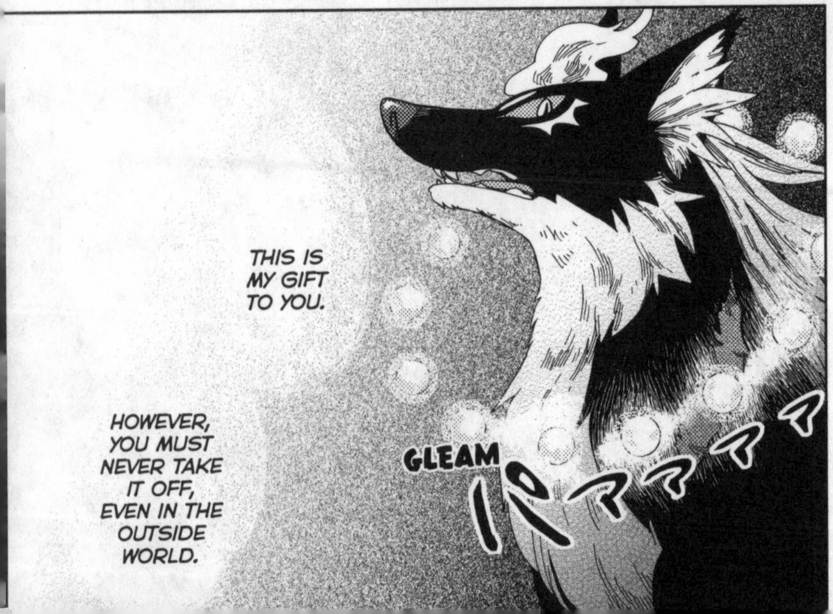
THIS IS MY GIFT TO YOU.
GLEAM
HOWEVER, YOU MUST NEVER TAKE IT OFF, EVEN IN THE OUTSIDE WORLD.

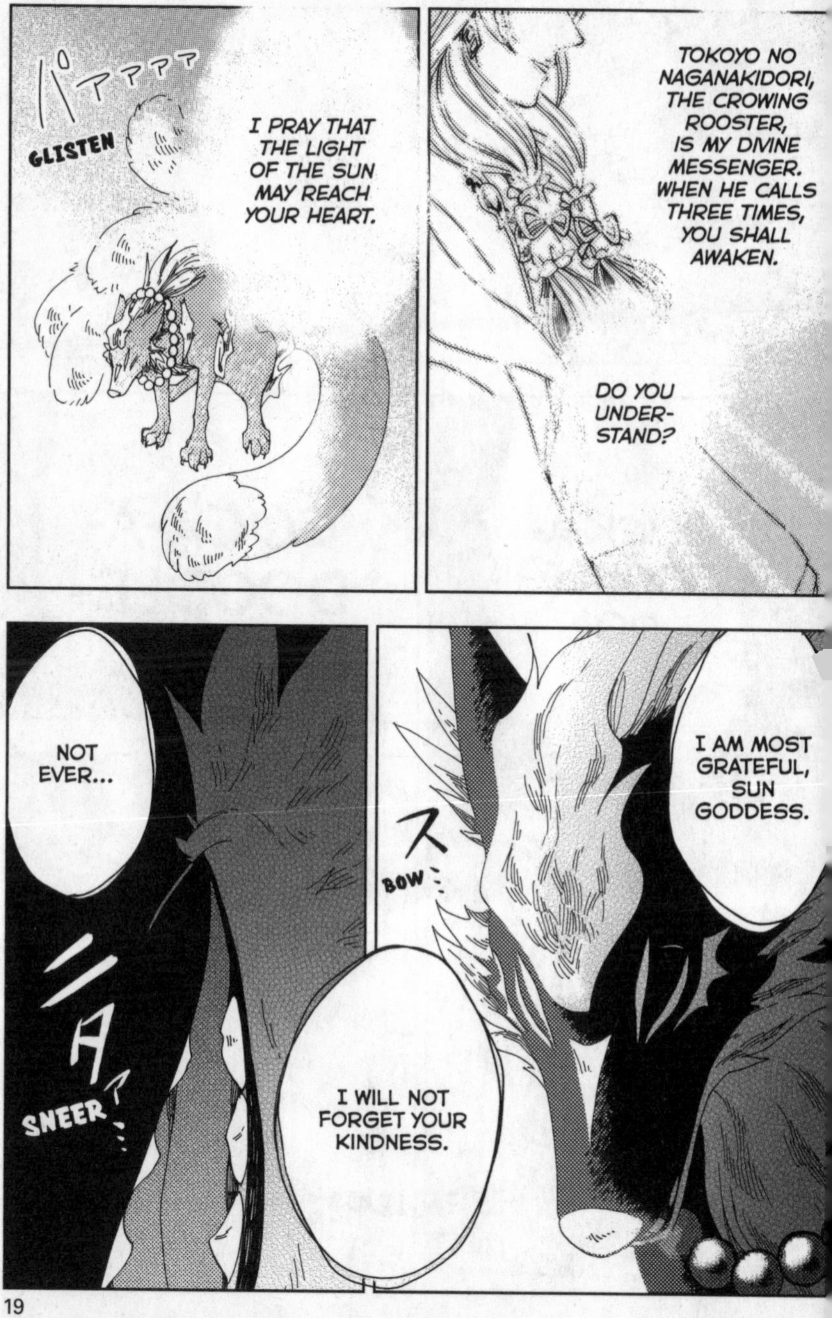
TOKOYO NO NAGANAKIDORI, THE CROWING ROOSTER, IS MY DIVINE MESSENGER. WHEN HE CALLS THREE TIMES, YOU SHALL AWAKEN.
DO YOU UNDER-STAND?
パァァァァ
GLISTEN
I PRAY THAT THE LIGHT OF THE SUN MAY REACH YOUR HEART.
I AM MOST GRATEFUL, SUN GODDESS.
ス
BOW
I WILL NOT FORGET YOUR KINDNESS.
NOT EVER...
ニヤァ
SNEER

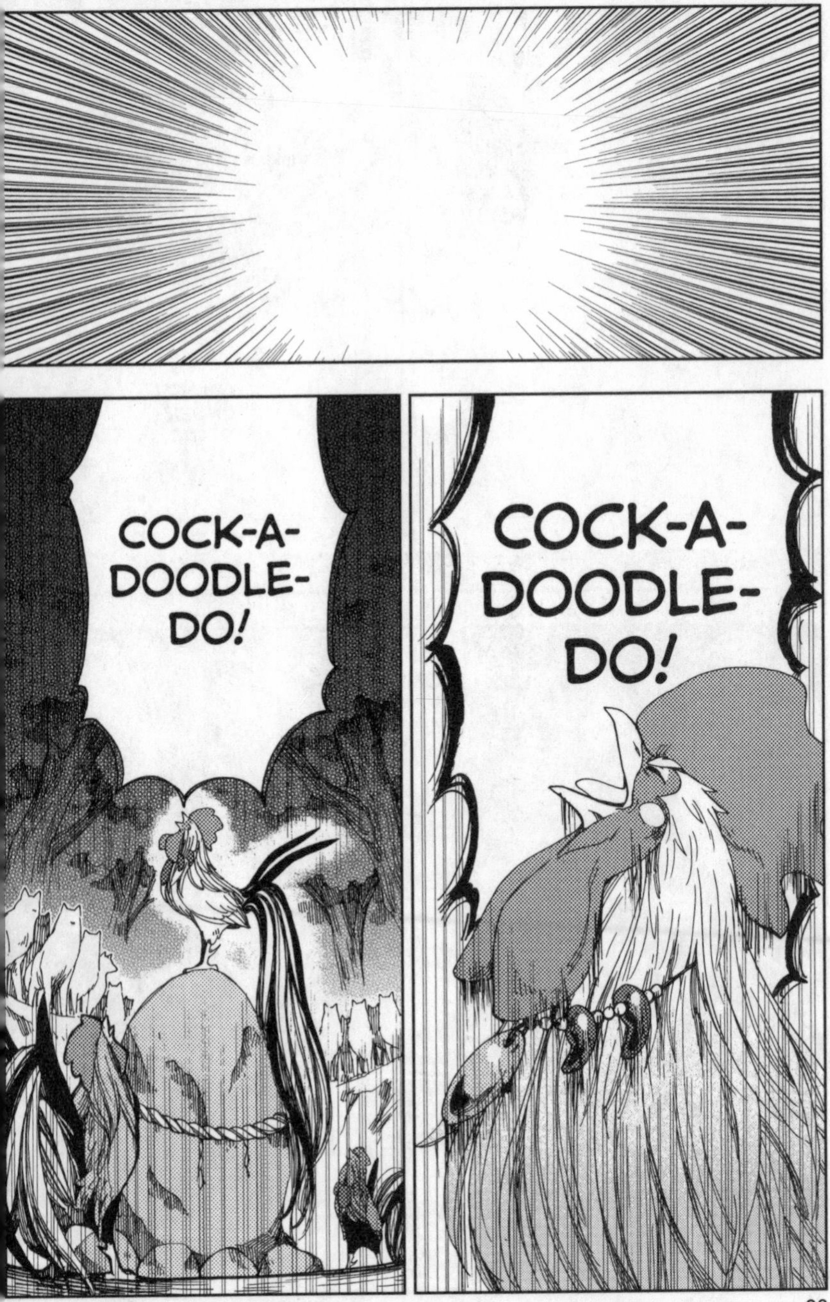
COCK-A-DOODLE-DO!
COCK-A-DOODLE-DO!

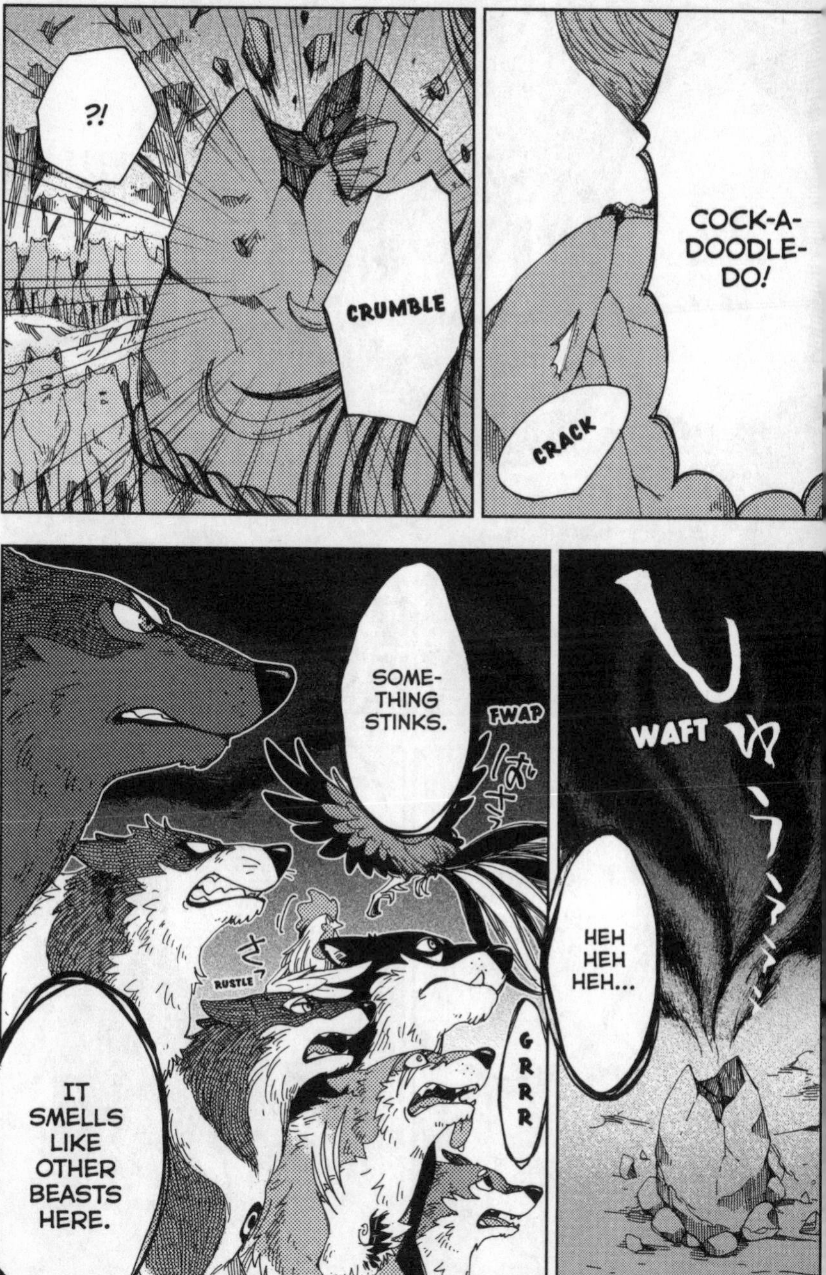
COCK-A-DOODLE-DO!
CRACK
?!
CRUMBLE
WAFT
HEH HEH HEH...
SOME-THING STINKS.
FWAP
RUSTLE
GRRR
IT SMELLS LIKE OTHER BEASTS HERE.

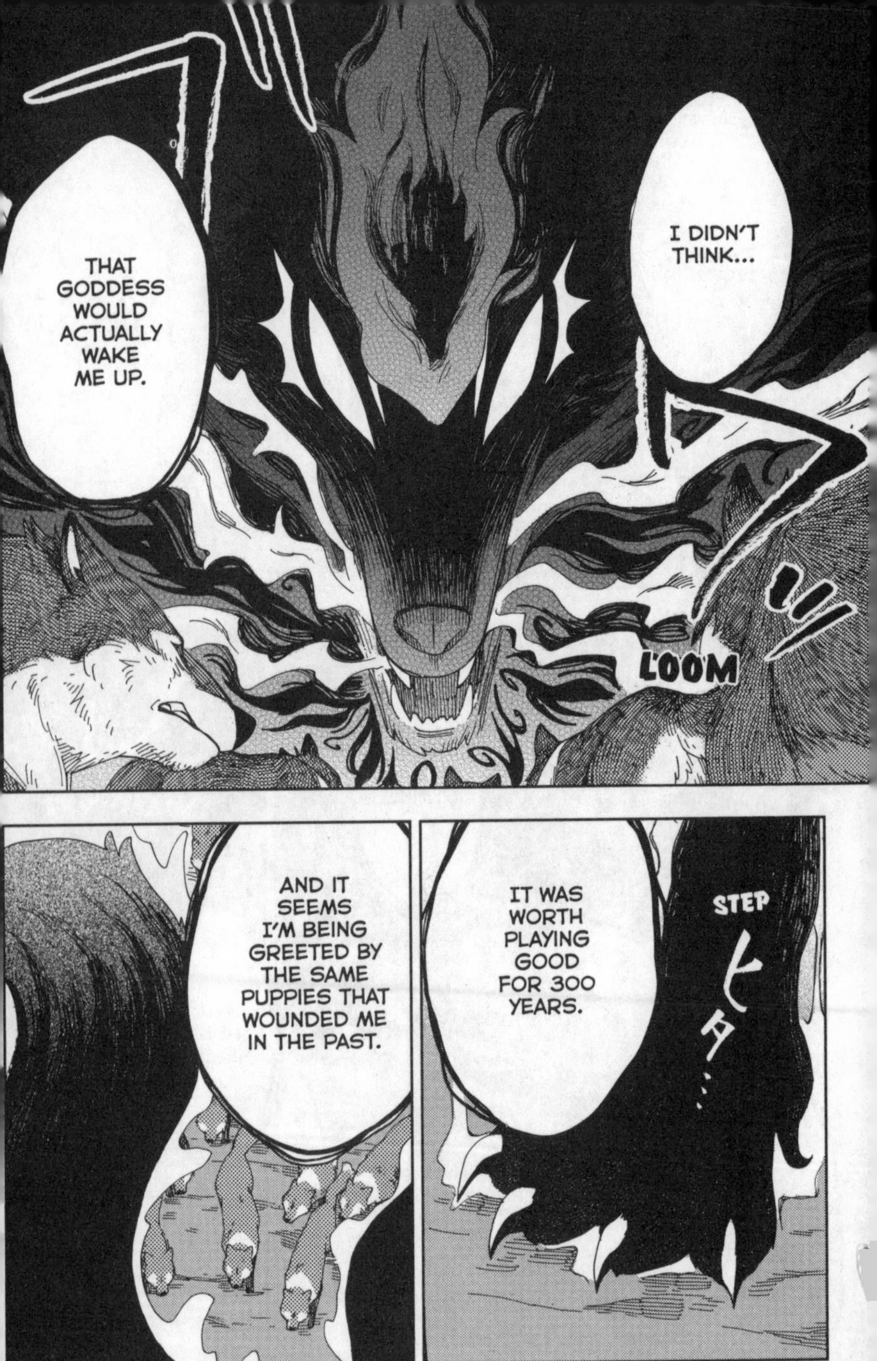
I DIDN'T THINK...
THAT GODDESS WOULD ACTUALLY WAKE ME UP.
LOOM
STEP
ヒタ…
IT WAS WORTH PLAYING GOOD FOR 300 YEARS.
AND IT SEEMS I'M BEING GREETED BY THE SAME PUPPIES THAT WOUNDED ME IN THE PAST.

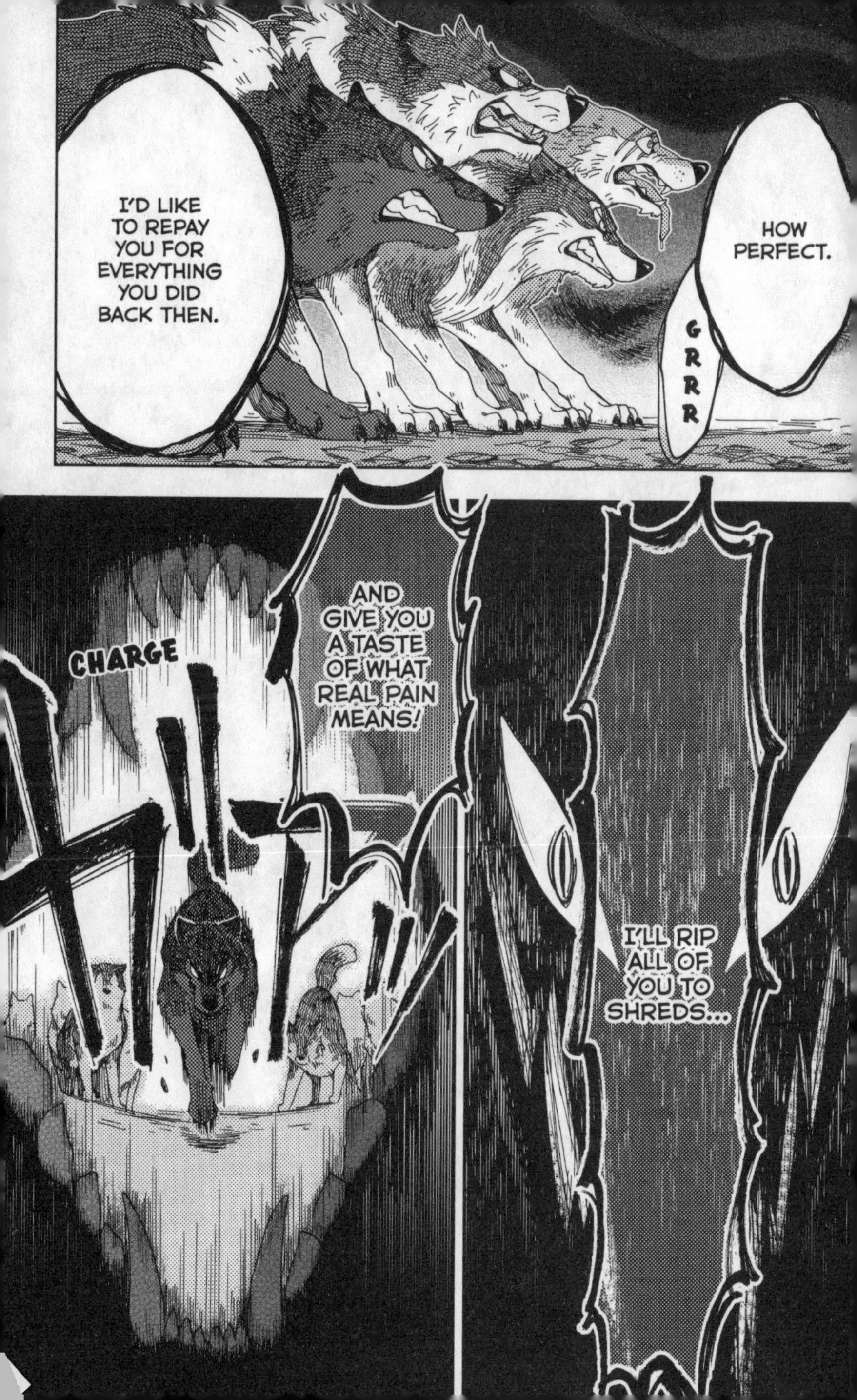

HOW PERFECT.
GRRR
I'D LIKE TO REPAY YOU FOR EVERYTHING YOU DID BACK THEN.
I'LL RIP ALL OF YOU TO SHREDS...
AND GIVE YOU A TASTE OF WHAT REAL PAIN MEANS!
CHARGE

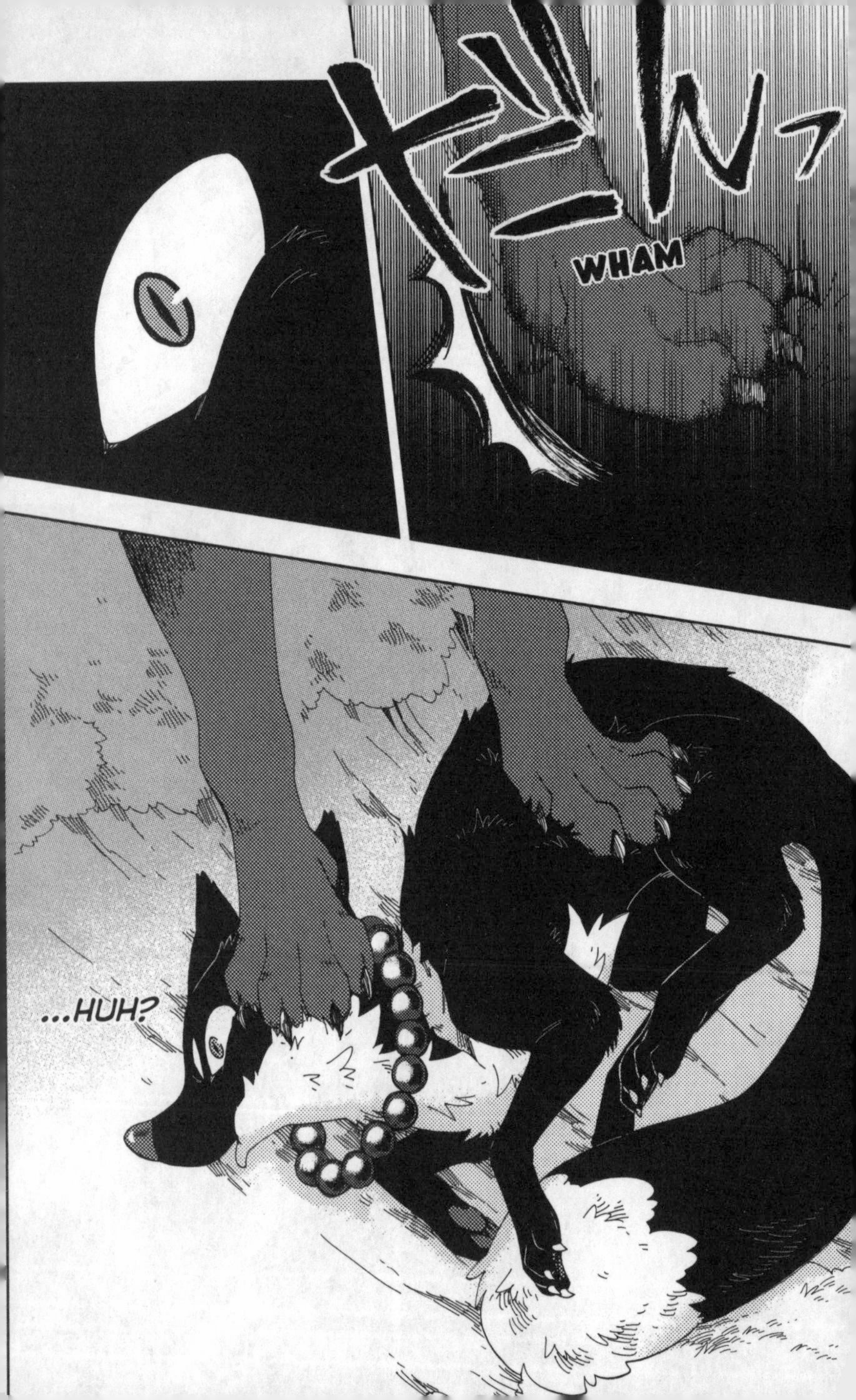
WHAM
...HUH?

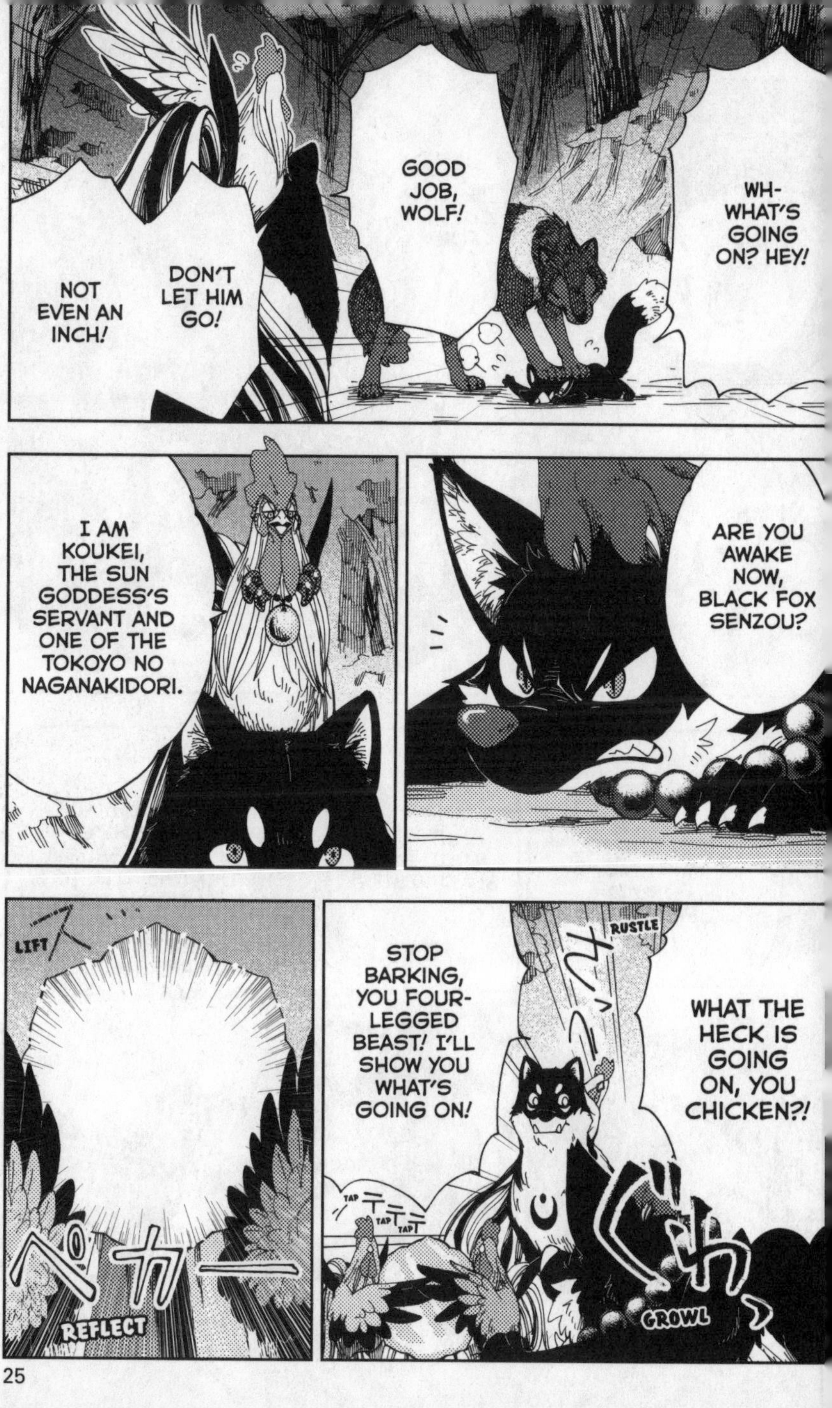
WH- WHAT'S GOING ON? HEY!
GOOD JOB, WOLF!
DON'T LET HIM GO!
NOT EVEN AN INCH!
ARE YOU AWAKE NOW, BLACK FOX SENZOU?
I AM KOUKEI, THE SUN GODDESS'S SERVANT AND ONE OF THE TOKOYO NO NAGANAKIDORI.
RUSTLE
WHAT THE HECK IS GOING ON, YOU CHICKEN?!
STOP BARKING, YOU FOUR-LEGGED BEAST! I'LL SHOW YOU WHAT'S GOING ON!
TAP TAP TAP
GROWL
LIFT
REFLECT

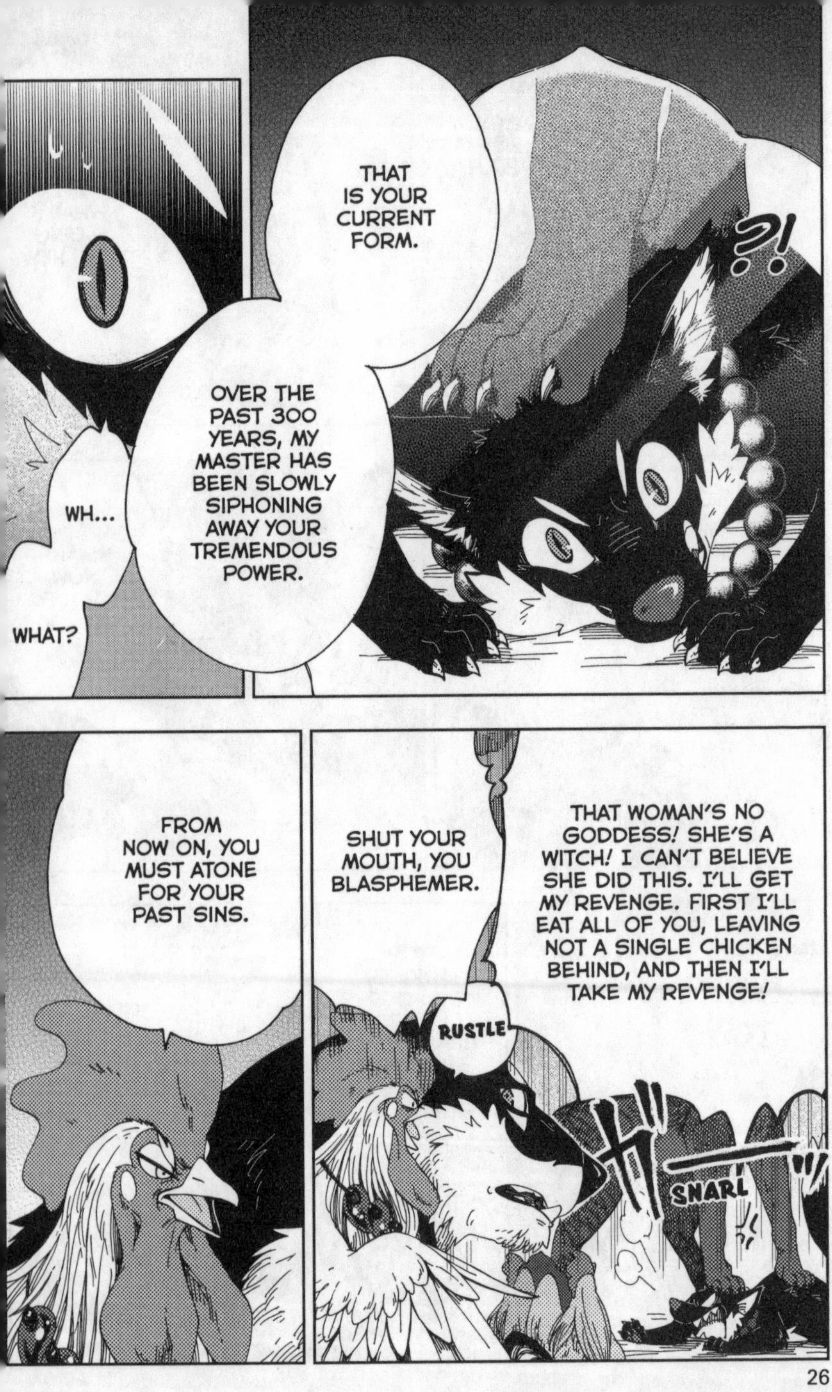
THAT IS YOUR CURRENT FORM.
?!
OVER THE PAST 300 YEARS, MY MASTER HAS BEEN SLOWLY SIPHONING AWAY YOUR TREMENDOUS POWER.
WH...
WHAT?
THAT WOMAN'S NO GODDESS! SHE'S A WITCH! I CAN'T BELIEVE SHE DID THIS. I'LL GET MY REVENGE. FIRST I'LL EAT ALL OF YOU, LEAVING NOT A SINGLE CHICKEN BEHIND, AND THEN I'LL TAKE MY REVENGE!
SHUT YOUR MOUTH, YOU BLASPHEMER.
RUSTLE
SNARL
FROM NOW ON, YOU MUST ATONE FOR YOUR PAST SINS.

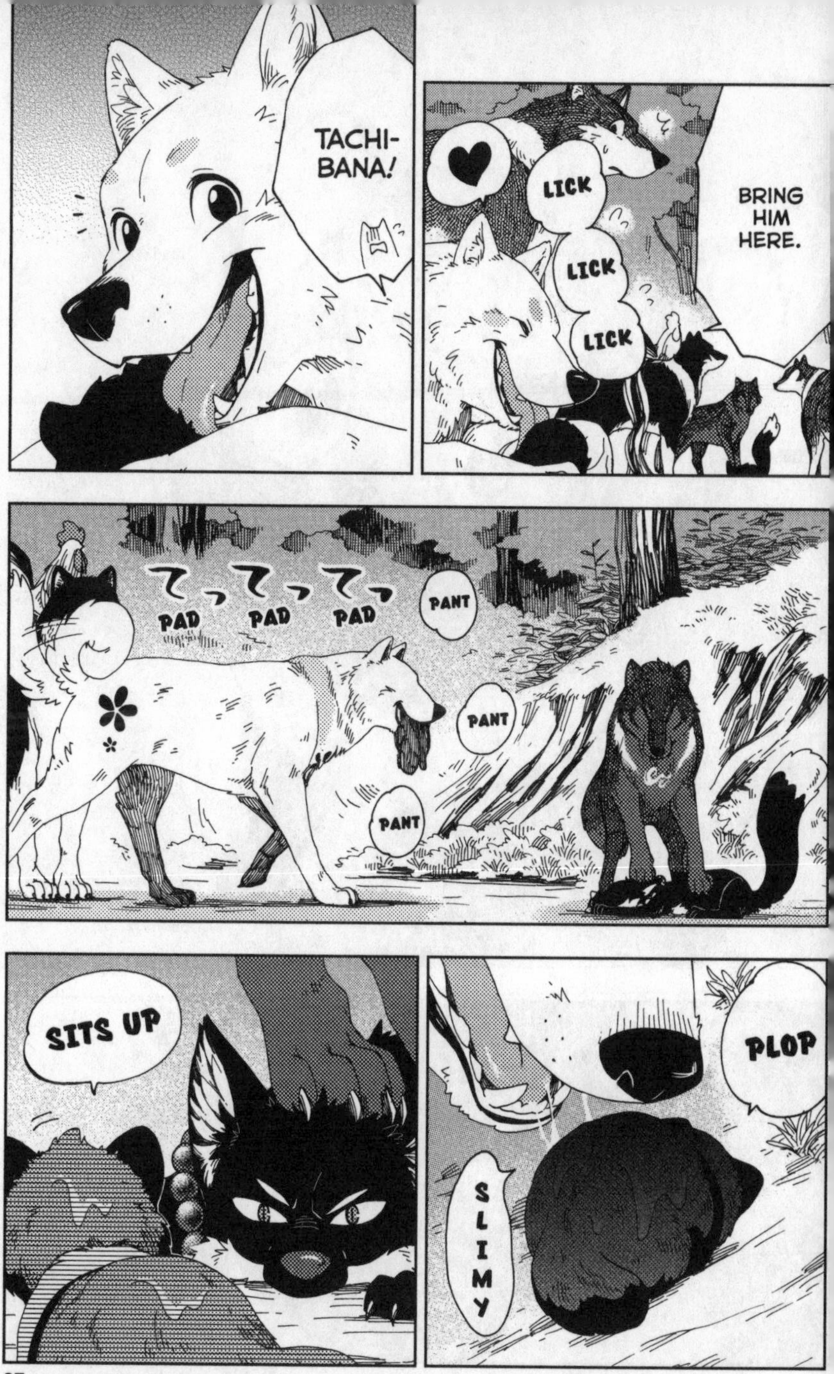
BRING HIM HERE.
LICK
LICK
LICK
TACHI-BANA!
PANT
PANT
てっ てっ てっ
PAD PAD PAD
PANT
PLOP
SLIMY
SITS UP

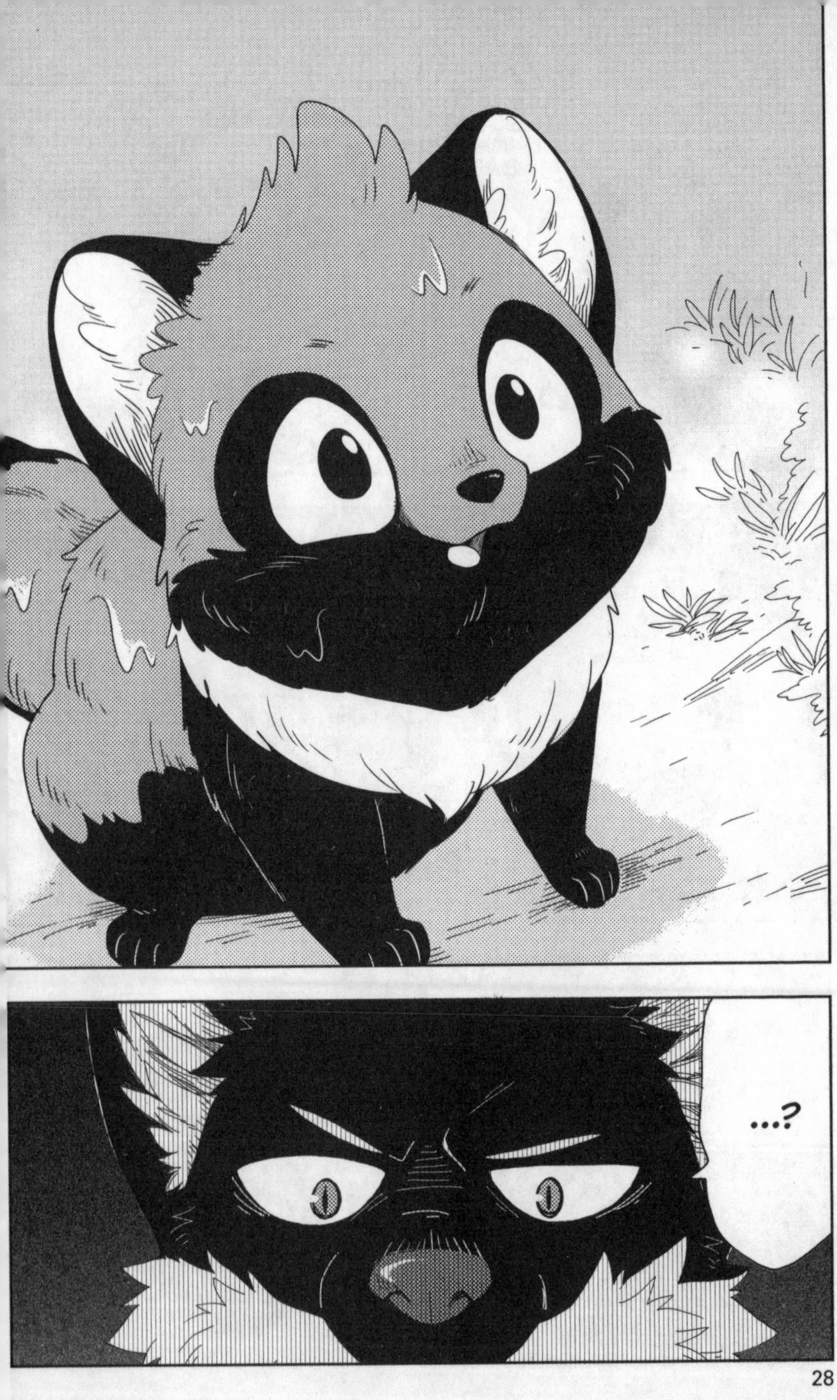
...?

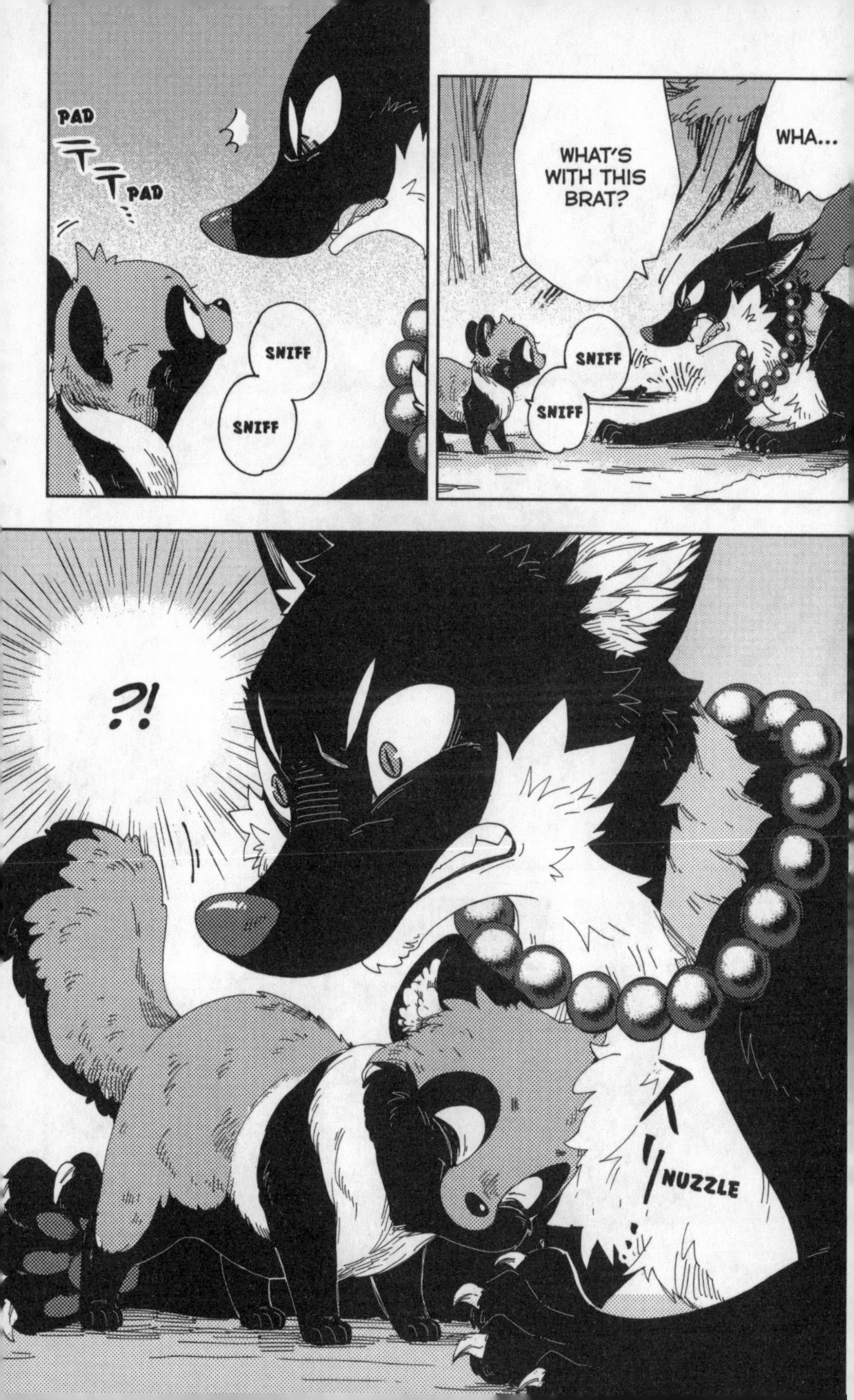
WHA...
WHAT'S WITH THIS BRAT?
SNIFF
SNIFF
PAD PAD
SNIFF
SNIFF
?!
NUZZLE

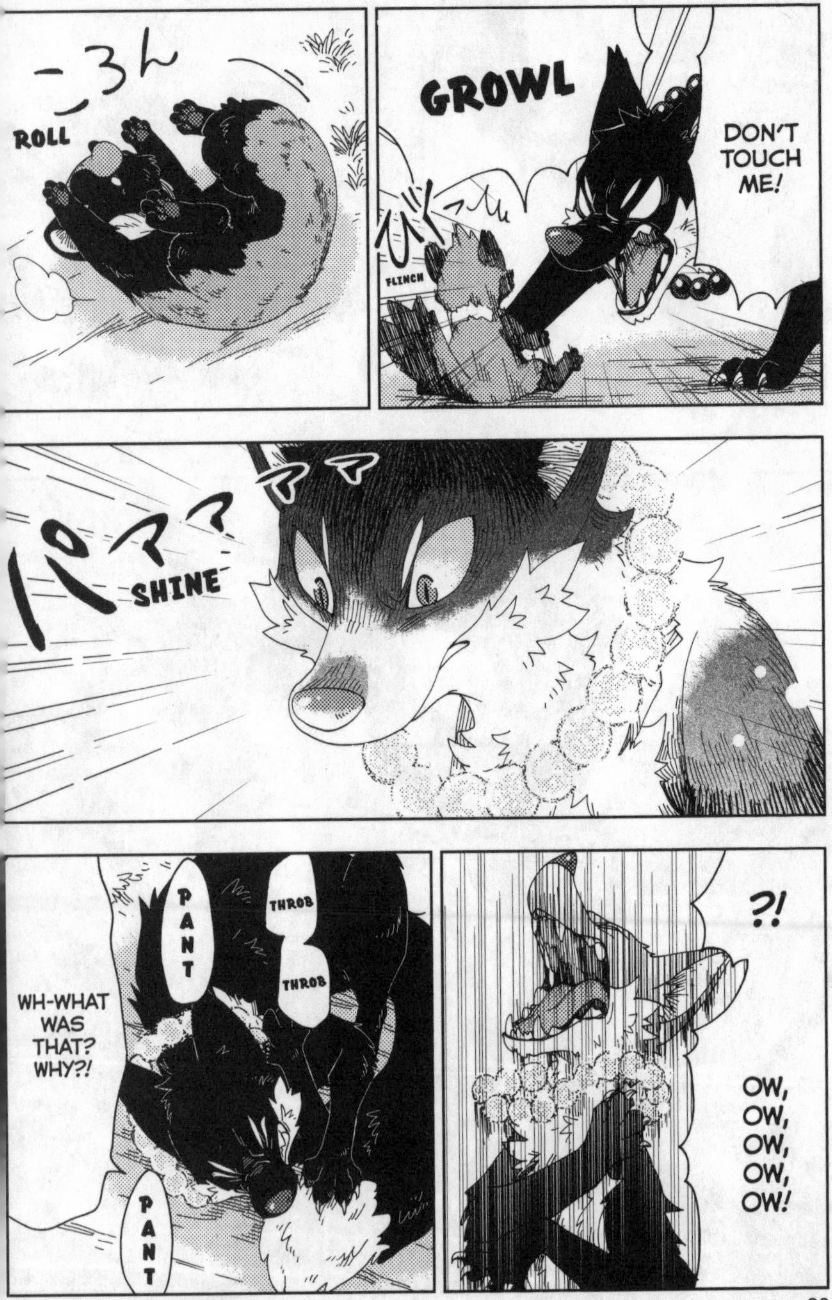
GROWL
DON'T TOUCH ME!
FLINCH
ころん
ROLL
SHINE
?!
OW, OW, OW, OW, OW!
PANT
THROB
THROB
WH-WHAT WAS THAT? WHY?!
PANT

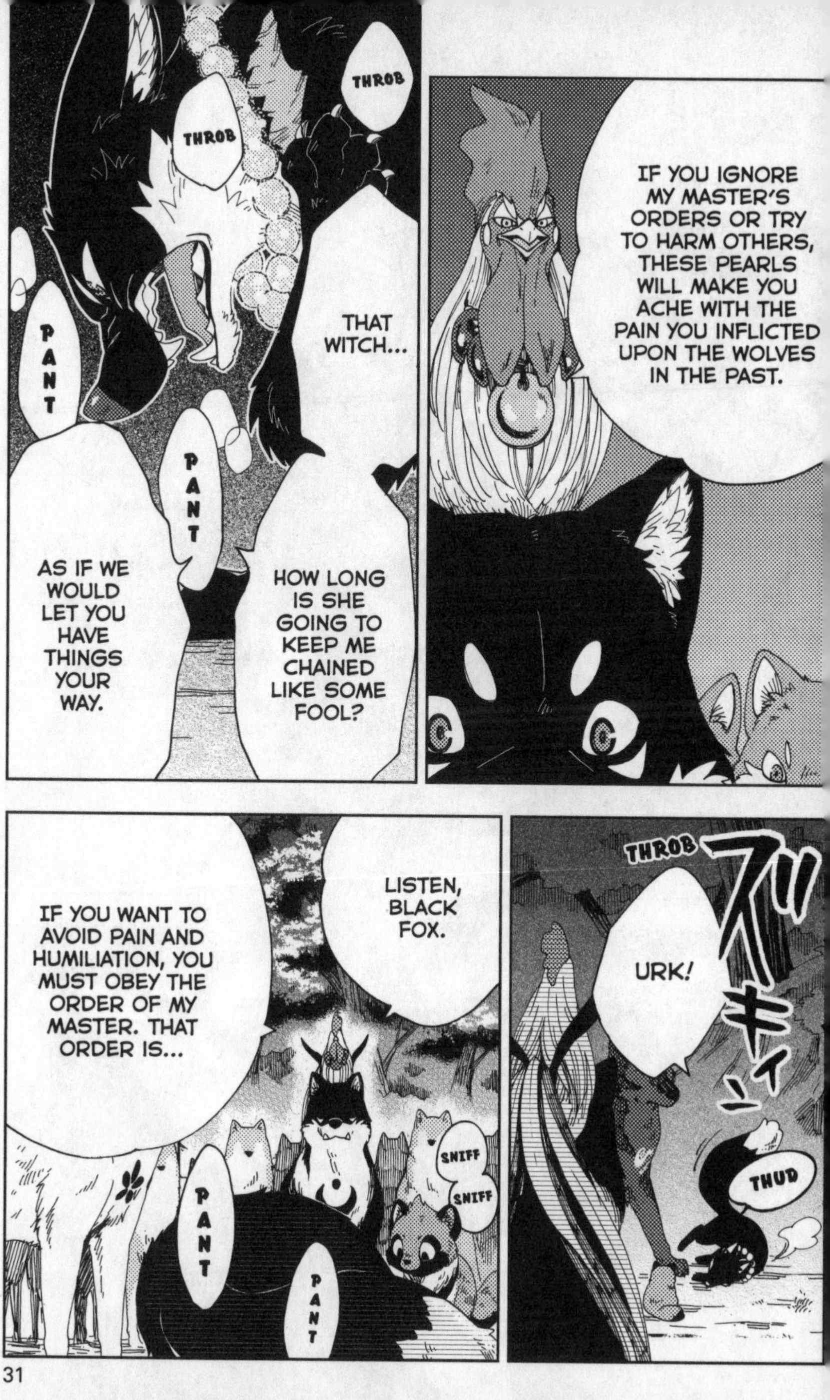
IF YOU IGNORE MY MASTER'S ORDERS OR TRY TO HARM OTHERS, THESE PEARLS WILL MAKE YOU ACHE WITH THE PAIN YOU INFLICTED UPON THE WOLVES IN THE PAST.
THROB
THROB
THAT WITCH...
PANT
HOW LONG IS SHE GOING TO KEEP ME CHAINED LIKE SOME FOOL?
PANT
AS IF WE WOULD LET YOU HAVE THINGS YOUR WAY.
THROB
URK!
THUD
LISTEN, BLACK FOX.
IF YOU WANT TO AVOID PAIN AND HUMILIATION, YOU MUST OBEY THE ORDER OF MY MASTER. THAT ORDER IS...
SNIFF
SNIFF
PANT
PANT

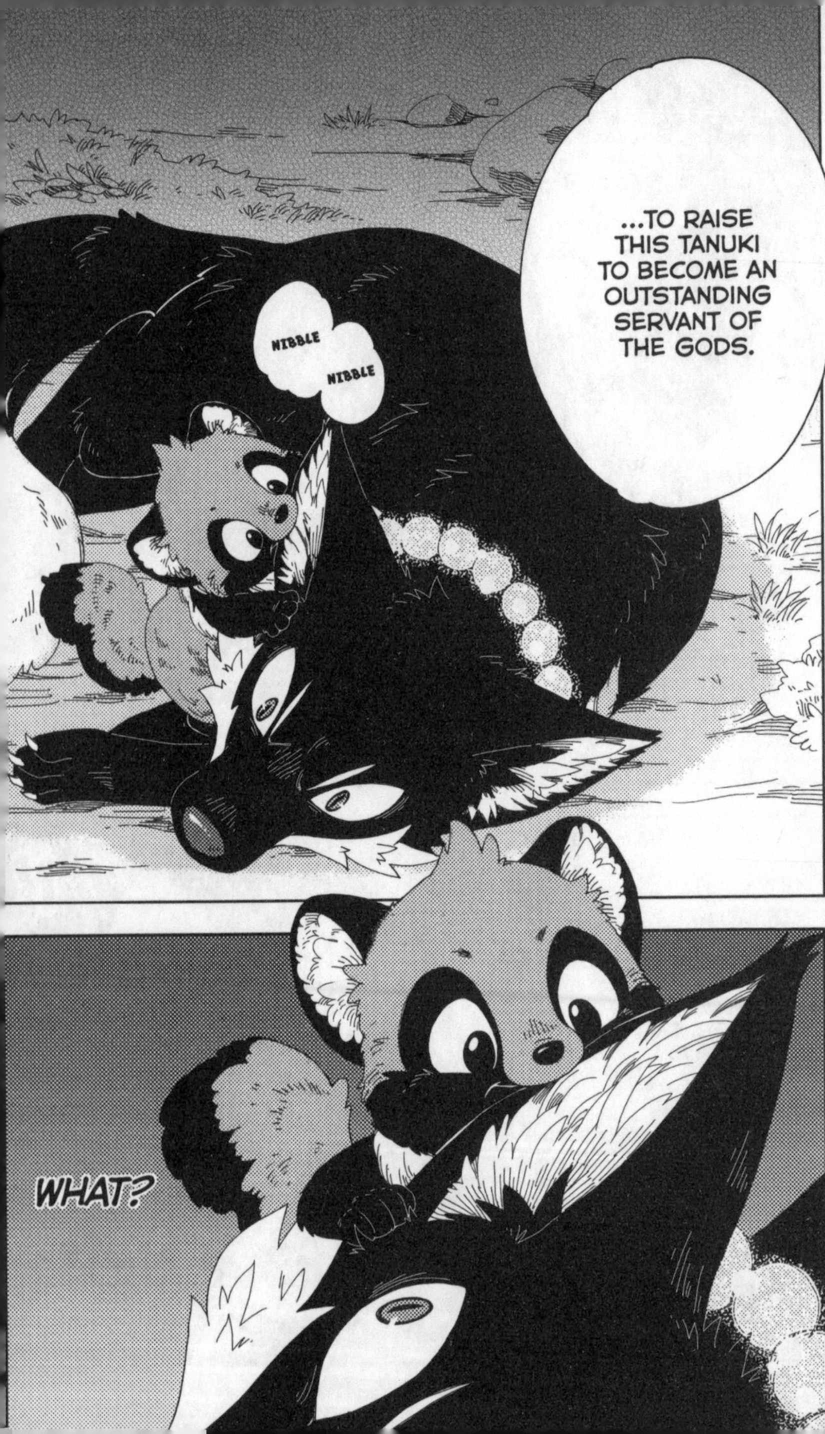
...TO RAISE THIS TANUKI TO BECOME AN OUTSTANDING SERVANT OF THE GODS.
NIBBLE
NIBBLE
WHAT?

The Bakemono Field Guide

#1

Bakegitsune
(Fox)

The most famous of bakemono. Kitsune (foxes) have the power to transform into a human and can cause calamities and natural disasters. Although the black foxes and the white foxes that act as servants to the deity Inari are the same species, they do not get along.

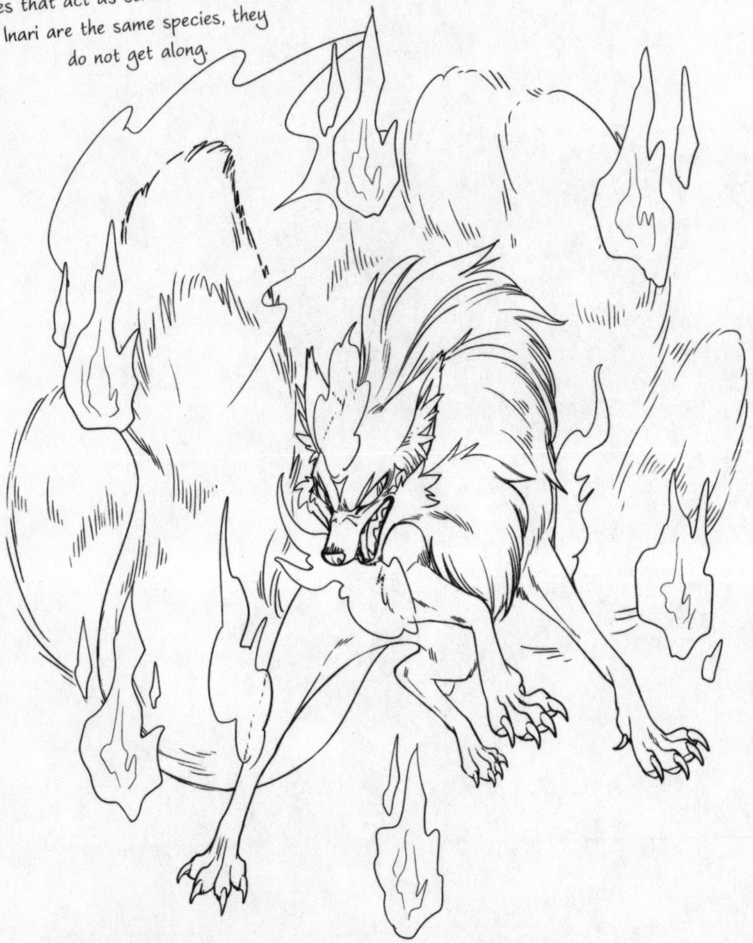

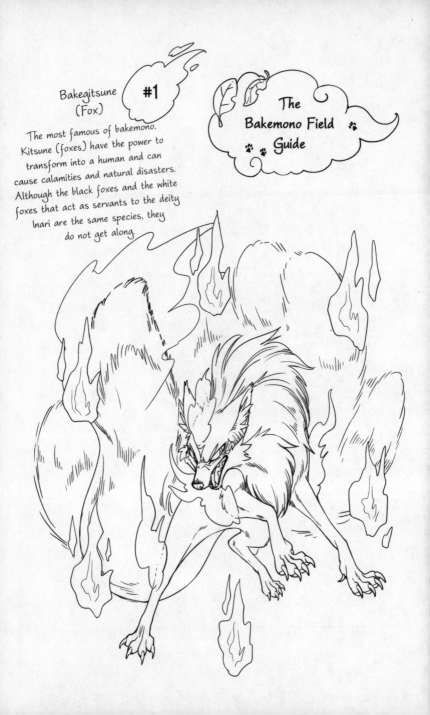

Chapter 2

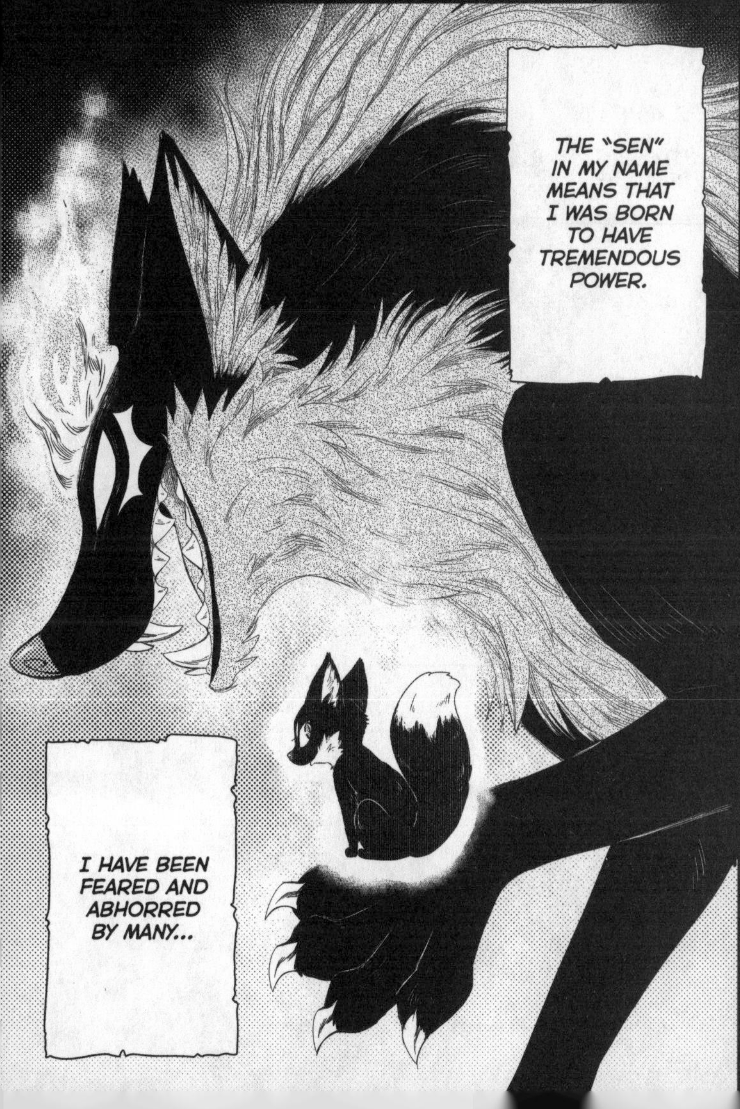
THE "SEN" IN MY NAME MEANS THAT I WAS BORN TO HAVE TREMENDOUS POWER.
I HAVE BEEN FEARED AND ABHORRED BY MANY...

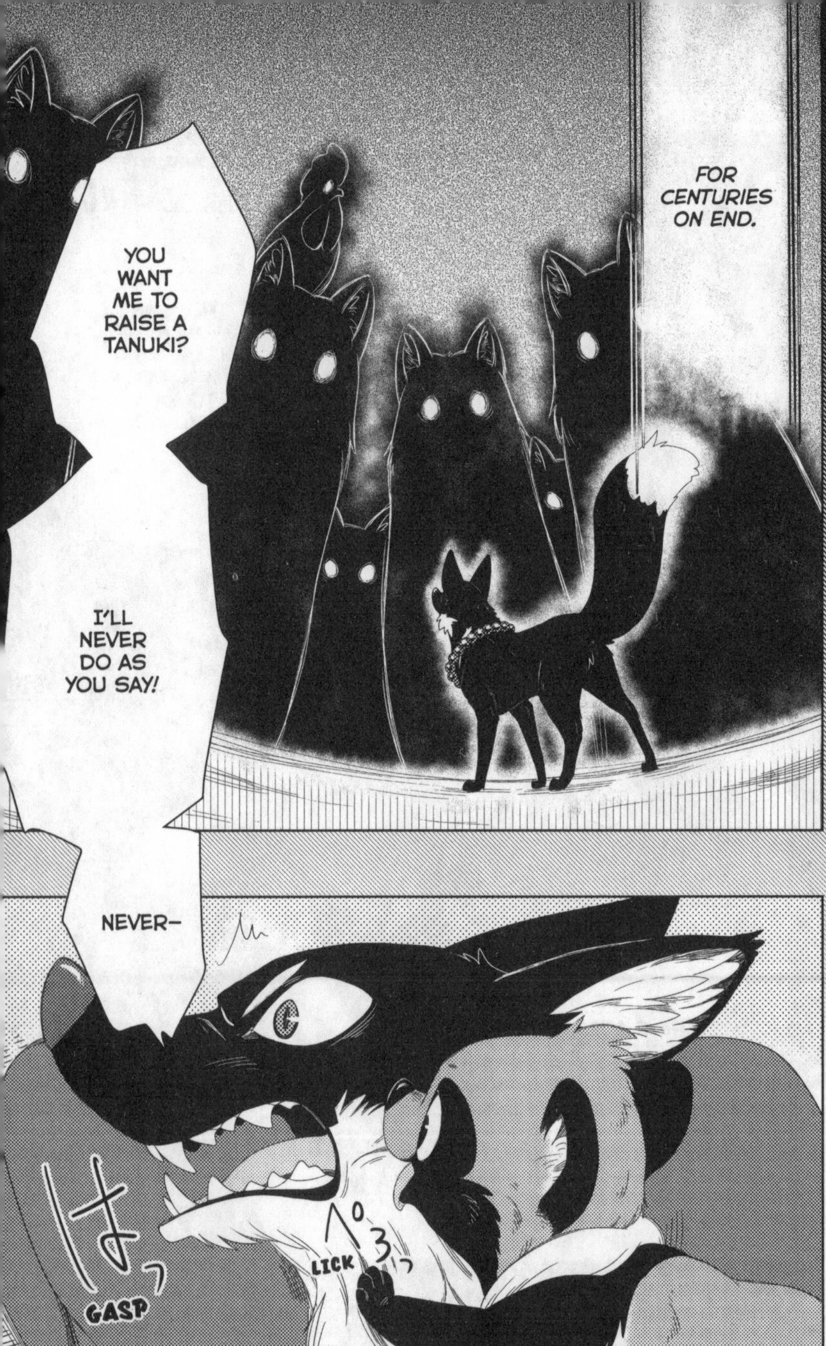

FOR CENTURIES ON END.
YOU WANT ME TO RAISE A TANUKI?
I'LL NEVER DO AS YOU SAY!
NEVER–
LICK
はっ
GASP

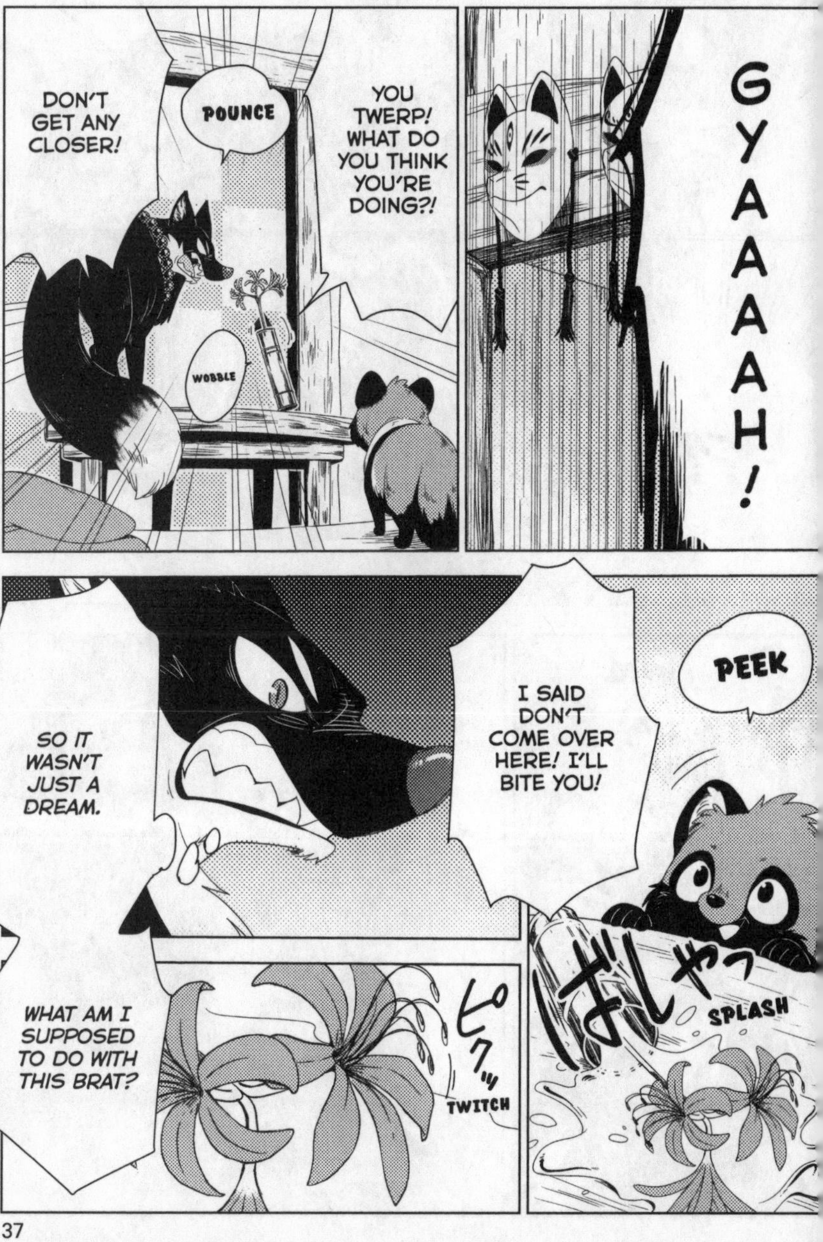
GYAAAAH!
YOU TWERP! WHAT DO YOU THINK YOU'RE DOING?!
POUNCE
DON'T GET ANY CLOSER!
WOBBLE
PEEK
ばしゃっ
SPLASH
I SAID DON'T COME OVER HERE! I'LL BITE YOU!
SO IT WASN'T JUST A DREAM.
ピクッ
TWITCH
WHAT AM I SUPPOSED TO DO WITH THIS BRAT?

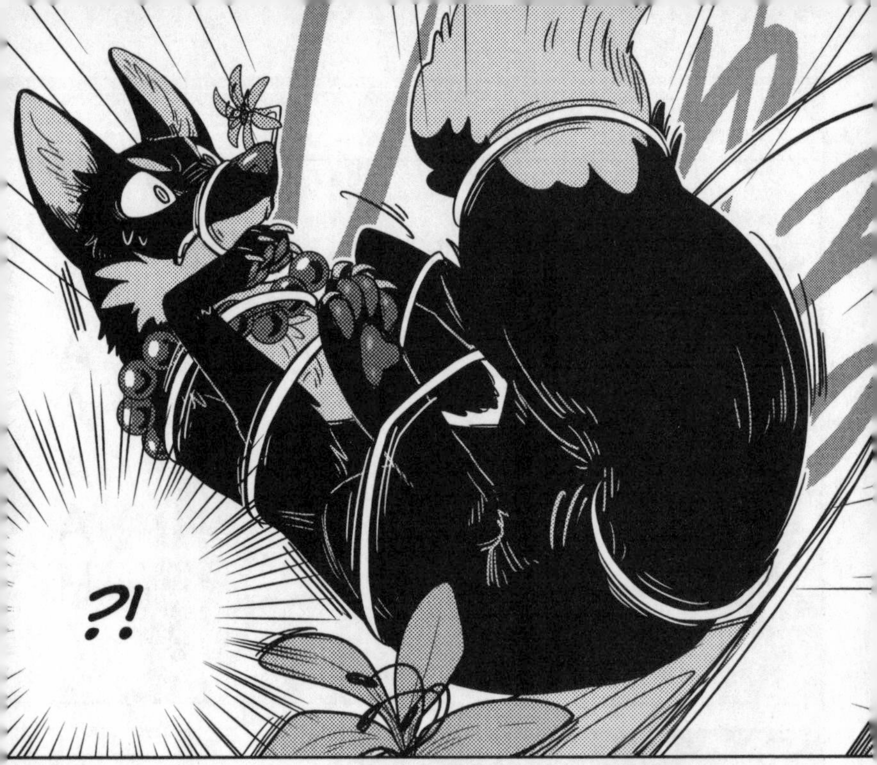
?!

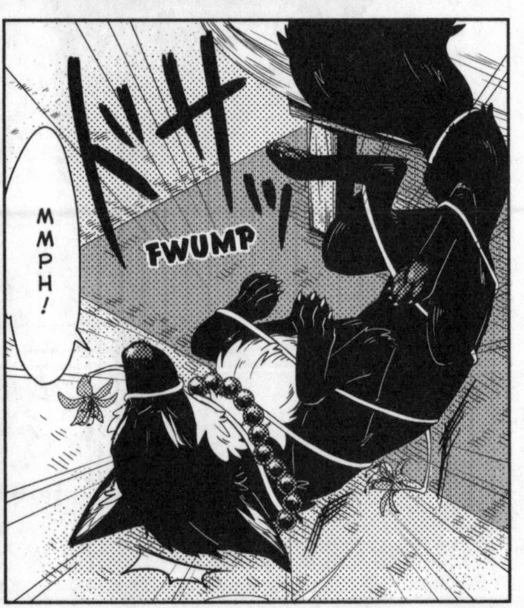
ドサッ
MMPH!
FWUMP

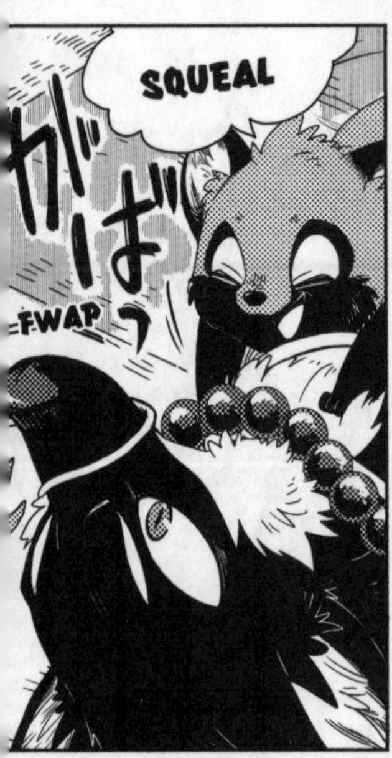
SQUEAL
がばっ
FWAP

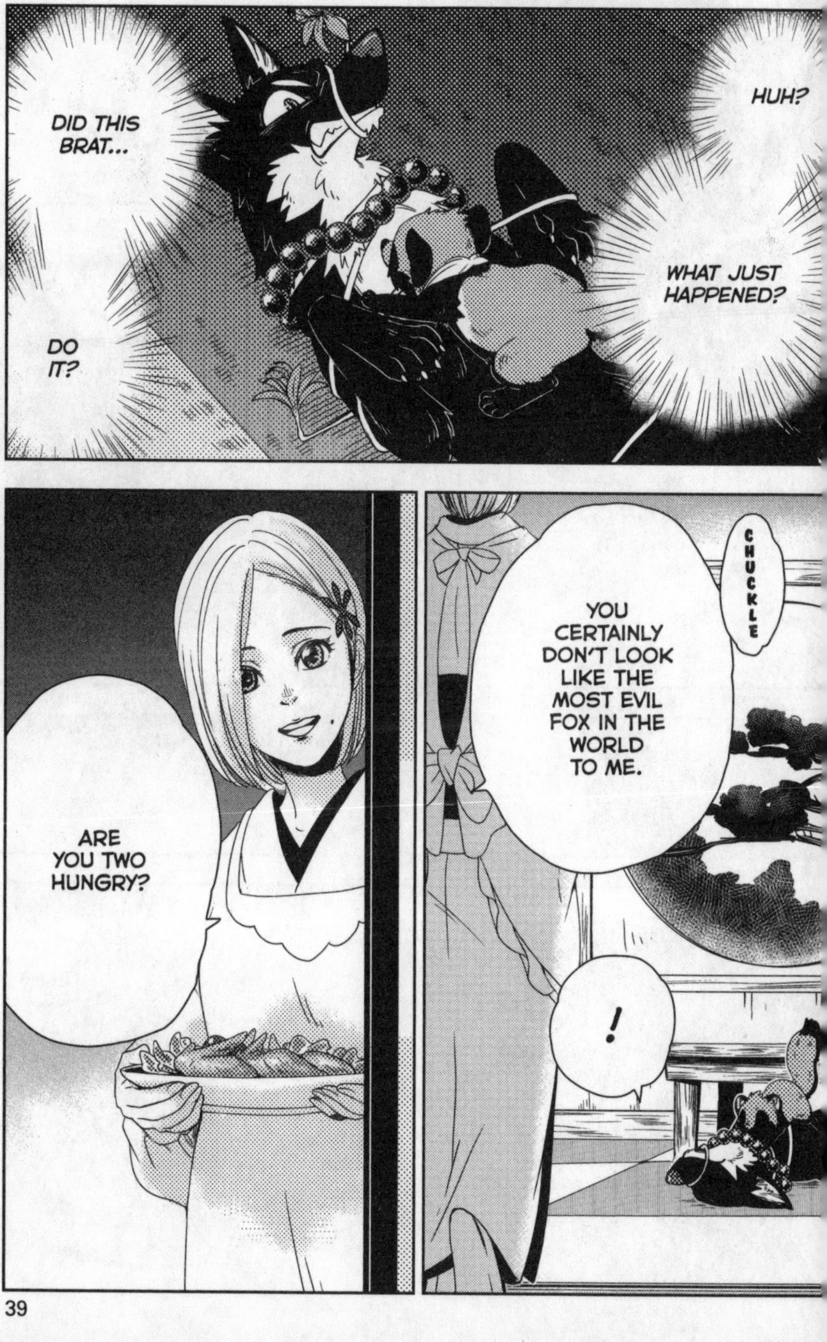
HUH?
WHAT JUST HAPPENED?
DID THIS BRAT...
DO IT?
CHUCKLE
YOU CERTAINLY DON'T LOOK LIKE THE MOST EVIL FOX IN THE WORLD TO ME.
!
ARE YOU TWO HUNGRY?

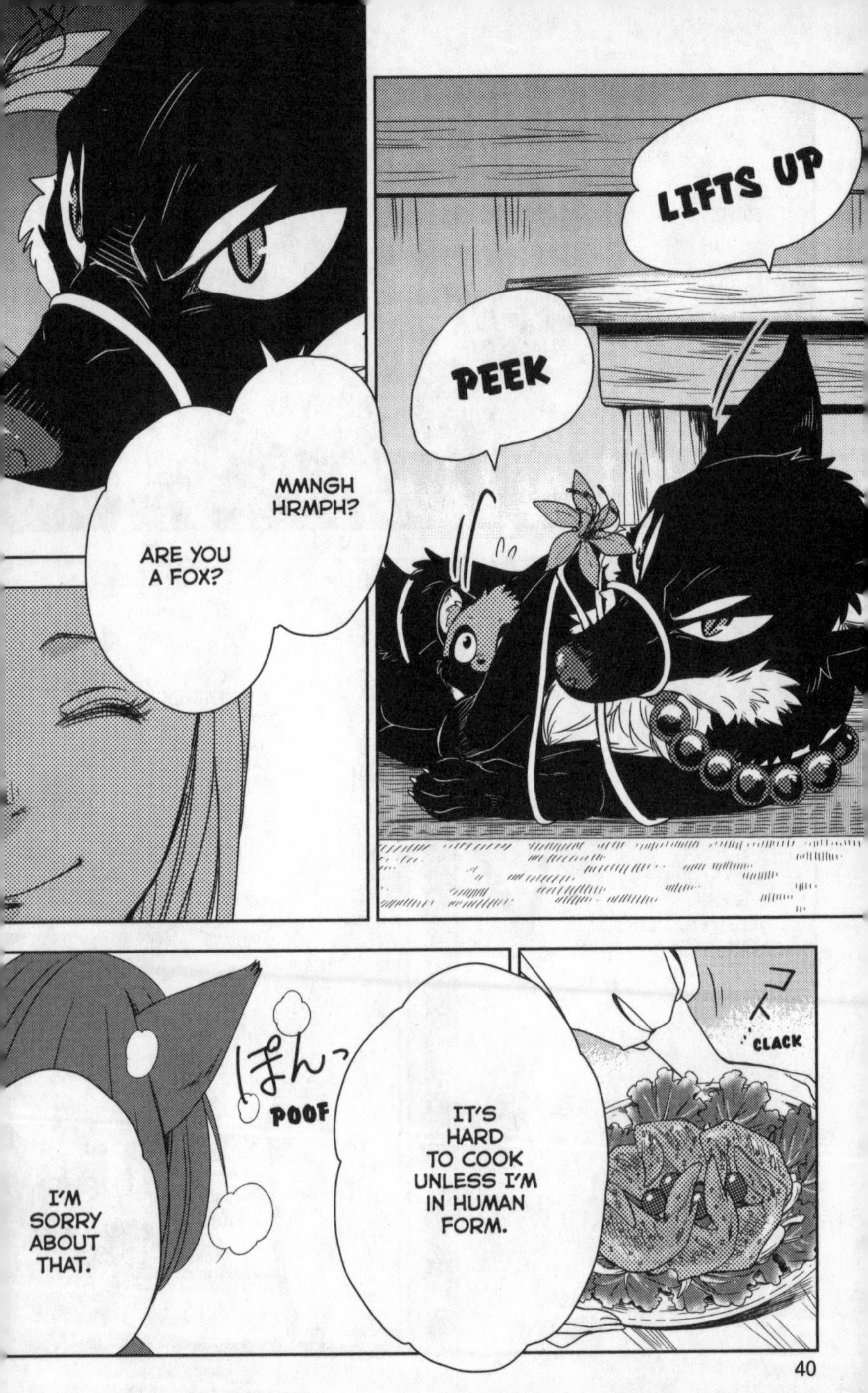
LIFTS UP
PEEK
MMNGH HRMPH?
ARE YOU A FOX?
コト
CLACK
IT'S HARD TO COOK UNLESS I'M IN HUMAN FORM.
ぽんっ
POOF
I'M SORRY ABOUT THAT.

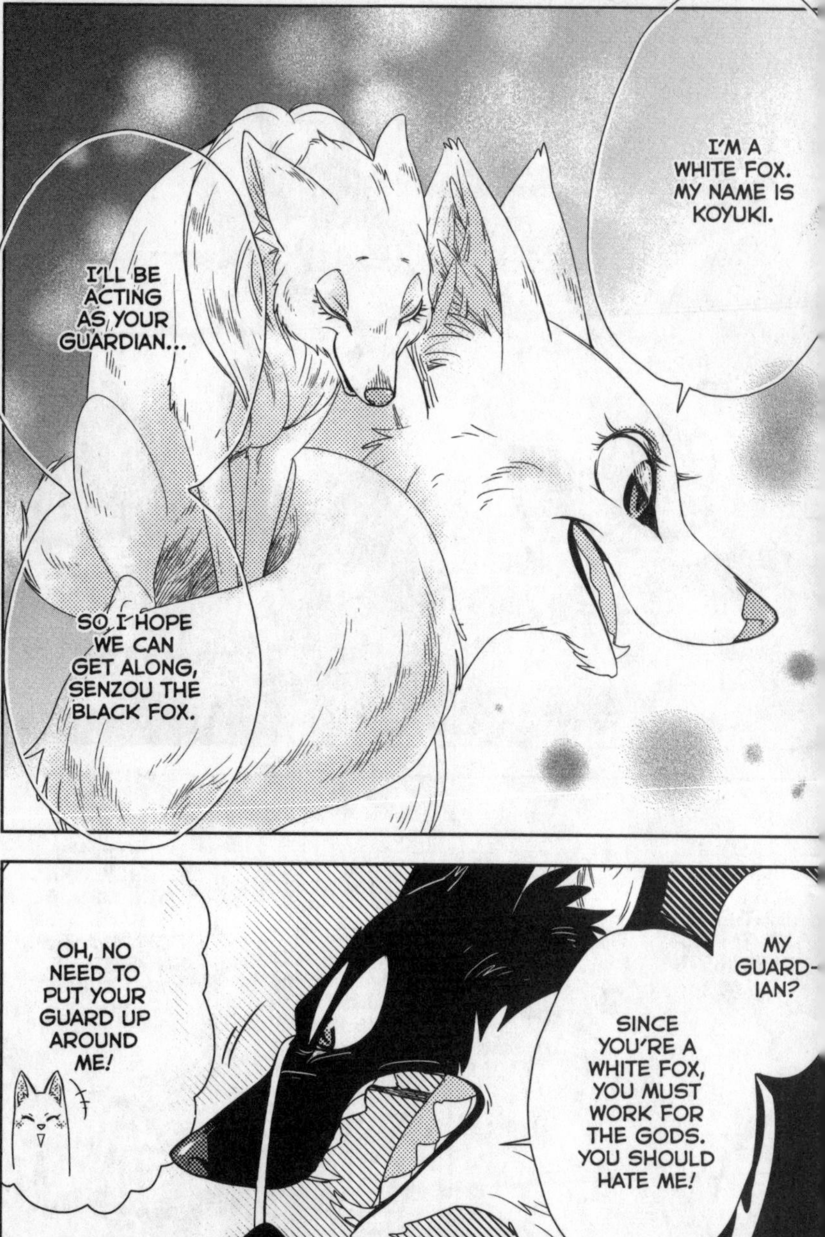
I'M A WHITE FOX. MY NAME IS KOYUKI.
I'LL BE ACTING AS YOUR GUARDIAN...
SO I HOPE WE CAN GET ALONG, SENZOU THE BLACK FOX.
MY GUARD-IAN?
SINCE YOU'RE A WHITE FOX, YOU MUST WORK FOR THE GODS. YOU SHOULD HATE ME!
OH, NO NEED TO PUT YOUR GUARD UP AROUND ME!

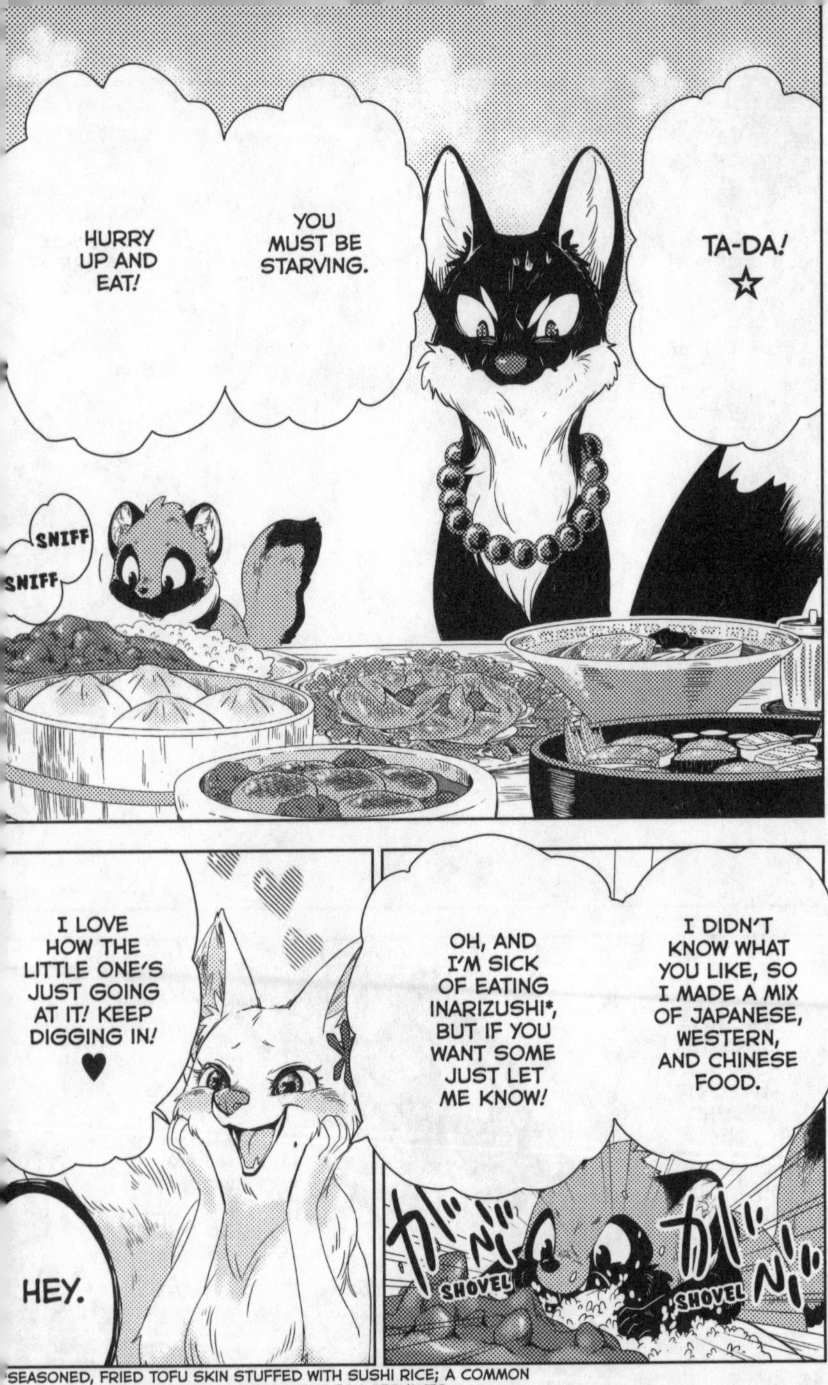
TA-DA! ☆
YOU MUST BE STARVING.
HURRY UP AND EAT!
SNIFF SNIFF
I DIDN'T KNOW WHAT YOU LIKE, SO I MADE A MIX OF JAPANESE, WESTERN, AND CHINESE FOOD.
OH, AND I'M SICK OF EATING INARIZUSHI*, BUT IF YOU WANT SOME JUST LET ME KNOW!
SHOVEL
SHOVEL
I LOVE HOW THE LITTLE ONE'S JUST GOING AT IT! KEEP DIGGING IN! ♥
HEY.

*SEASONED, FRIED TOFU SKIN STUFFED WITH SUSHI RICE; A COMMON OFFERING TO THE DEITY INARI AND INARI'S FOX SERVANTS

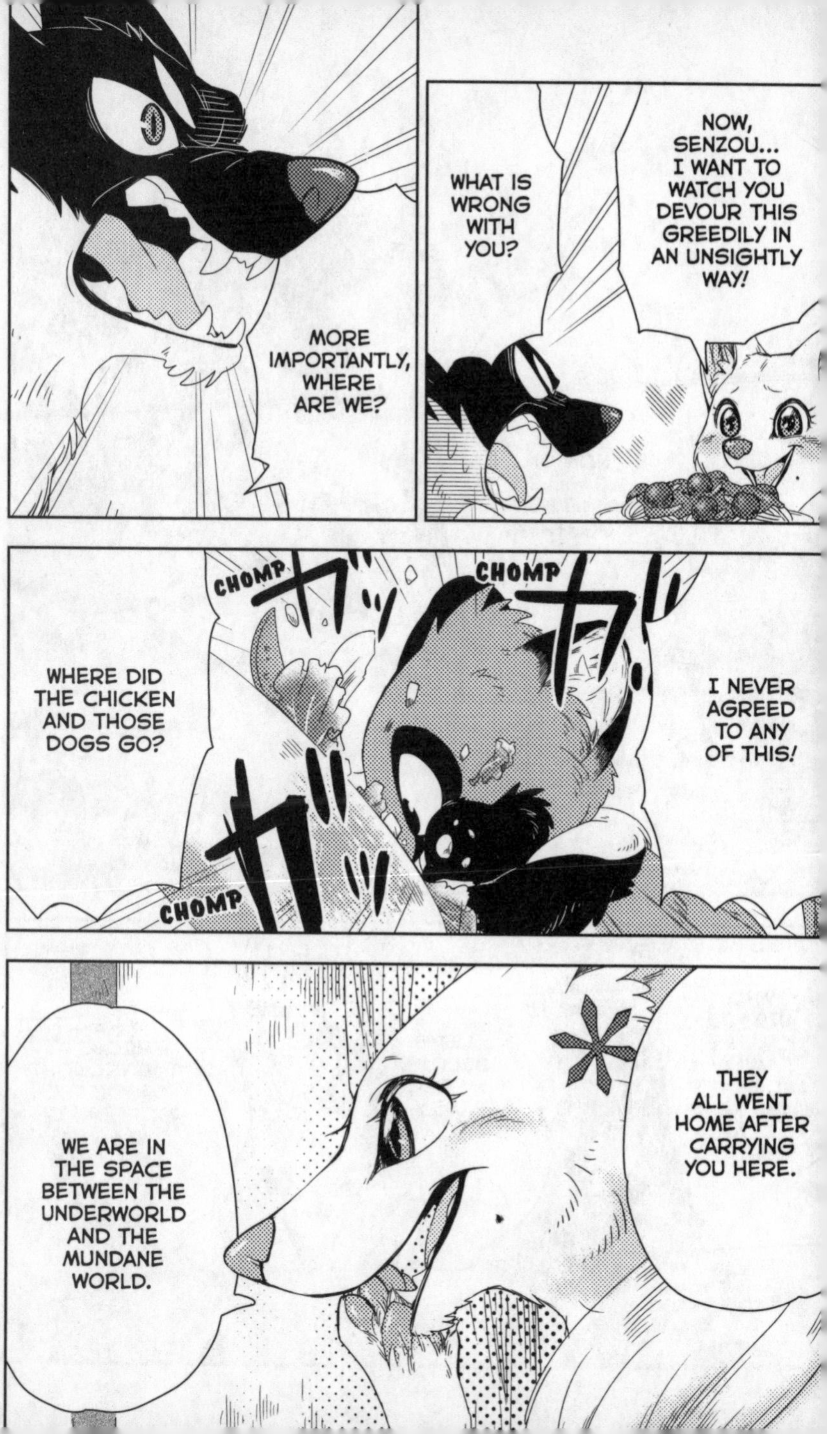
NOW, SENZOU... I WANT TO WATCH YOU DEVOUR THIS GREEDILY IN AN UNSIGHTLY WAY!
WHAT IS WRONG WITH YOU?
MORE IMPORTANTLY, WHERE ARE WE?
I NEVER AGREED TO ANY OF THIS!
CHOMP
CHOMP
WHERE DID THE CHICKEN AND THOSE DOGS GO?
CHOMP
THEY ALL WENT HOME AFTER CARRYING YOU HERE.
WE ARE IN THE SPACE BETWEEN THE UNDERWORLD AND THE MUNDANE WORLD.

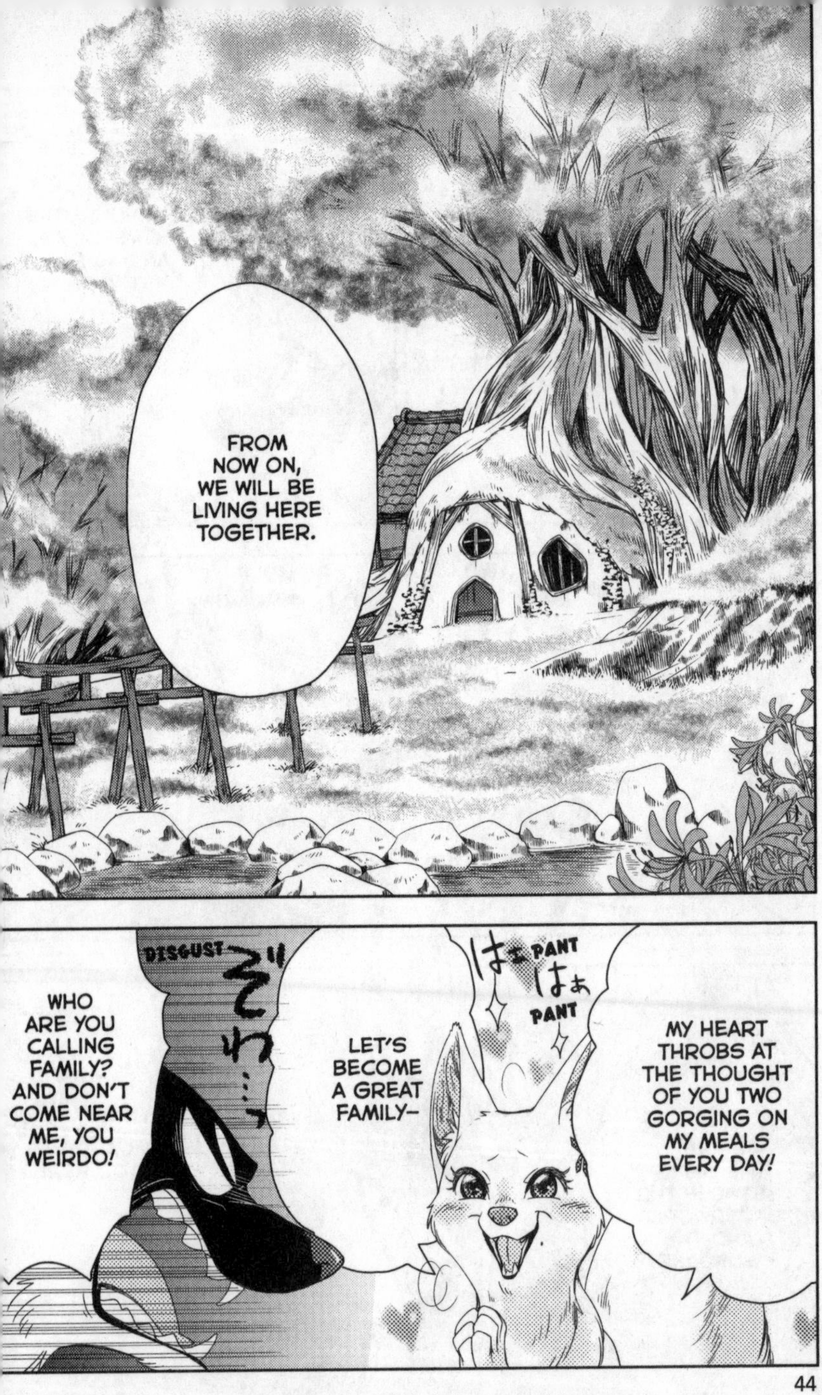
FROM NOW ON, WE WILL BE LIVING HERE TOGETHER.
MY HEART THROBS AT THE THOUGHT OF YOU TWO GORGING ON MY MEALS EVERY DAY!
はぁ PANT
はぁ PANT
LET'S BECOME A GREAT FAMILY–
ぞわ… DISGUST
WHO ARE YOU CALLING FAMILY? AND DON'T COME NEAR ME, YOU WEIRDO!

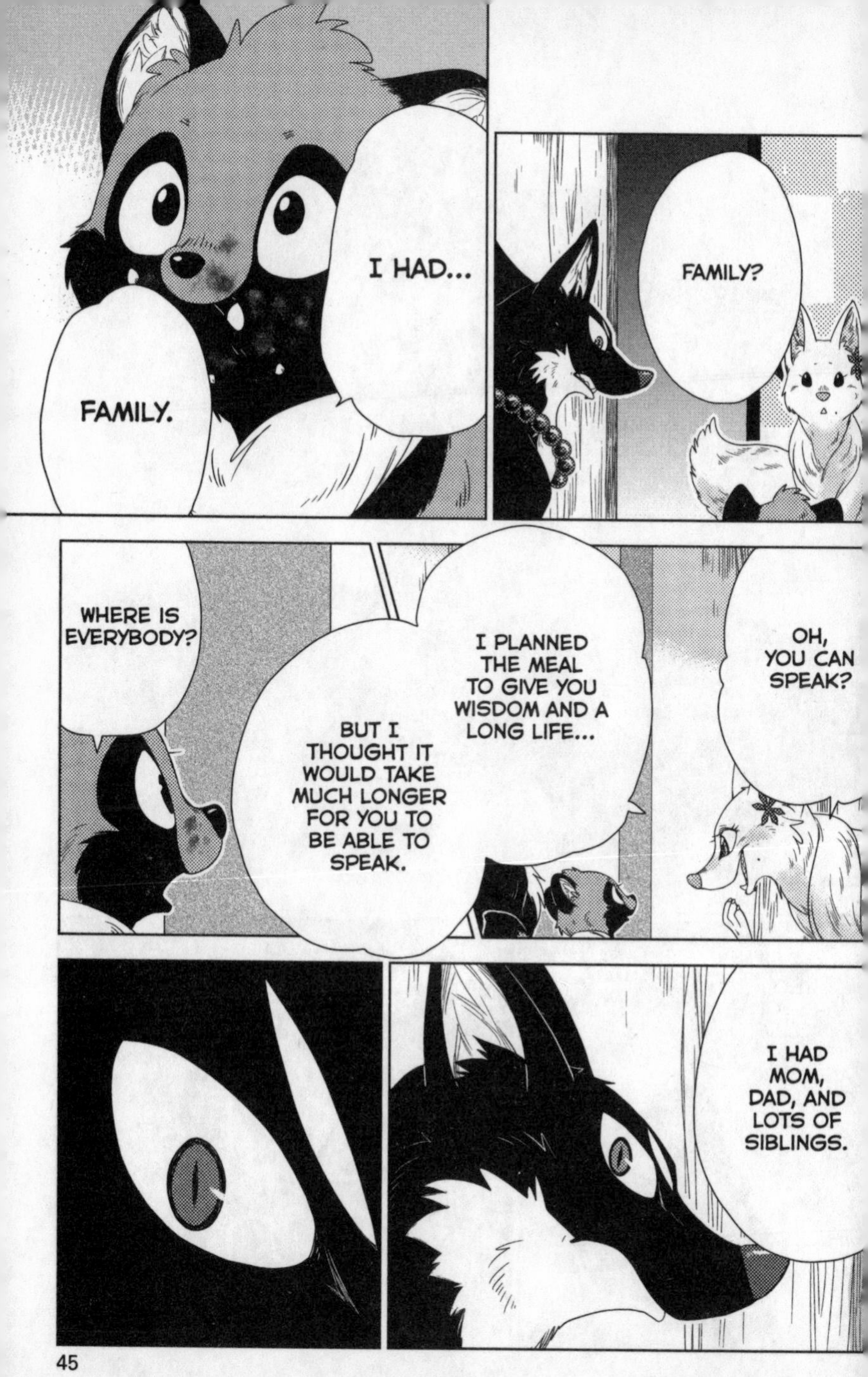
FAMILY?
I HAD...
FAMILY.
OH, YOU CAN SPEAK?
I PLANNED THE MEAL TO GIVE YOU WISDOM AND A LONG LIFE...
BUT I THOUGHT IT WOULD TAKE MUCH LONGER FOR YOU TO BE ABLE TO SPEAK.
WHERE IS EVERYBODY?
I HAD MOM, DAD, AND LOTS OF SIBLINGS.

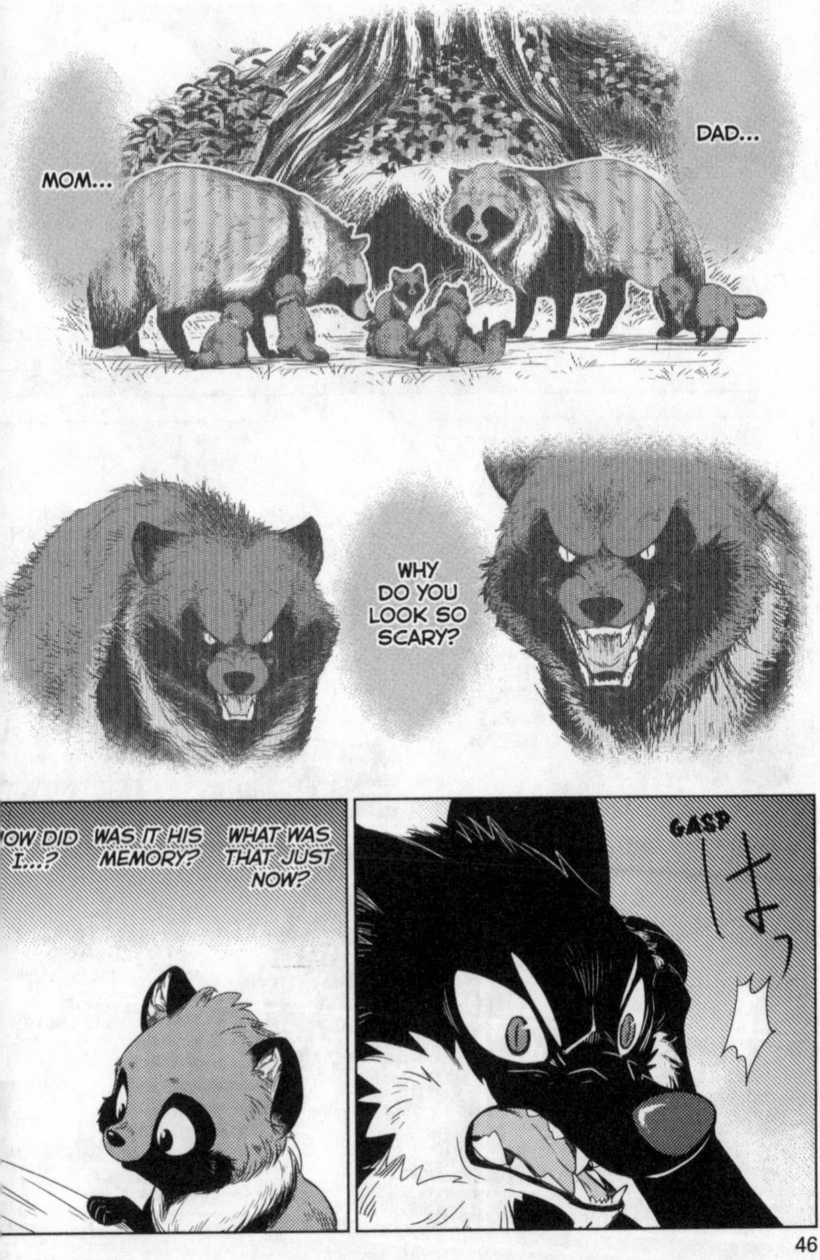
DAD...
MOM...
WHY DO YOU LOOK SO SCARY?
GASP
はっ
WHAT WAS THAT JUST NOW?
WAS IT HIS MEMORY?
OW DID I...?

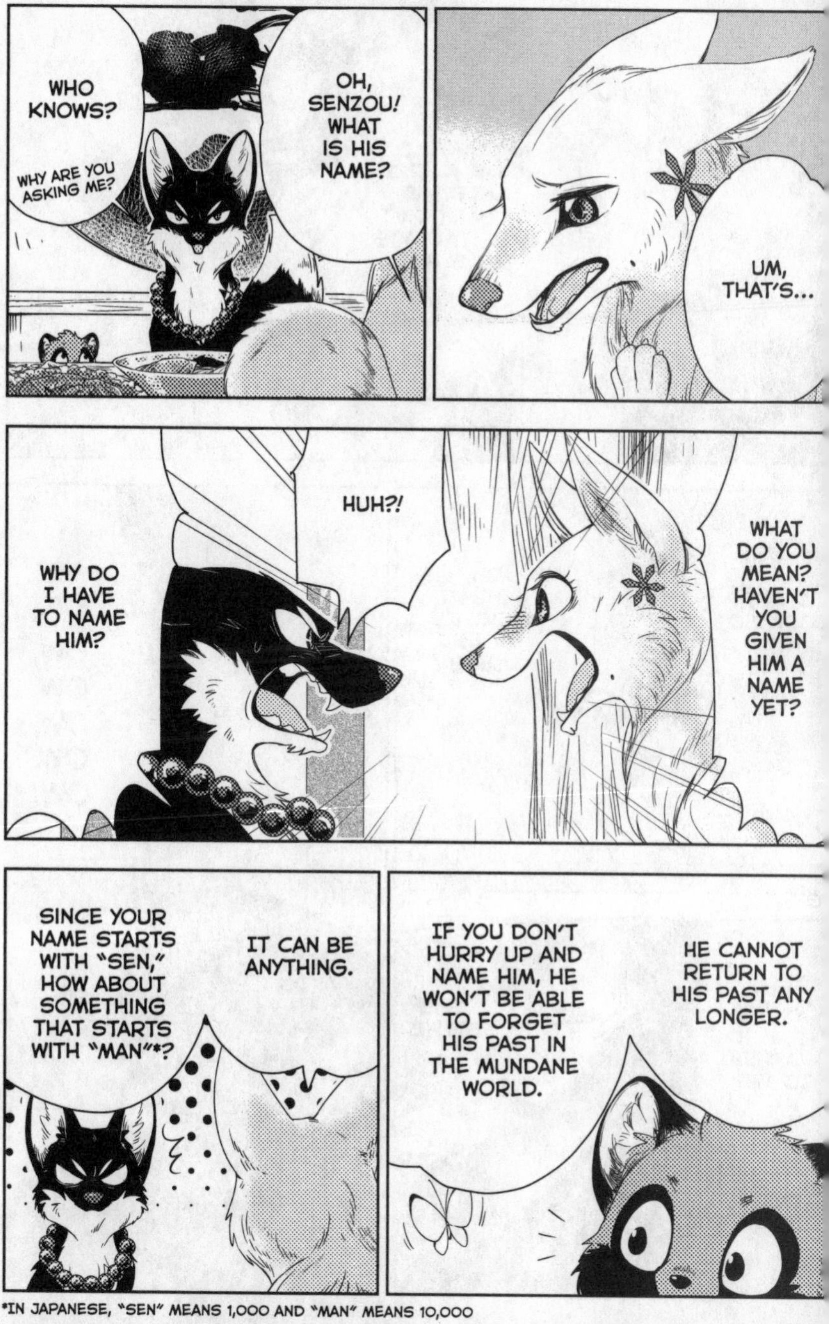
UM, THAT'S...
OH, SENZOU! WHAT IS HIS NAME?
WHO KNOWS?
WHY ARE YOU ASKING ME?
WHAT DO YOU MEAN? HAVEN'T YOU GIVEN HIM A NAME YET?
HUH?!
WHY DO I HAVE TO NAME HIM?
HE CANNOT RETURN TO HIS PAST ANY LONGER.
IF YOU DON'T HURRY UP AND NAME HIM, HE WON'T BE ABLE TO FORGET HIS PAST IN THE MUNDANE WORLD.
IT CAN BE ANYTHING.
SINCE YOUR NAME STARTS WITH "SEN," HOW ABOUT SOMETHING THAT STARTS WITH "MAN"*?

*IN JAPANESE, "SEN" MEANS 1,000 AND "MAN" MEANS 10,000

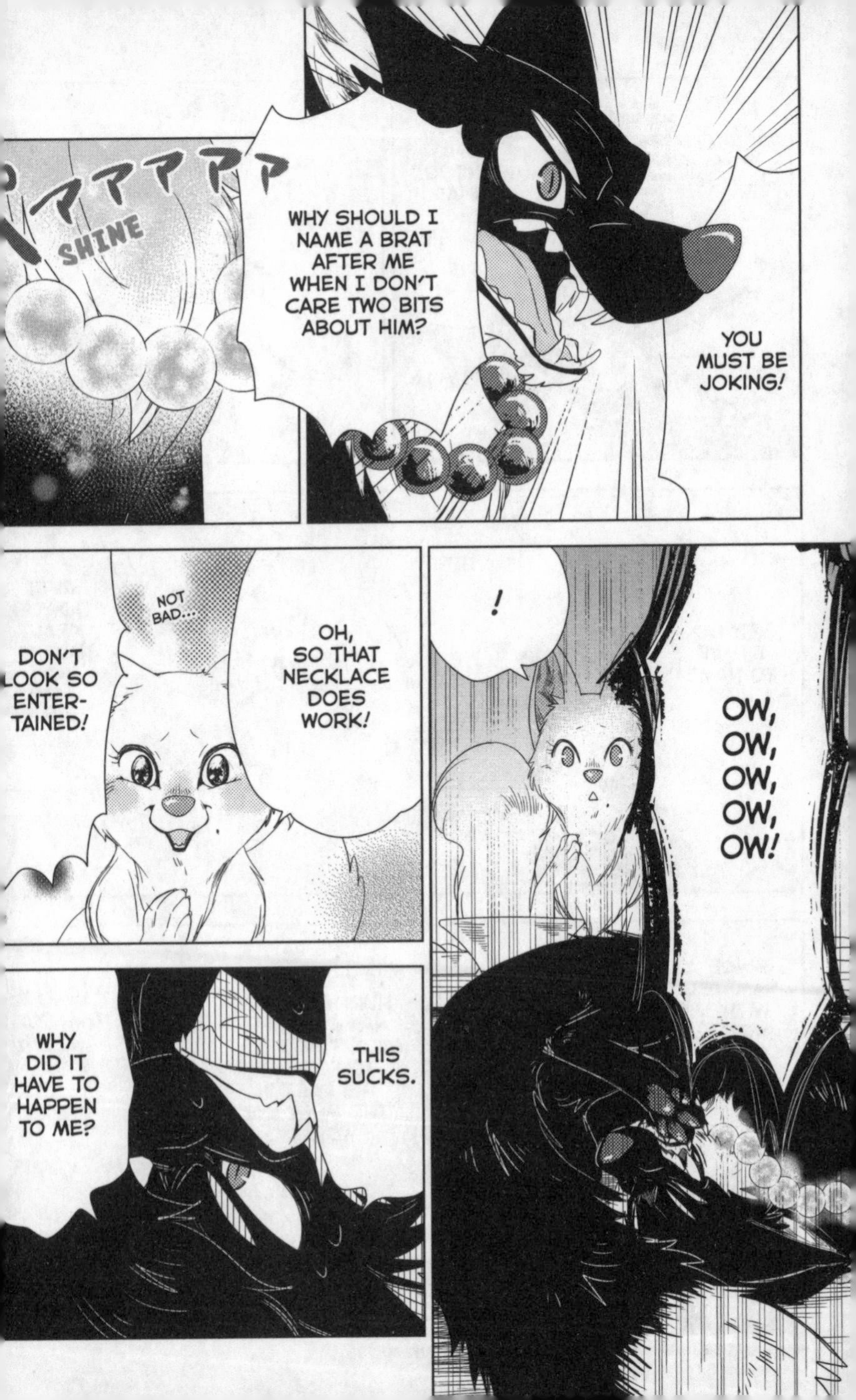
YOU MUST BE JOKING!
WHY SHOULD I NAME A BRAT AFTER ME WHEN I DON'T CARE TWO BITS ABOUT HIM?
SHINE
!
OW, OW, OW, OW, OW!
OH, SO THAT NECKLACE DOES WORK!
NOT BAD...
DON'T LOOK SO ENTERTAINED!
THIS SUCKS.
WHY DID IT HAVE TO HAPPEN TO ME?

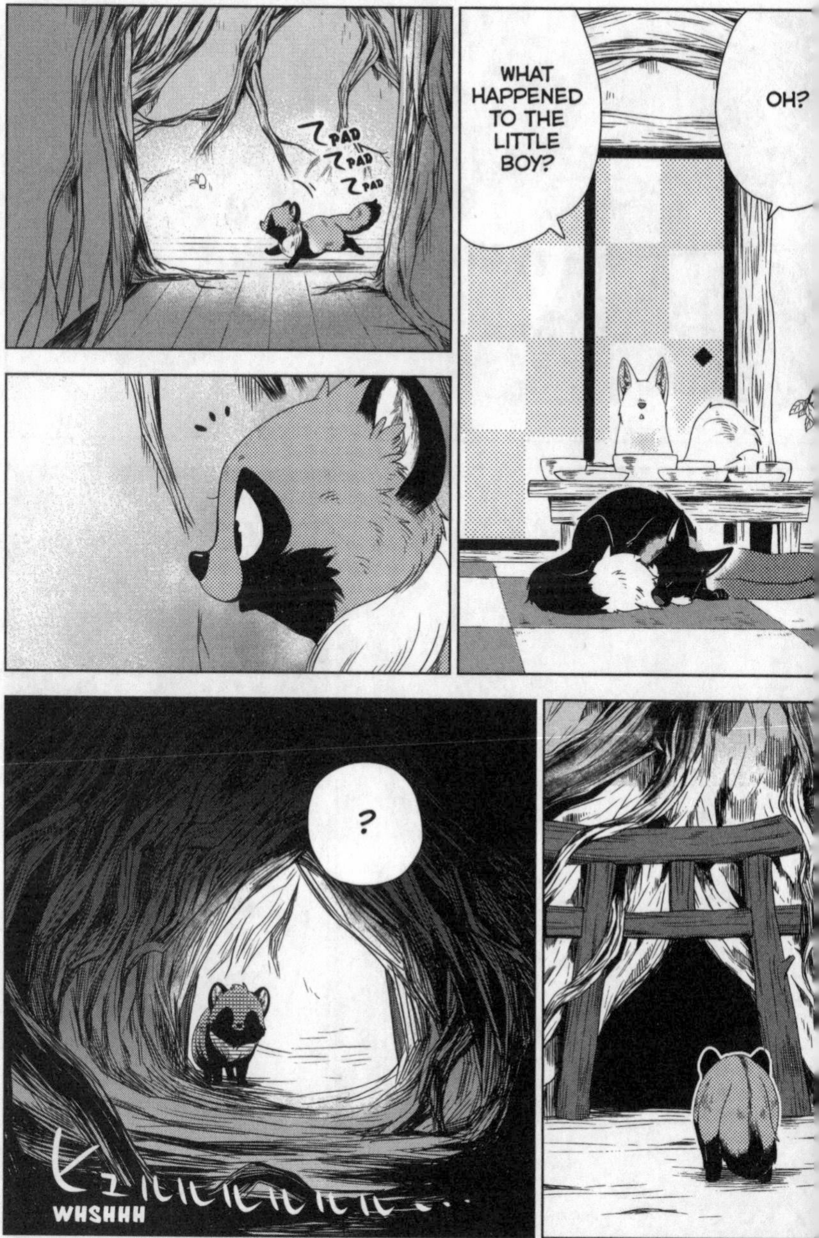
OH?
WHAT HAPPENED TO THE LITTLE BOY?
PAD
PAD
PAD
?
WHSHHH

SNIFF

TROT

HEY, I SMELL MY FAMILY!

TWEET ピㇱ…

!

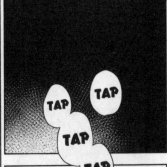

TAP

TAP

TAP

TAP

BRIGHT パァァァァァ

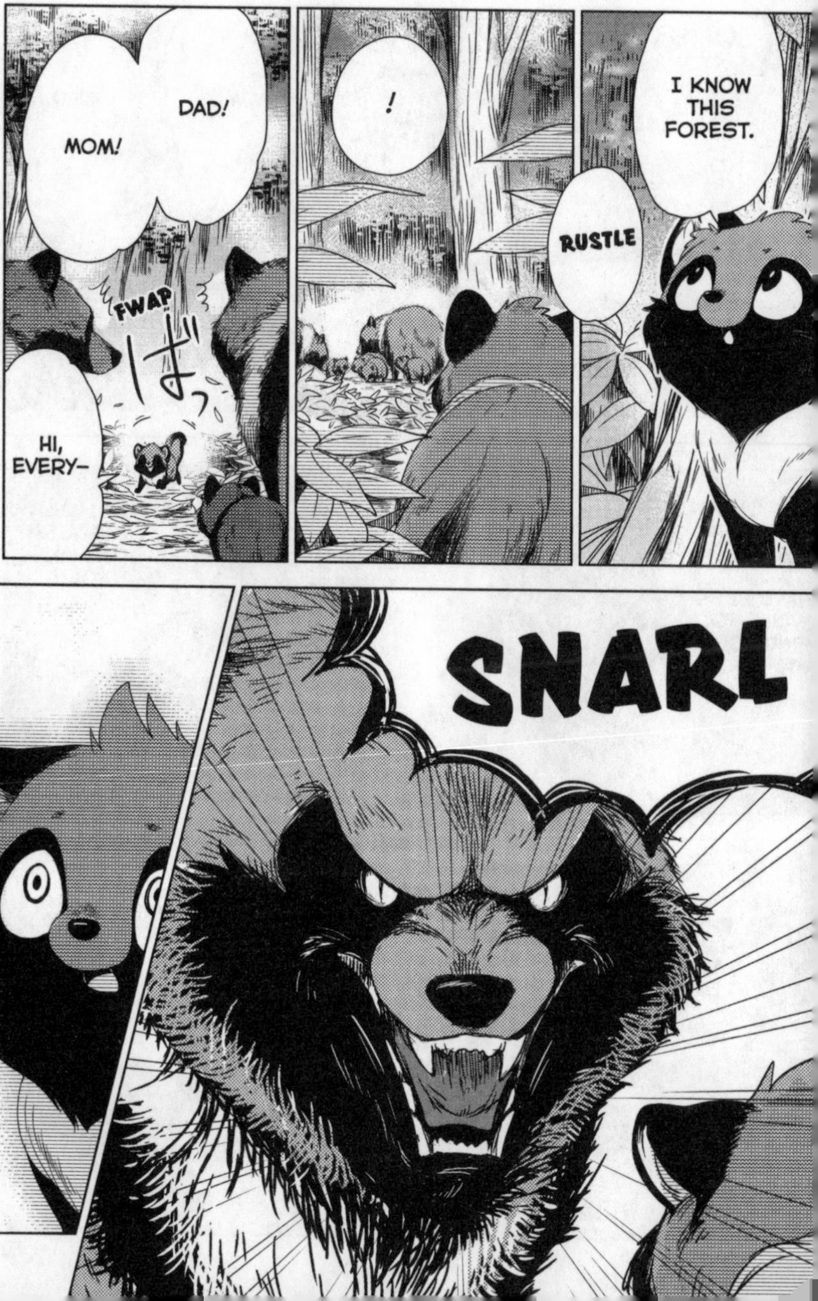
I KNOW THIS FOREST.
RUSTLE
!
DAD!
MOM!
FWAP
HI, EVERY–
SNARL

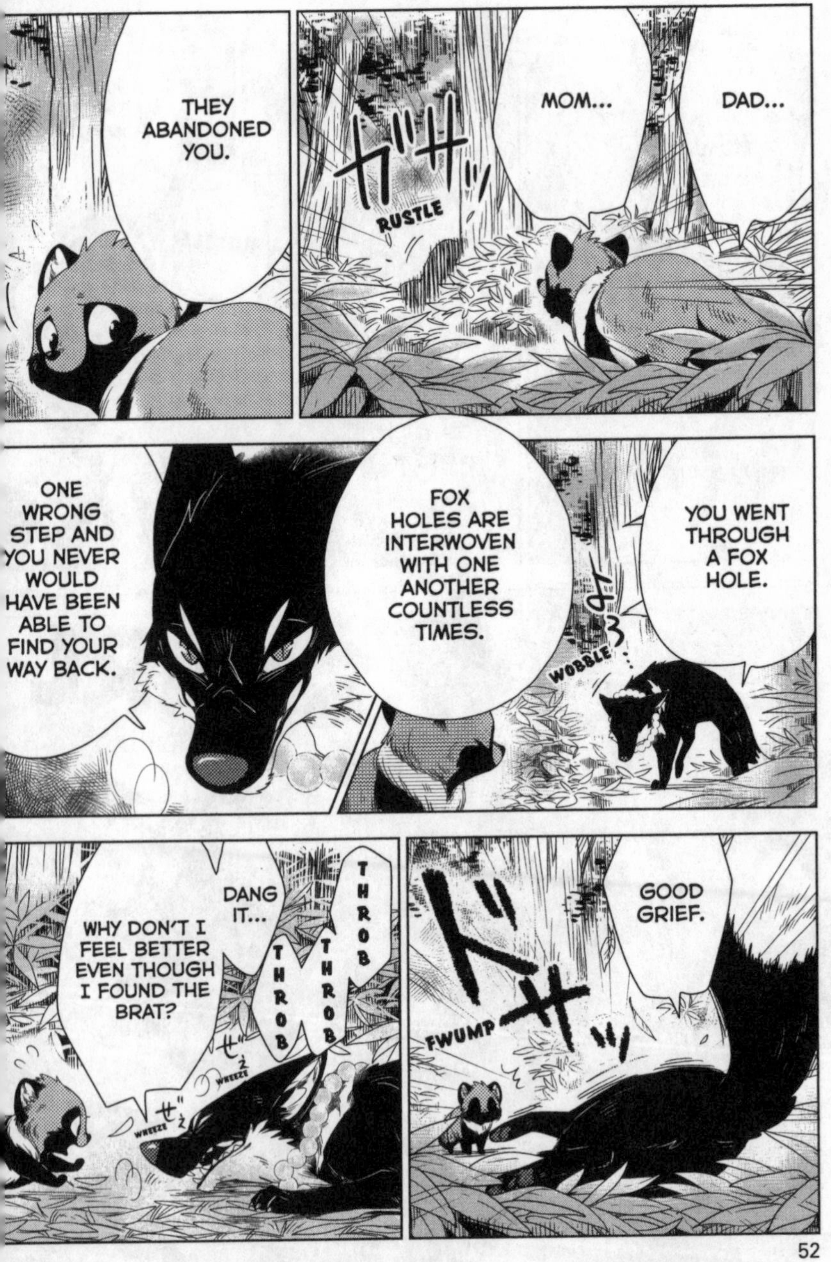
MOM... DAD...
ガサッ
RUSTLE
THEY ABANDONED YOU.
YOU WENT THROUGH A FOX HOLE.
WOBBLE
FOX HOLES ARE INTERWOVEN WITH ONE ANOTHER COUNTLESS TIMES.
ONE WRONG STEP AND YOU NEVER WOULD HAVE BEEN ABLE TO FIND YOUR WAY BACK.
GOOD GRIEF.
ドサッ
FWUMP
THROB
THROB
DANG IT...
THROB
WHY DON'T I FEEL BETTER EVEN THOUGH I FOUND THE BRAT?
WHEEZE
WHEEZE

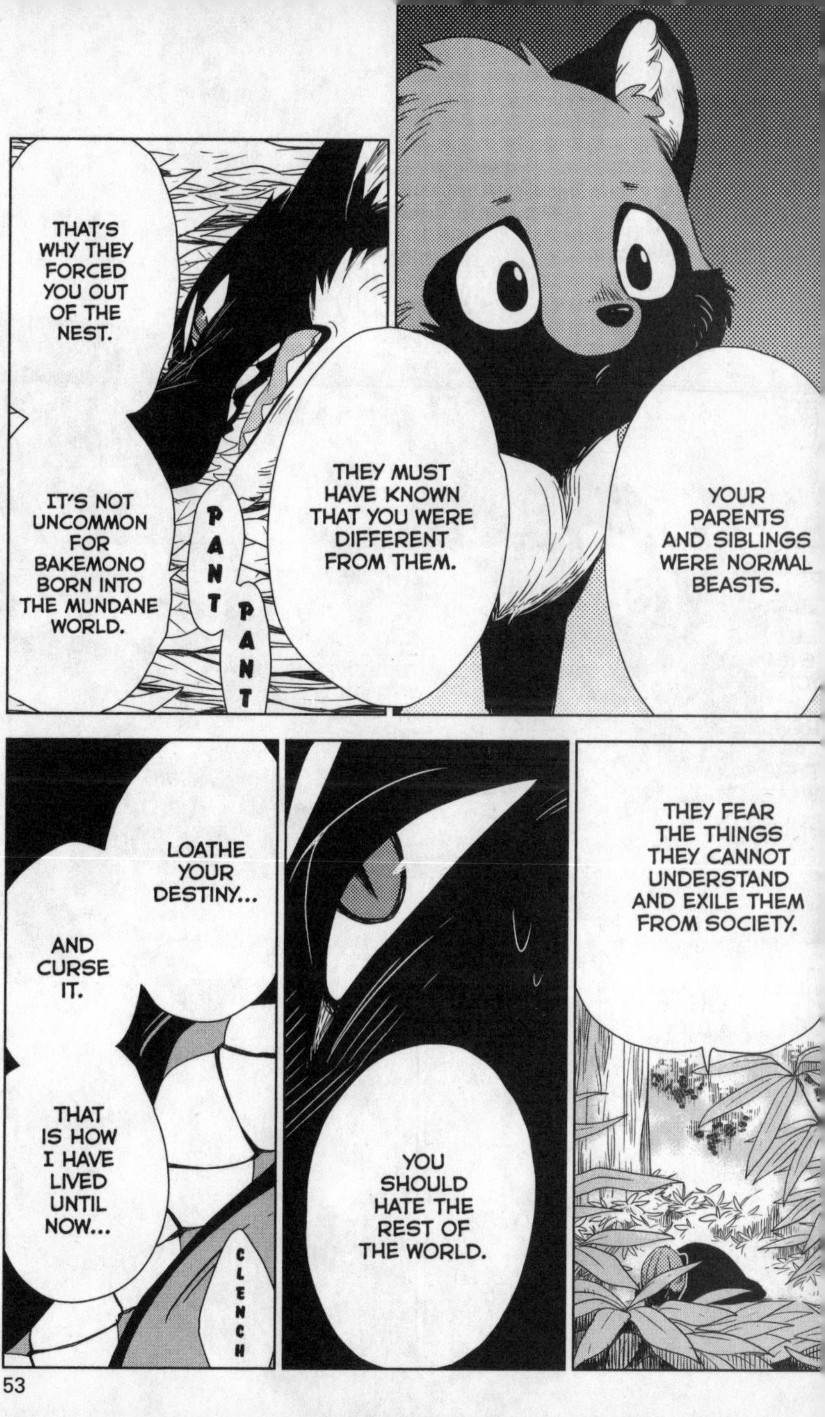
YOUR PARENTS AND SIBLINGS WERE NORMAL BEASTS.
THEY MUST HAVE KNOWN THAT YOU WERE DIFFERENT FROM THEM.
THAT'S WHY THEY FORCED YOU OUT OF THE NEST.
PANT PANT
IT'S NOT UNCOMMON FOR BAKEMONO BORN INTO THE MUNDANE WORLD.
THEY FEAR THE THINGS THEY CANNOT UNDERSTAND AND EXILE THEM FROM SOCIETY.
YOU SHOULD HATE THE REST OF THE WORLD.
LOATHE YOUR DESTINY...
AND CURSE IT.
CLENCH
THAT IS HOW I HAVE LIVED UNTIL NOW...

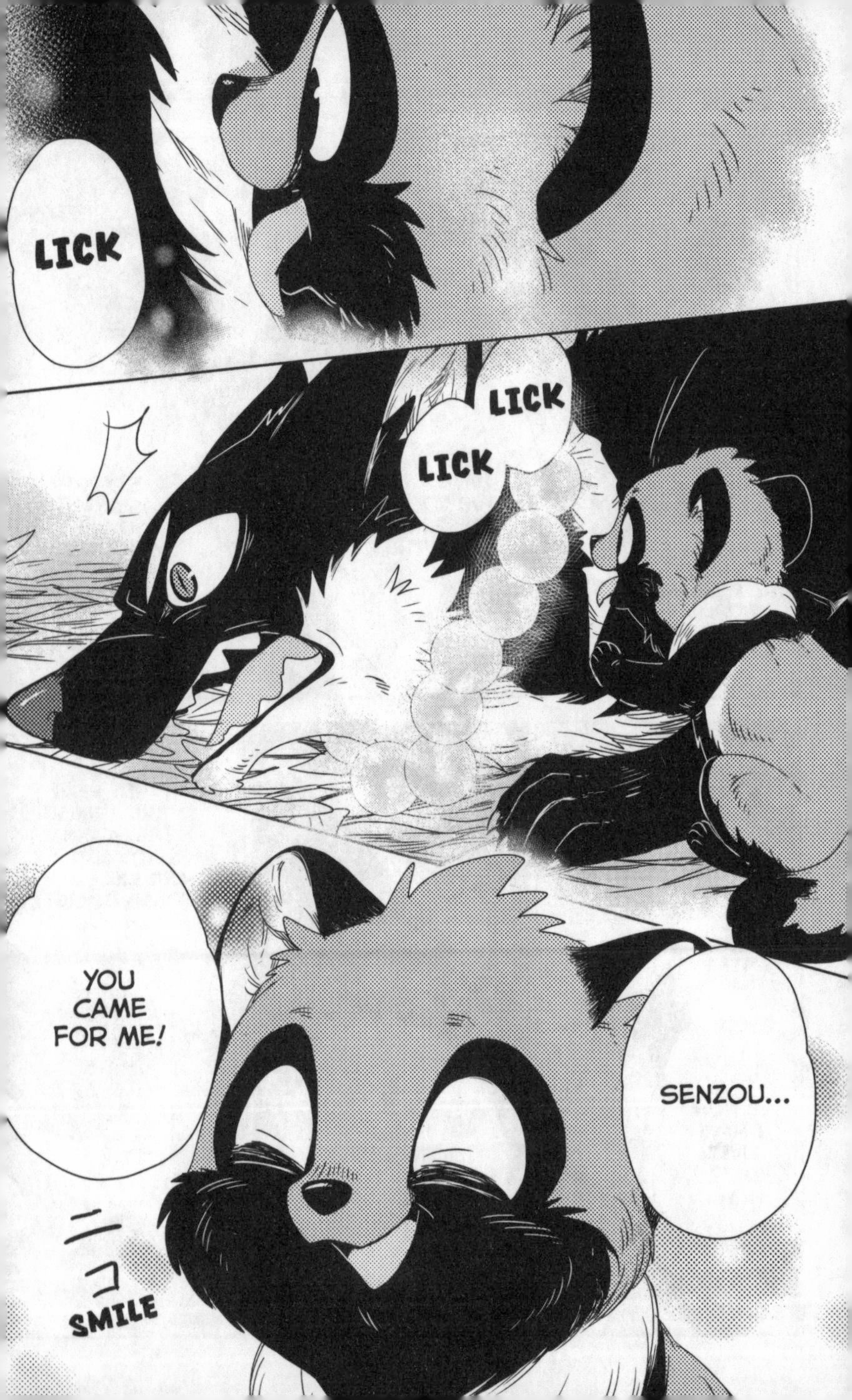
LICK
LICK
LICK
SENZOU...
YOU CAME FOR ME!
ニコ
SMILE

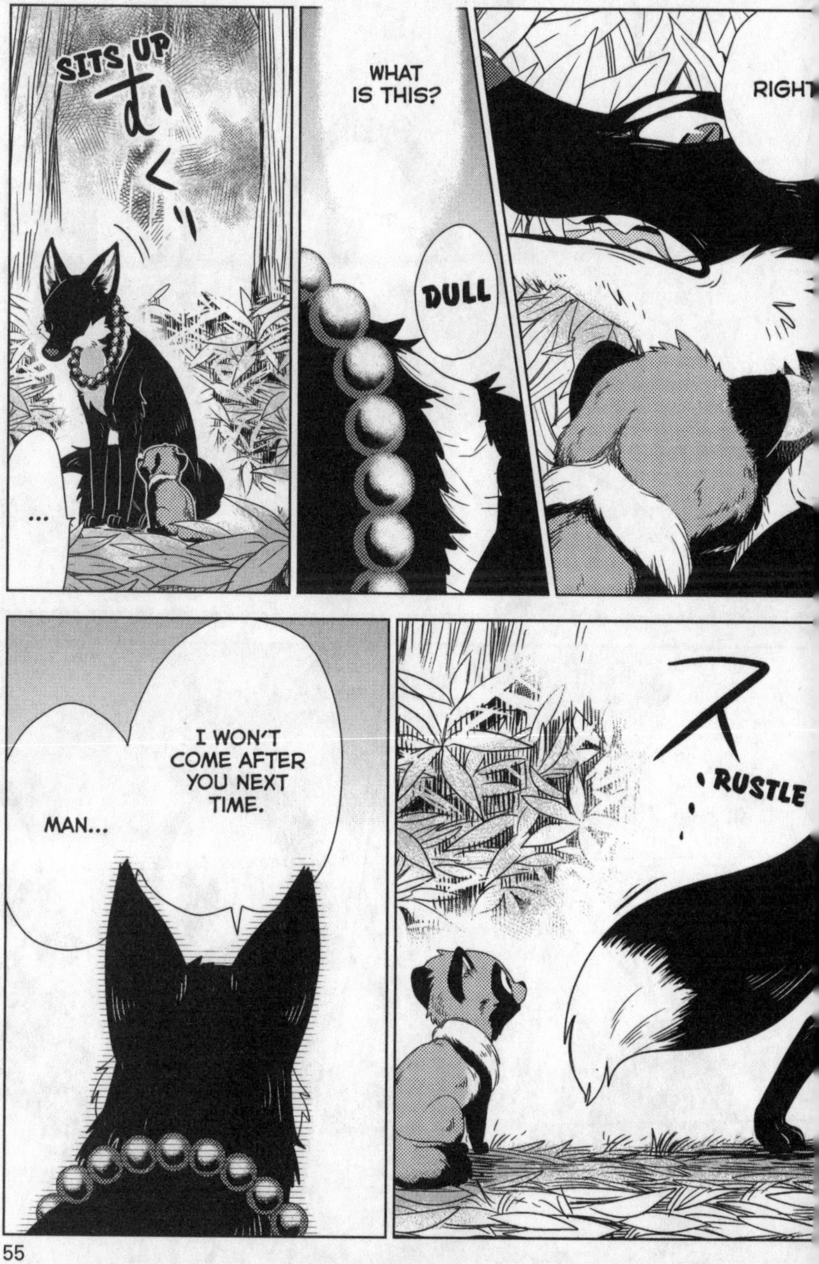
RIGHT
WHAT IS THIS?
DULL
SITS UP
むくり
...
ス
RUSTLE
I WON'T COME AFTER YOU NEXT TIME.
MAN...

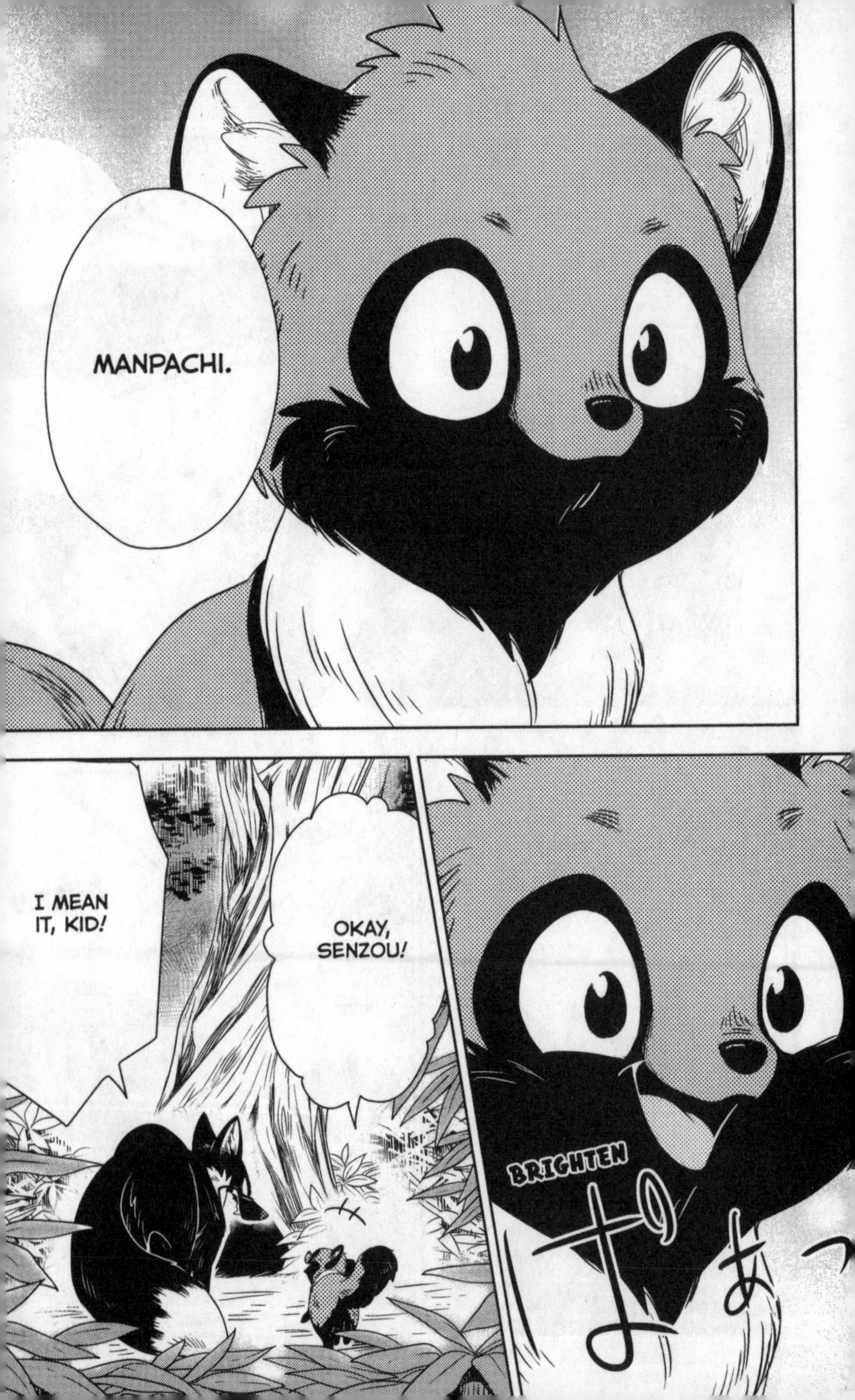
MANPACHI.
BRIGHTEN
I MEAN IT, KID!
OKAY, SENZOU!

#2

The Bakemono Field Guide

Bakedanuki (Tanuki)

They are like the mascots of bakemono. Beloved in Japan for centuries, tanuki appear in many old stories and are known for being quiet and a little on the dumb side... but they're better at transforming than kitsune are!

Chapter 3

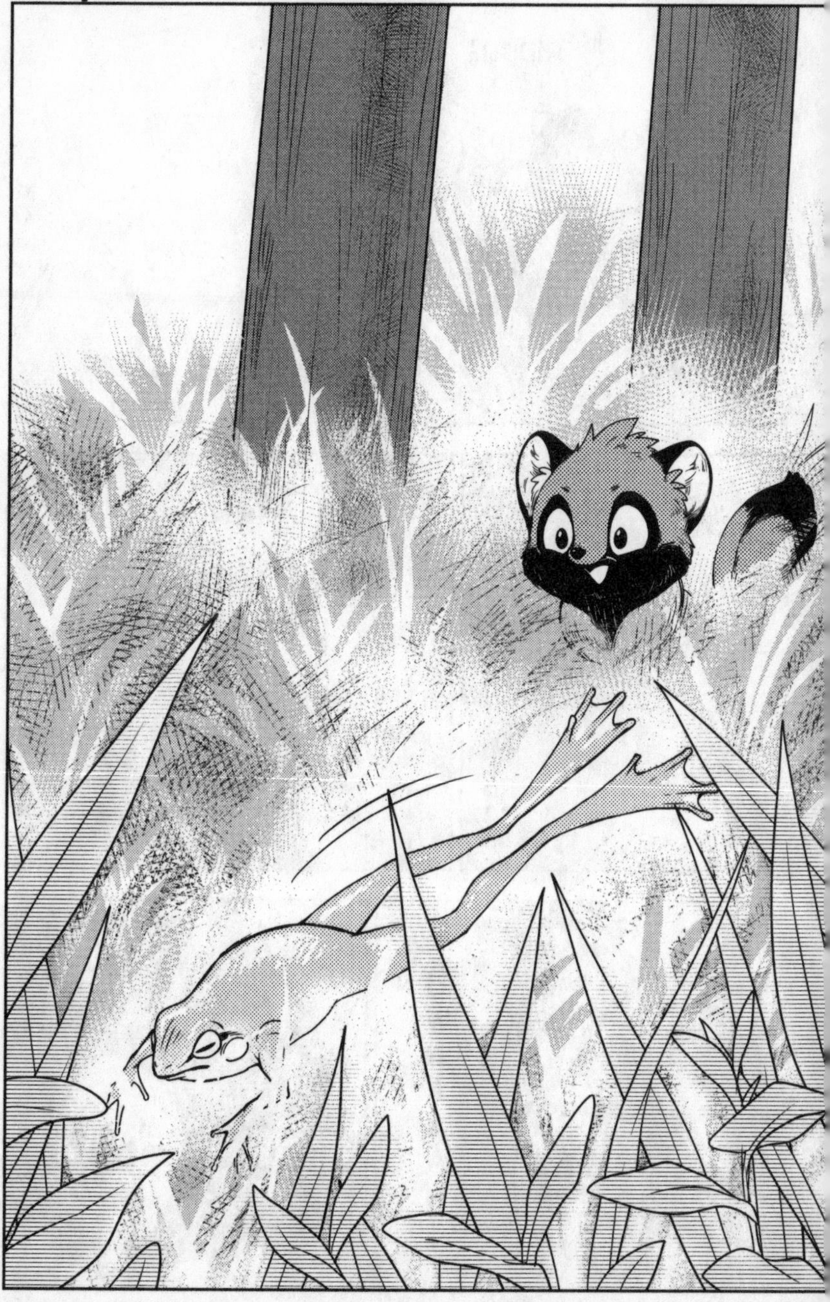

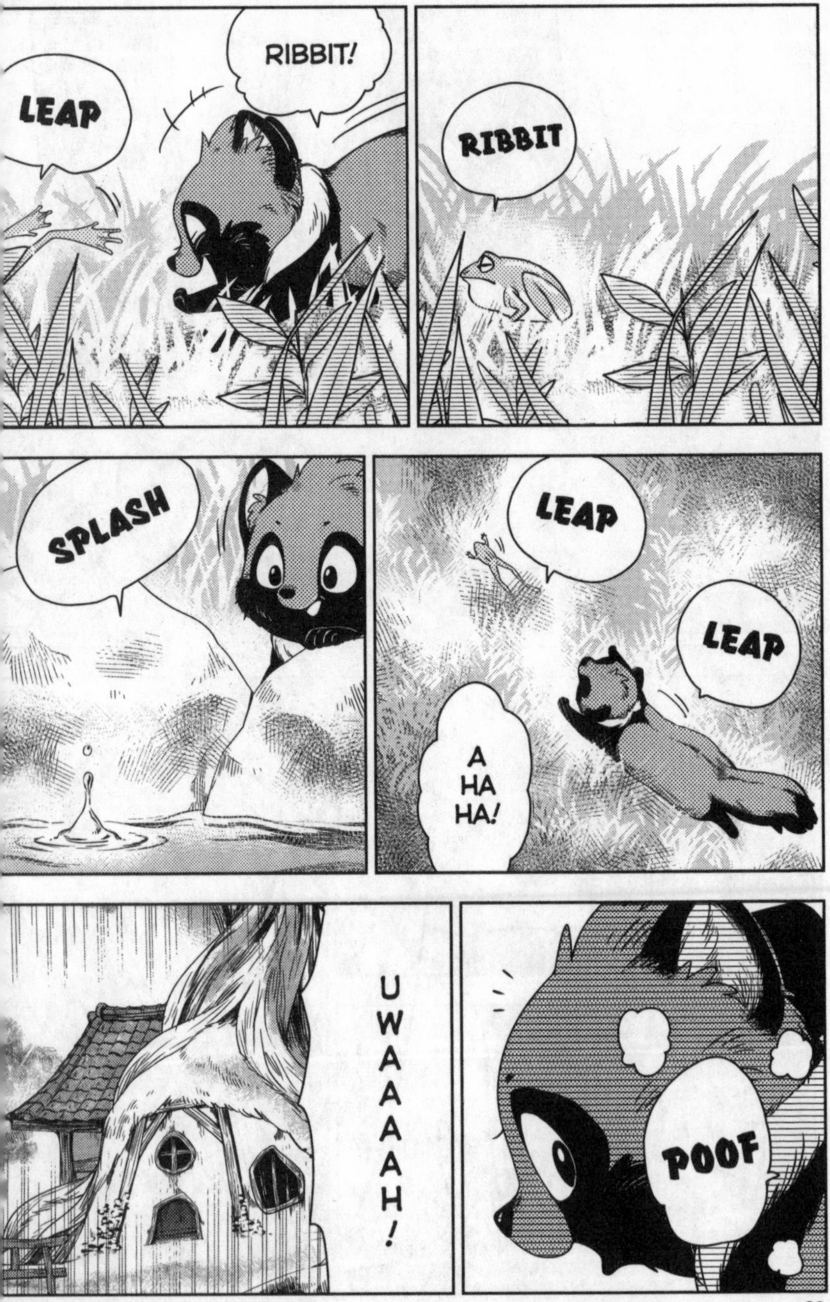
RIBBIT
RIBBIT!
LEAP
LEAP
LEAP
A HA HA!
SPLASH
POOF
UWAAAAAH!

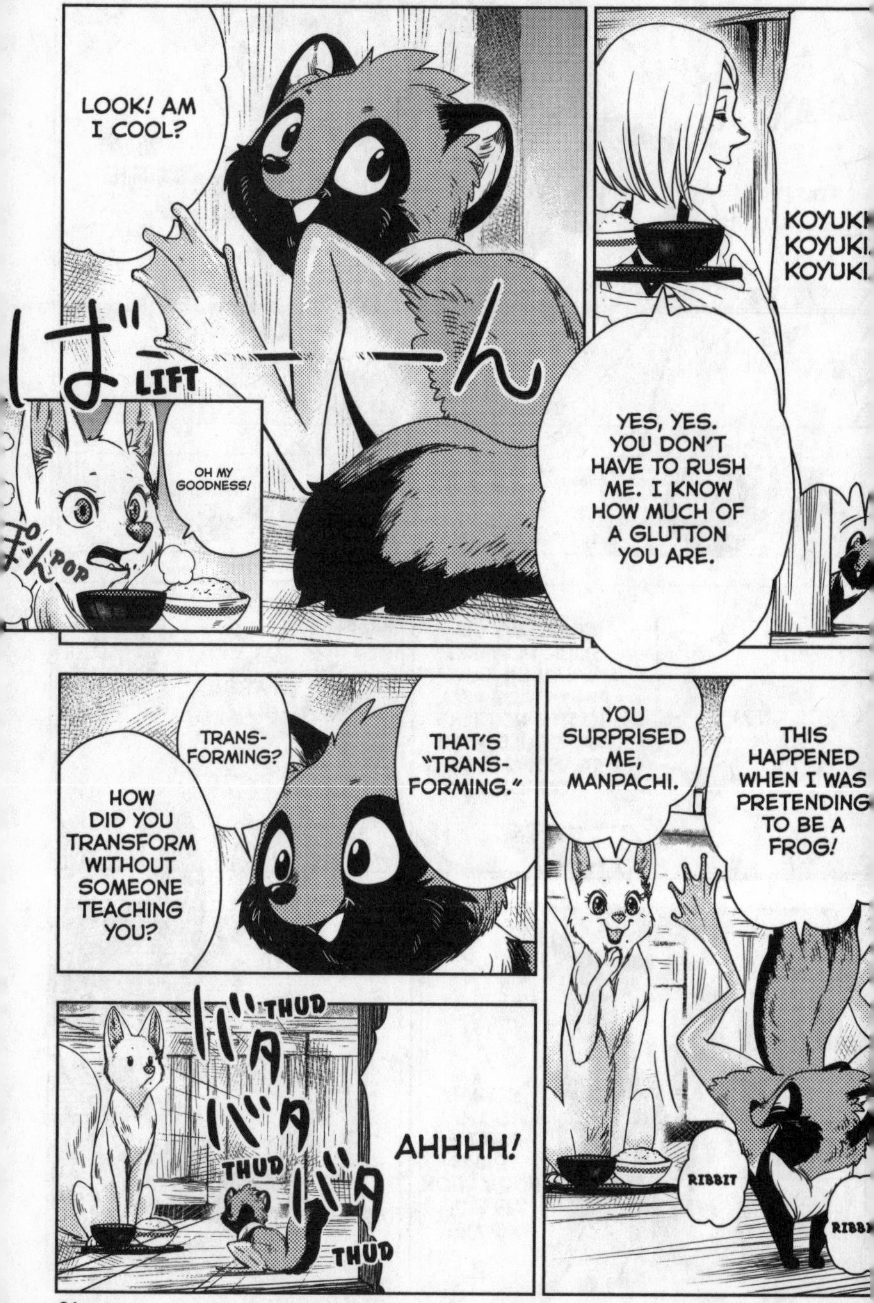
KOYUKI
KOYUKI.
KOYUKI.
YES, YES. YOU DON'T HAVE TO RUSH ME. I KNOW HOW MUCH OF A GLUTTON YOU ARE.
LOOK! AM I COOL?
ばーーん
LIFT
OH MY GOODNESS!
ぽん
POP
THIS HAPPENED WHEN I WAS PRETENDING TO BE A FROG!
YOU SURPRISED ME, MANPACHI.
RIBBIT
RIBBI
THAT'S "TRANS-FORMING."
TRANS-FORMING?
HOW DID YOU TRANSFORM WITHOUT SOMEONE TEACHING YOU?
AHHHH!
バタ
THUD
バタ
THUD
バタ
THUD

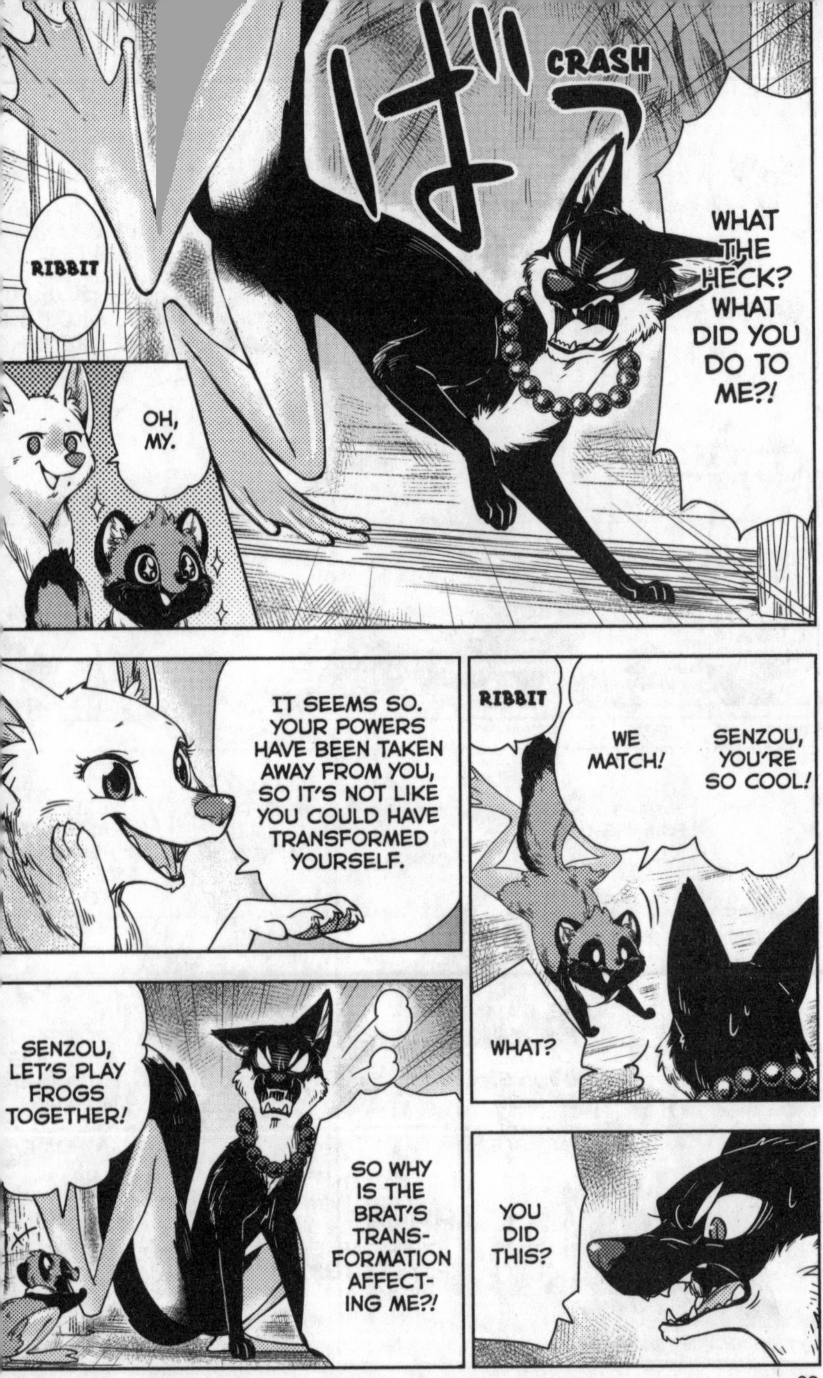
CRASH
ばっ
WHAT THE HECK? WHAT DID YOU DO TO ME?!
RIBBIT
OH, MY.
SENZOU, YOU'RE SO COOL!
WE MATCH!
RIBBIT
WHAT?
IT SEEMS SO. YOUR POWERS HAVE BEEN TAKEN AWAY FROM YOU, SO IT'S NOT LIKE YOU COULD HAVE TRANSFORMED YOURSELF.
YOU DID THIS?
SO WHY IS THE BRAT'S TRANS-FORMATION AFFECT-ING ME?!
SENZOU, LET'S PLAY FROGS TOGETHER!

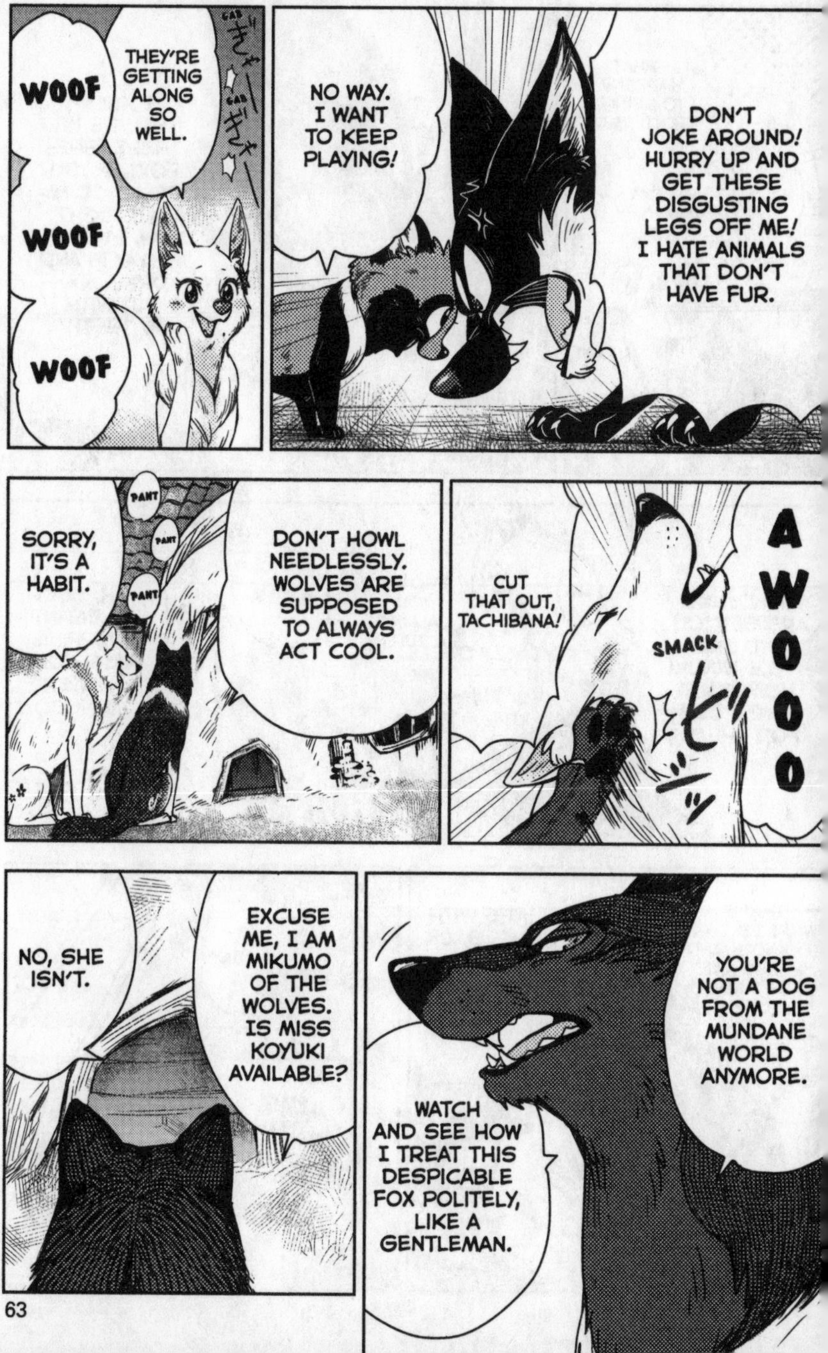
DON'T JOKE AROUND! HURRY UP AND GET THESE DISGUSTING LEGS OFF ME! I HATE ANIMALS THAT DON'T HAVE FUR.
NO WAY. I WANT TO KEEP PLAYING!
GAB GAB
THEY'RE GETTING ALONG SO WELL.
WOOF
WOOF
WOOF
AWOOO
SMACK
CUT THAT OUT, TACHIBANA!
DON'T HOWL NEEDLESSLY. WOLVES ARE SUPPOSED TO ALWAYS ACT COOL.
PANT
PANT
PANT
SORRY, IT'S A HABIT.
YOU'RE NOT A DOG FROM THE MUNDANE WORLD ANYMORE.
WATCH AND SEE HOW I TREAT THIS DESPICABLE FOX POLITELY, LIKE A GENTLEMAN.
EXCUSE ME, I AM MIKUMO OF THE WOLVES. IS MISS KOYUKI AVAILABLE?
NO, SHE ISN'T.

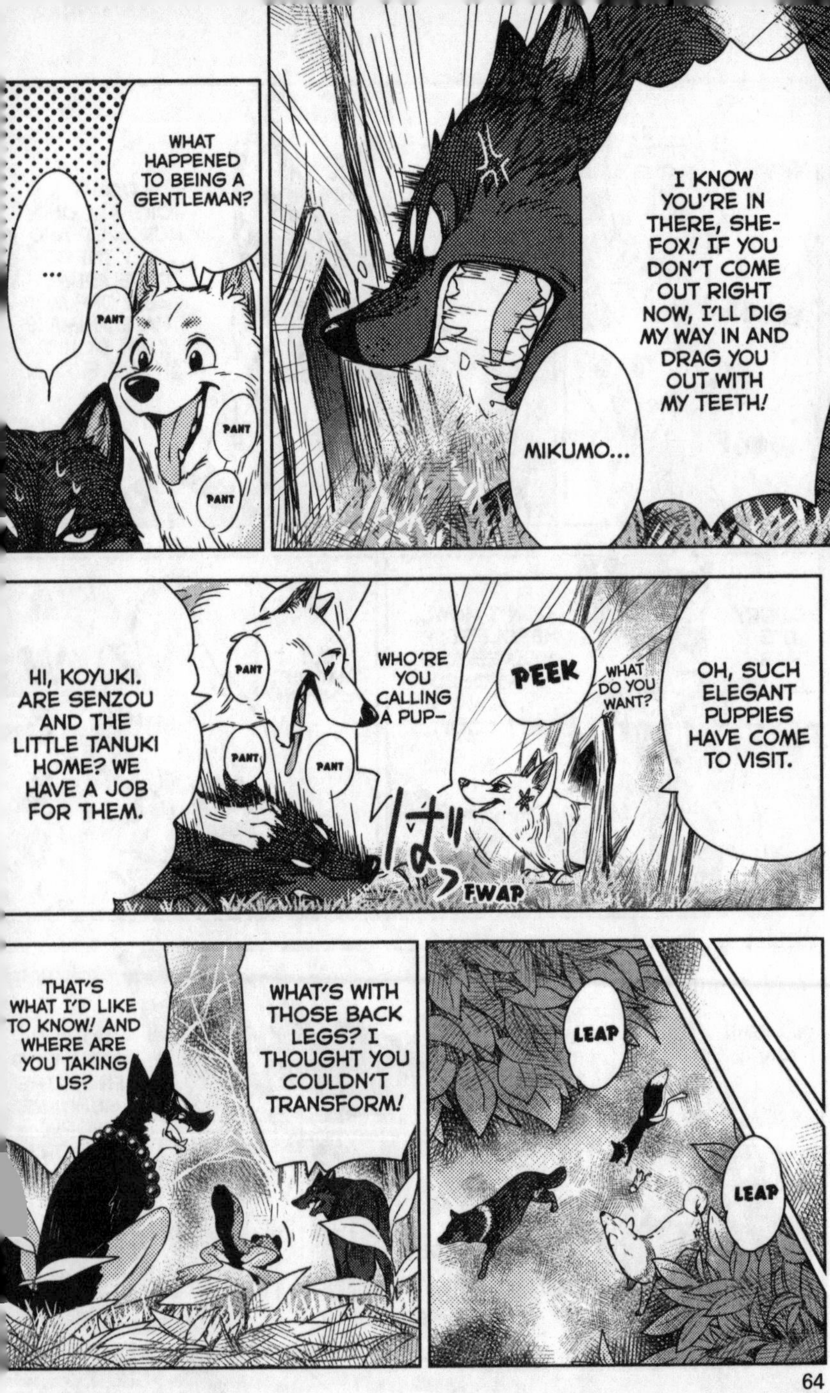
I KNOW YOU'RE IN THERE, SHE-FOX! IF YOU DON'T COME OUT RIGHT NOW, I'LL DIG MY WAY IN AND DRAG YOU OUT WITH MY TEETH!
MIKUMO...
WHAT HAPPENED TO BEING A GENTLEMAN?
...
PANT
PANT
PANT
OH, SUCH ELEGANT PUPPIES HAVE COME TO VISIT.
WHAT DO YOU WANT?
PEEK
WHO'RE YOU CALLING A PUP—
FWAP
PANT
PANT
PANT
HI, KOYUKI. ARE SENZOU AND THE LITTLE TANUKI HOME? WE HAVE A JOB FOR THEM.
LEAP
LEAP
WHAT'S WITH THOSE BACK LEGS? I THOUGHT YOU COULDN'T TRANSFORM!
THAT'S WHAT I'D LIKE TO KNOW! AND WHERE ARE YOU TAKING US?

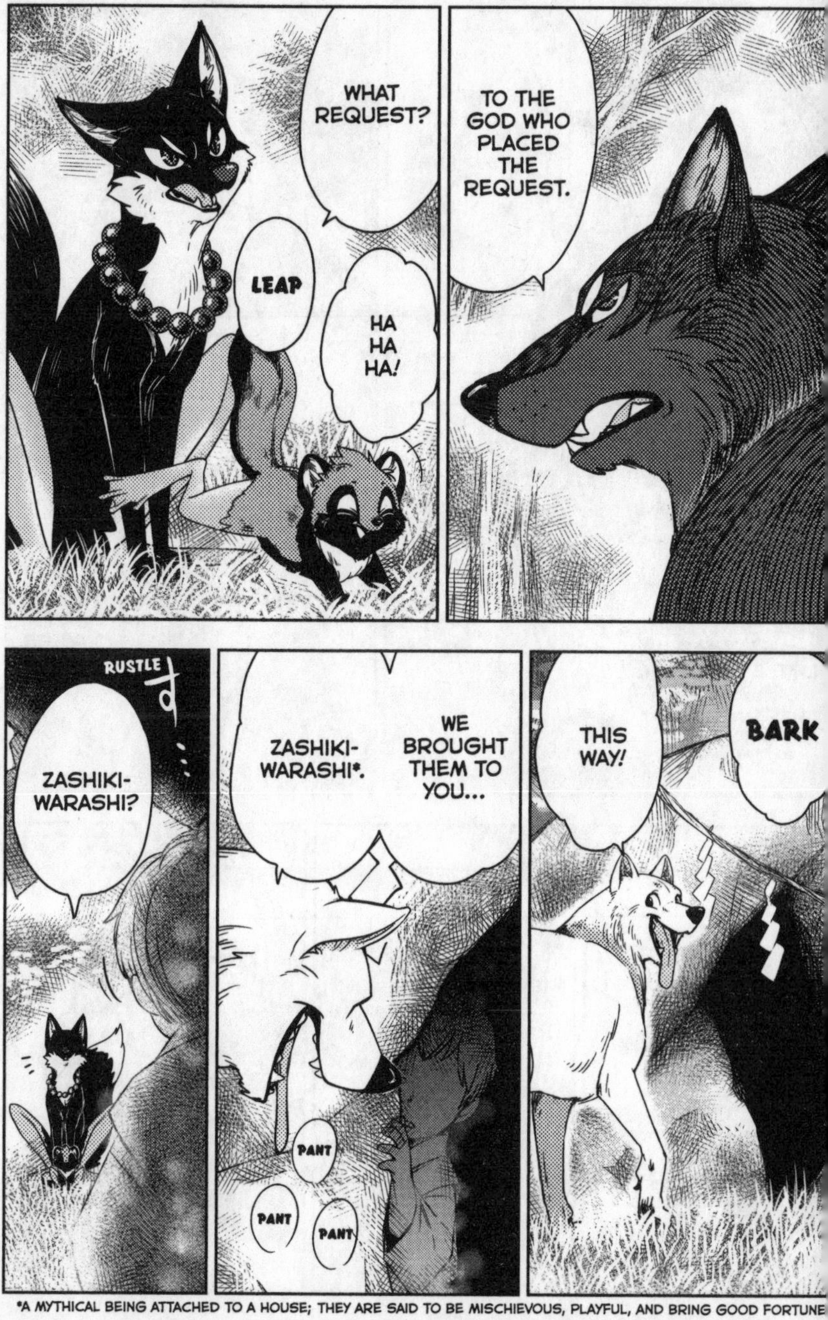
TO THE GOD WHO PLACED THE REQUEST.
WHAT REQUEST?
HA HA HA!
LEAP
BARK
THIS WAY!
WE BROUGHT THEM TO YOU...
ZASHIKI-WARASHI*.
PANT
PANT
PANT
RUSTLE
ZASHIKI-WARASHI?

*A MYTHICAL BEING ATTACHED TO A HOUSE; THEY ARE SAID TO BE MISCHIEVOUS, PLAYFUL, AND BRING GOOD FORTUNE

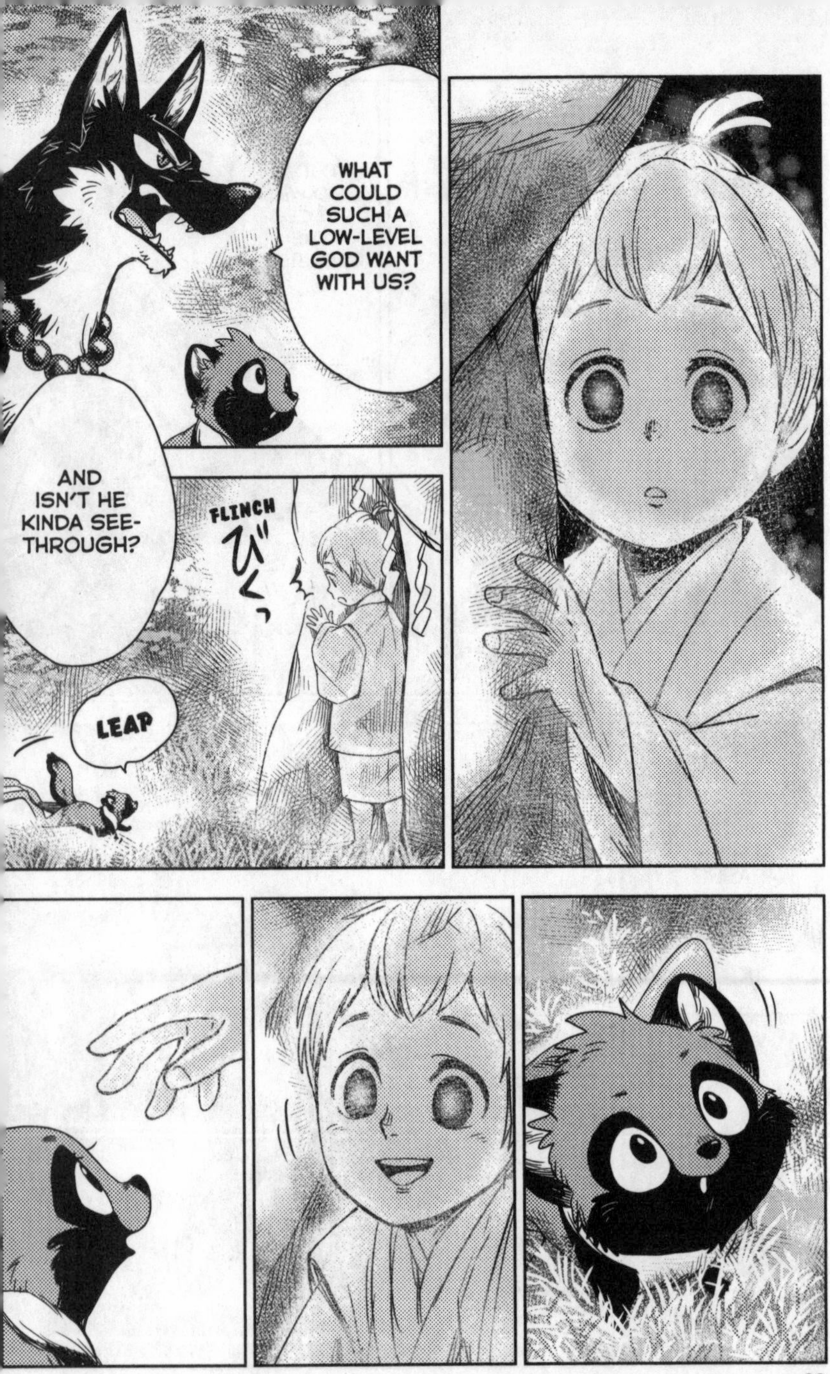
WHAT COULD SUCH A LOW-LEVEL GOD WANT WITH US?
AND ISN'T HE KINDA SEE-THROUGH?
FLINCH
びくっ
LEAP

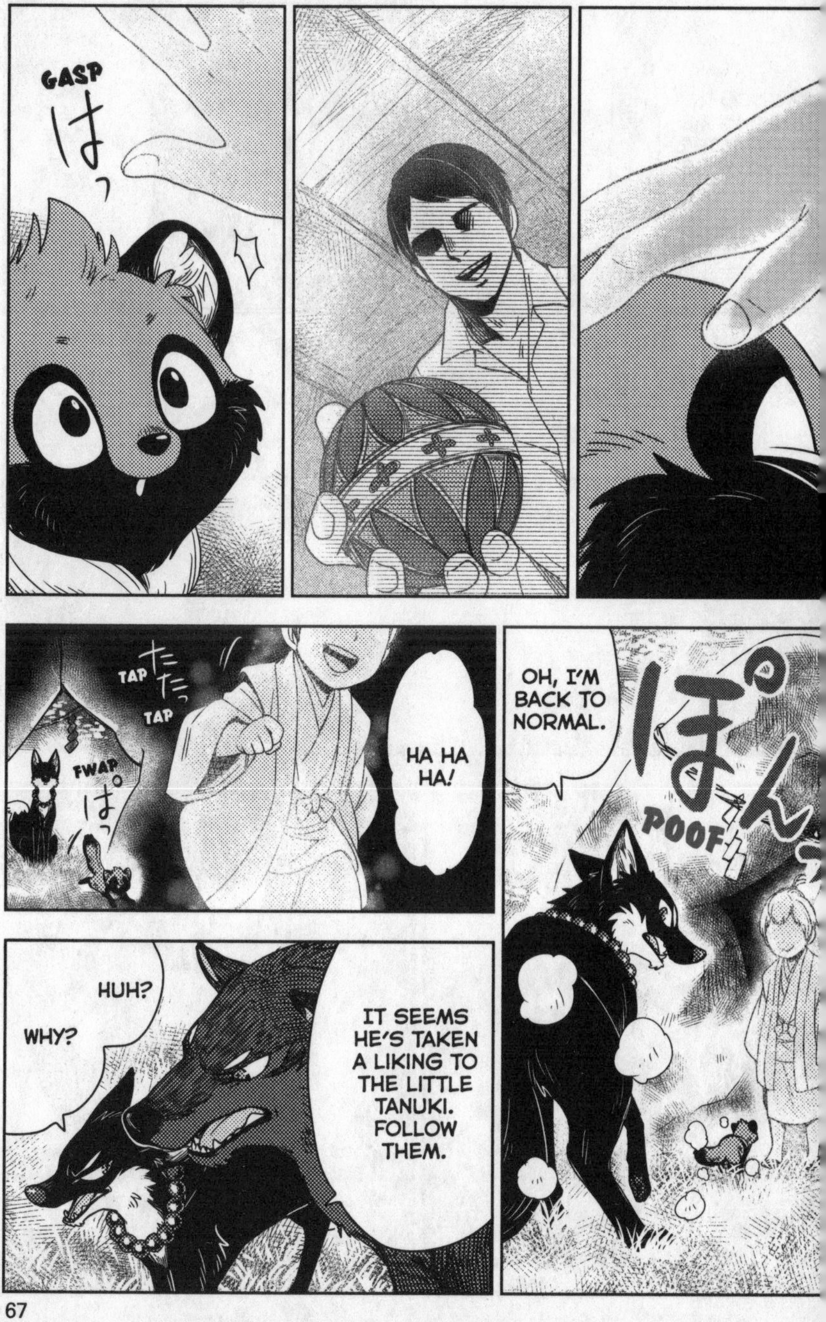
GASP
はっ
OH, I'M BACK TO NORMAL.
ぽんっ
POOF
HA HA HA!
TAP
たたっ
TAP
FWAP
ぱっ
IT SEEMS HE'S TAKEN A LIKING TO THE LITTLE TANUKI. FOLLOW THEM.
HUH?
WHY?

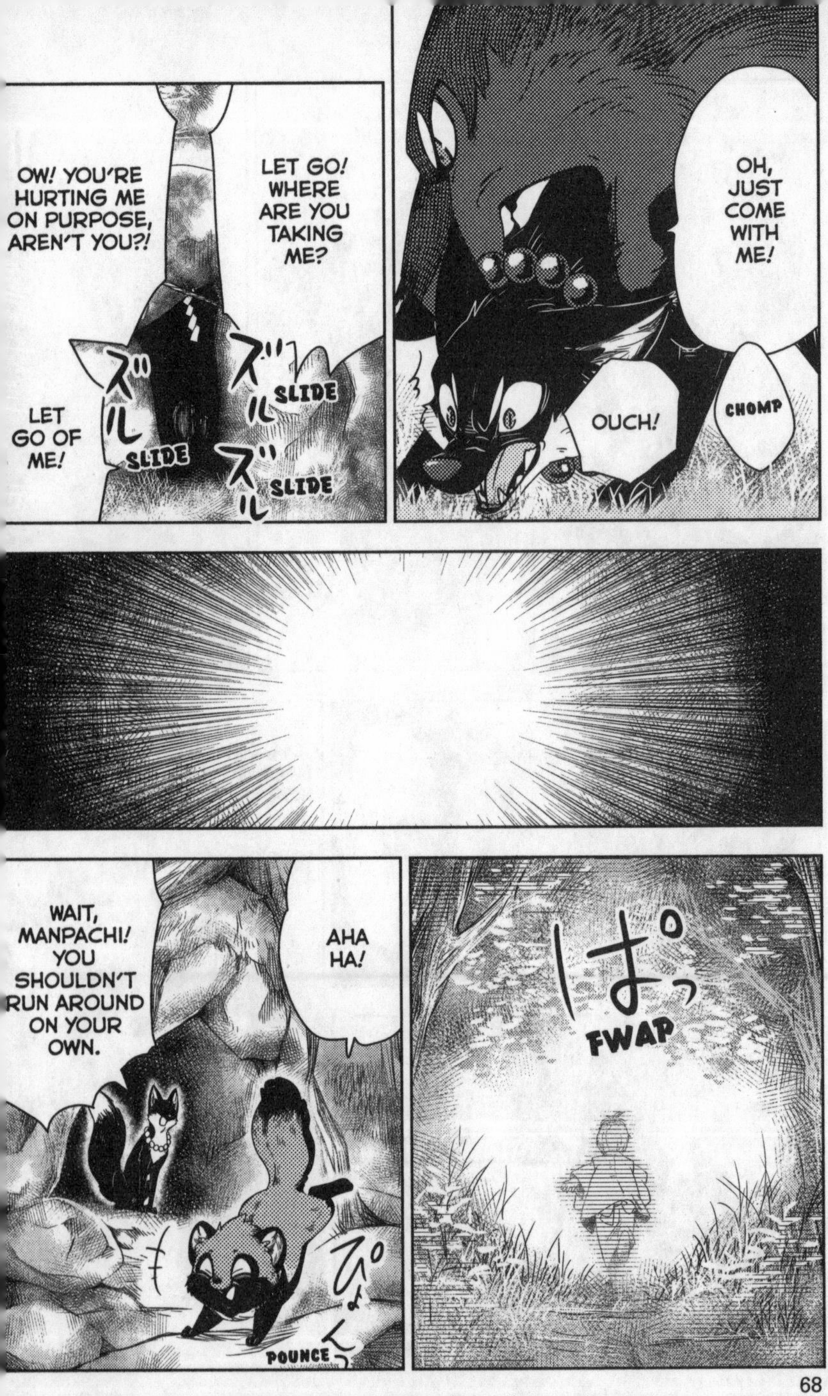
OH, JUST COME WITH ME!
CHOMP
OUCH!
LET GO! WHERE ARE YOU TAKING ME?
OW! YOU'RE HURTING ME ON PURPOSE, AREN'T YOU?!
ズル
SLIDE
ズル
SLIDE
ズル
SLIDE
LET GO OF ME!
ぱっ
FWAP
AHA HA!
WAIT, MANPACHI! YOU SHOULDN'T RUN AROUND ON YOUR OWN.
ぴょん
POUNCE

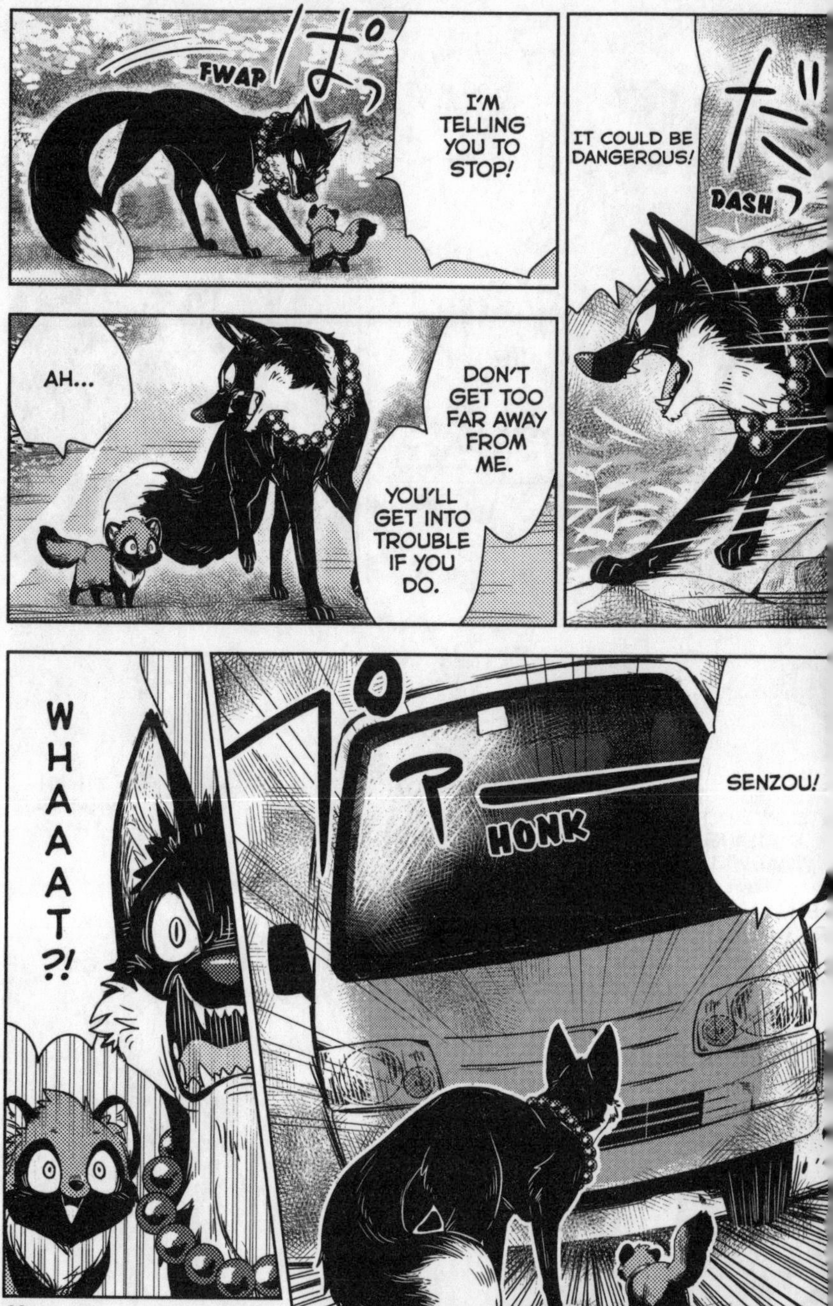
IT COULD BE DANGEROUS!
DASH
FWAP
I'M TELLING YOU TO STOP!
DON'T GET TOO FAR AWAY FROM ME.
YOU'LL GET INTO TROUBLE IF YOU DO.
AH...
SENZOU!
HONK
WHAAAT?!

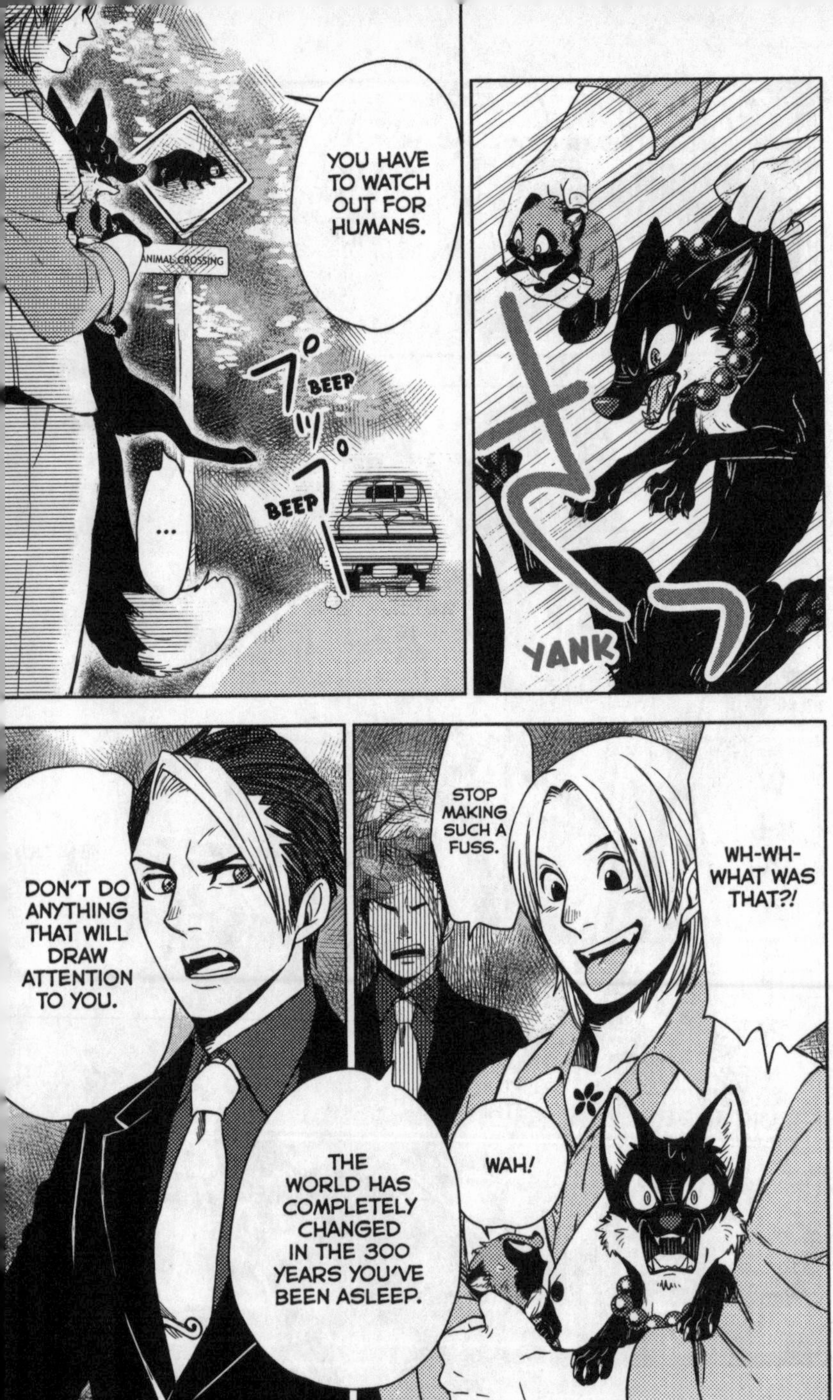
YANK
YOU HAVE TO WATCH OUT FOR HUMANS.
ANIMAL CROSSING
BEEP
BEEP
...
WH-WH-WHAT WAS THAT?!
STOP MAKING SUCH A FUSS.
WAH!
THE WORLD HAS COMPLETELY CHANGED IN THE 300 YEARS YOU'VE BEEN ASLEEP.
DON'T DO ANYTHING THAT WILL DRAW ATTENTION TO YOU.

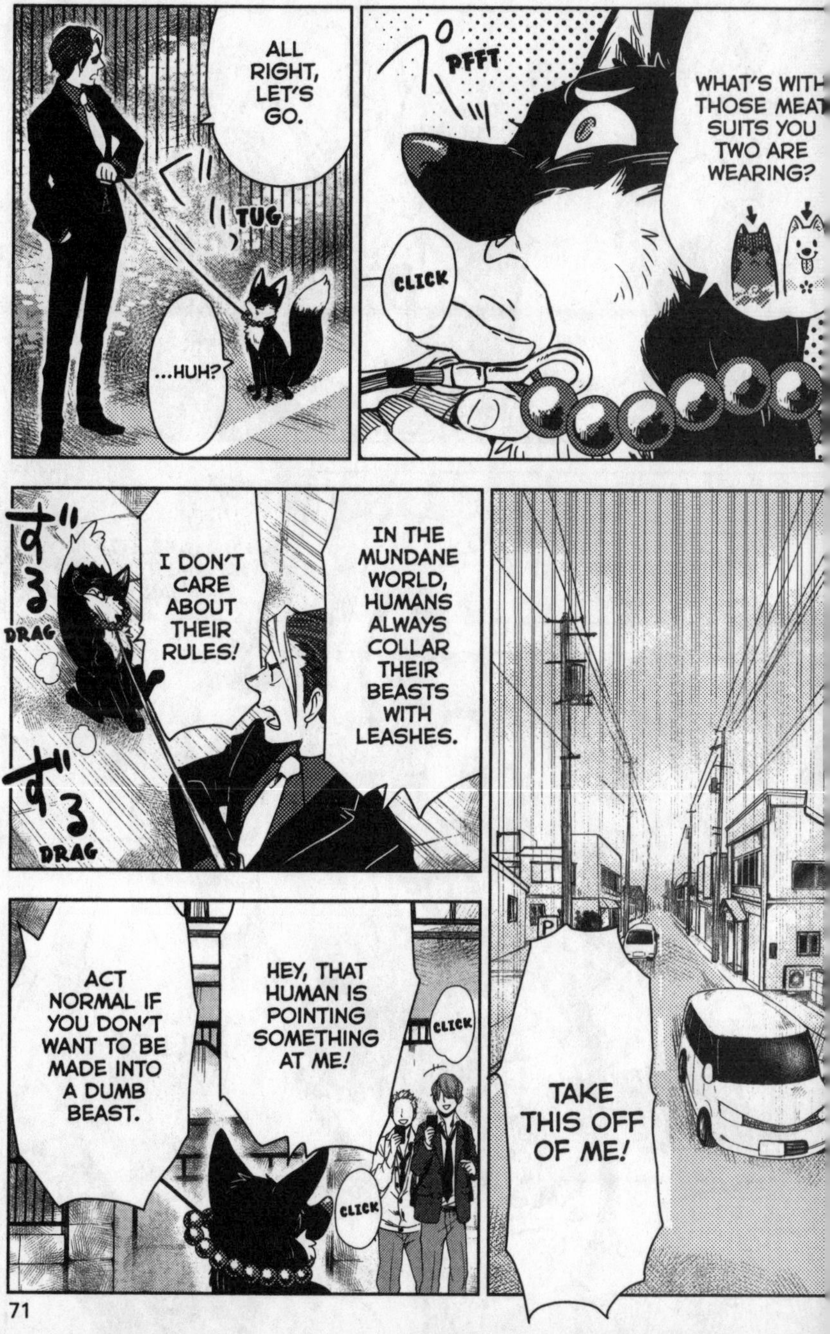
PFFT
WHAT'S WITH THOSE MEAT SUITS YOU TWO ARE WEARING?
CLICK
ALL RIGHT, LET'S GO.
TUG
...HUH?
TAKE THIS OFF OF ME!
IN THE MUNDANE WORLD, HUMANS ALWAYS COLLAR THEIR BEASTS WITH LEASHES.
I DON'T CARE ABOUT THEIR RULES!
ずる
DRAG
ずる
DRAG
HEY, THAT HUMAN IS POINTING SOMETHING AT ME!
CLICK
CLICK
ACT NORMAL IF YOU DON'T WANT TO BE MADE INTO A DUMB BEAST.

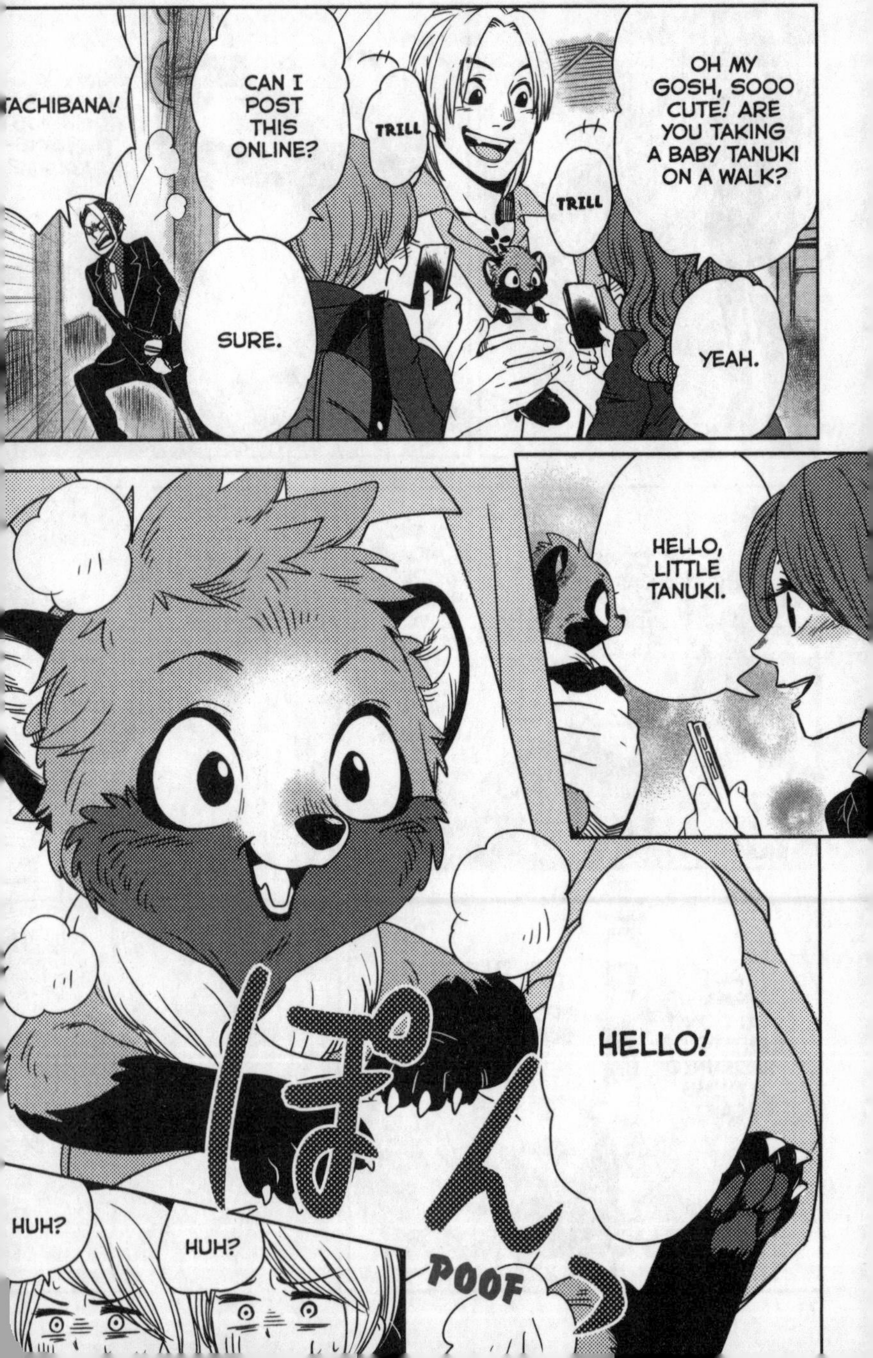
OH MY GOSH, SOOO CUTE! ARE YOU TAKING A BABY TANUKI ON A WALK?
TRILL
TRILL
CAN I POST THIS ONLINE?
YEAH.
SURE.
TACHIBANA!
HELLO, LITTLE TANUKI.
HELLO!
ぽん
POOF
HUH?
HUH?

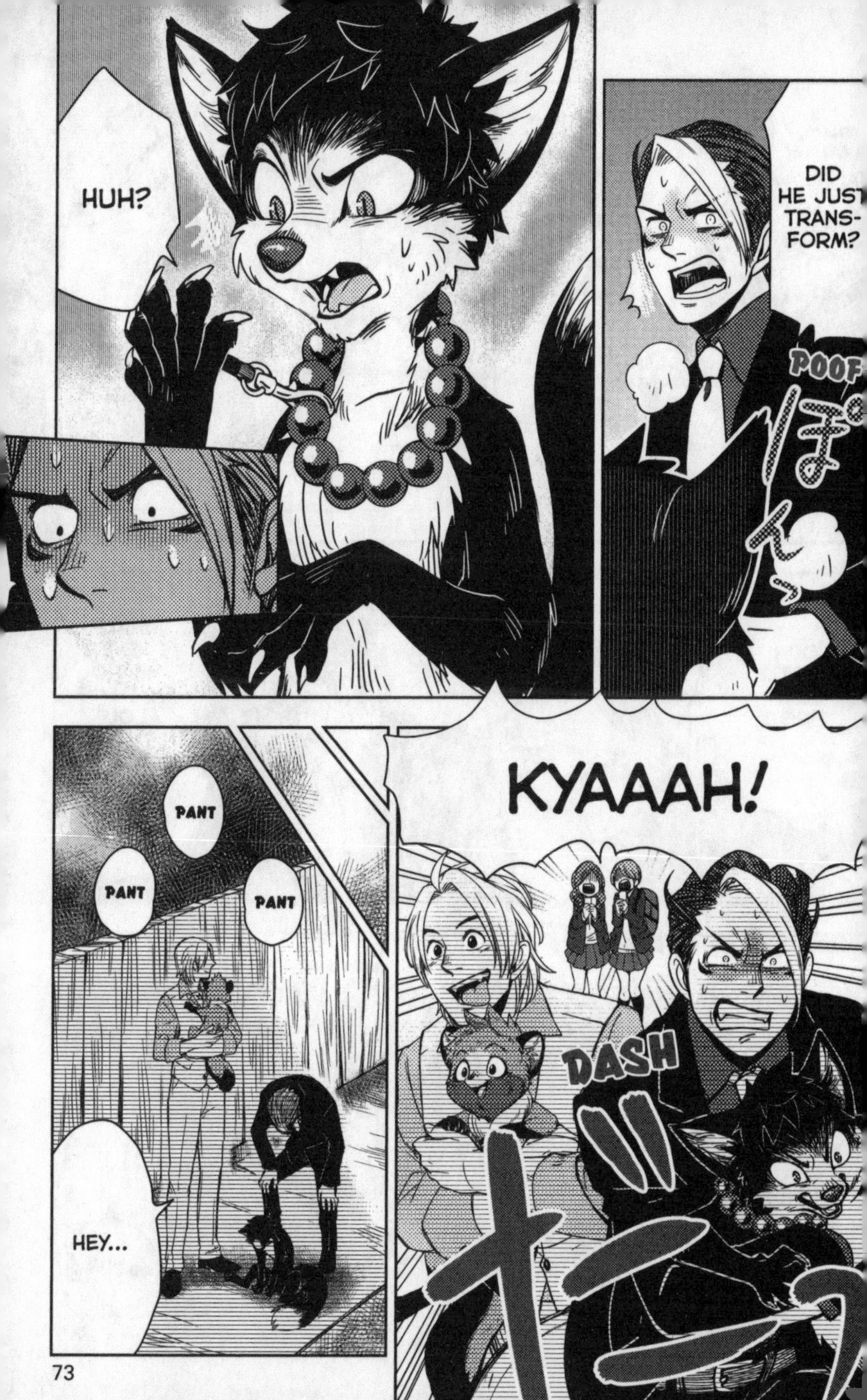
DID HE JUST TRANS-FORM?
POOF
HUH?
KYAAAH!
DASH
PANT
PANT
PANT
HEY...

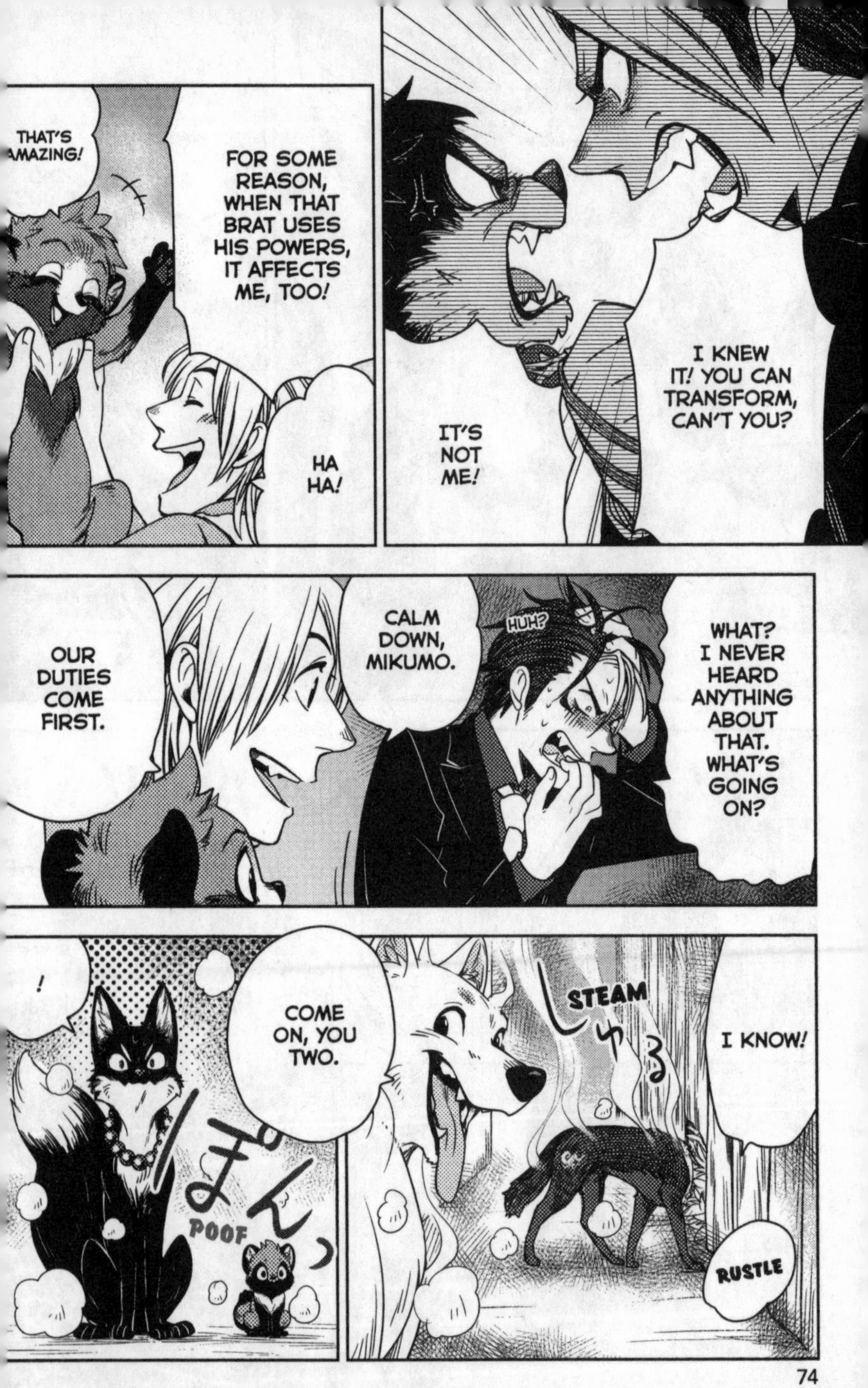
I KNEW IT! YOU CAN TRANSFORM, CAN'T YOU?
IT'S NOT ME!
FOR SOME REASON, WHEN THAT BRAT USES HIS POWERS, IT AFFECTS ME, TOO!
THAT'S AMAZING!
HA HA!
WHAT? I NEVER HEARD ANYTHING ABOUT THAT. WHAT'S GOING ON?
HUH?
CALM DOWN, MIKUMO.
OUR DUTIES COME FIRST.
I KNOW!
STEAM
COME ON, YOU TWO.
RUSTLE
!
POOF

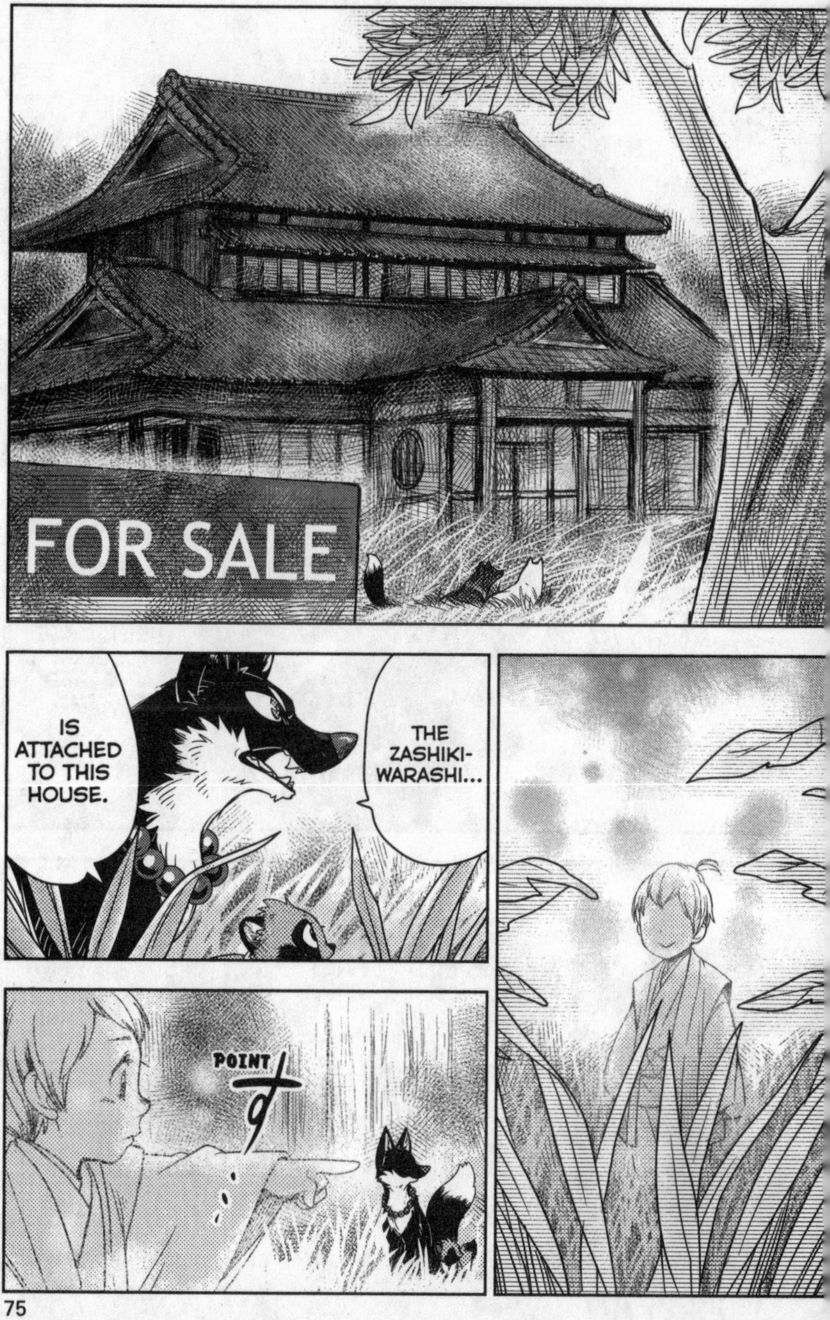
FOR SALE
THE ZASHIKI-WARASHI...
IS ATTACHED TO THIS HOUSE.
POINT
...

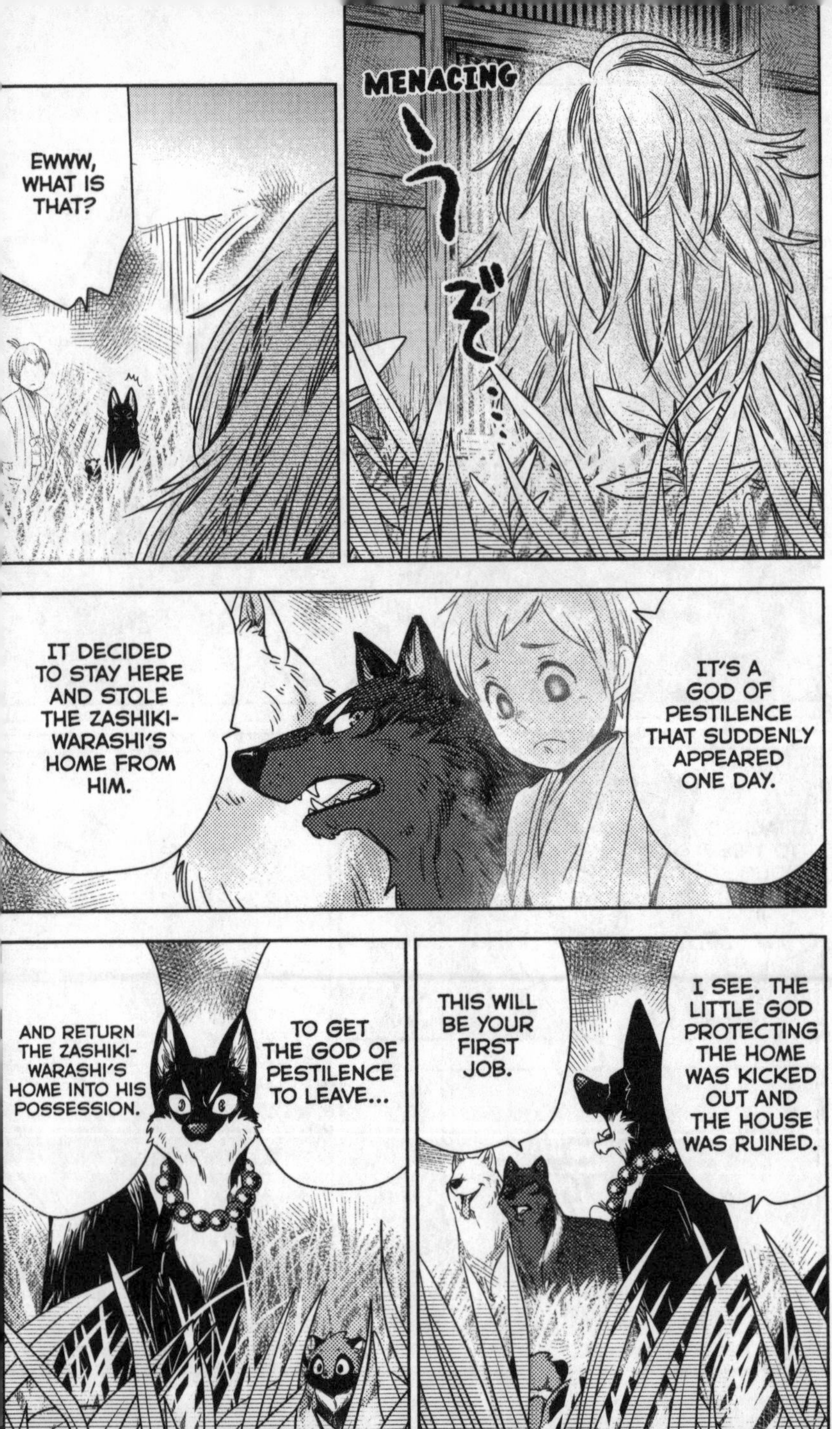
MENACING
EWWW, WHAT IS THAT?
IT'S A GOD OF PESTILENCE THAT SUDDENLY APPEARED ONE DAY.
IT DECIDED TO STAY HERE AND STOLE THE ZASHIKI-WARASHI'S HOME FROM HIM.
I SEE. THE LITTLE GOD PROTECTING THE HOME WAS KICKED OUT AND THE HOUSE WAS RUINED.
THIS WILL BE YOUR FIRST JOB.
TO GET THE GOD OF PESTILENCE TO LEAVE...
AND RETURN THE ZASHIKI-WARASHI'S HOME INTO HIS POSSESSION.

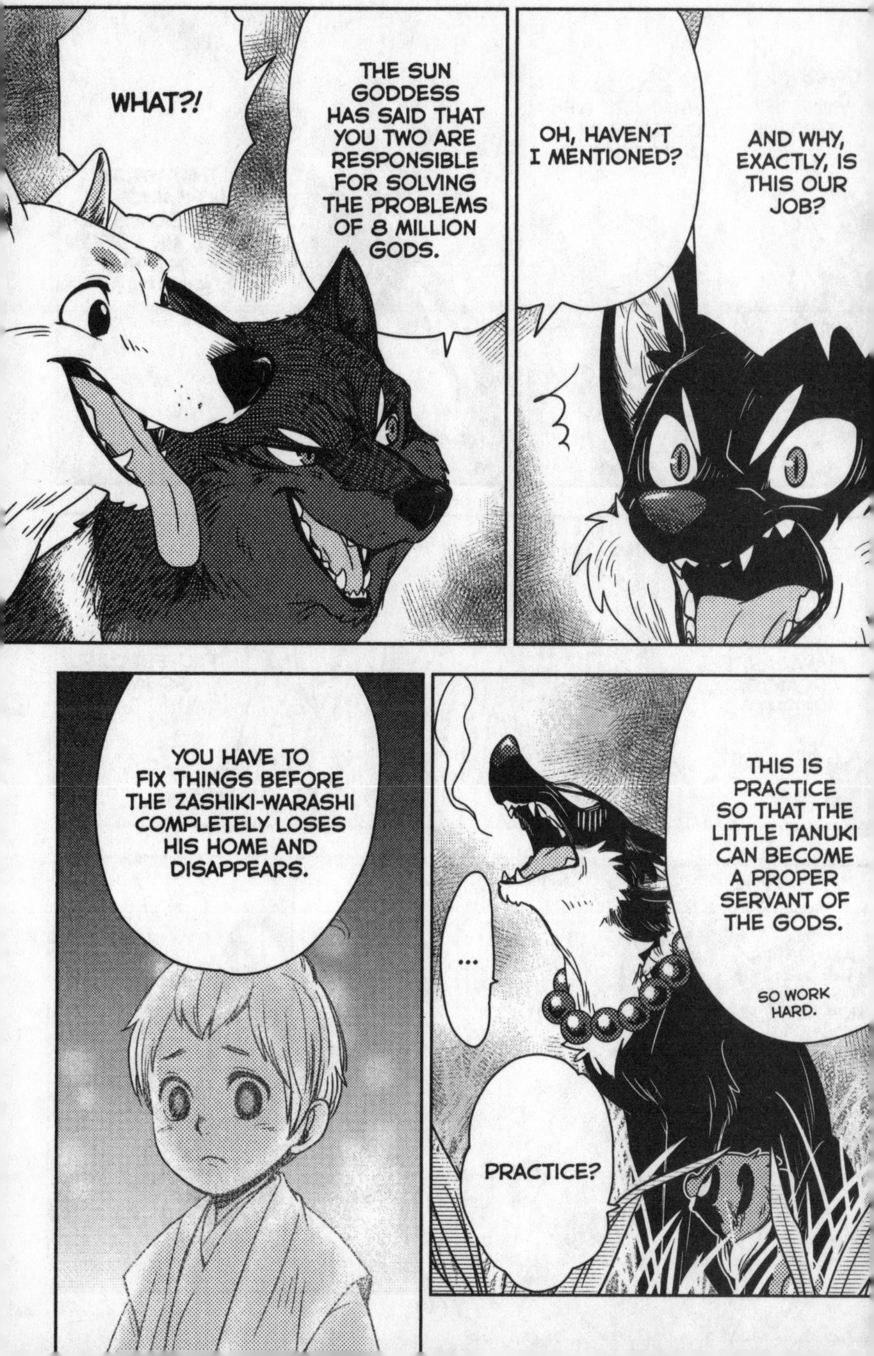
AND WHY, EXACTLY, IS THIS OUR JOB?
OH, HAVEN'T I MENTIONED?
THE SUN GODDESS HAS SAID THAT YOU TWO ARE RESPONSIBLE FOR SOLVING THE PROBLEMS OF 8 MILLION GODS.
WHAT?!
THIS IS PRACTICE SO THAT THE LITTLE TANUKI CAN BECOME A PROPER SERVANT OF THE GODS.
SO WORK HARD.
...
PRACTICE?
YOU HAVE TO FIX THINGS BEFORE THE ZASHIKI-WARASHI COMPLETELY LOSES HIS HOME AND DISAPPEARS.

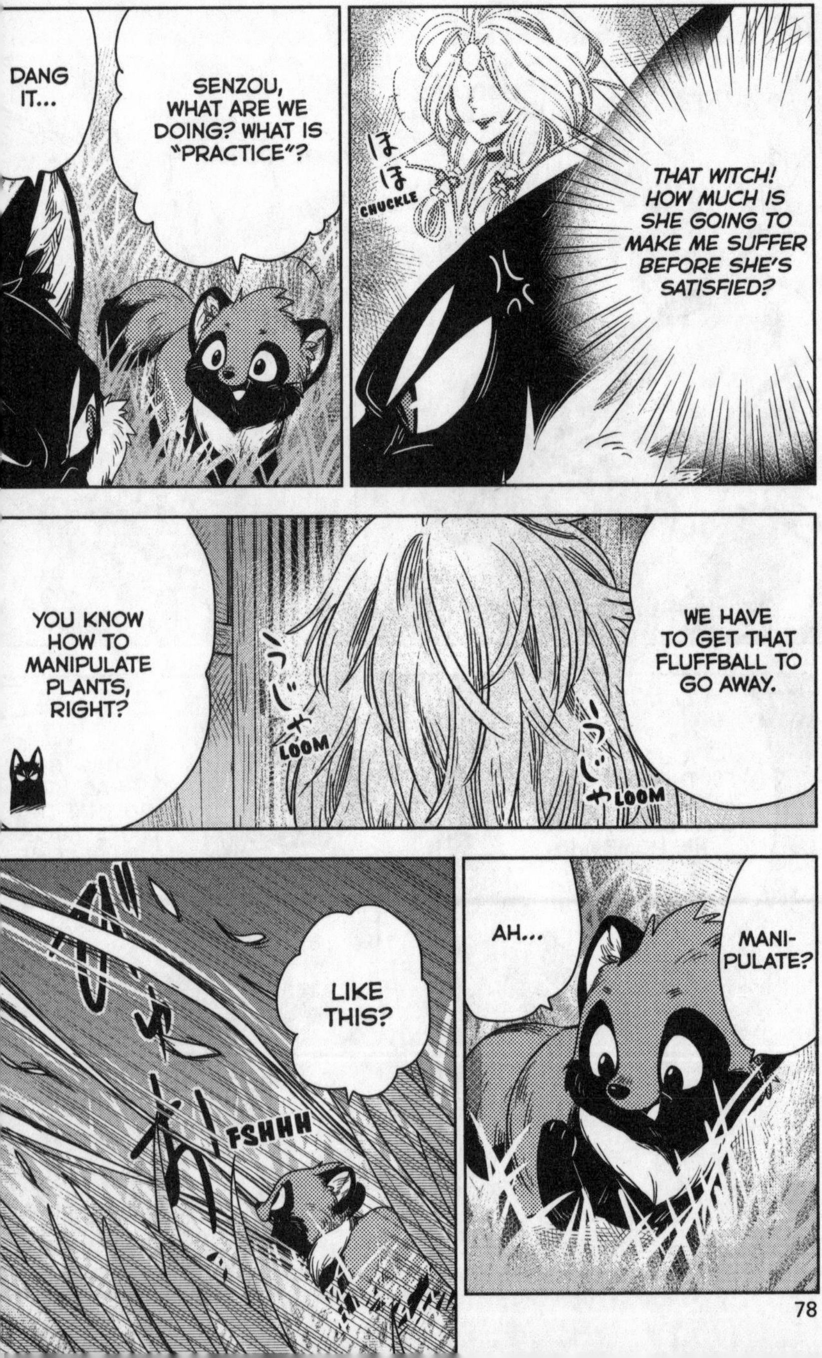
ほほ
CHUCKLE
THAT WITCH! HOW MUCH IS SHE GOING TO MAKE ME SUFFER BEFORE SHE'S SATISFIED?
SENZOU, WHAT ARE WE DOING? WHAT IS "PRACTICE"?
DANG IT...
WE HAVE TO GET THAT FLUFFBALL TO GO AWAY.
うじゃ LOOM
うじゃ LOOM
YOU KNOW HOW TO MANIPULATE PLANTS, RIGHT?
MANI-PULATE?
AH...
LIKE THIS?
FSHHH

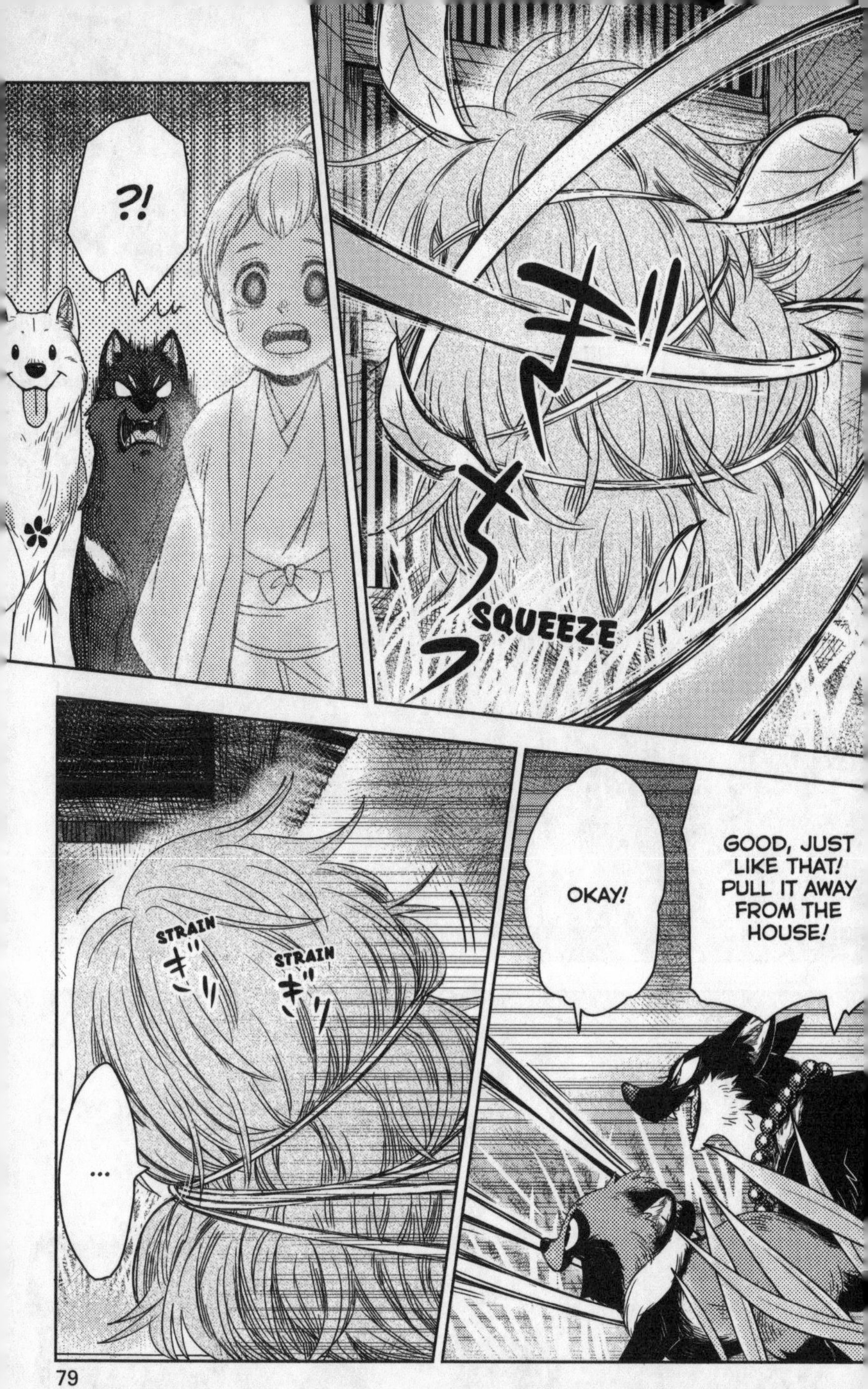
SQUEEZE
?!
GOOD, JUST LIKE THAT! PULL IT AWAY FROM THE HOUSE!
OKAY!
STRAIN
STRAIN
...

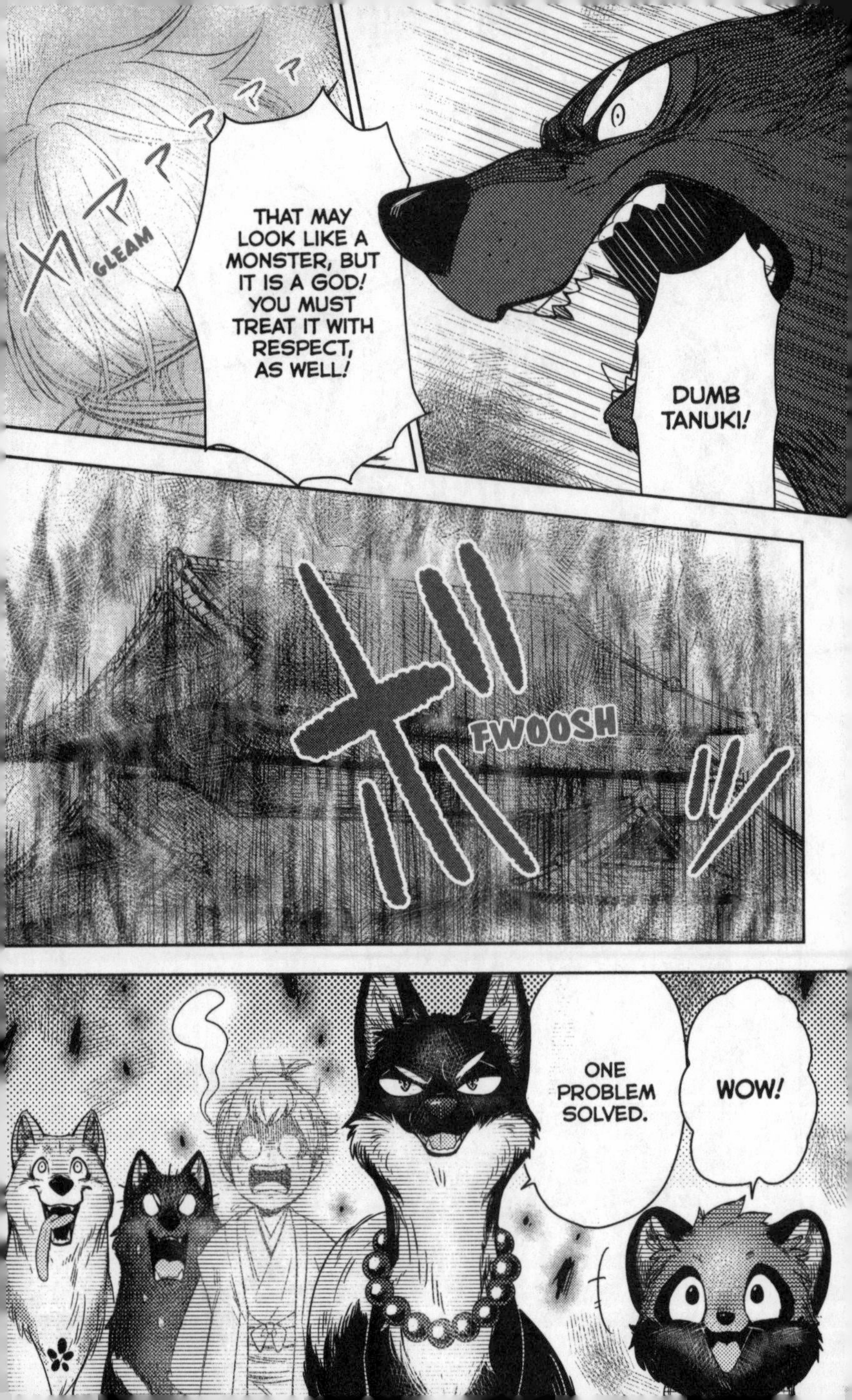
DUMB TANUKI!
THAT MAY LOOK LIKE A MONSTER, BUT IT IS A GOD! YOU MUST TREAT IT WITH RESPECT, AS WELL!
GLEAM
FWOOSH
WOW!
ONE PROBLEM SOLVED.

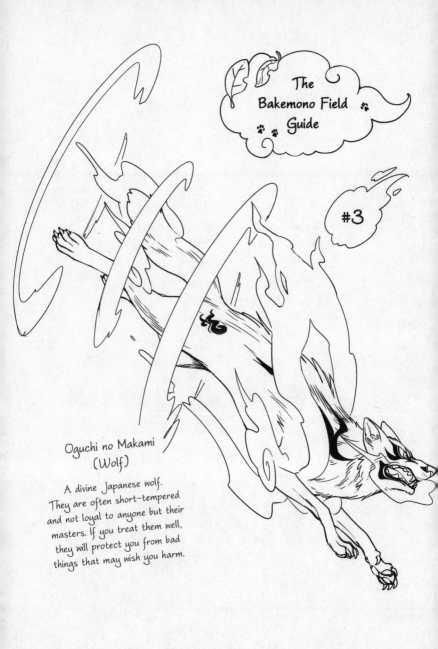

The Bakemono Field Guide

#3

Oguchi no Makami
(Wolf)

A divine Japanese wolf. They are often short-tempered and not loyal to anyone but their masters. If you treat them well, they will protect you from bad things that may wish you harm.

Chapter 4

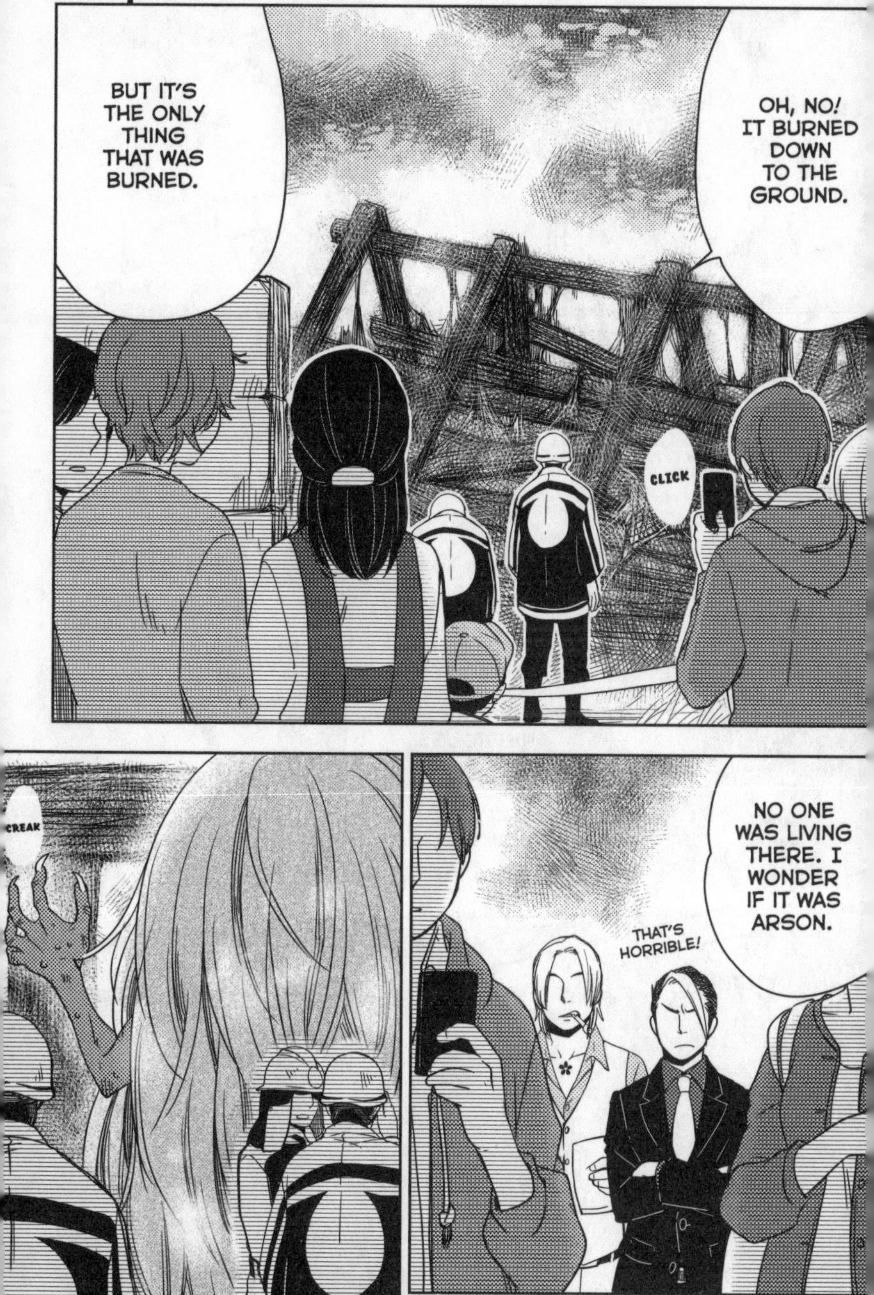
OH, NO! IT BURNED DOWN TO THE GROUND.
CLICK
BUT IT'S THE ONLY THING THAT WAS BURNED.
NO ONE WAS LIVING THERE. I WONDER IF IT WAS ARSON.
THAT'S HORRIBLE!
CREAK

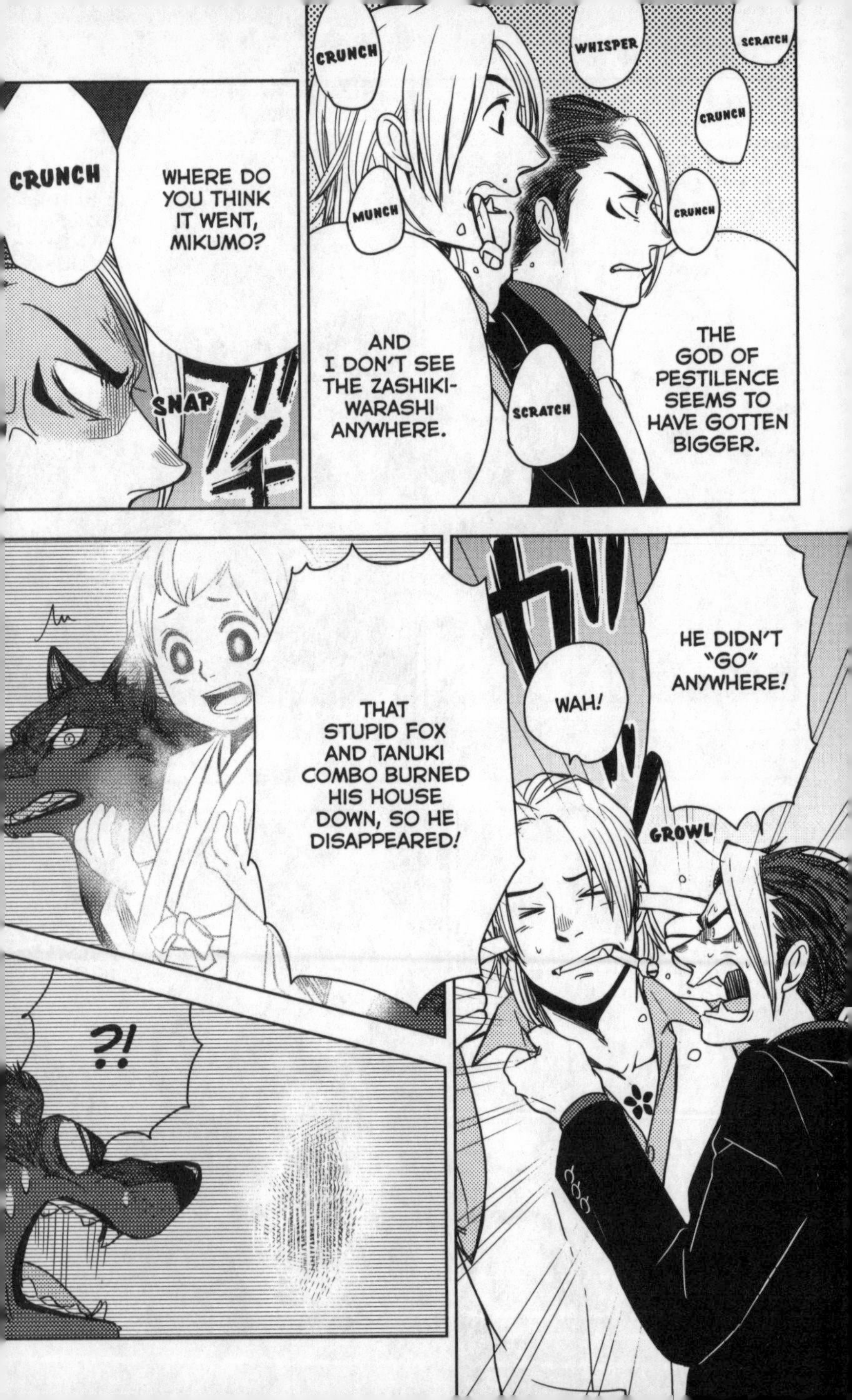

SCRATCH
WHISPER
CRUNCH
CRUNCH
CRUNCH
CRUNCH
MUNCH
THE GOD OF PESTILENCE SEEMS TO HAVE GOTTEN BIGGER.
AND I DON'T SEE THE ZASHIKI-WARASHI ANYWHERE.
SCRATCH
WHERE DO YOU THINK IT WENT, MIKUMO?
CRUNCH
SNAP
HE DIDN'T "GO" ANYWHERE!
WAH!
GROWL
THAT STUPID FOX AND TANUKI COMBO BURNED HIS HOUSE DOWN, SO HE DISAPPEARED!
?!

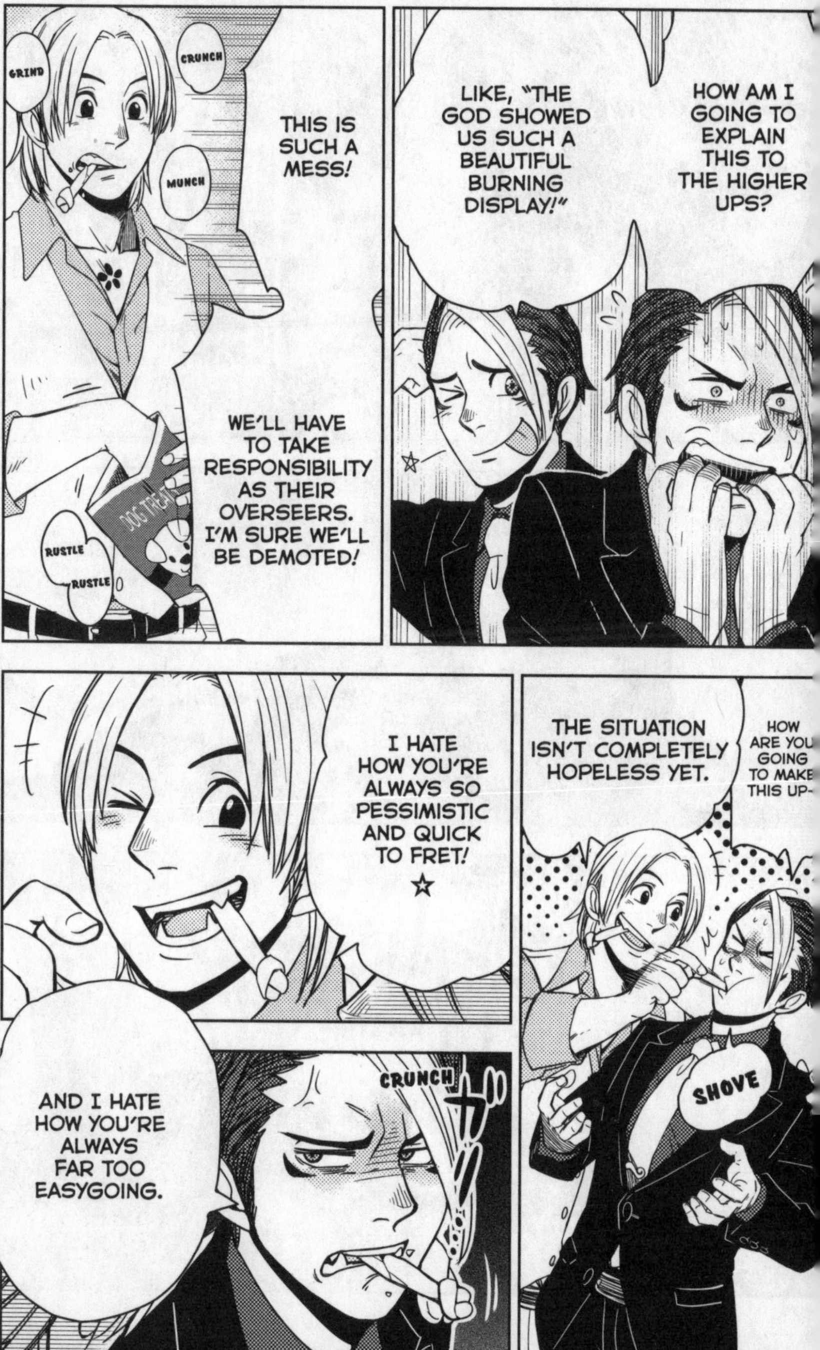
HOW AM I GOING TO EXPLAIN THIS TO THE HIGHER UPS?
LIKE, "THE GOD SHOWED US SUCH A BEAUTIFUL BURNING DISPLAY!"
THIS IS SUCH A MESS!
CRUNCH
GRIND
MUNCH
WE'LL HAVE TO TAKE RESPONSIBILITY AS THEIR OVERSEERS. I'M SURE WE'LL BE DEMOTED!
RUSTLE
RUSTLE
HOW ARE YOU GOING TO MAKE THIS UP-
THE SITUATION ISN'T COMPLETELY HOPELESS YET.
SHOVE
I HATE HOW YOU'RE ALWAYS SO PESSIMISTIC AND QUICK TO FRET! ☆
CRUNCH
AND I HATE HOW YOU'RE ALWAYS FAR TOO EASYGOING.

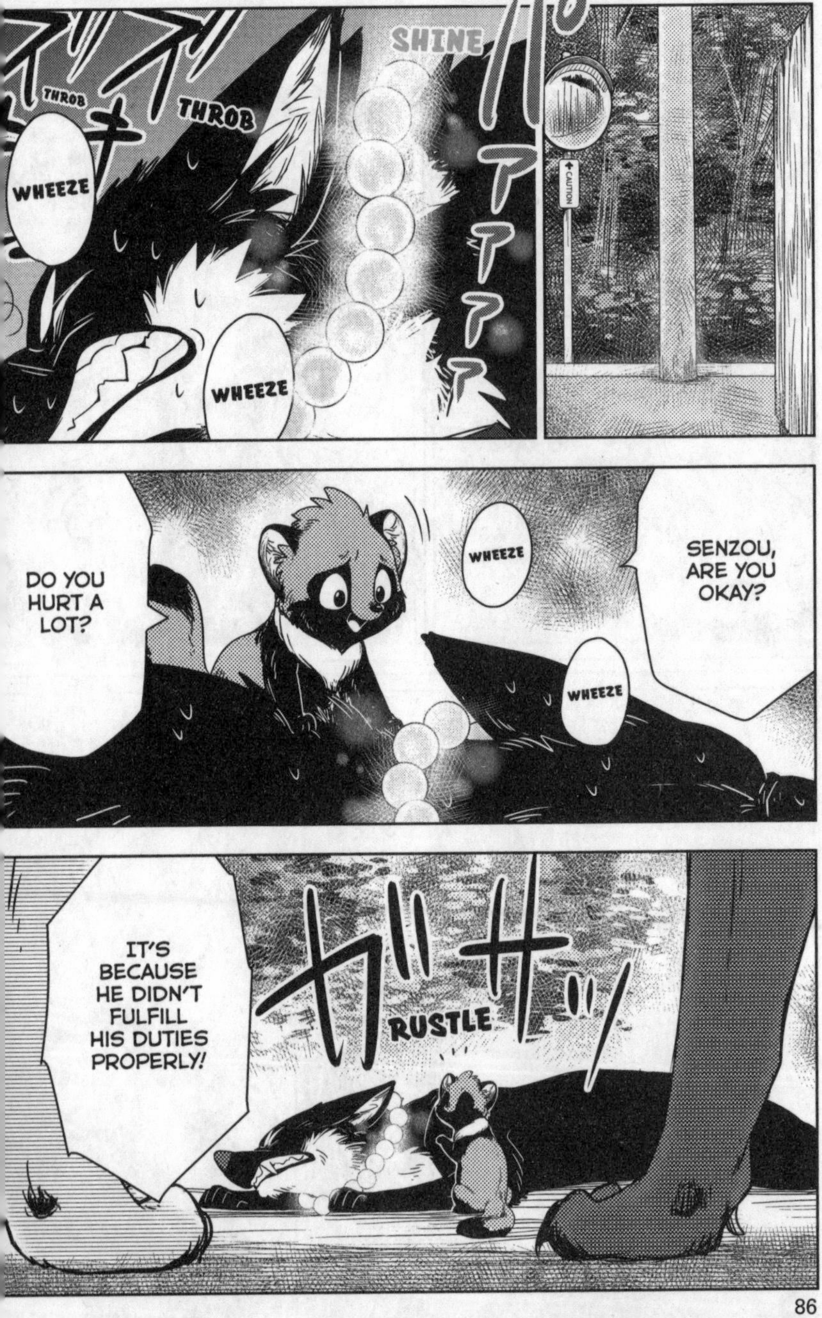

CAUTION
パァァァァ
SHINE
THROB
THROB
ズリズリ
WHEEZE
WHEEZE
SENZOU, ARE YOU OKAY?
WHEEZE
WHEEZE
DO YOU HURT A LOT?
ガサッ
RUSTLE
IT'S BECAUSE HE DIDN'T FULFILL HIS DUTIES PROPERLY!

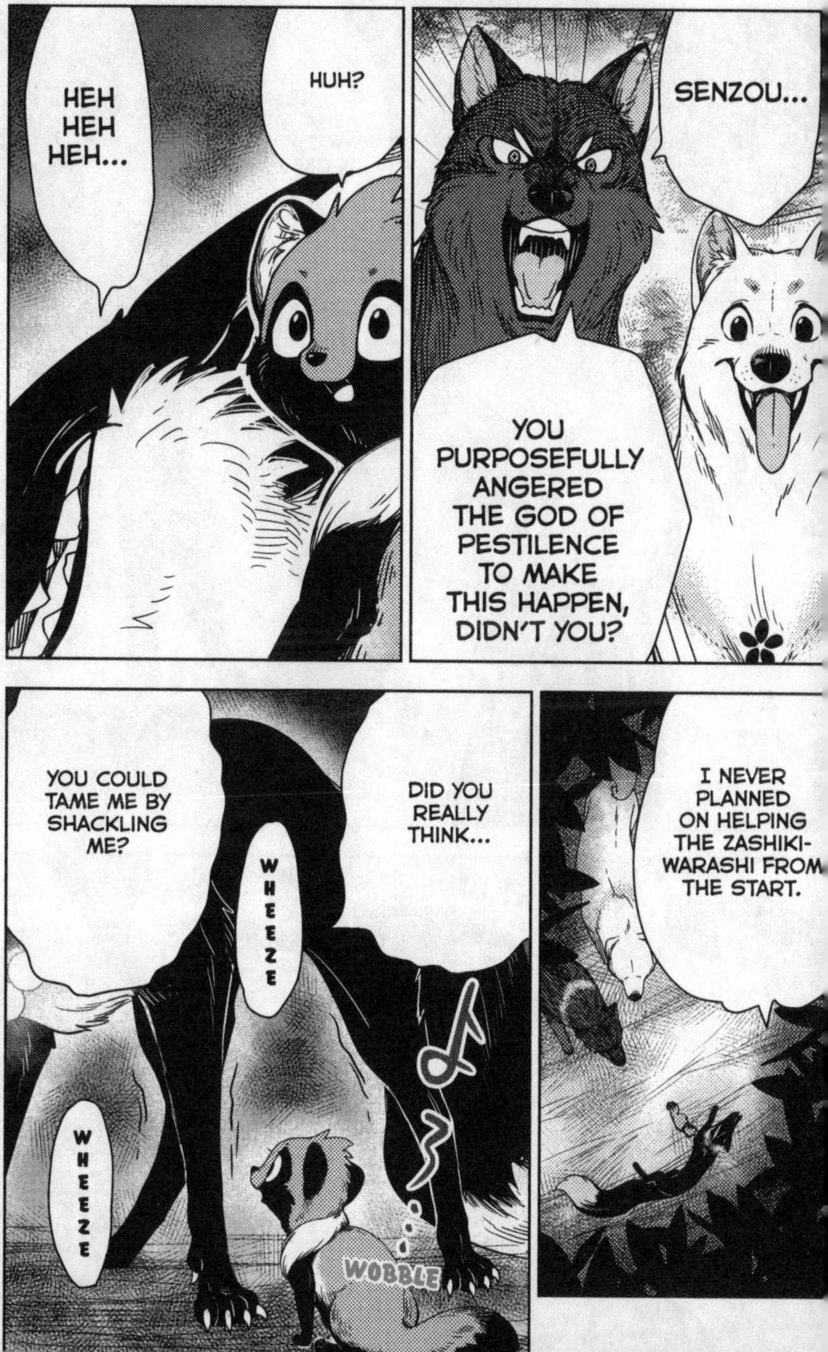
SENZOU...
YOU PURPOSEFULLY ANGERED THE GOD OF PESTILENCE TO MAKE THIS HAPPEN, DIDN'T YOU?
HUH?
HEH HEH HEH...
I NEVER PLANNED ON HELPING THE ZASHIKI-WARASHI FROM THE START.
DID YOU REALLY THINK...
YOU COULD TAME ME BY SHACKLING ME?
WHEEZE
WHEEZE
WOBBLE

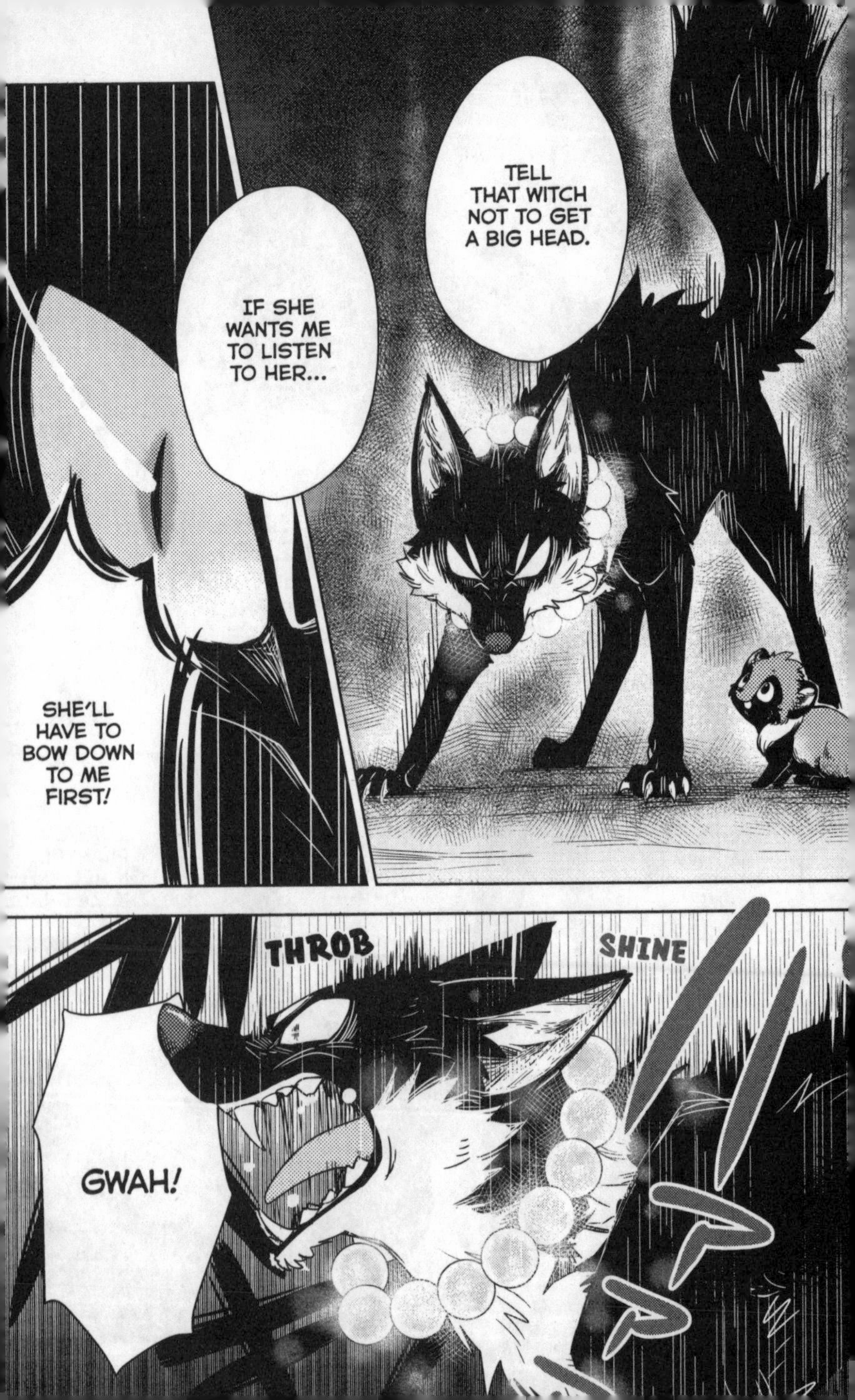
TELL THAT WITCH NOT TO GET A BIG HEAD.
IF SHE WANTS ME TO LISTEN TO HER...
SHE'LL HAVE TO BOW DOWN TO ME FIRST!
SHINE
THROB
GWAH!

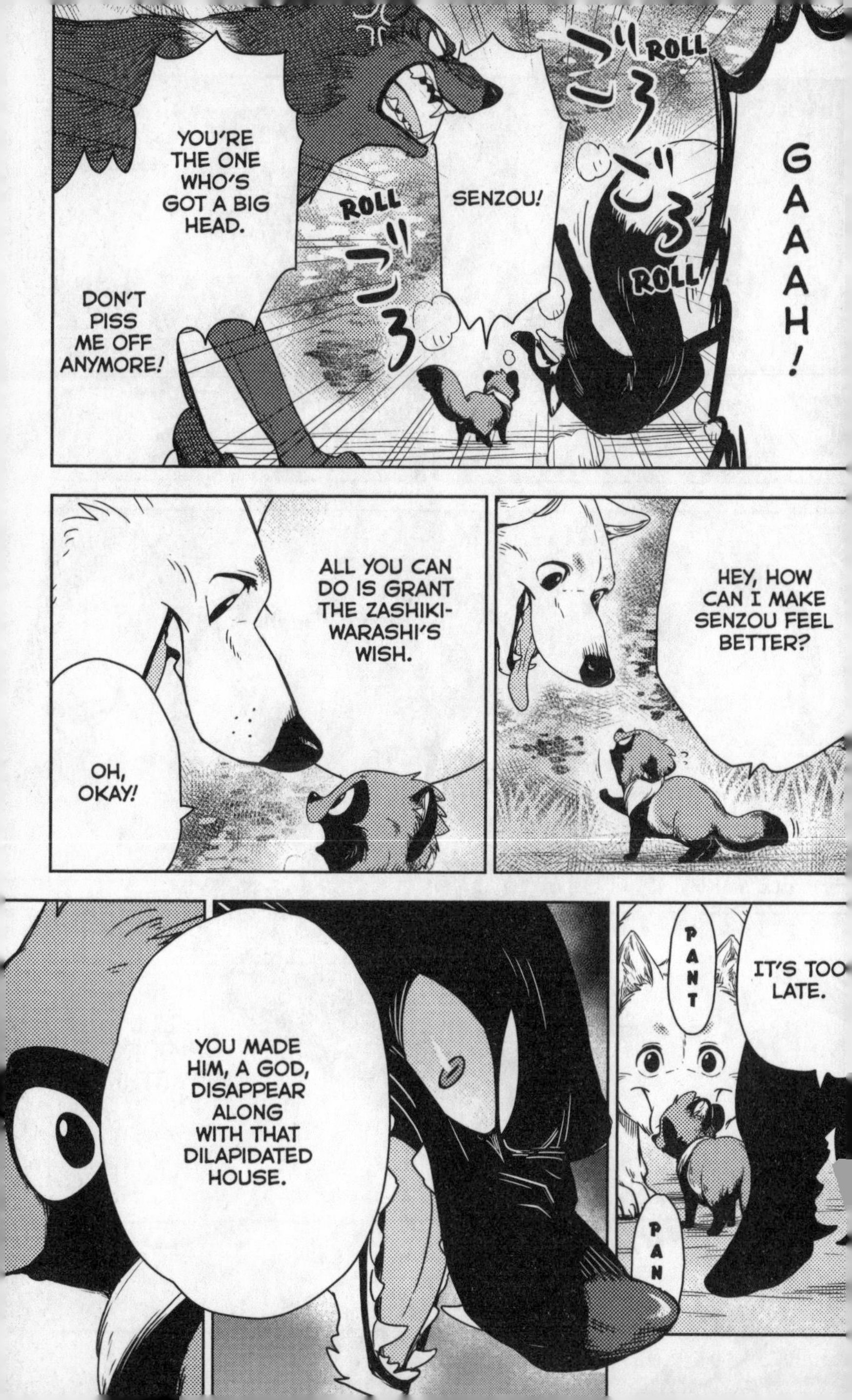
GAAAH!
ROLL
ROLL
SENZOU!
ROLL
YOU'RE THE ONE WHO'S GOT A BIG HEAD.
DON'T PISS ME OFF ANYMORE!
HEY, HOW CAN I MAKE SENZOU FEEL BETTER?
ALL YOU CAN DO IS GRANT THE ZASHIKI-WARASHI'S WISH.
OH, OKAY!
IT'S TOO LATE.
PANT
PAN
YOU MADE HIM, A GOD, DISAPPEAR ALONG WITH THAT DILAPIDATED HOUSE.

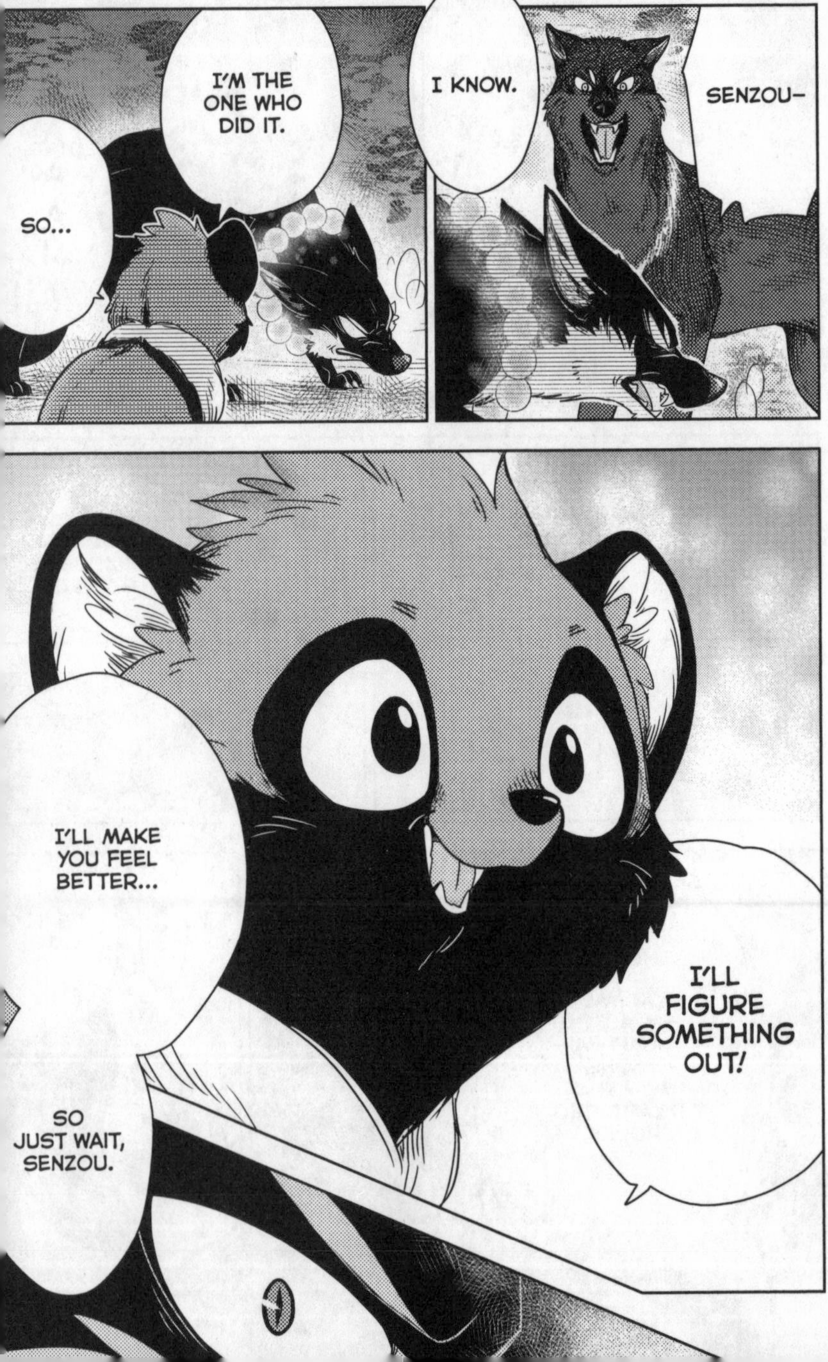
SENZOU–
I KNOW.
I'M THE ONE WHO DID IT.
SO...
I'LL MAKE YOU FEEL BETTER...
I'LL FIGURE SOMETHING OUT!
SO JUST WAIT, SENZOU.

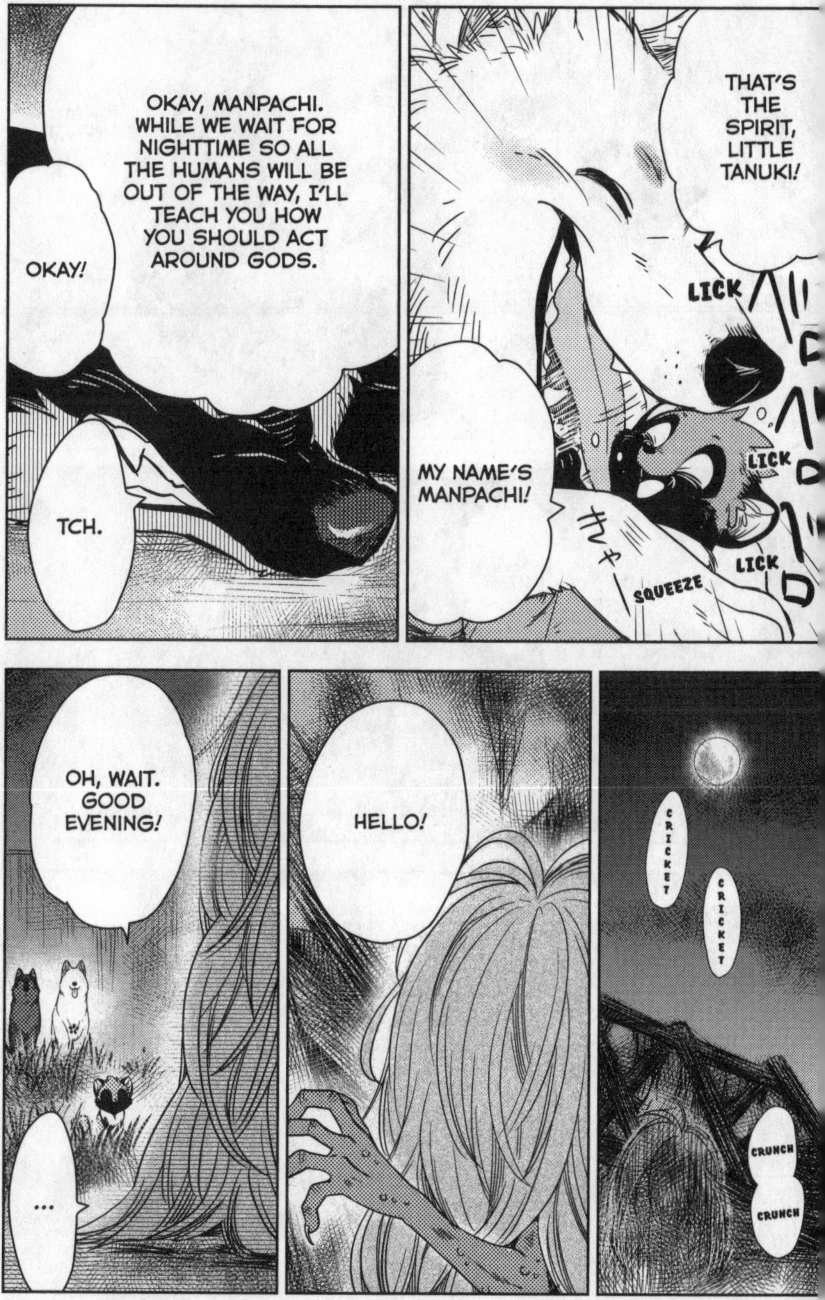

THAT'S THE SPIRIT, LITTLE TANUKI!
LICK
MY NAME'S MANPACHI!
LICK
LICK
きゃー
SQUEEZE
OKAY, MANPACHI. WHILE WE WAIT FOR NIGHTTIME SO ALL THE HUMANS WILL BE OUT OF THE WAY, I'LL TEACH YOU HOW YOU SHOULD ACT AROUND GODS.
OKAY!
TCH.
CRICKET
CRICKET
CRUNCH
CRUNCH
HELLO!
OH, WAIT. GOOD EVENING!
...

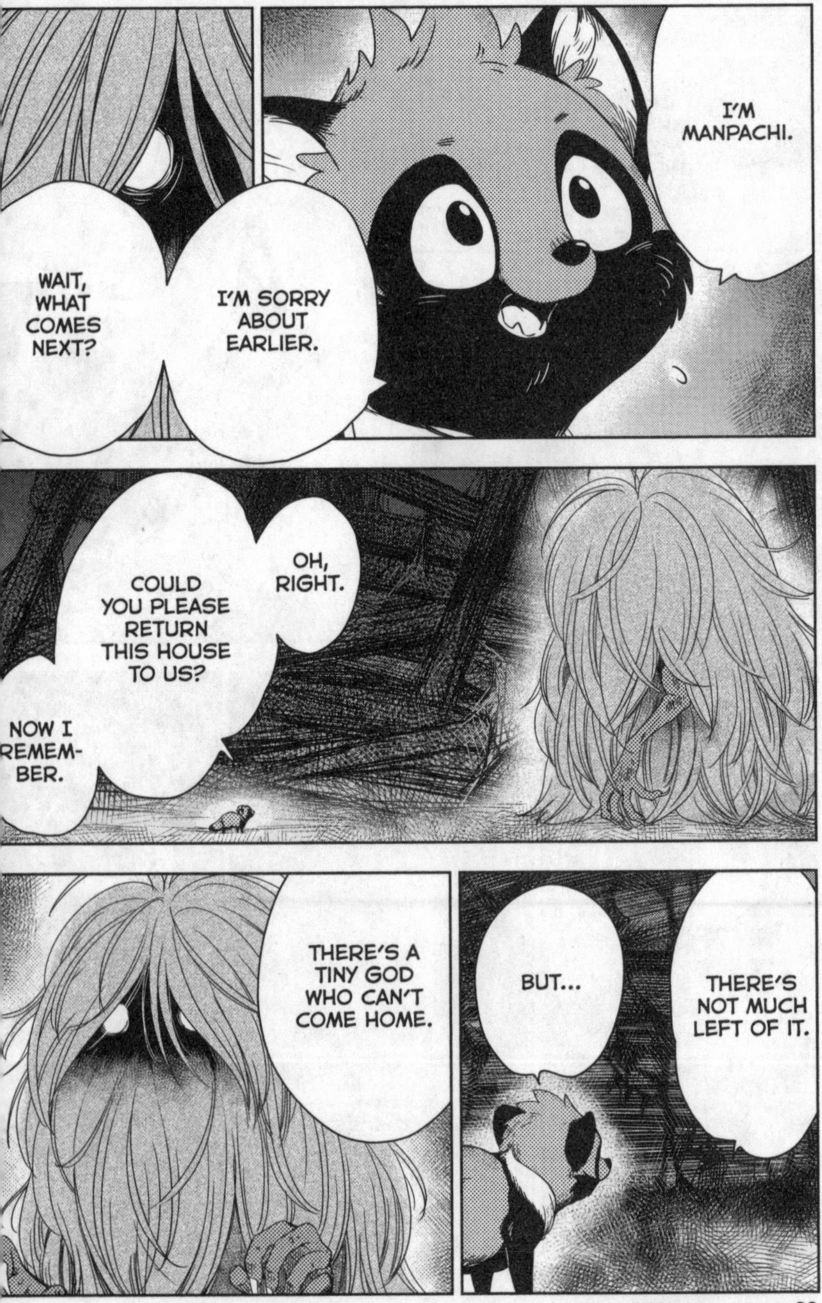
I'M MANPACHI.
I'M SORRY ABOUT EARLIER.
WAIT, WHAT COMES NEXT?
OH, RIGHT.
COULD YOU PLEASE RETURN THIS HOUSE TO US?
NOW I REMEM-BER.
THERE'S NOT MUCH LEFT OF IT.
BUT...
THERE'S A TINY GOD WHO CAN'T COME HOME.

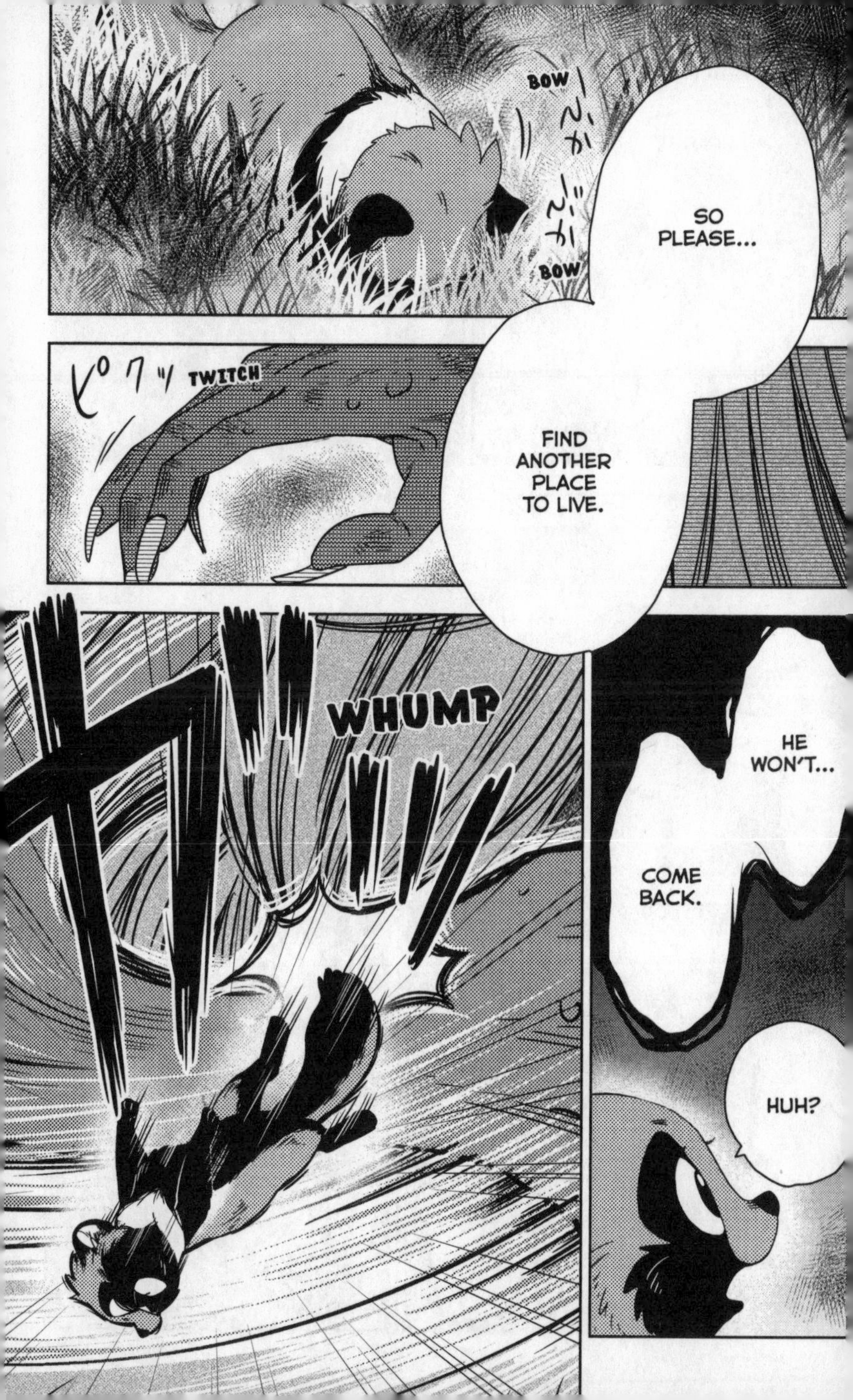

SO PLEASE...
BOW
BOW
FIND ANOTHER PLACE TO LIVE.
ピクッ
TWITCH
HE WON'T...
COME BACK.
HUH?
WHUMP

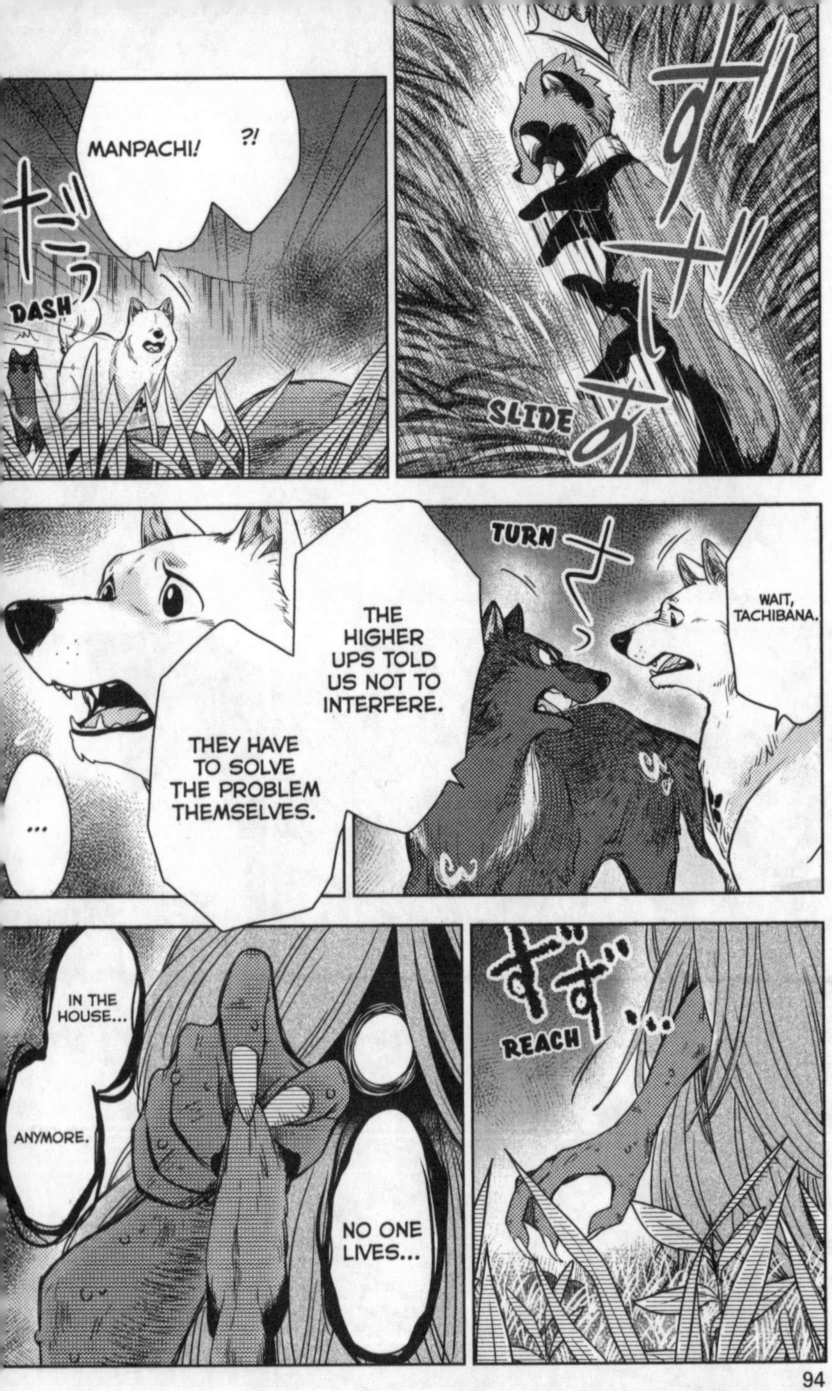
SLIDE
MANPACHI!
?!
DASH
TURN
WAIT, TACHIBANA.
THE HIGHER UPS TOLD US NOT TO INTERFERE.
THEY HAVE TO SOLVE THE PROBLEM THEMSELVES.
...
REACH
NO ONE LIVES...
IN THE HOUSE...
ANYMORE.

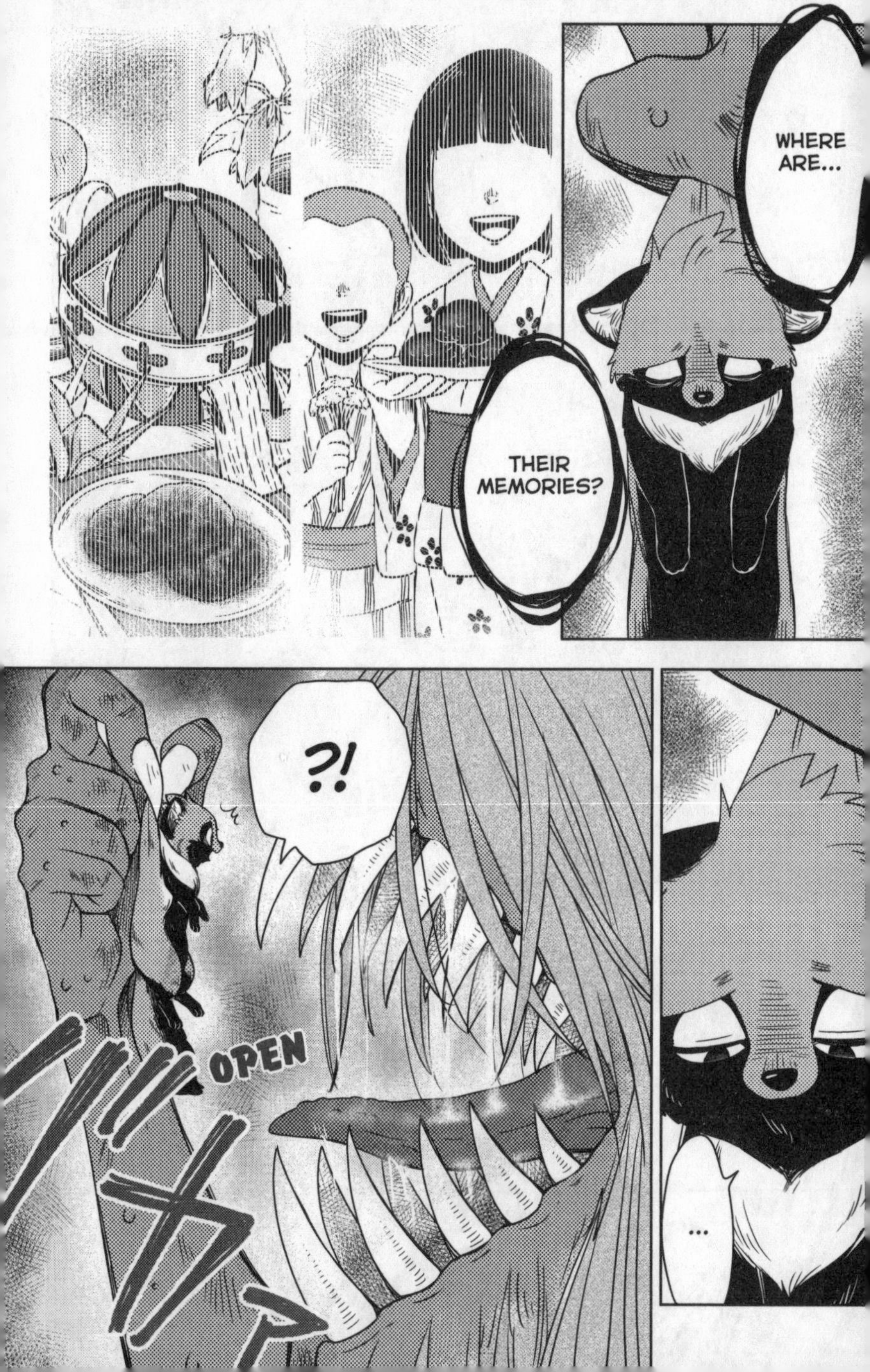
WHERE ARE...
THEIR MEMORIES?
...
?!
OPEN

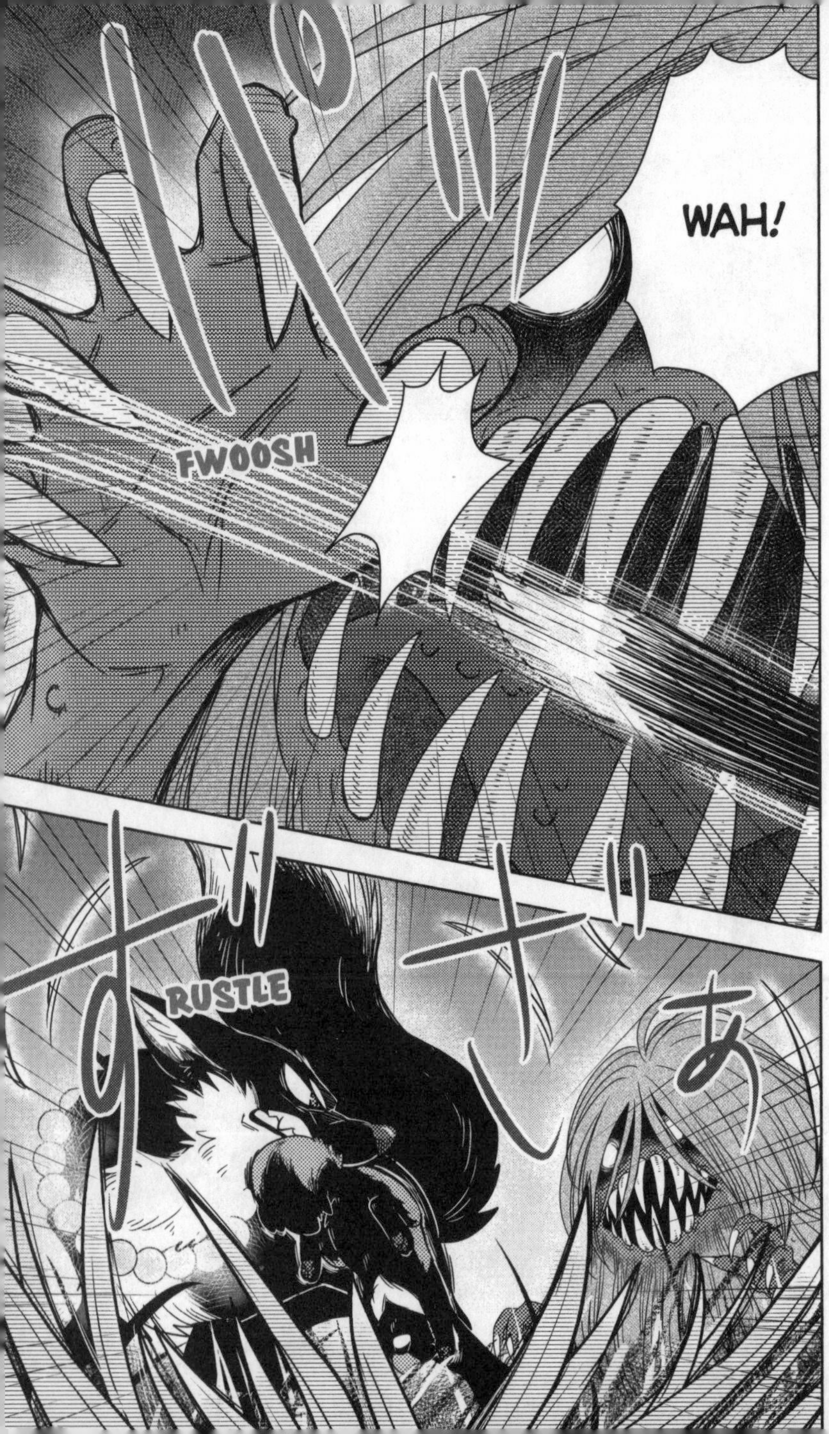
WAH!
FWOOSH
あ
RUSTLE

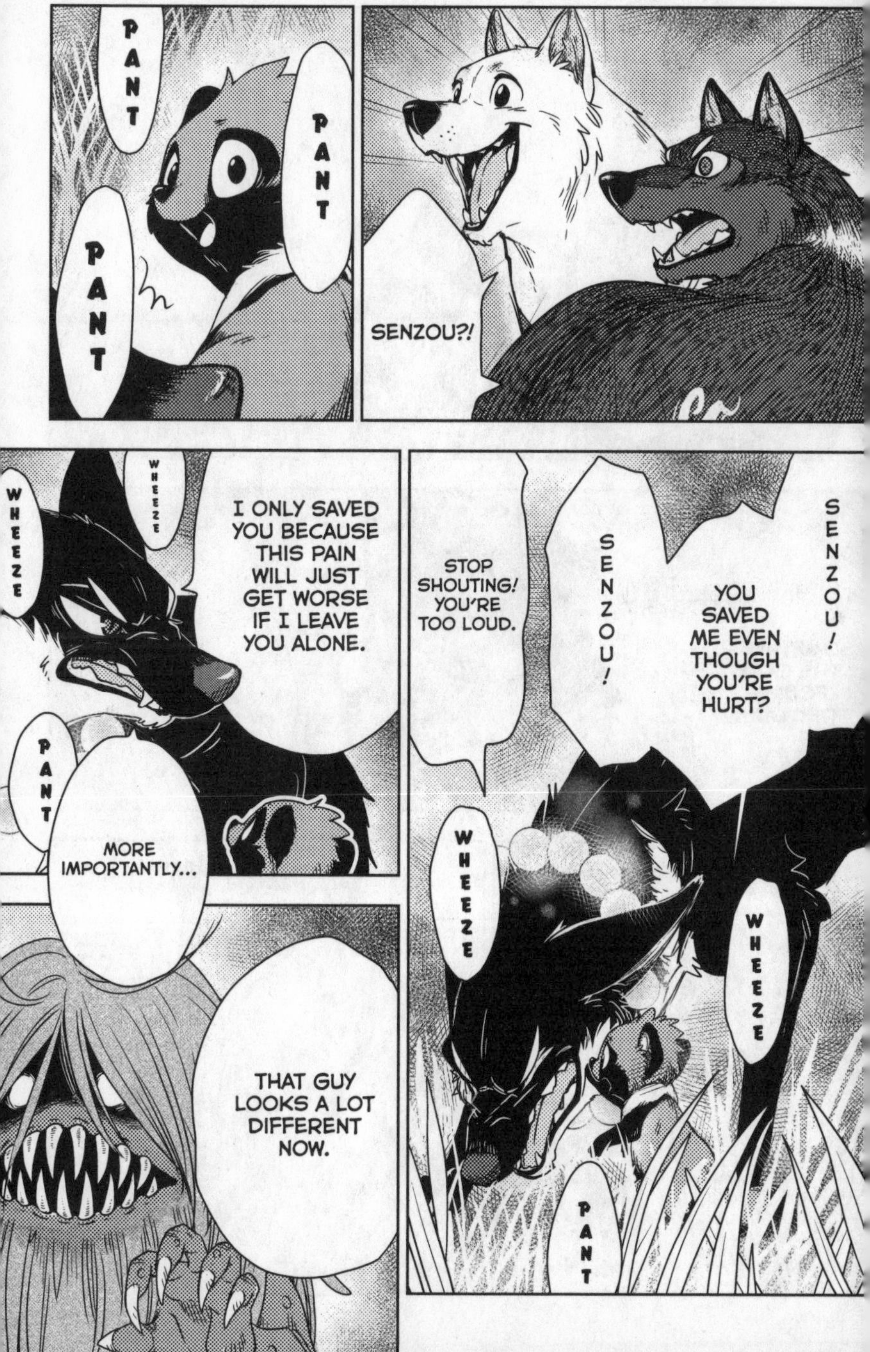
SENZOU?!
PANT
PANT
PANT
SENZOU!
YOU SAVED ME EVEN THOUGH YOU'RE HURT?
SENZOU!
STOP SHOUTING! YOU'RE TOO LOUD.
WHEEZE
WHEEZE
PANT
WHEEZE
I ONLY SAVED YOU BECAUSE THIS PAIN WILL JUST GET WORSE IF I LEAVE YOU ALONE.
WHEEZE
PANT
MORE IMPORTANTLY...
THAT GUY LOOKS A LOT DIFFERENT NOW.

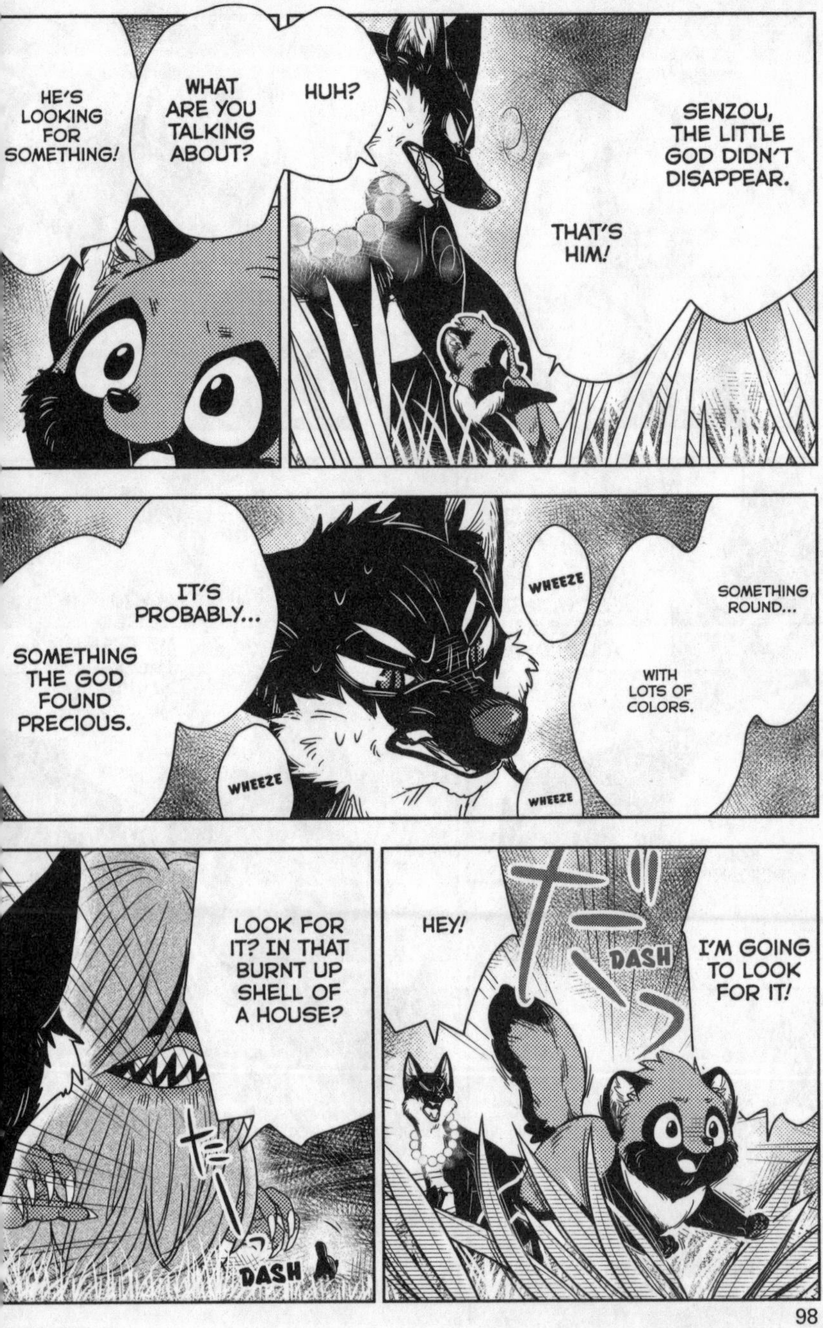
SENZOU, THE LITTLE GOD DIDN'T DISAPPEAR.
THAT'S HIM!
HUH?
WHAT ARE YOU TALKING ABOUT?
HE'S LOOKING FOR SOMETHING!
SOMETHING ROUND...
WITH LOTS OF COLORS.
WHEEZE
WHEEZE
IT'S PROBABLY...
SOMETHING THE GOD FOUND PRECIOUS.
WHEEZE
I'M GOING TO LOOK FOR IT!
DASH
HEY!
LOOK FOR IT? IN THAT BURNT UP SHELL OF A HOUSE?
DASH

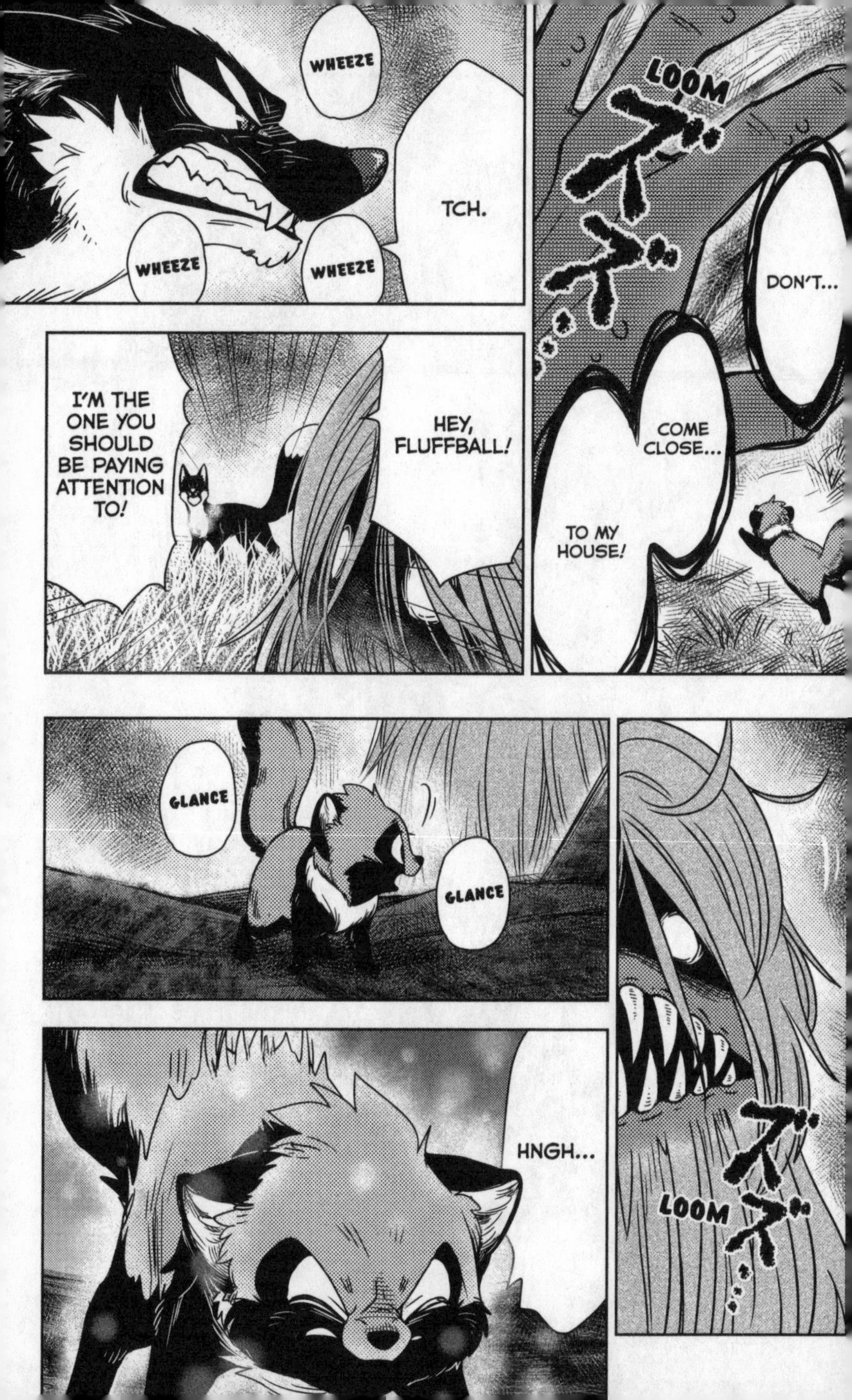
LOOM
DON'T...
COME CLOSE...
TO MY HOUSE!
WHEEZE
TCH.
WHEEZE
WHEEZE
HEY, FLUFFBALL!
I'M THE ONE YOU SHOULD BE PAYING ATTENTION TO!
LOOM
GLANCE
GLANCE
HNGH...

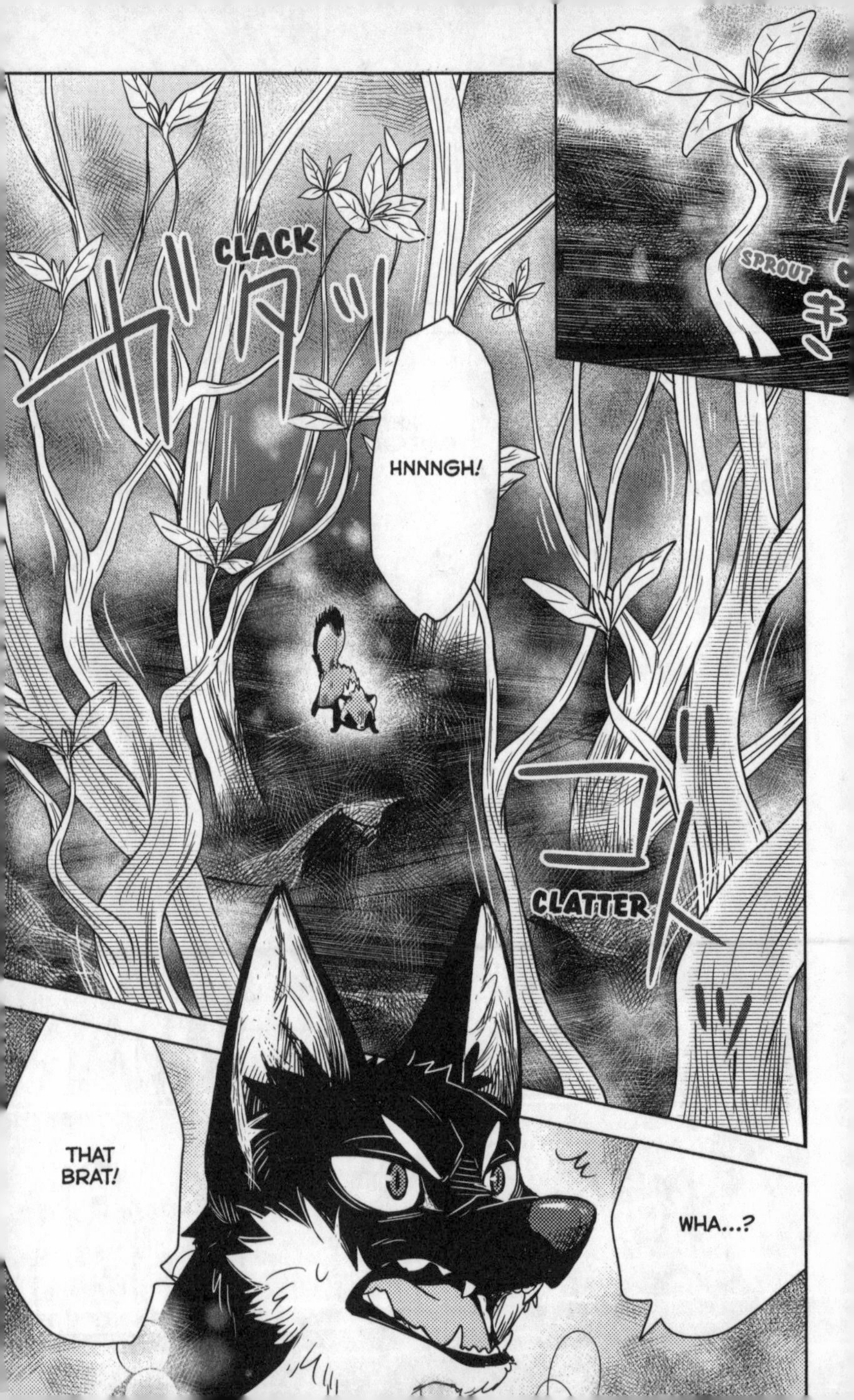
SPROUT
CLACK
HNNNGH!
CLATTER
WHA...?
THAT BRAT!

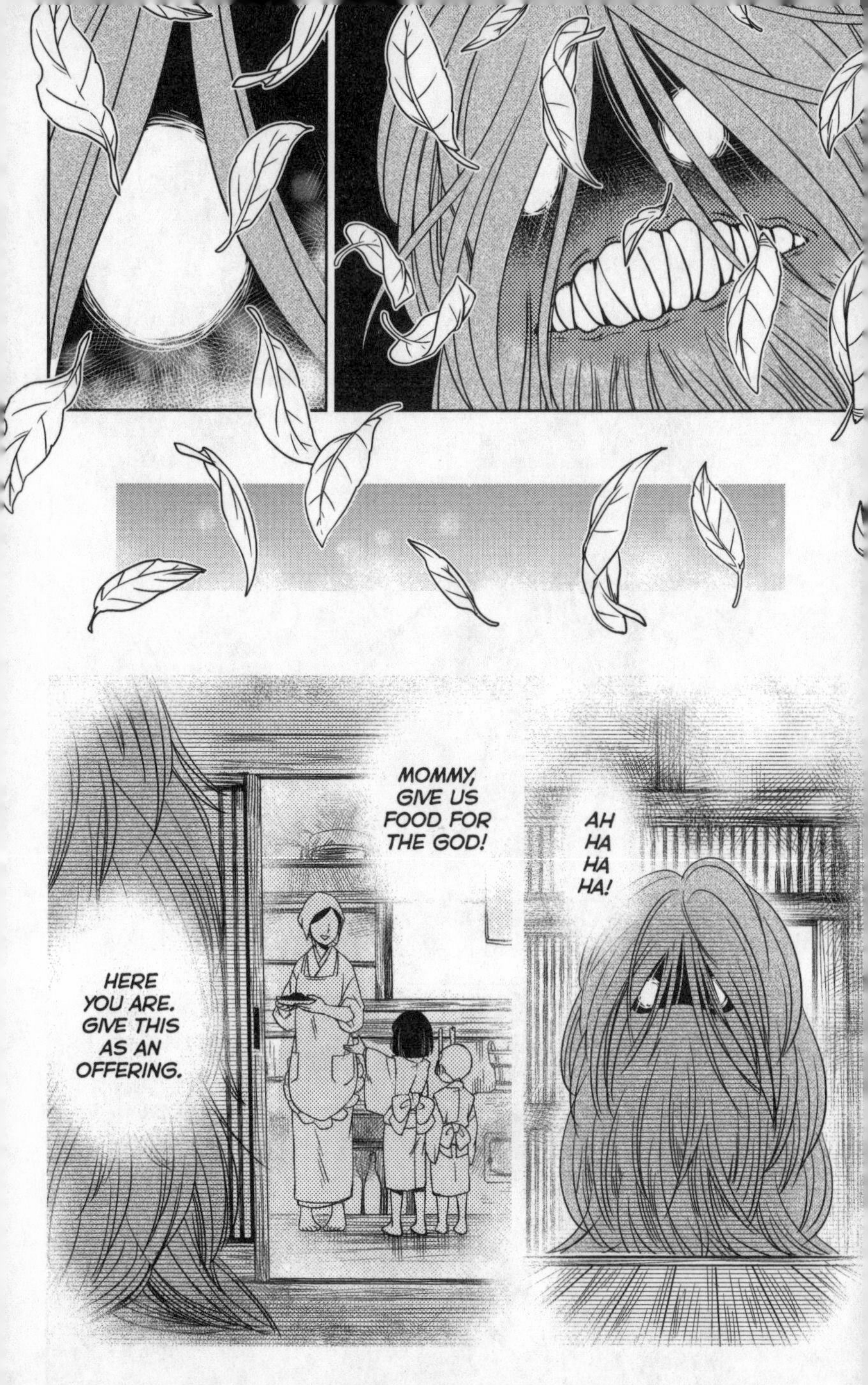
AH HA HA HA!
MOMMY, GIVE US FOOD FOR THE GOD!
HERE YOU ARE. GIVE THIS AS AN OFFERING.

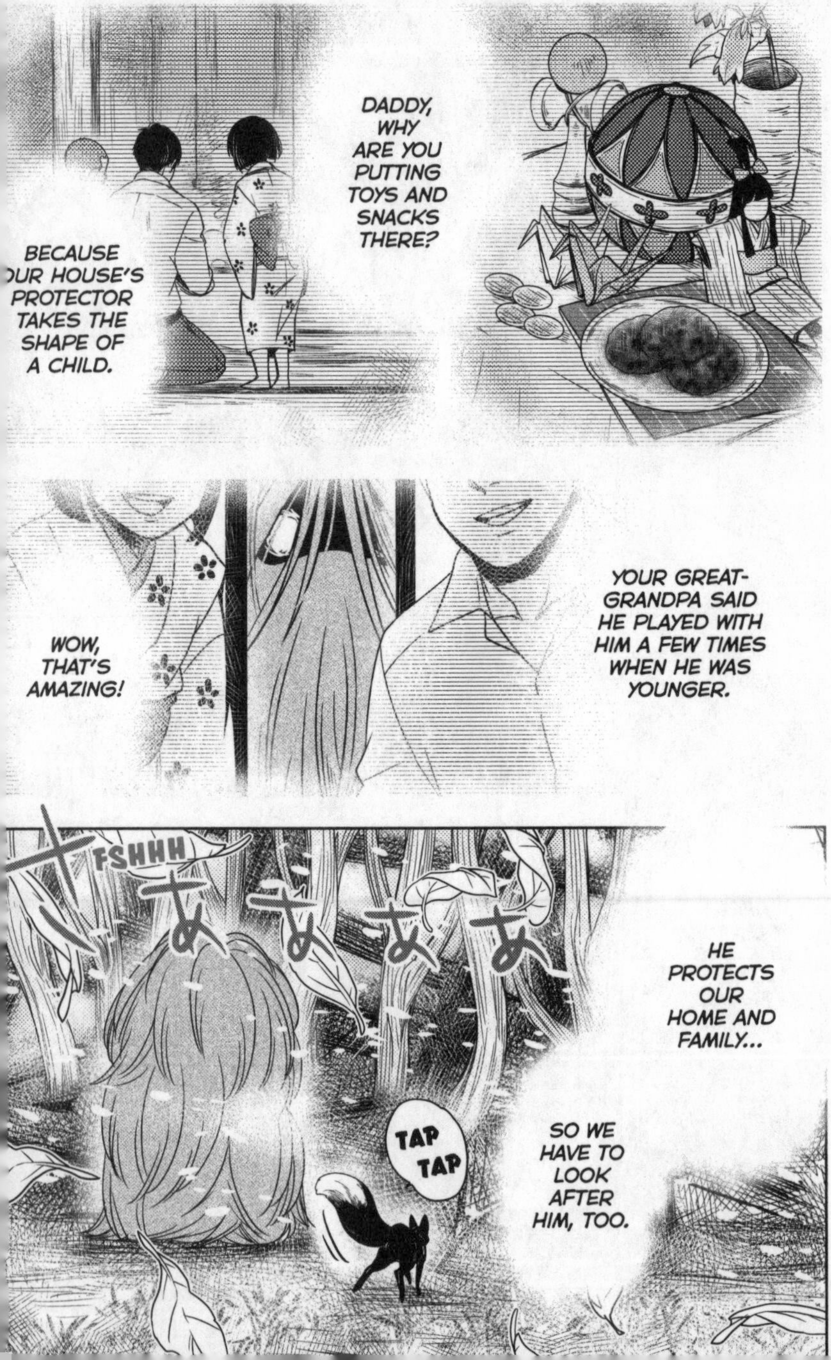
DADDY, WHY ARE YOU PUTTING TOYS AND SNACKS THERE?
BECAUSE OUR HOUSE'S PROTECTOR TAKES THE SHAPE OF A CHILD.
YOUR GREAT-GRANDPA SAID HE PLAYED WITH HIM A FEW TIMES WHEN HE WAS YOUNGER.
WOW, THAT'S AMAZING!
HE PROTECTS OUR HOME AND FAMILY...
FSHHH
ああああ
SO WE HAVE TO LOOK AFTER HIM, TOO.
TAP TAP

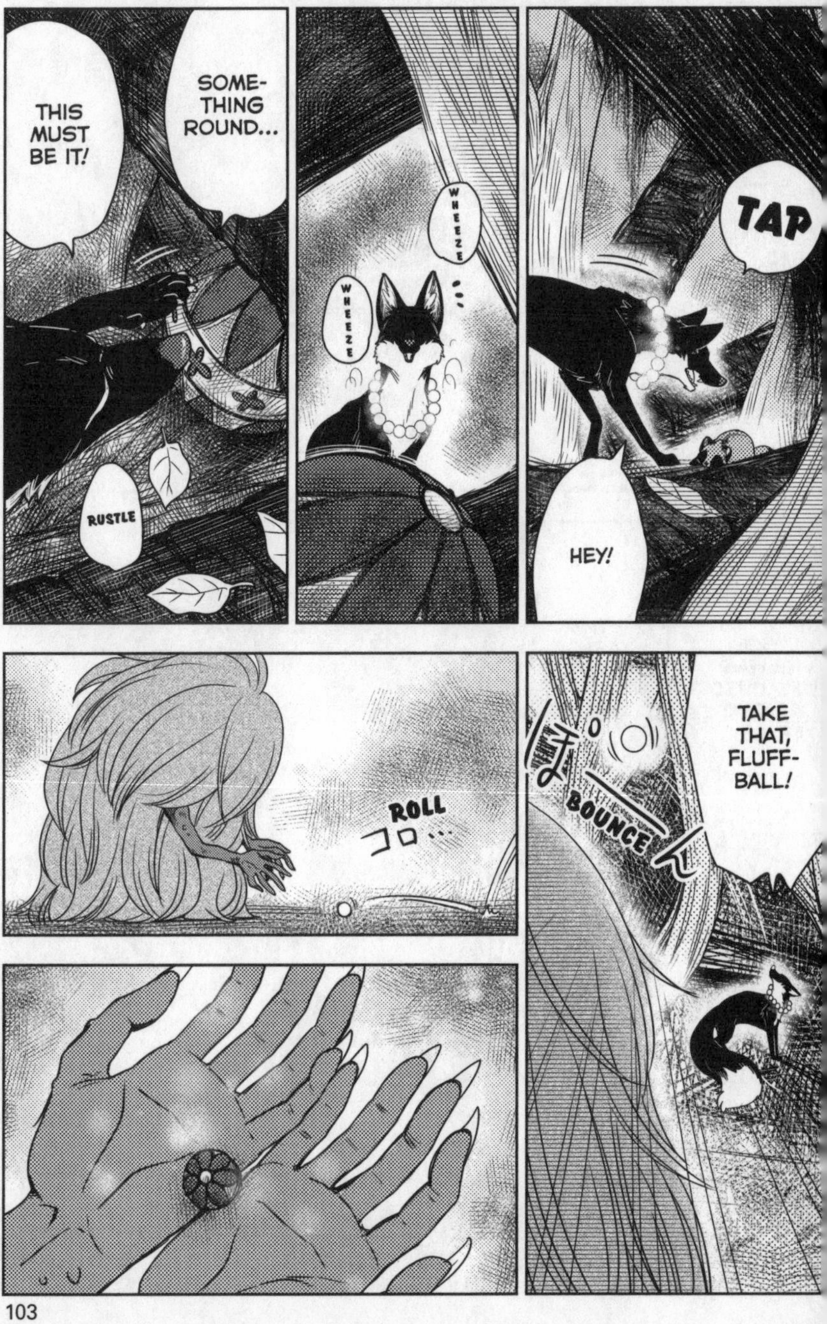
TAP
HEY!
WHEEZE
WHEEZE
SOME-THING ROUND...
THIS MUST BE IT!
RUSTLE
TAKE THAT, FLUFF-BALL!
BOUNCE
ROLL
コロ…

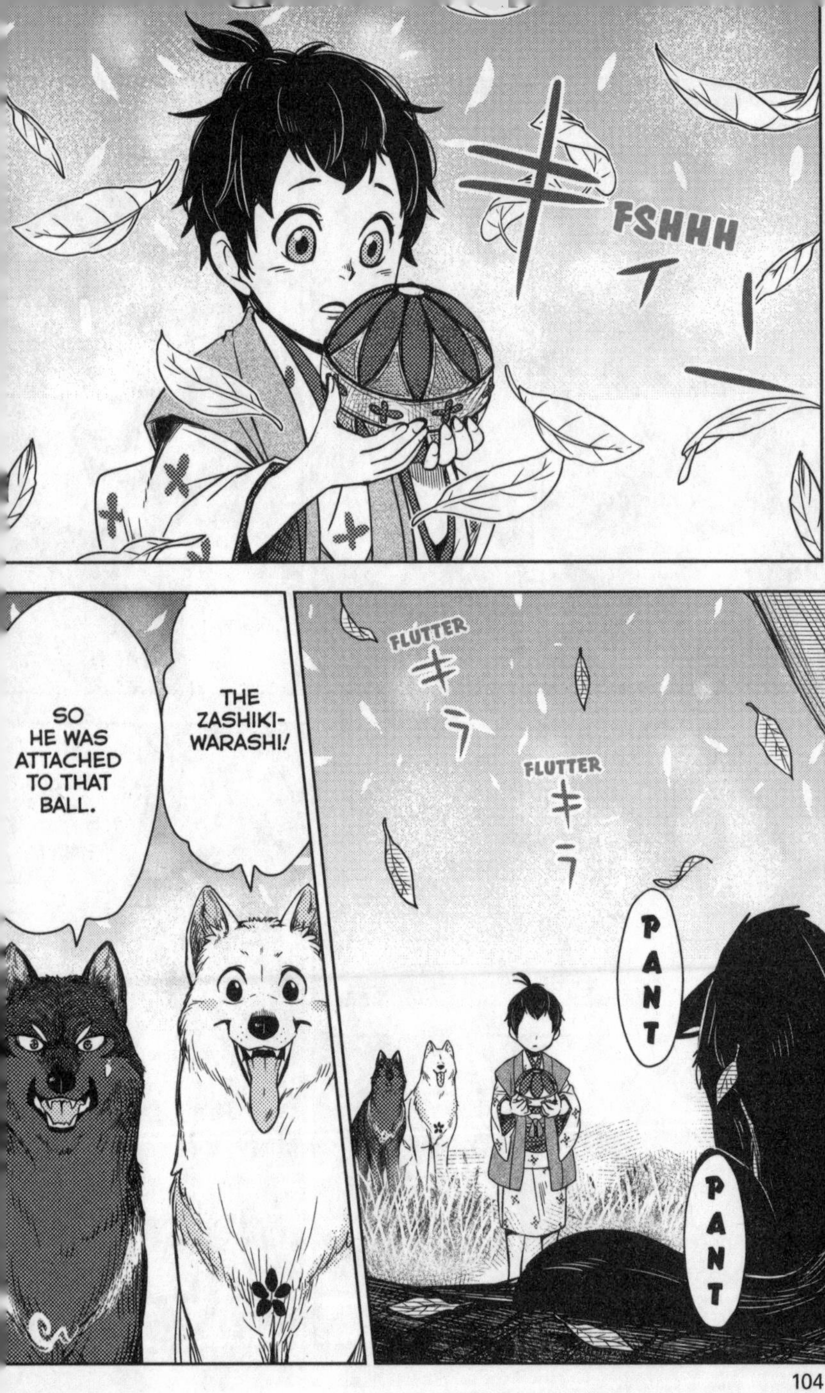
FSHHH
FLUTTER
キラ
FLUTTER
キラ
PANT
PANT
THE ZASHIKI-WARASHI!
SO HE WAS ATTACHED TO THAT BALL.

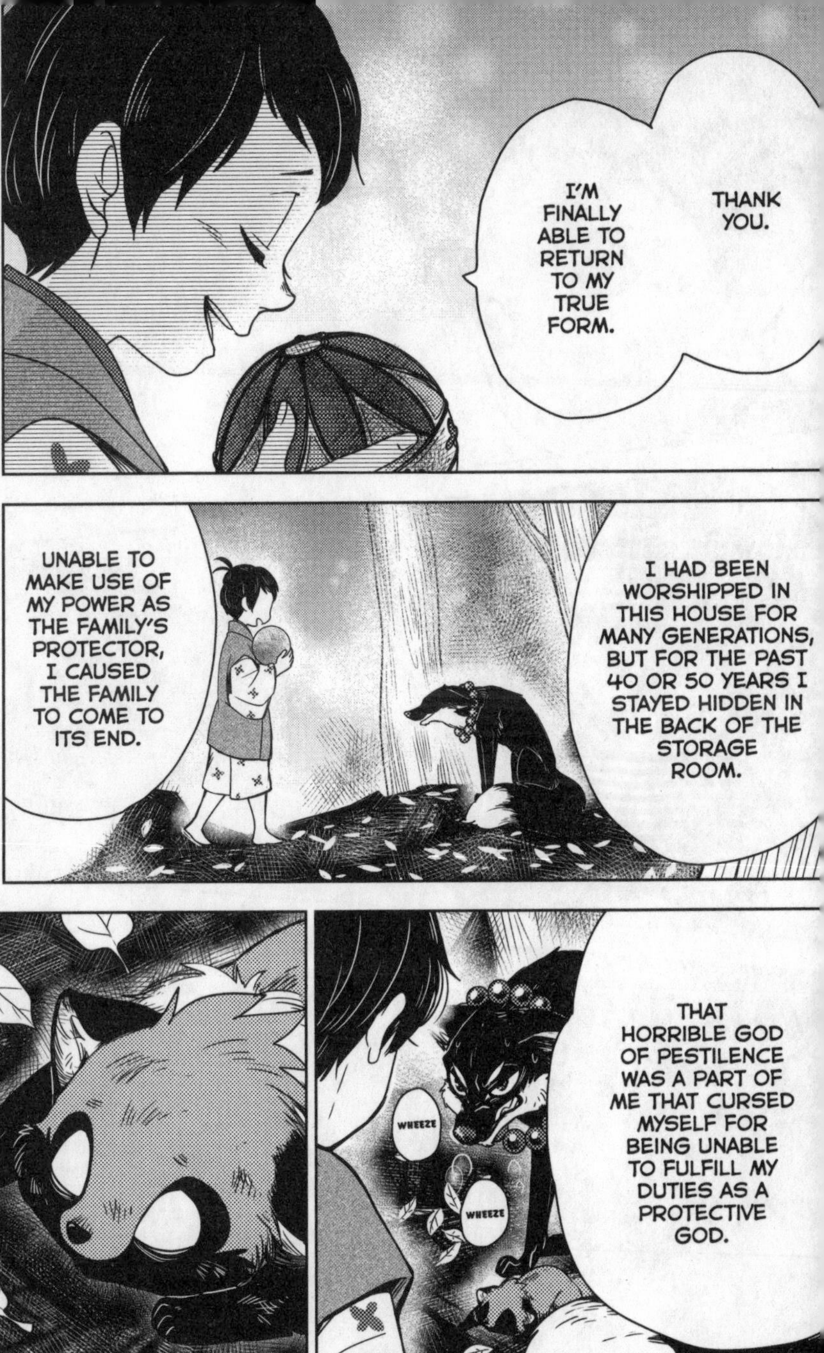
THANK YOU.
I'M FINALLY ABLE TO RETURN TO MY TRUE FORM.
I HAD BEEN WORSHIPPED IN THIS HOUSE FOR MANY GENERATIONS, BUT FOR THE PAST 40 OR 50 YEARS I STAYED HIDDEN IN THE BACK OF THE STORAGE ROOM.
UNABLE TO MAKE USE OF MY POWER AS THE FAMILY'S PROTECTOR, I CAUSED THE FAMILY TO COME TO ITS END.
THAT HORRIBLE GOD OF PESTILENCE WAS A PART OF ME THAT CURSED MYSELF FOR BEING UNABLE TO FULFILL MY DUTIES AS A PROTECTIVE GOD.
WHEEZE
WHEEZE

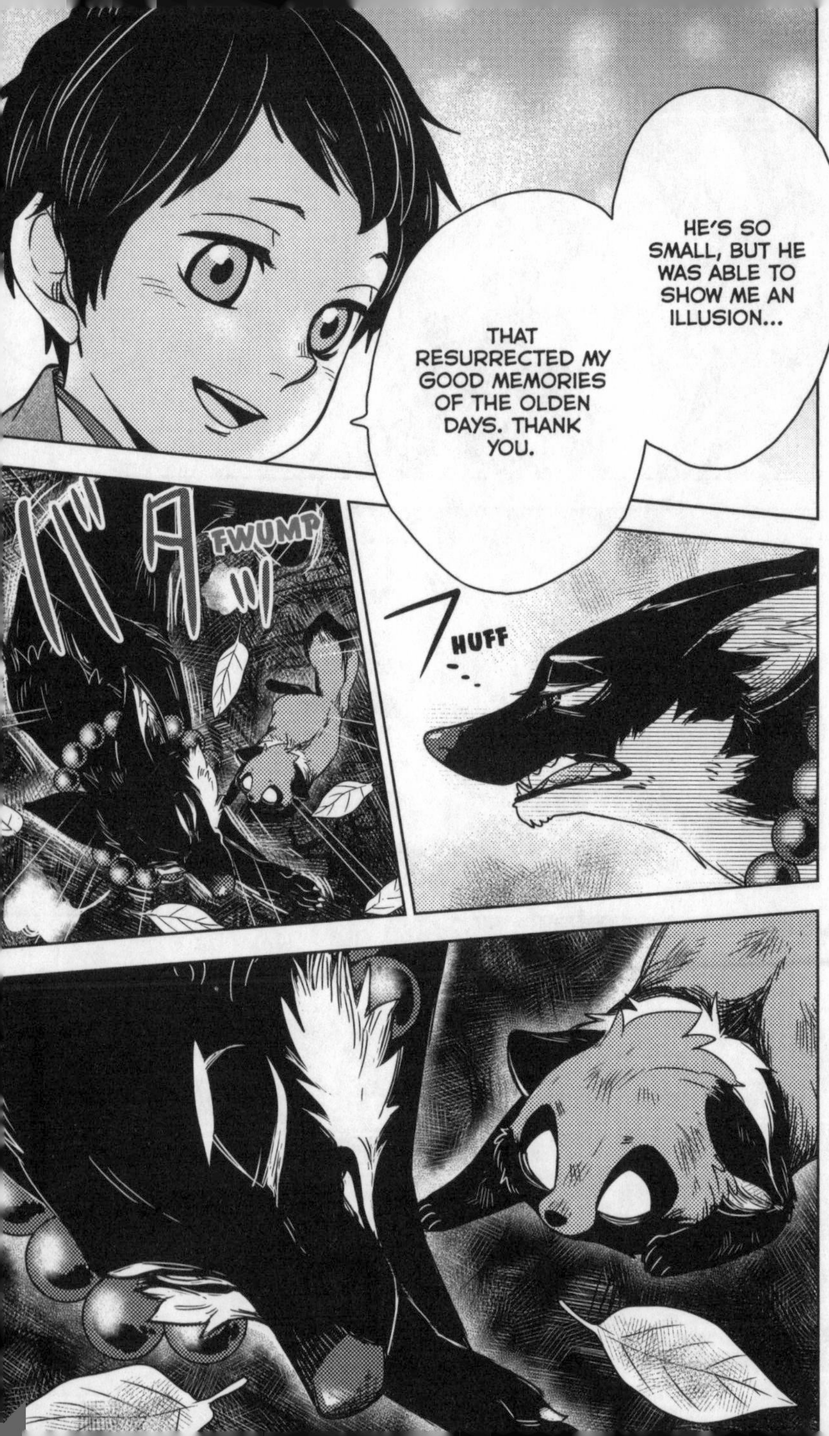
HE'S SO SMALL, BUT HE WAS ABLE TO SHOW ME AN ILLUSION...
THAT RESURRECTED MY GOOD MEMORIES OF THE OLDEN DAYS. THANK YOU.
HUFF
FWUMP

The Bakemono Field Guide

#4

Tokoyo no Naganakidori (Rooster)

A servant of the most highly ranked goddess in Japan, the sun goddess, Amaterasu Omikami. In the famous legend of "Amano Iwato," the sun goddess hides and the Tokoyo no Naganakidori calls her out once more, bringing the morning sun. These bakemono are known as sacred roosters whose cries can rid the world of darkness.

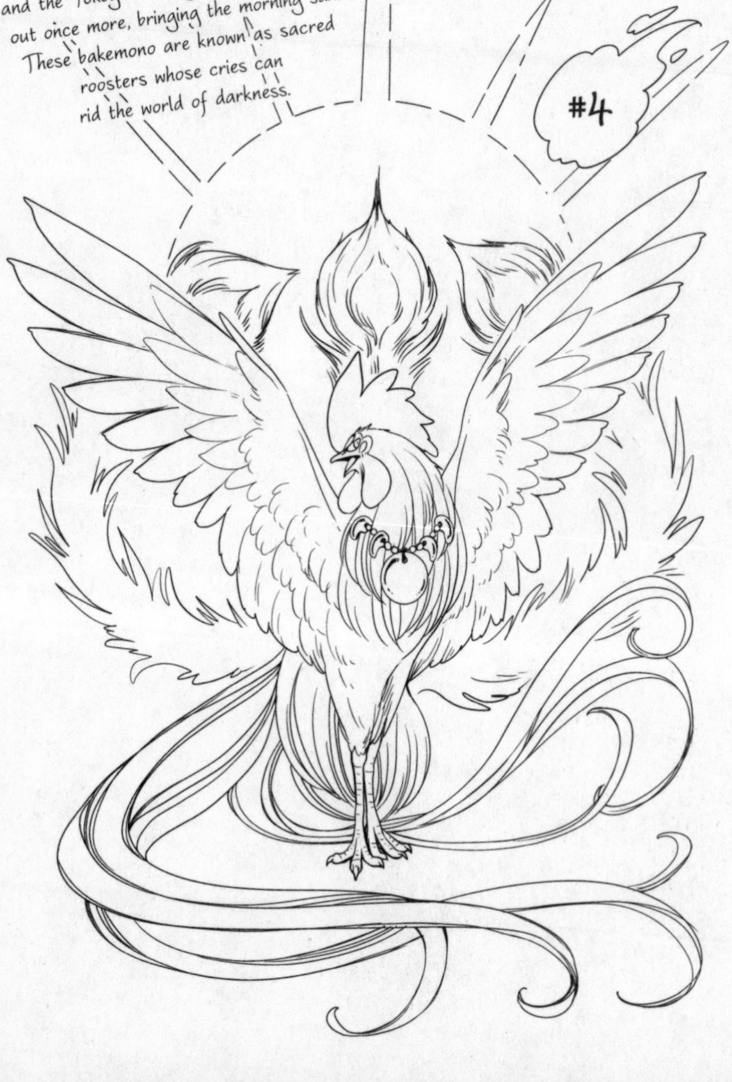

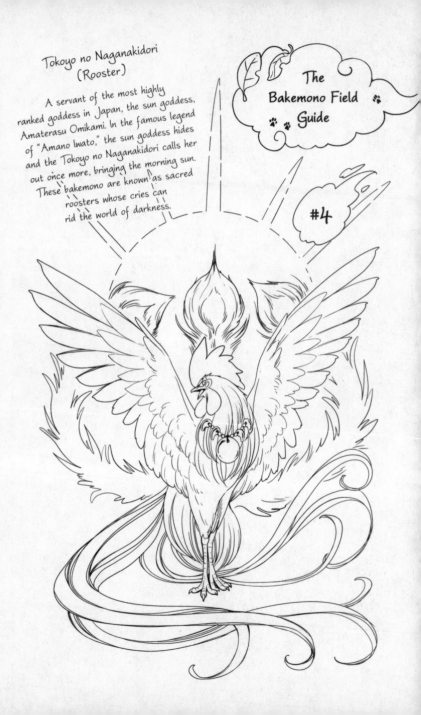

Chapter 5

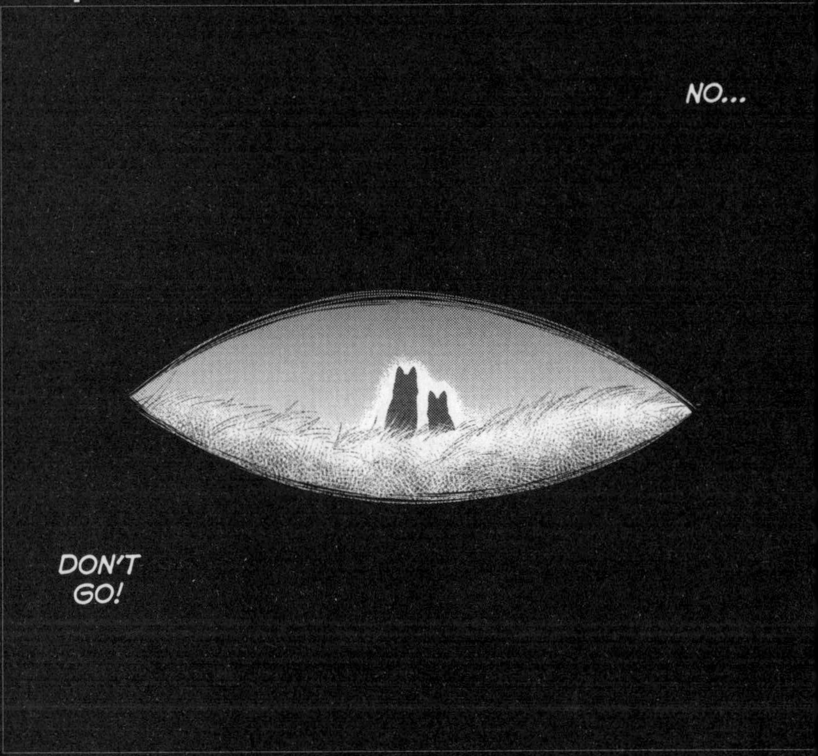
NO...
DON'T GO!

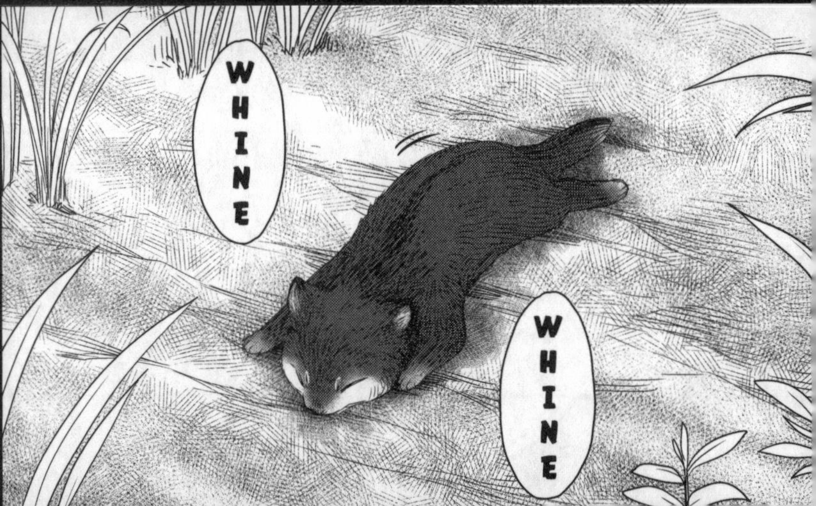
WHINE
WHINE

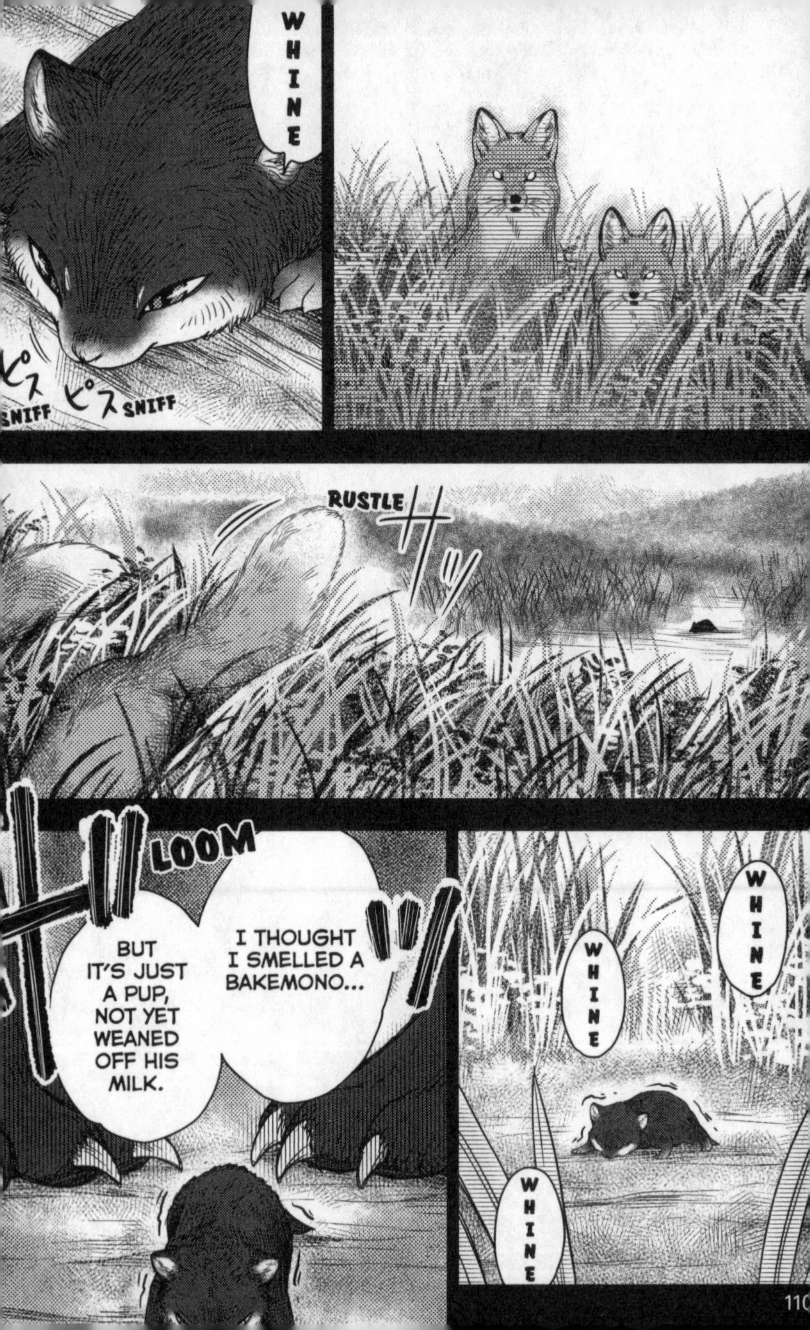
WHINE
ピス ピス
SNIFF SNIFF
RUSTLE
サッ
WHINE
WHINE
WHINE
LOOM
I THOUGHT I SMELLED A BAKEMONO...
BUT IT'S JUST A PUP, NOT YET WEANED OFF HIS MILK.

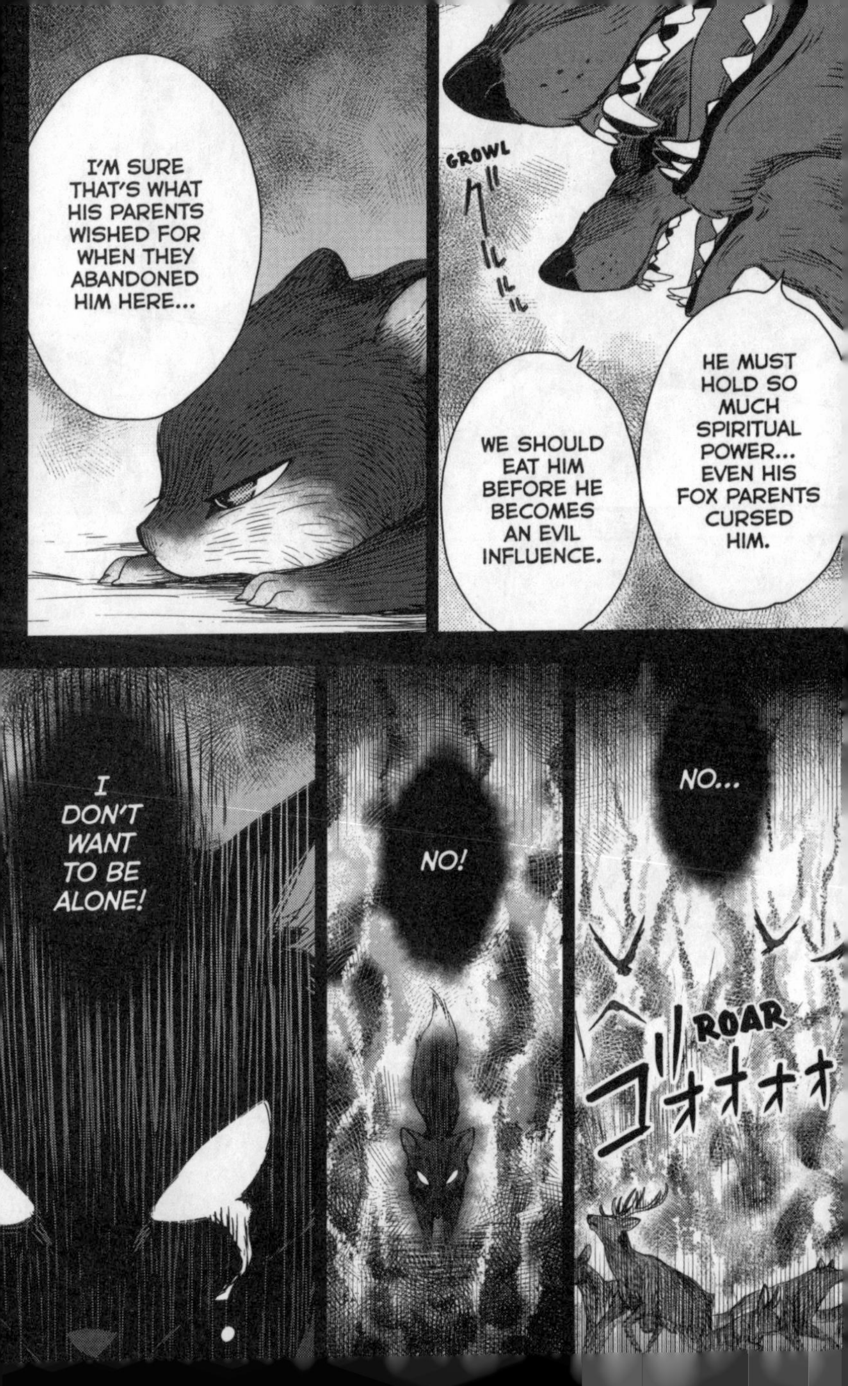
GROWL
グルルル
HE MUST HOLD SO MUCH SPIRITUAL POWER... EVEN HIS FOX PARENTS CURSED HIM.
WE SHOULD EAT HIM BEFORE HE BECOMES AN EVIL INFLUENCE.
I'M SURE THAT'S WHAT HIS PARENTS WISHED FOR WHEN THEY ABANDONED HIM HERE...
NO...
ROAR
ゴオオオオ
NO!
I DON'T WANT TO BE ALONE!

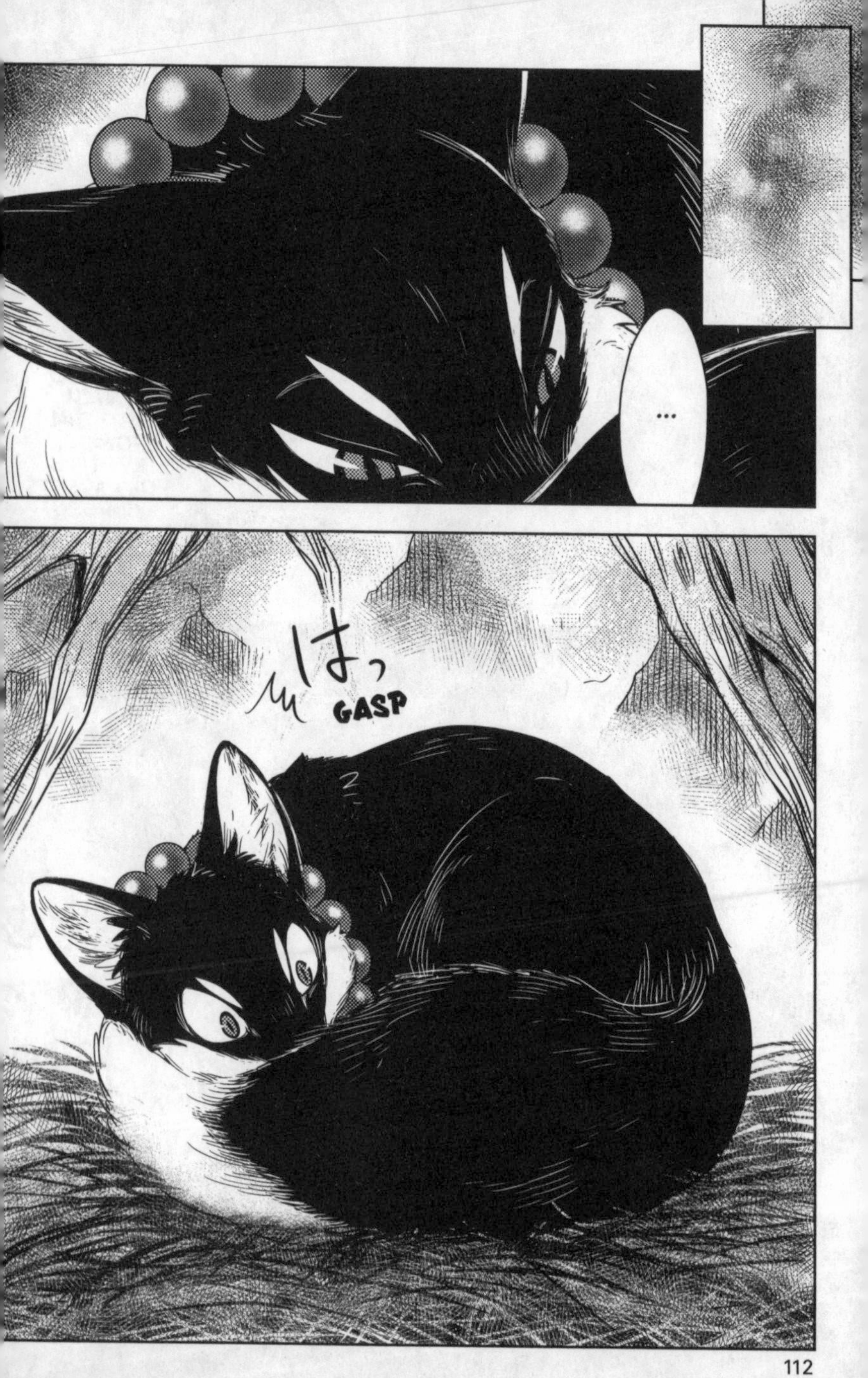
...
はっ
GASP

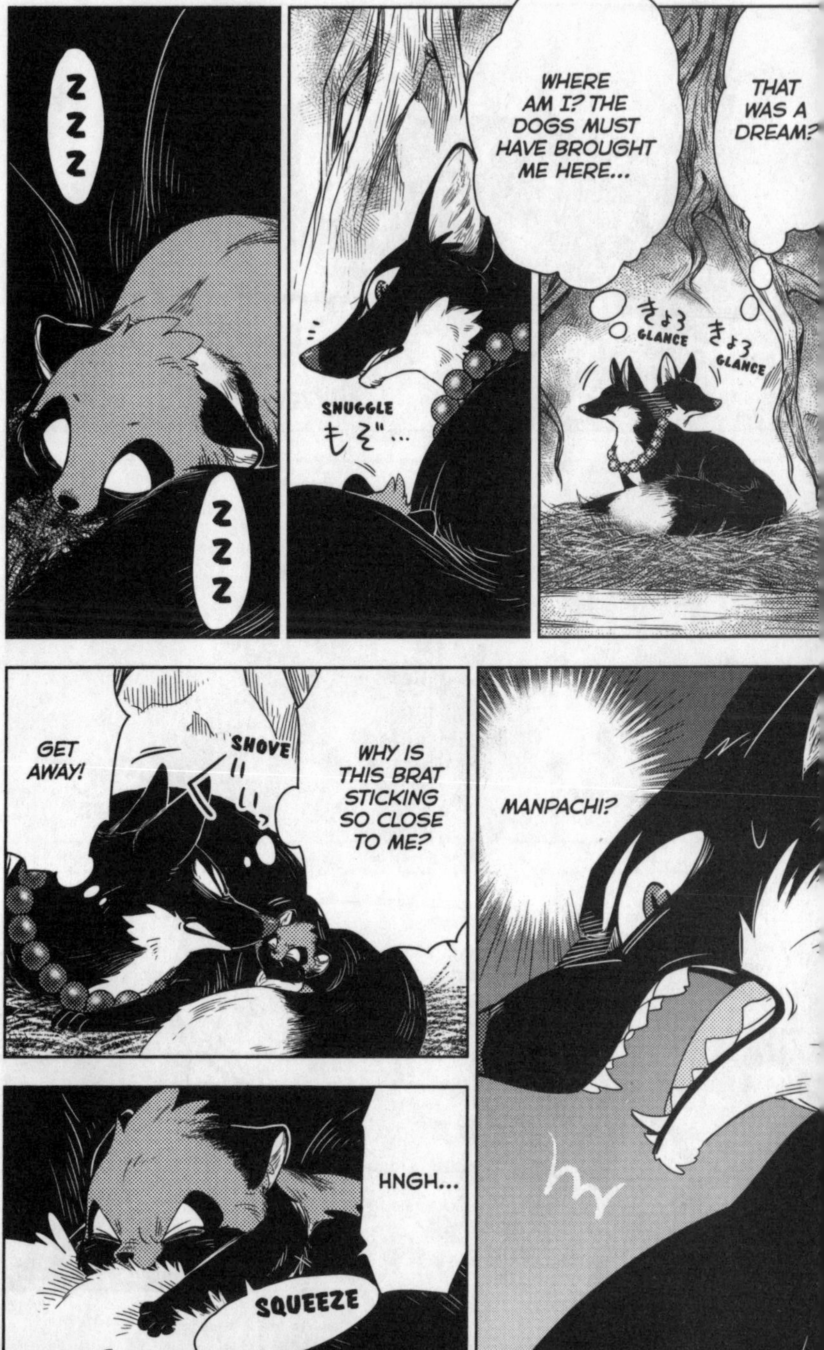
THAT WAS A DREAM?
WHERE AM I? THE DOGS MUST HAVE BROUGHT ME HERE...
きょろ GLANCE
きょろ GLANCE
SNUGGLE もぞ...
ZZZ
ZZZ
MANPACHI?
WHY IS THIS BRAT STICKING SO CLOSE TO ME?
SHOVE
GET AWAY!
HNGH...
SQUEEZE

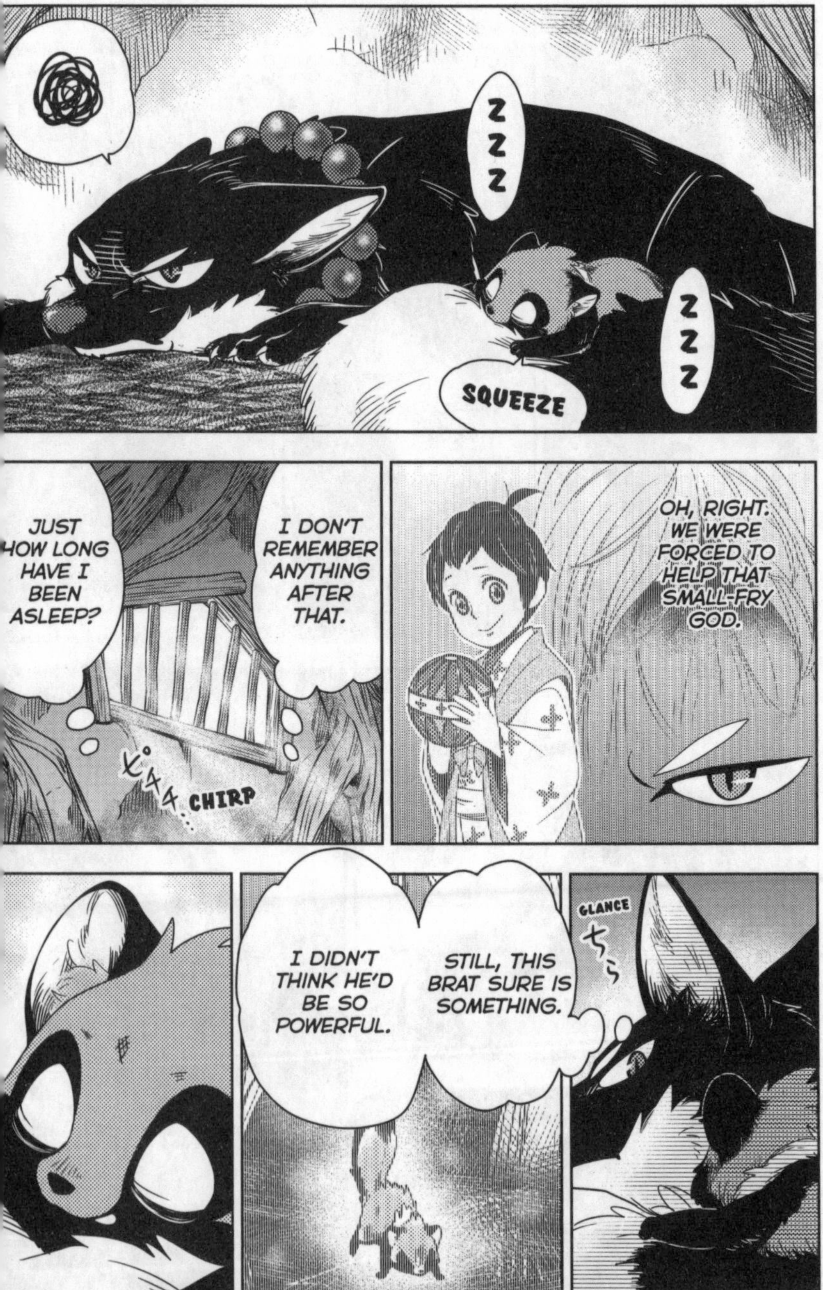
Z Z Z
Z Z Z
SQUEEZE
OH, RIGHT. WE WERE FORCED TO HELP THAT SMALL-FRY GOD.
I DON'T REMEMBER ANYTHING AFTER THAT.
JUST HOW LONG HAVE I BEEN ASLEEP?
ピィィ… CHIRP
GLANCE ちら
STILL, THIS BRAT SURE IS SOMETHING.
I DIDN'T THINK HE'D BE SO POWERFUL.

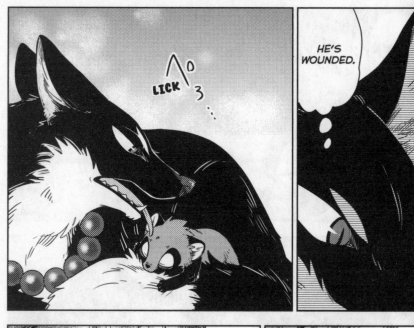

LICK

HE'S WOUNDED.

OH?

FLINCH

TREMBLE TREMBLE

TREMBLE

ZZZ ZZZ ZZZ

...

TAP

?!

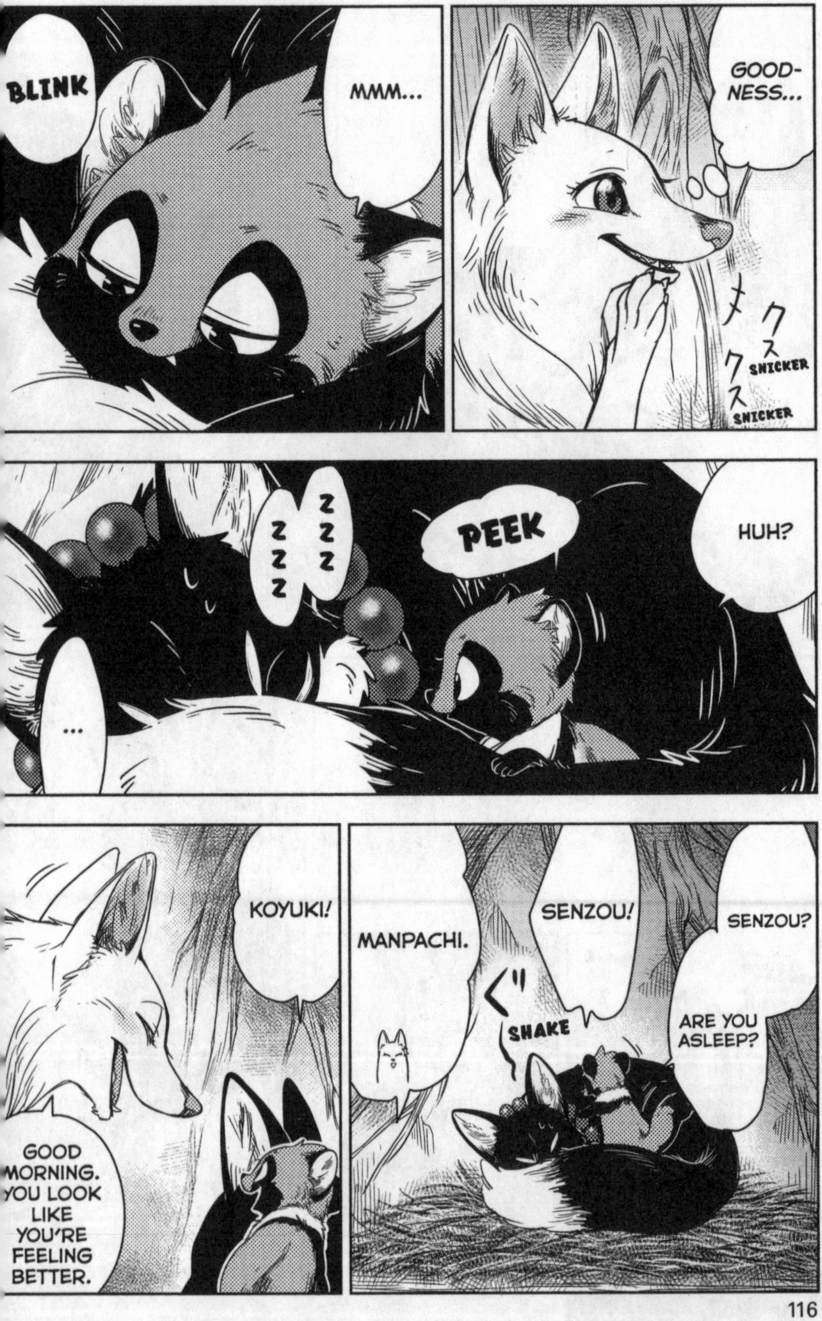
GOOD-
NESS...
クス
SNICKER
クス
SNICKER
MMM...
BLINK
HUH?
PEEK
ZZZ
ZZZ
...
SENZOU?
ARE YOU ASLEEP?
SENZOU!
ぐ
SHAKE
MANPACHI.
KOYUKI!
GOOD MORNING. YOU LOOK LIKE YOU'RE FEELING BETTER.

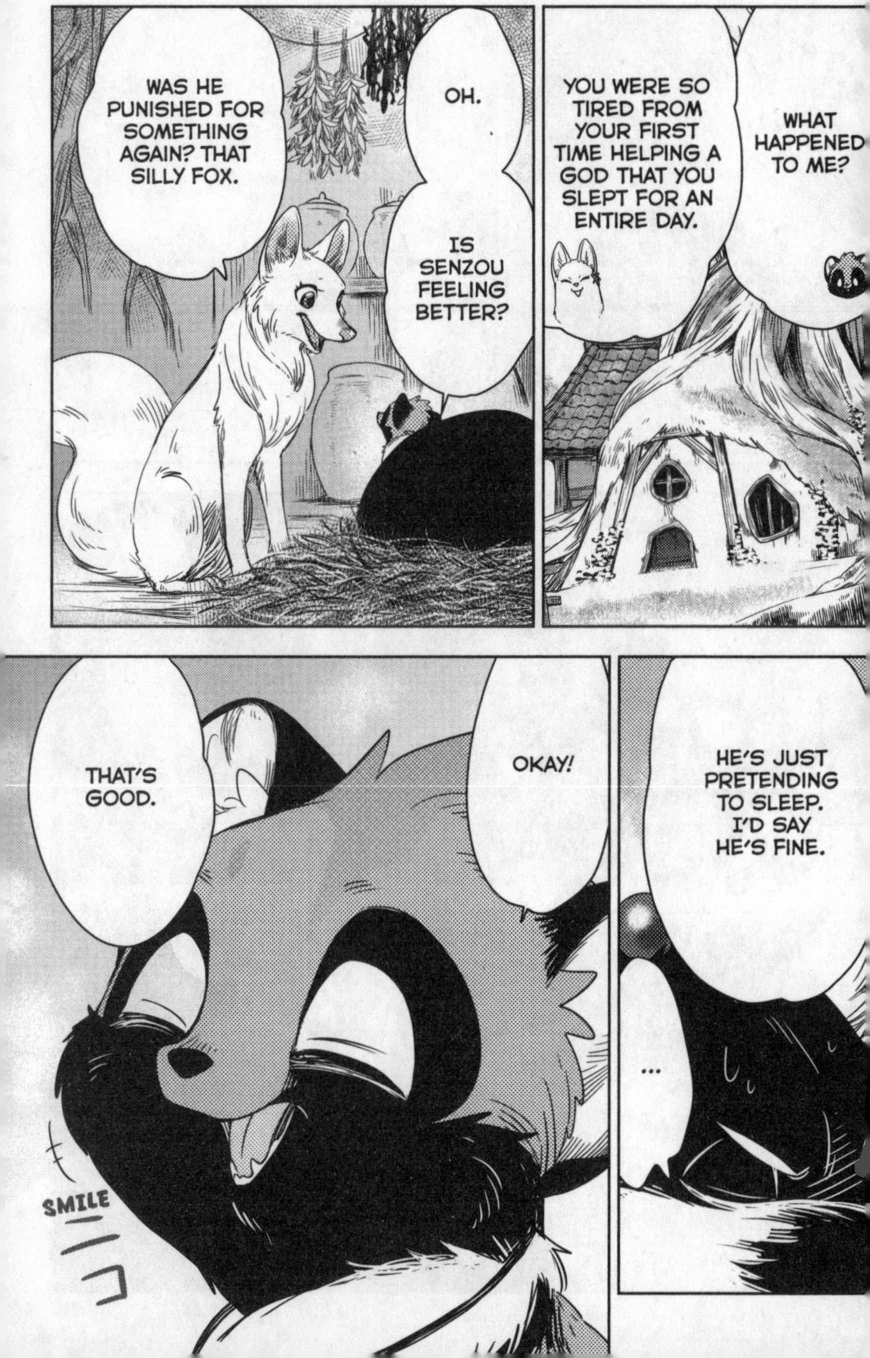
WHAT HAPPENED TO ME?
YOU WERE SO TIRED FROM YOUR FIRST TIME HELPING A GOD THAT YOU SLEPT FOR AN ENTIRE DAY.
OH.
IS SENZOU FEELING BETTER?
WAS HE PUNISHED FOR SOMETHING AGAIN? THAT SILLY FOX.
HE'S JUST PRETENDING TO SLEEP. I'D SAY HE'S FINE.
...
OKAY!
THAT'S GOOD.
SMILE

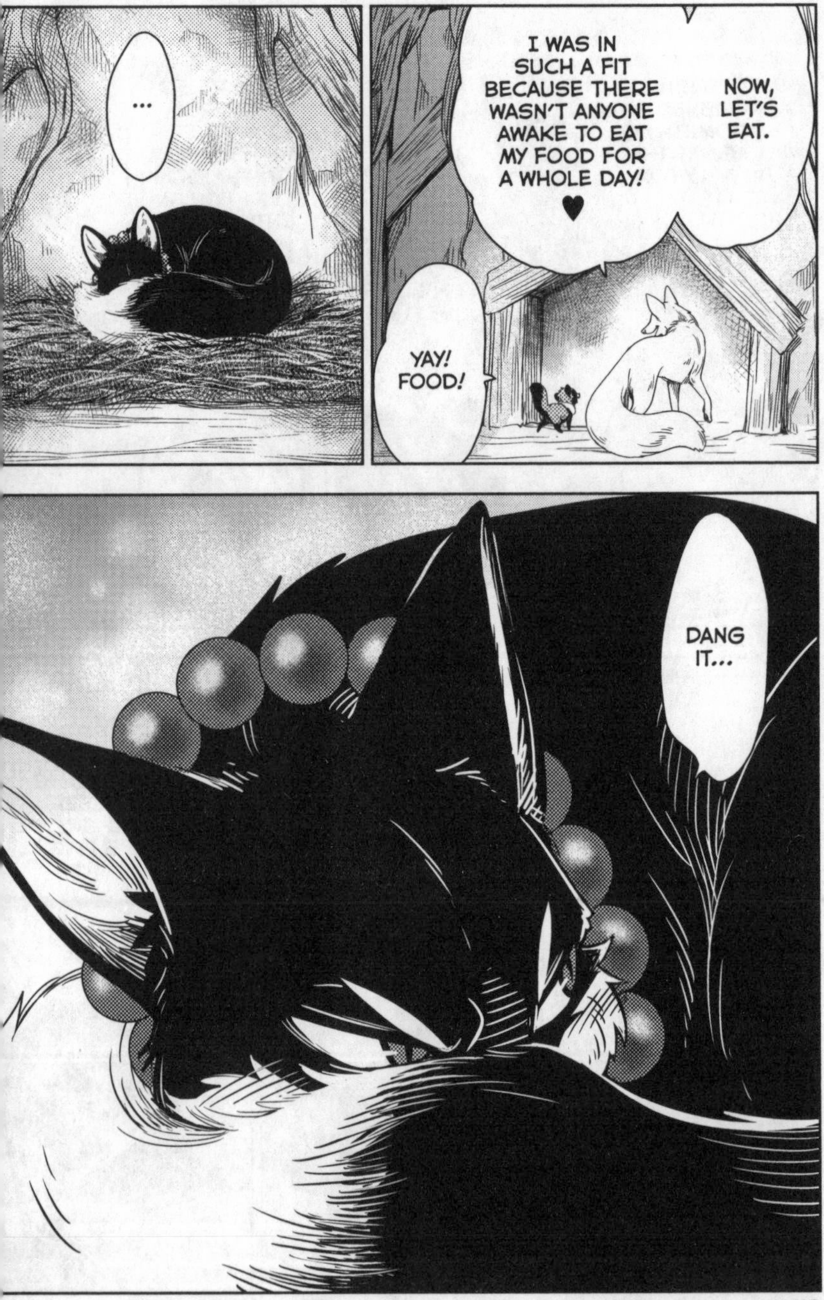
NOW, LET'S EAT.
I WAS IN SUCH A FIT BECAUSE THERE WASN'T ANYONE AWAKE TO EAT MY FOOD FOR A WHOLE DAY! ♥
YAY! FOOD!
...
DANG IT...

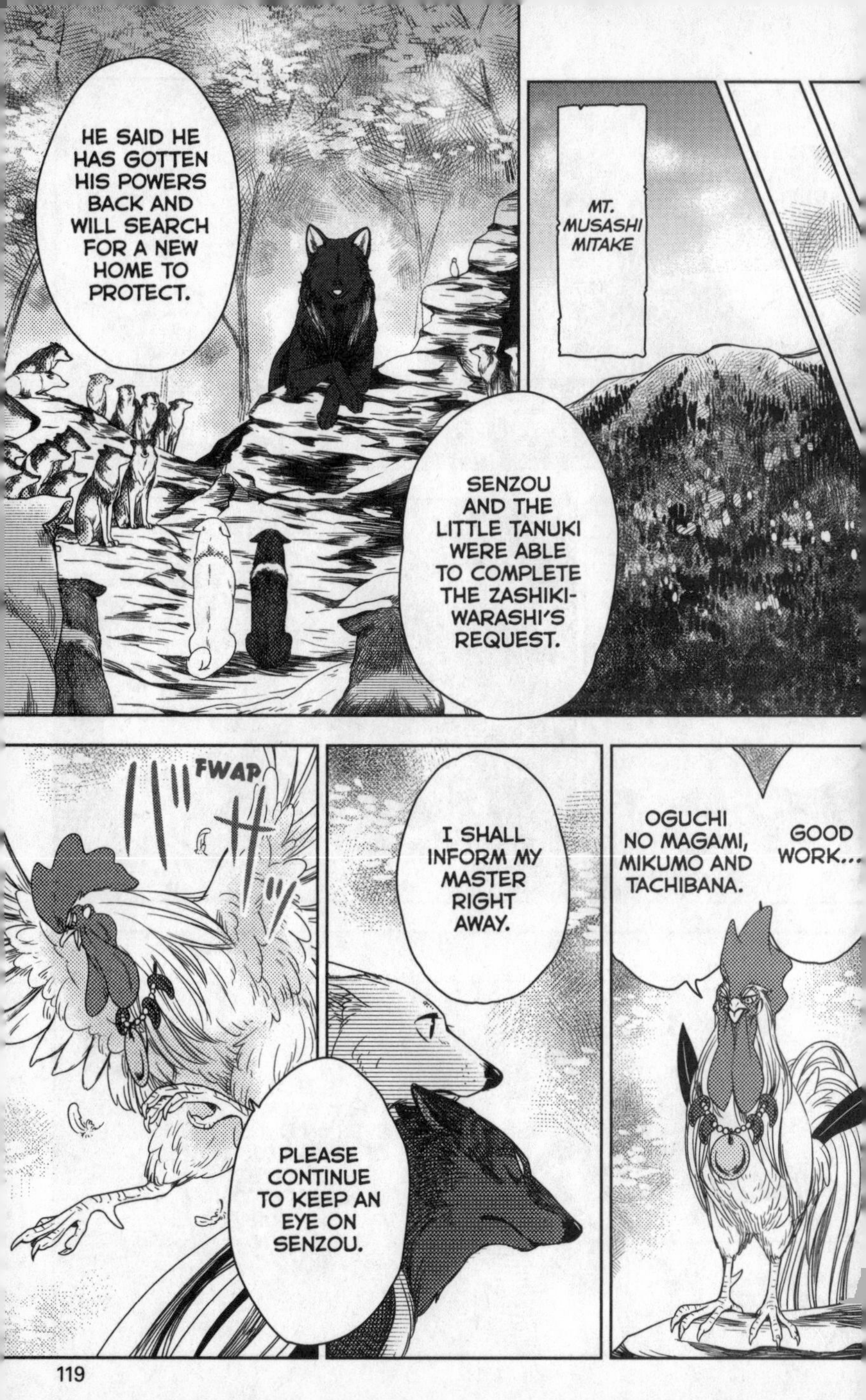
MT. MUSASHI MITAKE
SENZOU AND THE LITTLE TANUKI WERE ABLE TO COMPLETE THE ZASHIKI-WARASHI'S REQUEST.
HE SAID HE HAS GOTTEN HIS POWERS BACK AND WILL SEARCH FOR A NEW HOME TO PROTECT.
GOOD WORK...
OGUCHI NO MAGAMI, MIKUMO AND TACHIBANA.
I SHALL INFORM MY MASTER RIGHT AWAY.
PLEASE CONTINUE TO KEEP AN EYE ON SENZOU.
FWAP

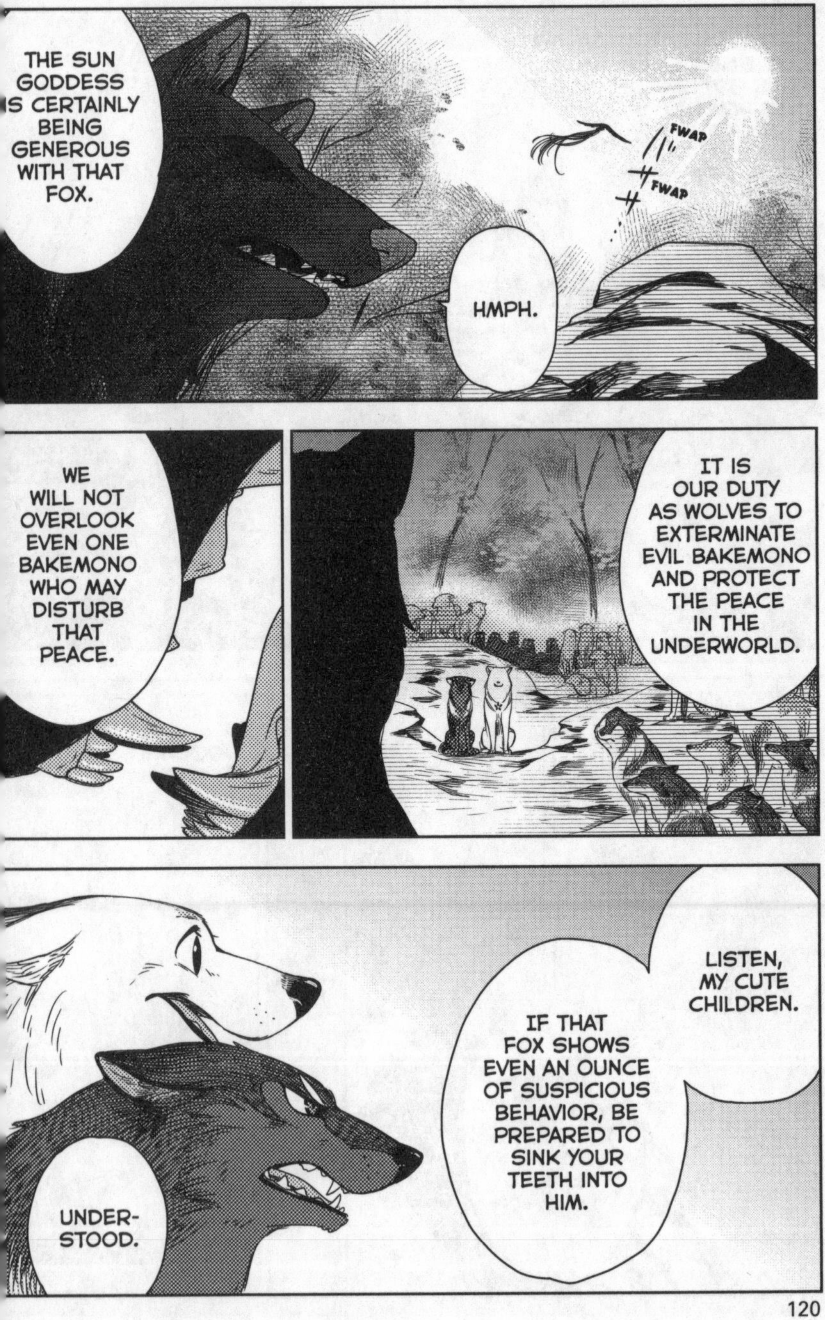
FWAP
FWAP
HMPH.
THE SUN GODDESS IS CERTAINLY BEING GENEROUS WITH THAT FOX.
IT IS OUR DUTY AS WOLVES TO EXTERMINATE EVIL BAKEMONO AND PROTECT THE PEACE IN THE UNDERWORLD.
WE WILL NOT OVERLOOK EVEN ONE BAKEMONO WHO MAY DISTURB THAT PEACE.
LISTEN, MY CUTE CHILDREN.
IF THAT FOX SHOWS EVEN AN OUNCE OF SUSPICIOUS BEHAVIOR, BE PREPARED TO SINK YOUR TEETH INTO HIM.
UNDER-STOOD.

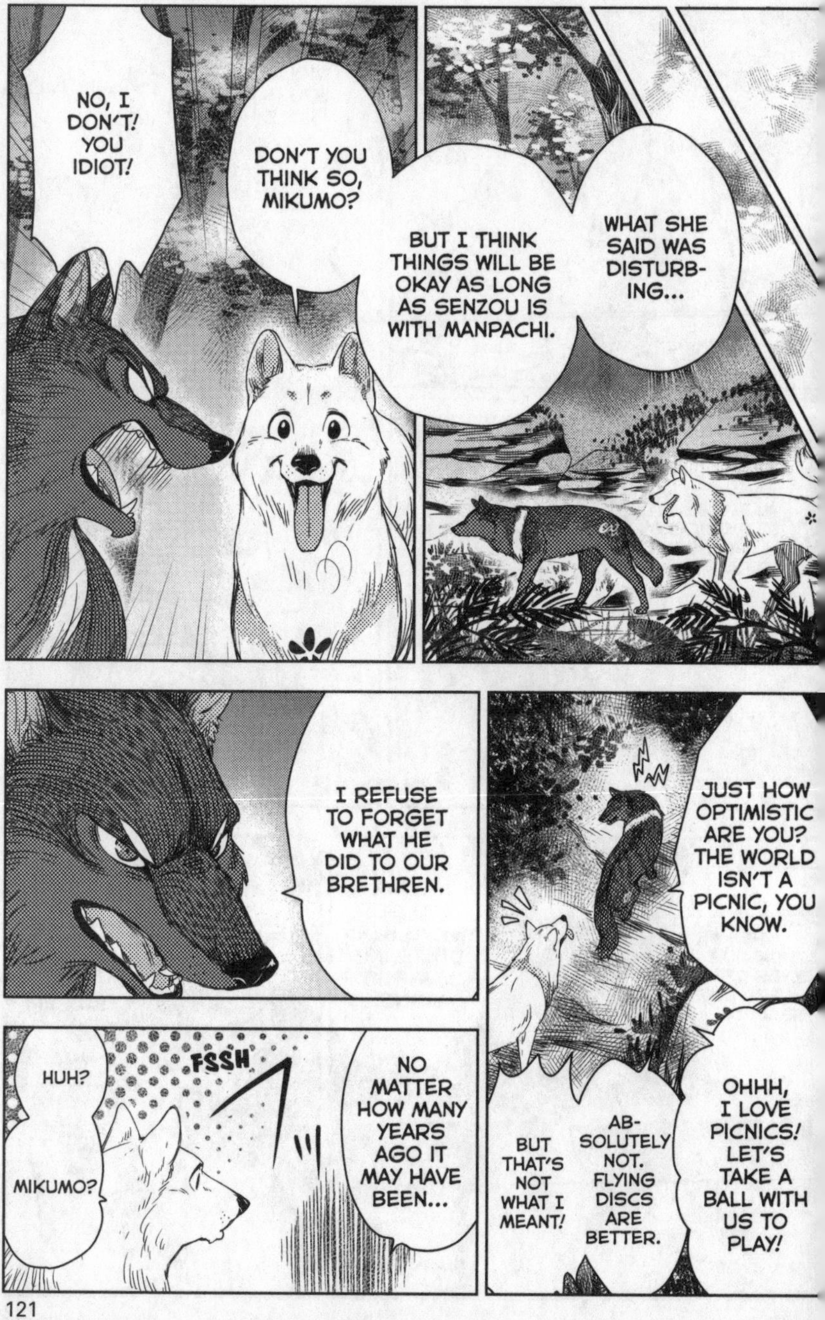
WHAT SHE SAID WAS DISTURB-ING...
BUT I THINK THINGS WILL BE OKAY AS LONG AS SENZOU IS WITH MANPACHI.
DON'T YOU THINK SO, MIKUMO?
NO, I DON'T! YOU IDIOT!
JUST HOW OPTIMISTIC ARE YOU? THE WORLD ISN'T A PICNIC, YOU KNOW.
I REFUSE TO FORGET WHAT HE DID TO OUR BRETHREN.
OHHH, I LOVE PICNICS! LET'S TAKE A BALL WITH US TO PLAY!
AB-SOLUTELY NOT. FLYING DISCS ARE BETTER.
BUT THAT'S NOT WHAT I MEANT!
NO MATTER HOW MANY YEARS AGO IT MAY HAVE BEEN...
FSSH
HUH?
MIKUMO?

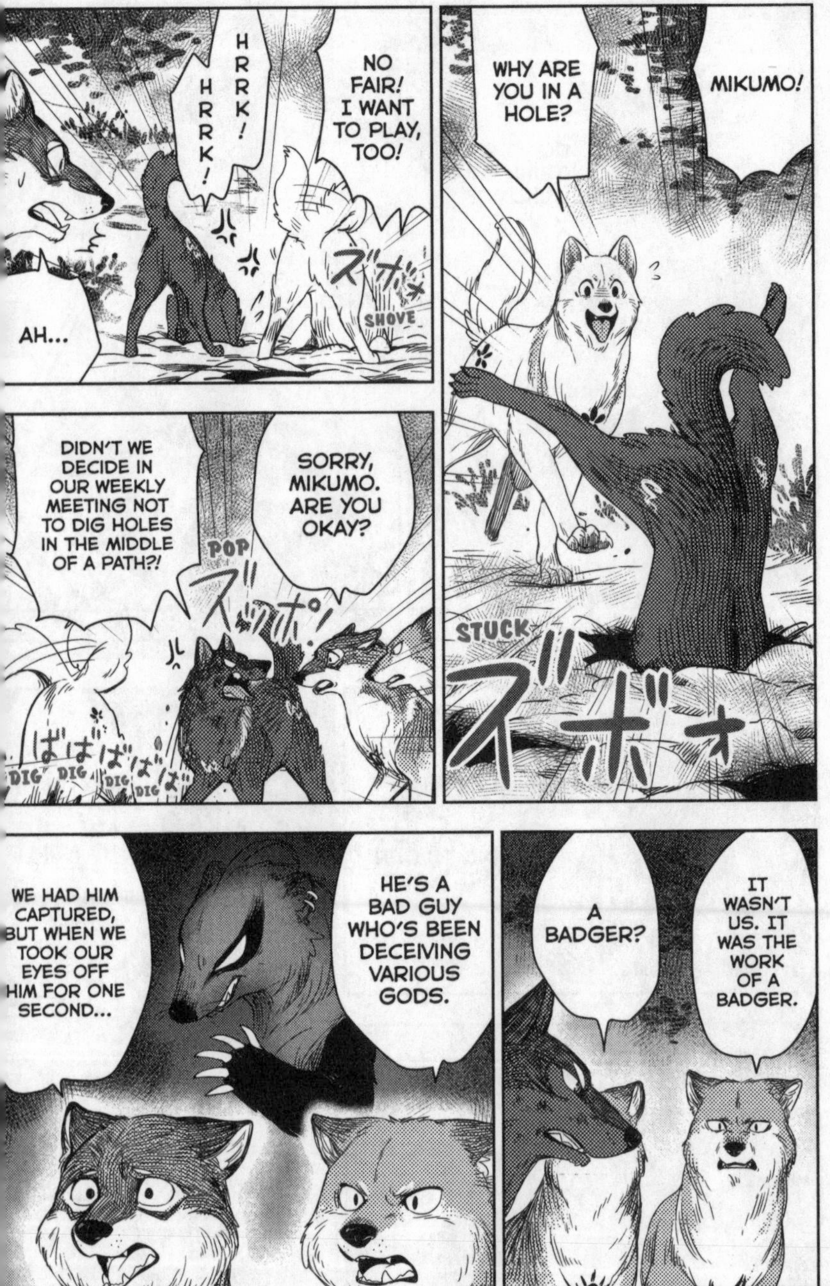

MIKUMO!
WHY ARE YOU IN A HOLE?
STUCK
ズボォ
NO FAIR! I WANT TO PLAY, TOO!
HRRK! HRRK!
ズオ
SHOVE
AH...
SORRY, MIKUMO. ARE YOU OKAY?
DIDN'T WE DECIDE IN OUR WEEKLY MEETING NOT TO DIG HOLES IN THE MIDDLE OF A PATH?!
POP
ズッポ!
ばばばばば
DIG DIG DIG DIG
IT WASN'T US. IT WAS THE WORK OF A BADGER.
A BADGER?
HE'S A BAD GUY WHO'S BEEN DECEIVING VARIOUS GODS.
WE HAD HIM CAPTURED, BUT WHEN WE TOOK OUR EYES OFF HIM FOR ONE SECOND...

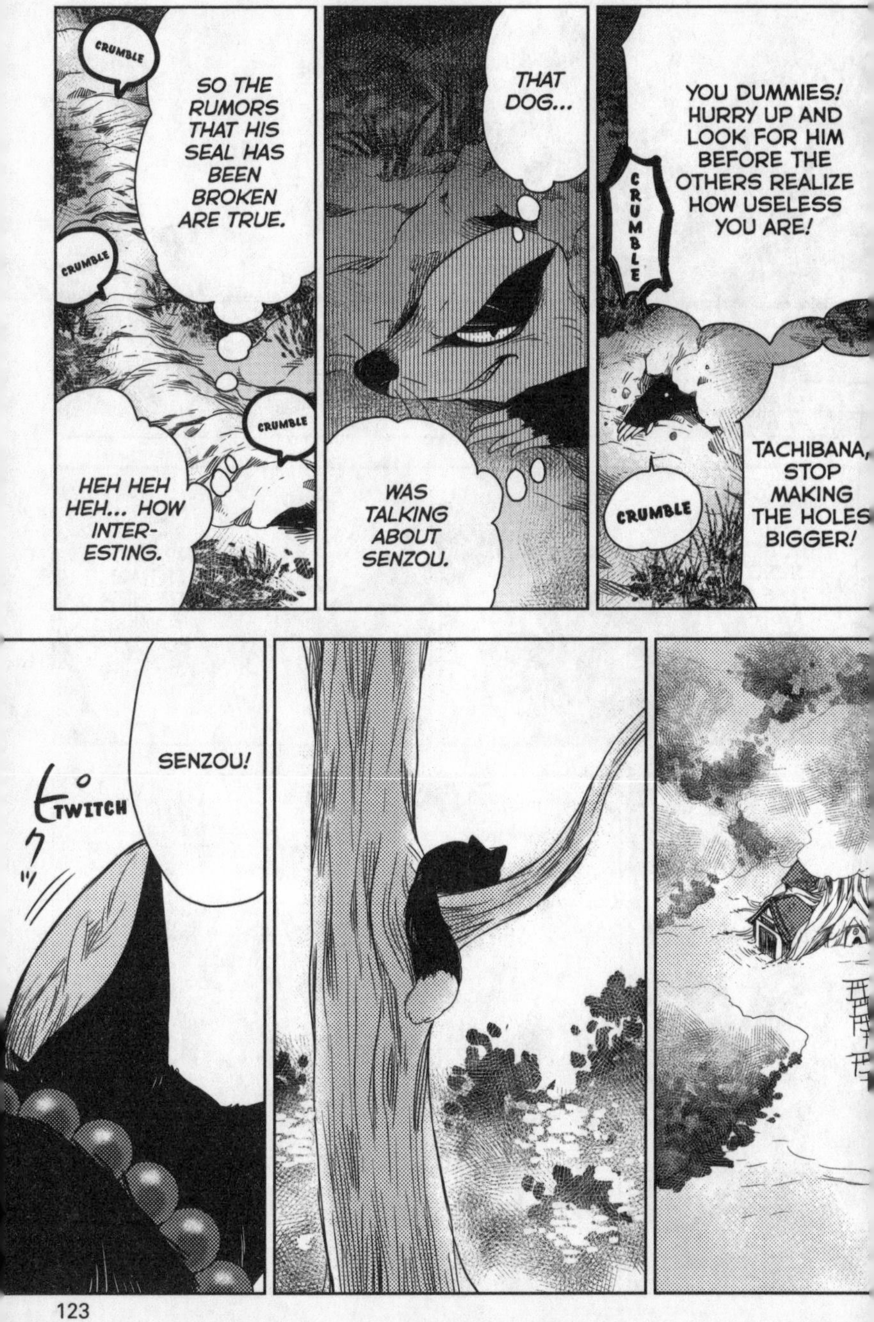
CRUMBLE
YOU DUMMIES! HURRY UP AND LOOK FOR HIM BEFORE THE OTHERS REALIZE HOW USELESS YOU ARE!
TACHIBANA, STOP MAKING THE HOLES BIGGER!
CRUMBLE
THAT DOG...
WAS TALKING ABOUT SENZOU.
CRUMBLE
SO THE RUMORS THAT HIS SEAL HAS BEEN BROKEN ARE TRUE.
CRUMBLE
CRUMBLE
HEH HEH HEH... HOW INTER-ESTING.
SENZOU!
TWITCH

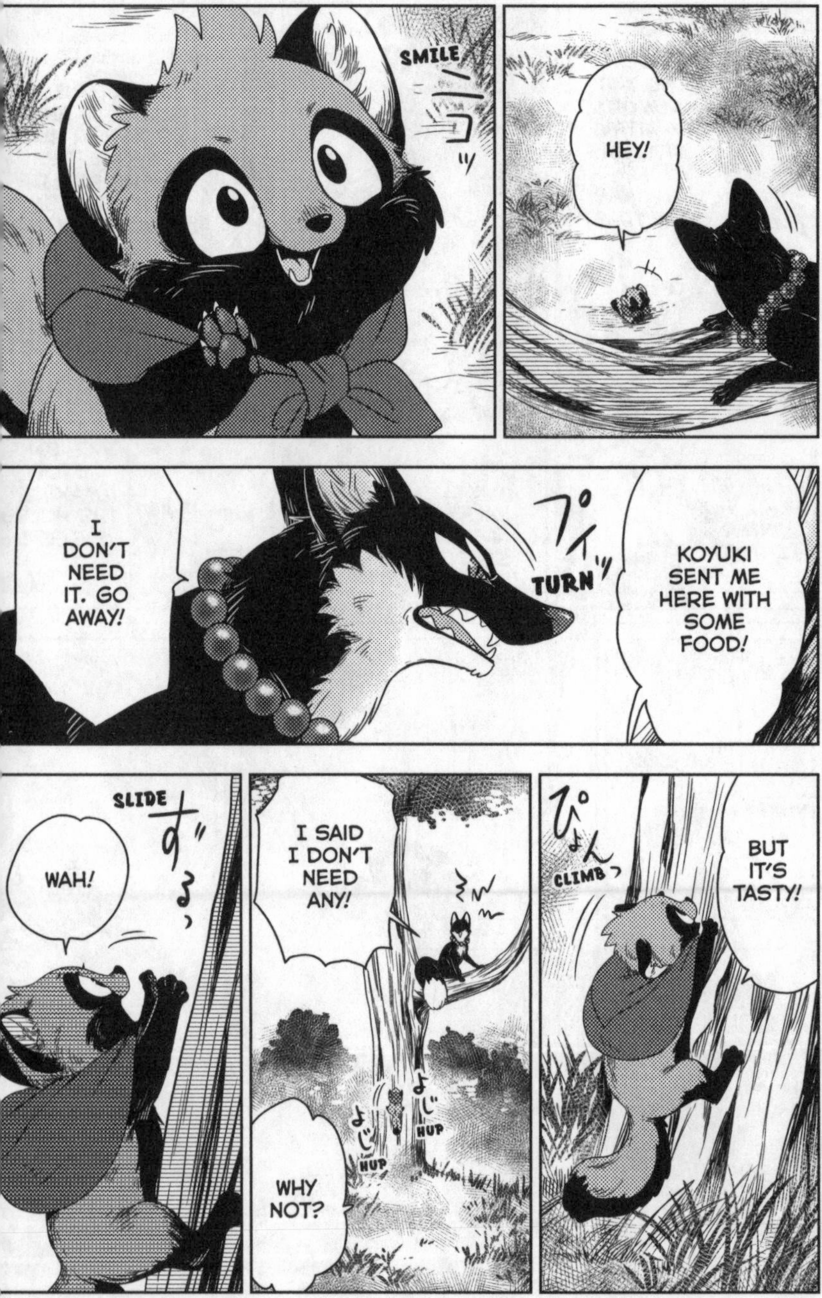
HEY!
SMILE
ニコッ
KOYUKI SENT ME HERE WITH SOME FOOD!
プイッ
TURN
I DON'T NEED IT. GO AWAY!
BUT IT'S TASTY!
ぴょん
CLIMB
I SAID I DON'T NEED ANY!
よじ
HUP
よじ
HUP
WHY NOT?
SLIDE
ずるっ
WAH!

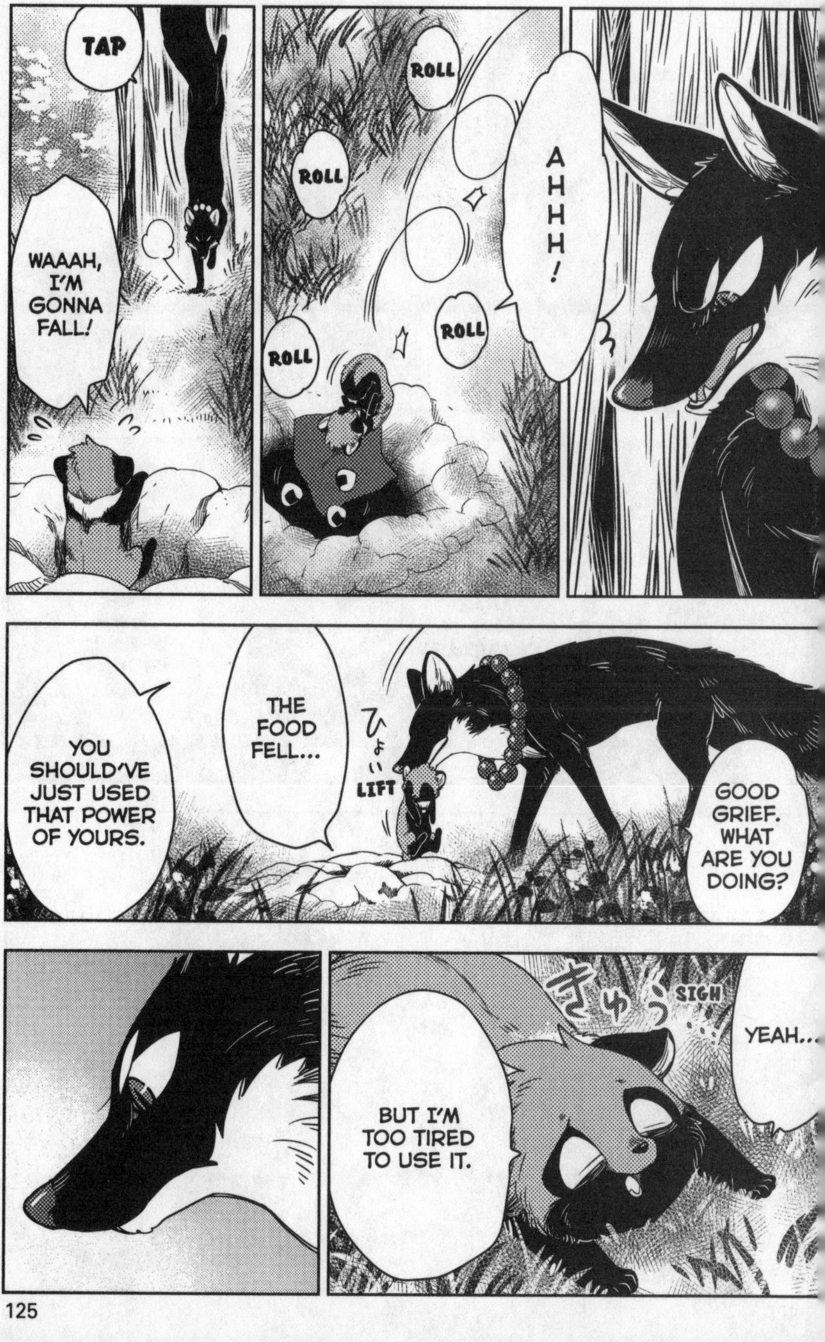
AHHH!
ROLL
ROLL
ROLL
ROLL
TAP
WAAAH, I'M GONNA FALL!
GOOD GRIEF. WHAT ARE YOU DOING?
ひょい
LIFT
THE FOOD FELL...
YOU SHOULD'VE JUST USED THAT POWER OF YOURS.
YEAH...
きゅう
SIGH
BUT I'M TOO TIRED TO USE IT.

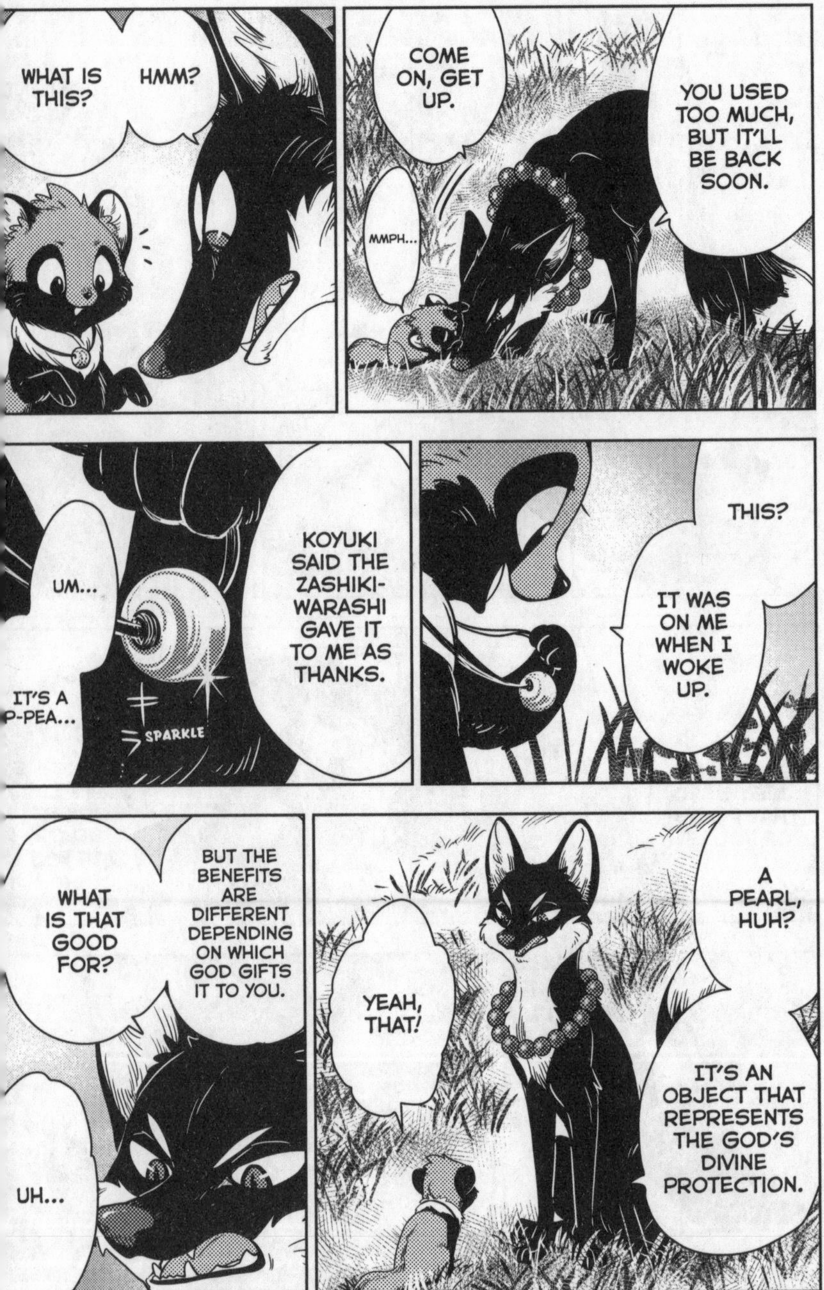
YOU USED TOO MUCH, BUT IT'LL BE BACK SOON.
COME ON, GET UP.
MMPH...
HMM?
WHAT IS THIS?
THIS?
IT WAS ON ME WHEN I WOKE UP.
KOYUKI SAID THE ZASHIKI-WARASHI GAVE IT TO ME AS THANKS.
UM...
SPARKLE
IT'S A P-PEA...
A PEARL, HUH?
YEAH, THAT!
IT'S AN OBJECT THAT REPRESENTS THE GOD'S DIVINE PROTECTION.
BUT THE BENEFITS ARE DIFFERENT DEPENDING ON WHICH GOD GIFTS IT TO YOU.
WHAT IS THAT GOOD FOR?
UH...

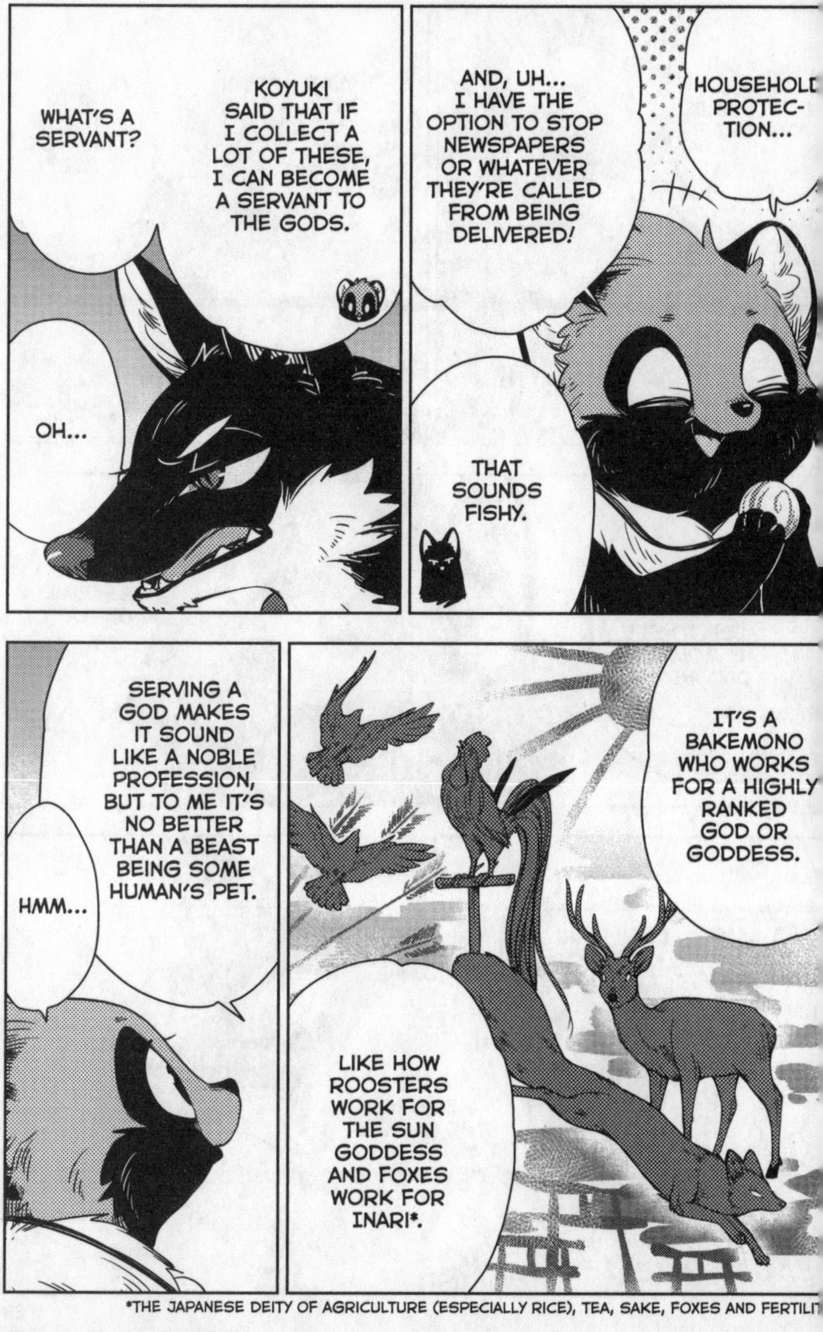
HOUSEHOLD PROTECTION...
AND, UH... I HAVE THE OPTION TO STOP NEWSPAPERS OR WHATEVER THEY'RE CALLED FROM BEING DELIVERED!
THAT SOUNDS FISHY.
KOYUKI SAID THAT IF I COLLECT A LOT OF THESE, I CAN BECOME A SERVANT TO THE GODS.
WHAT'S A SERVANT?
OH...
IT'S A BAKEMONO WHO WORKS FOR A HIGHLY RANKED GOD OR GODDESS.
LIKE HOW ROOSTERS WORK FOR THE SUN GODDESS AND FOXES WORK FOR INARI*.
SERVING A GOD MAKES IT SOUND LIKE A NOBLE PROFESSION, BUT TO ME IT'S NO BETTER THAN A BEAST BEING SOME HUMAN'S PET.
HMM...

*THE JAPANESE DEITY OF AGRICULTURE (ESPECIALLY RICE), TEA, SAKE, FOXES AND FERTILIT

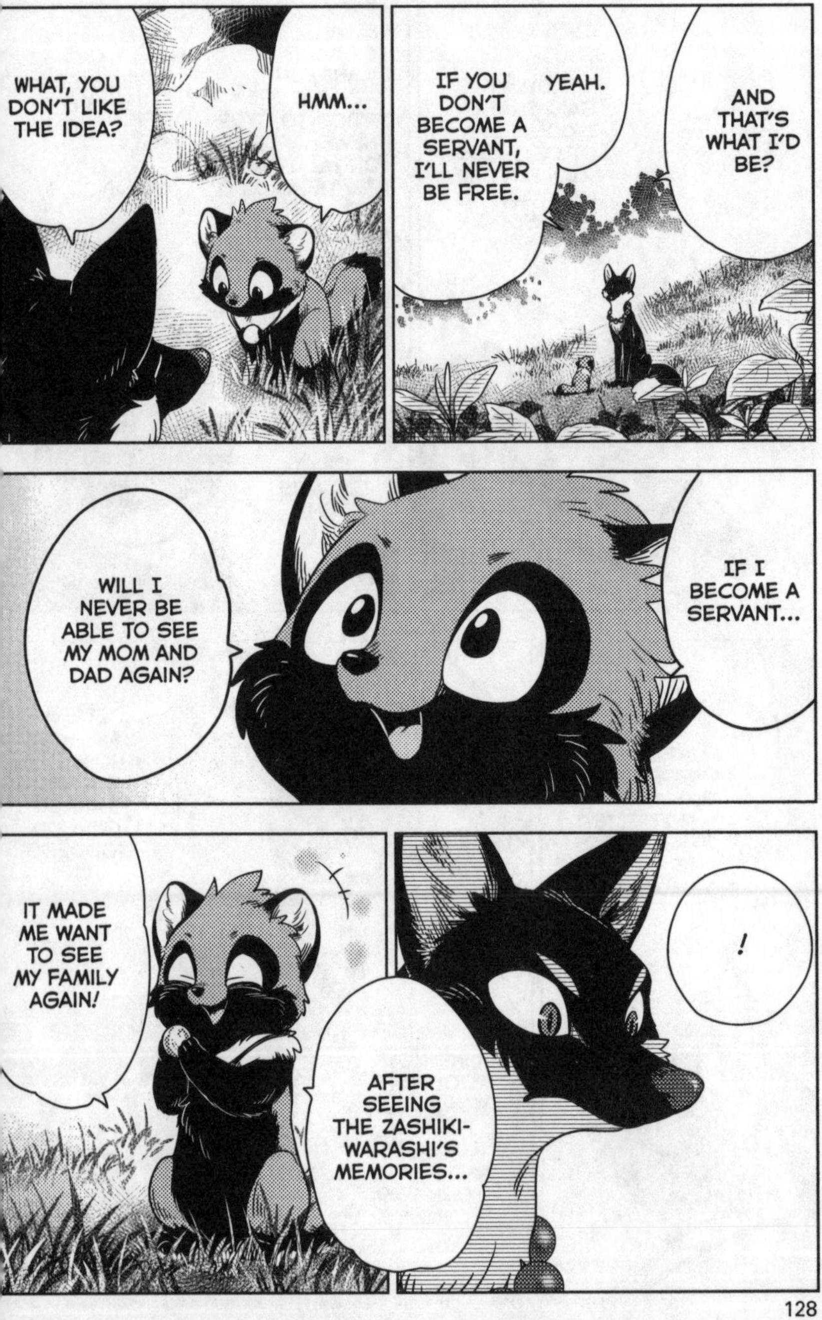
AND THAT'S WHAT I'D BE?
YEAH.
IF YOU DON'T BECOME A SERVANT, I'LL NEVER BE FREE.
HMM...
WHAT, YOU DON'T LIKE THE IDEA?
IF I BECOME A SERVANT...
WILL I NEVER BE ABLE TO SEE MY MOM AND DAD AGAIN?
!
AFTER SEEING THE ZASHIKI-WARASHI'S MEMORIES...
IT MADE ME WANT TO SEE MY FAMILY AGAIN!

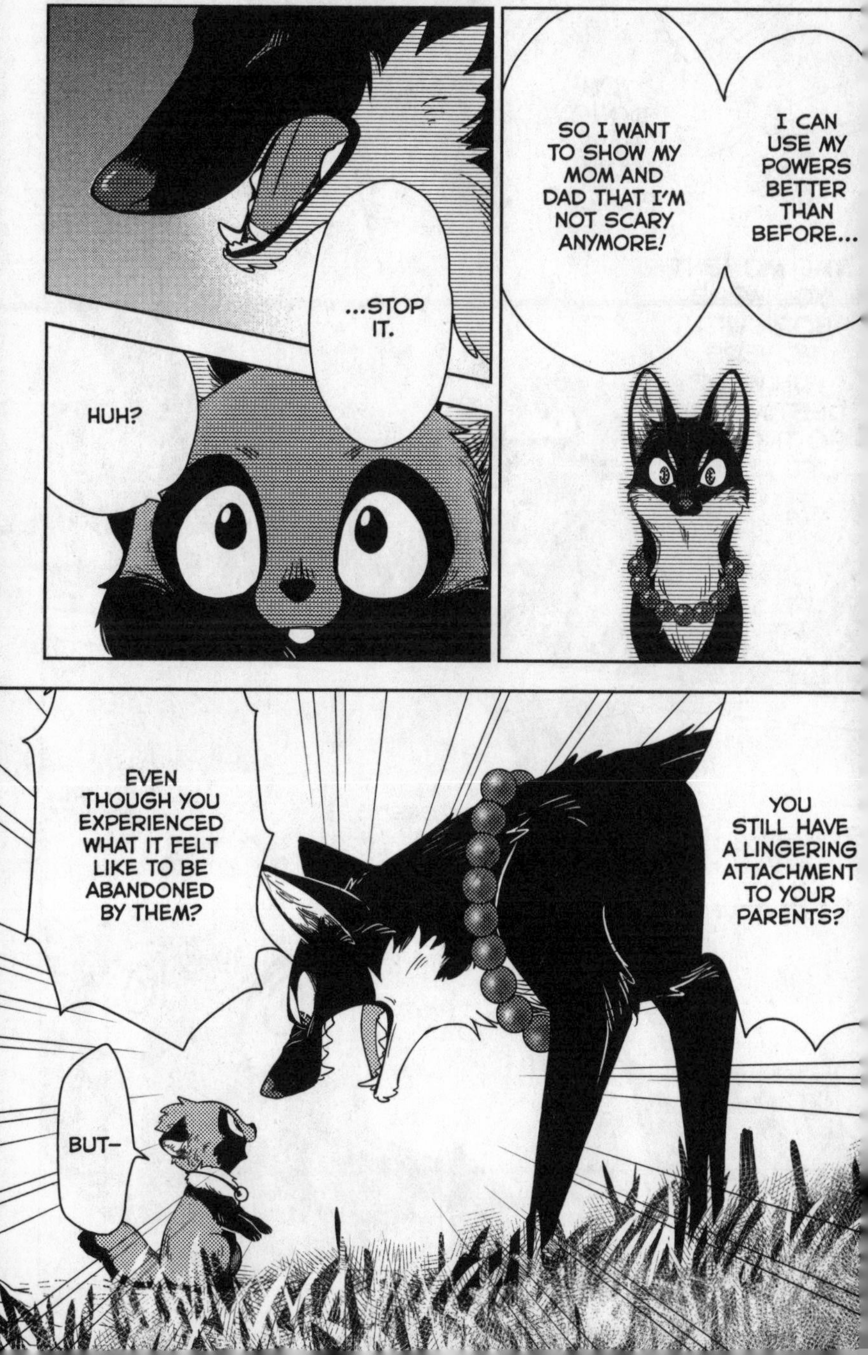
I CAN USE MY POWERS BETTER THAN BEFORE...
SO I WANT TO SHOW MY MOM AND DAD THAT I'M NOT SCARY ANYMORE!
...STOP IT.
HUH?
YOU STILL HAVE A LINGERING ATTACHMENT TO YOUR PARENTS?
EVEN THOUGH YOU EXPERIENCED WHAT IT FELT LIKE TO BE ABANDONED BY THEM?
BUT–

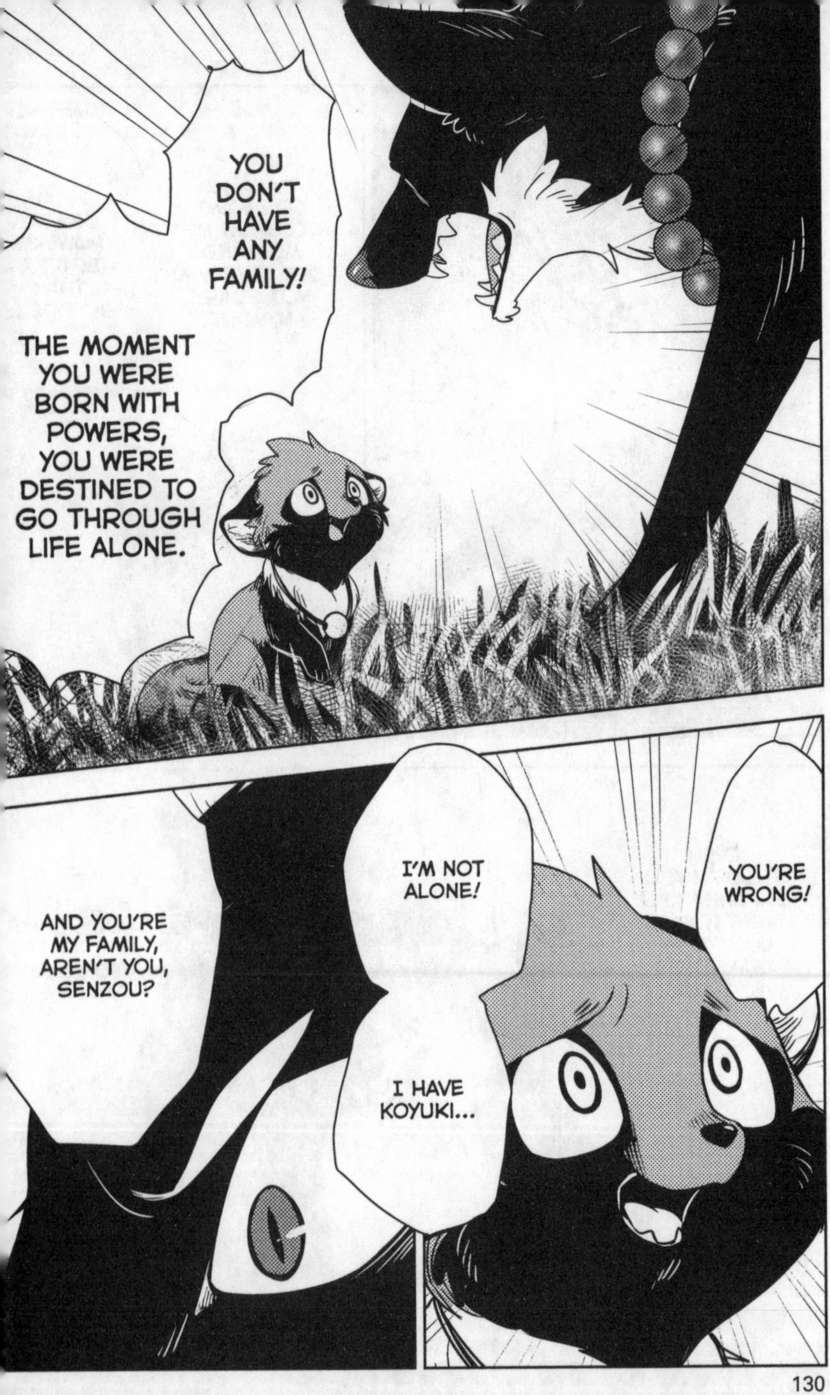
YOU DON'T HAVE ANY FAMILY!
THE MOMENT YOU WERE BORN WITH POWERS, YOU WERE DESTINED TO GO THROUGH LIFE ALONE.
YOU'RE WRONG!
I'M NOT ALONE!
I HAVE KOYUKI...
AND YOU'RE MY FAMILY, AREN'T YOU, SENZOU?

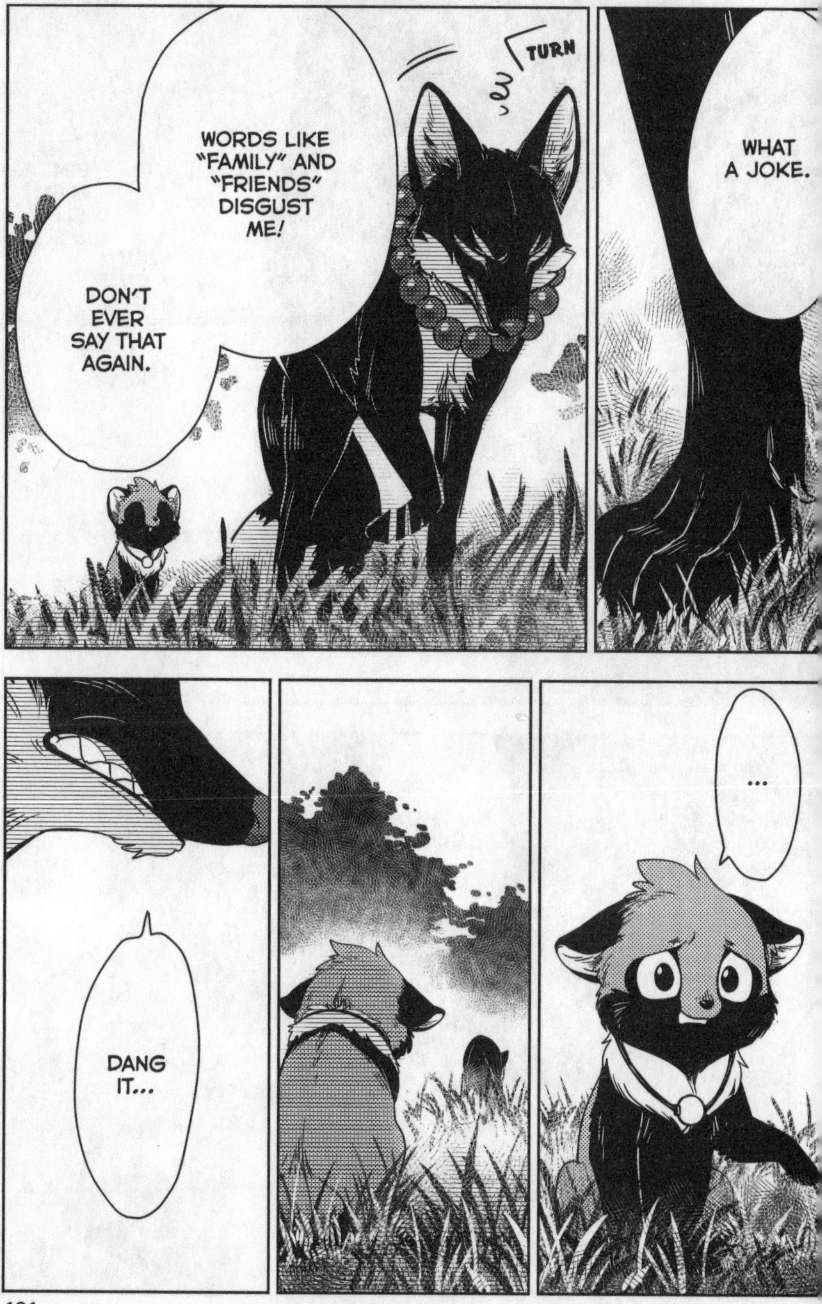
WHAT A JOKE.
TURN
WORDS LIKE "FAMILY" AND "FRIENDS" DISGUST ME!
DON'T EVER SAY THAT AGAIN.
...
DANG IT...

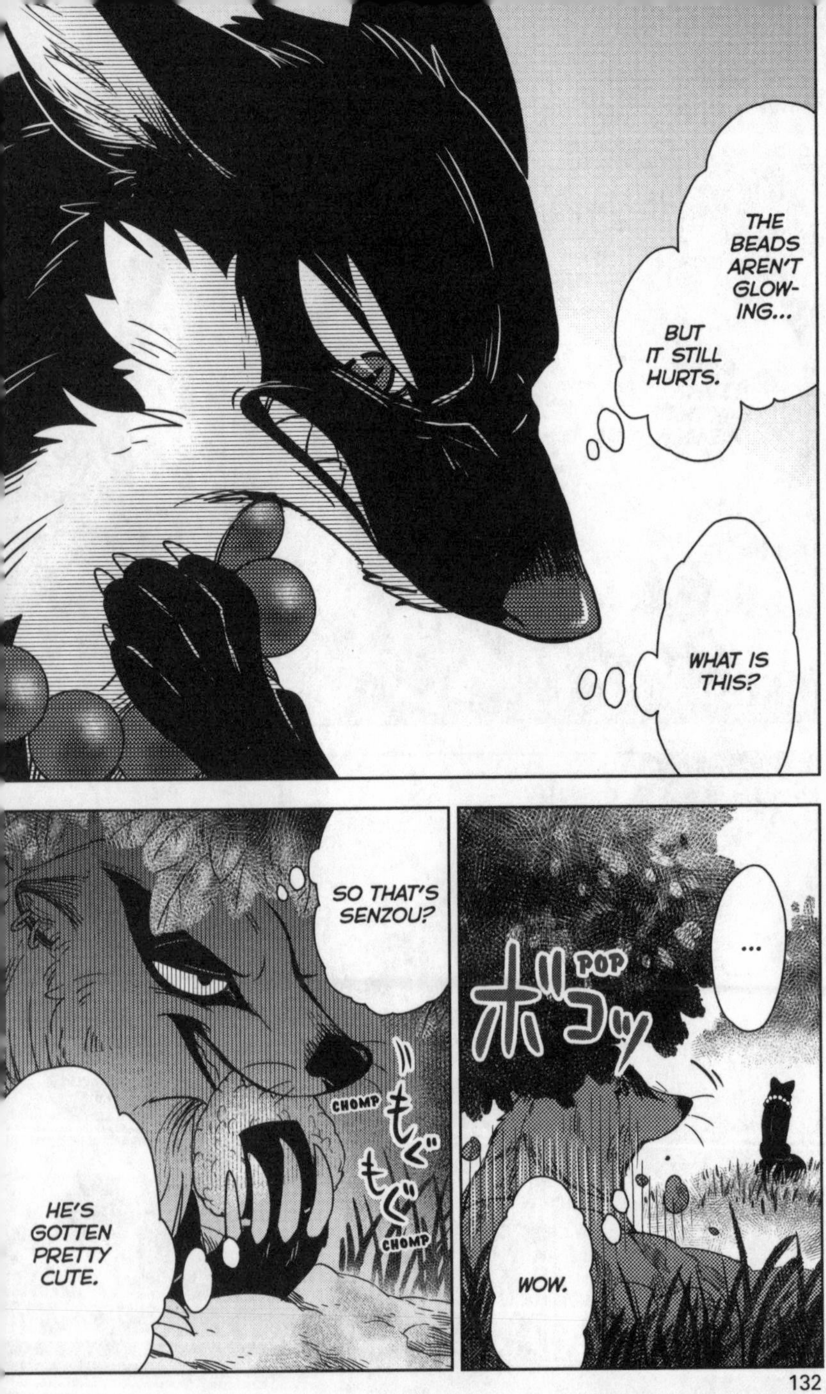
THE BEADS AREN'T GLOWING...
BUT IT STILL HURTS.
WHAT IS THIS?
...
ボコッ
POP
WOW.
SO THAT'S SENZOU?
もぐもぐ
CHOMP
CHOMP
HE'S GOTTEN PRETTY CUTE.

The Bakemono Field Guide

Reiken
(Spirit Dogs)

They are great at chasing down evil bakemono and sometimes mix with the wolves. There are times when they become attached to a person. If that person returns their affection, they will be greatly blessed.

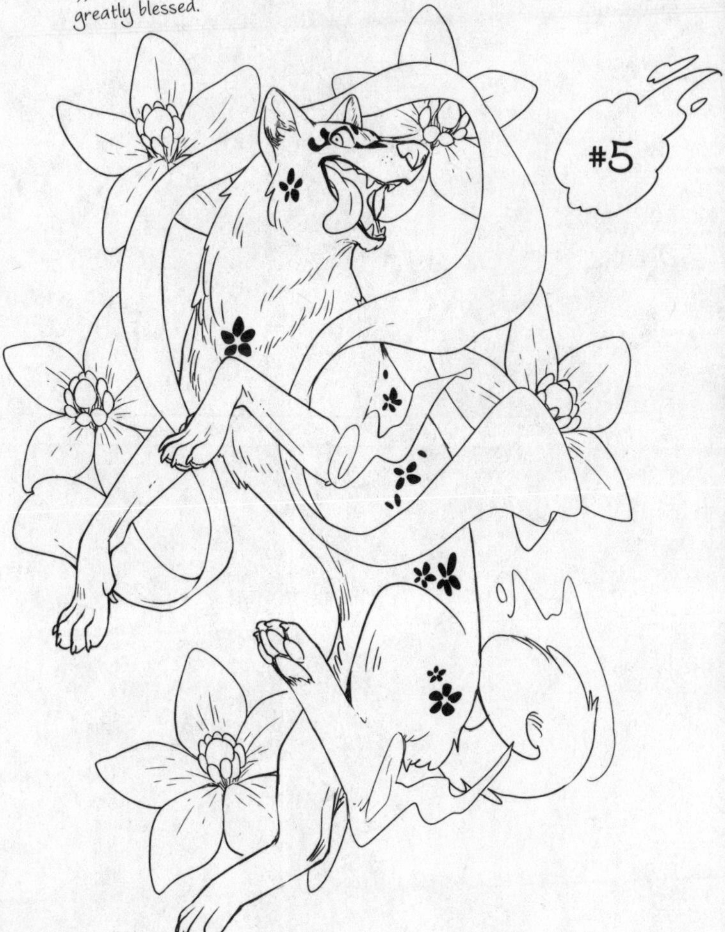
#5

Chapter 6

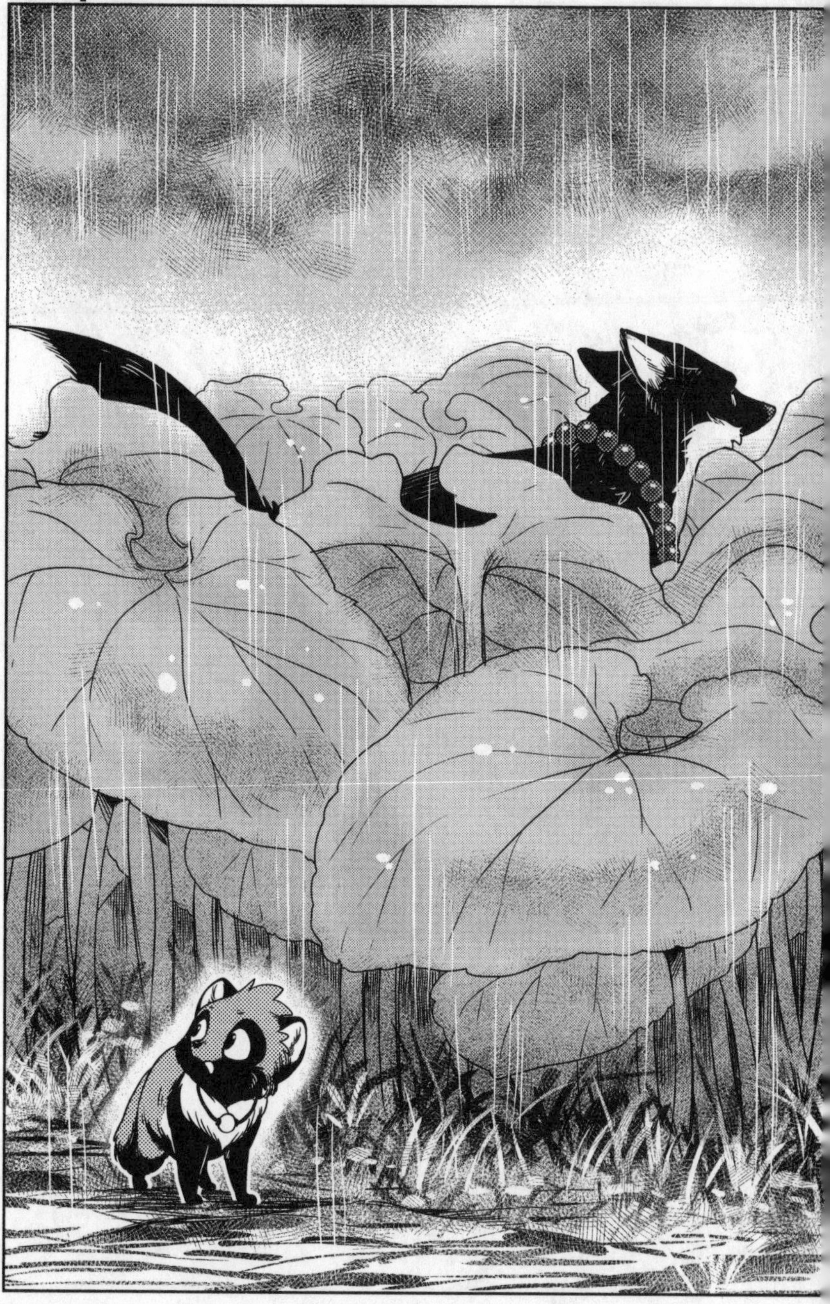

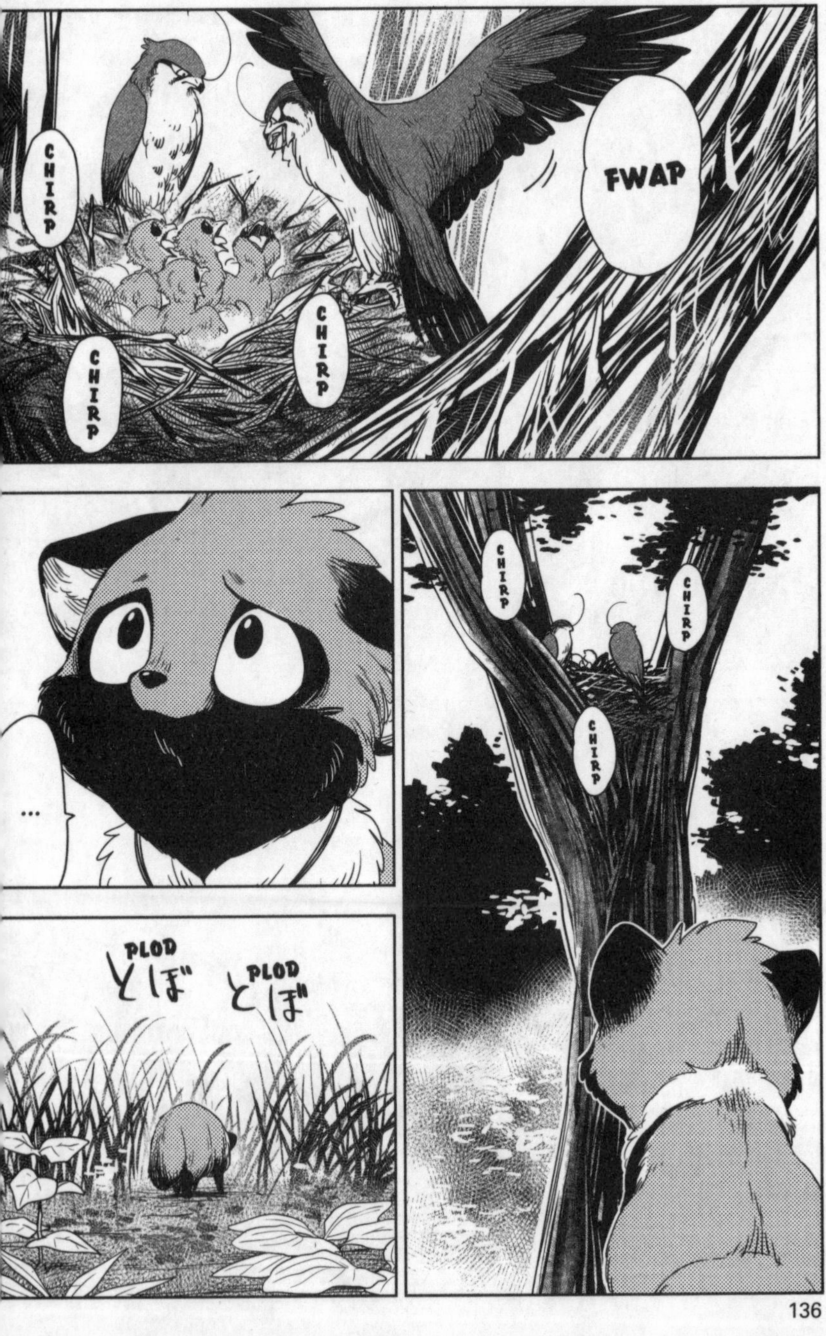
FWAP
CHIRP
CHIRP
CHIRP
CHIRP
CHIRP
CHIRP
...
PLOD とぼ
PLOD とぼ

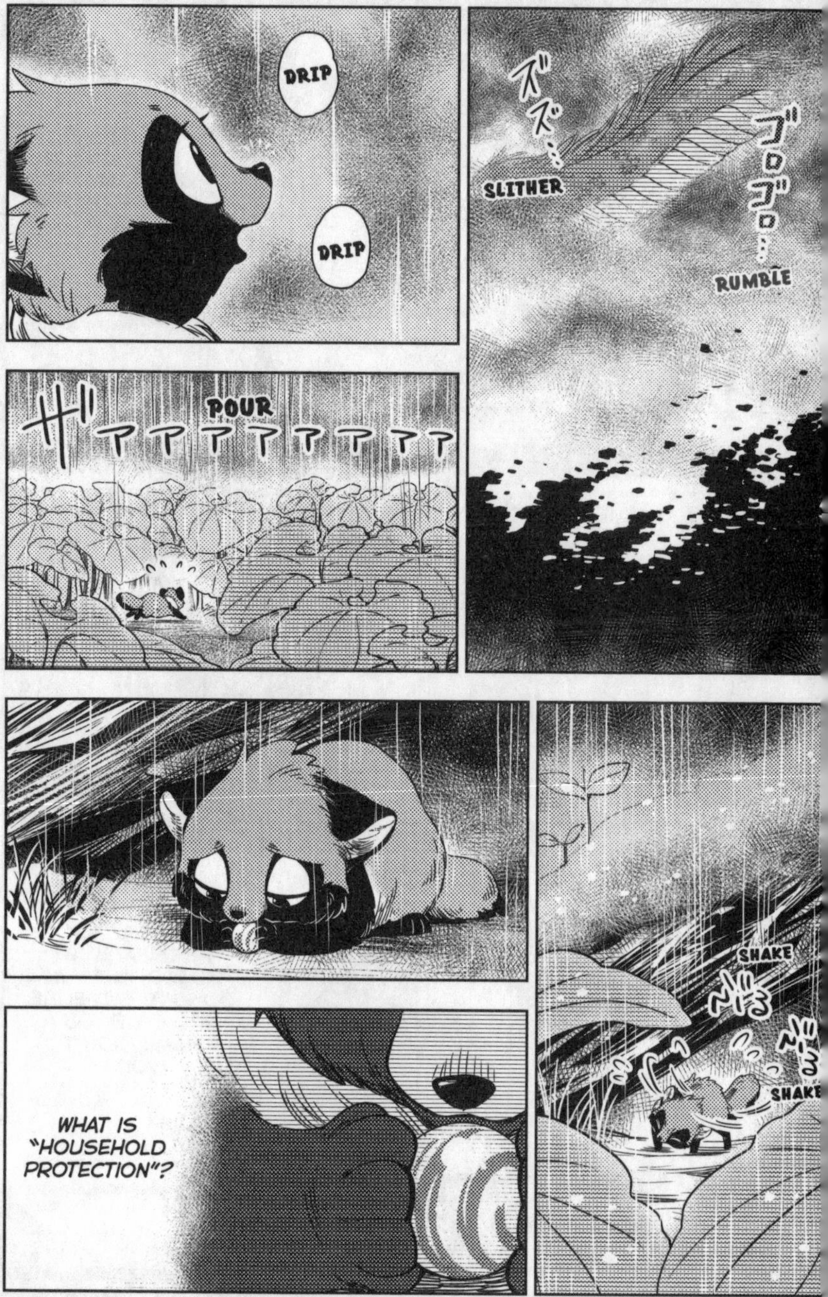
ズズ…
SLITHER
ゴロゴロ…
RUMBLE
DRIP
DRIP
ザアアアアアアアアア
POUR
SHAKE
ぶる
ぶる
SHAKE
WHAT IS "HOUSEHOLD PROTECTION"?

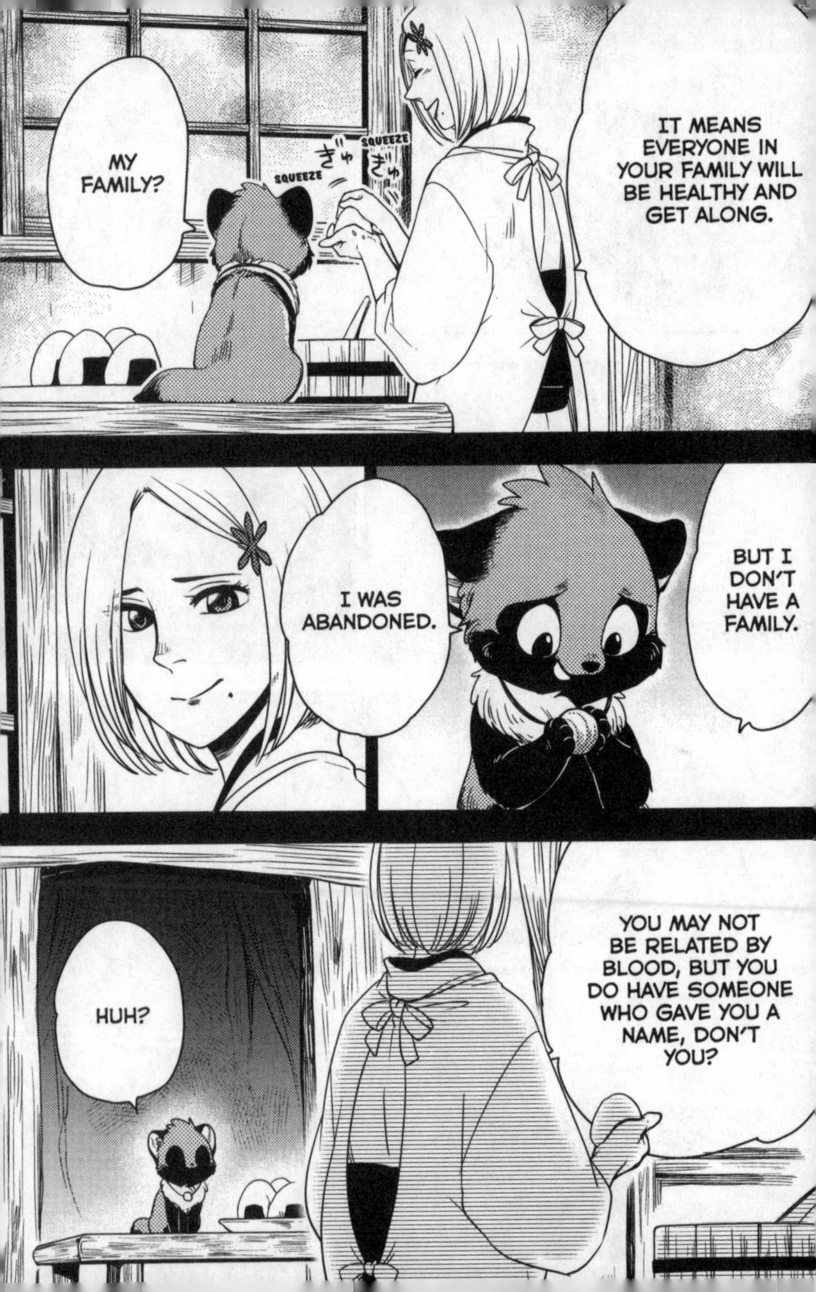
IT MEANS EVERYONE IN YOUR FAMILY WILL BE HEALTHY AND GET ALONG.
ぎゅ SQUEEZE
ぎゅ SQUEEZE
MY FAMILY?
BUT I DON'T HAVE A FAMILY.
I WAS ABANDONED.
YOU MAY NOT BE RELATED BY BLOOD, BUT YOU DO HAVE SOMEONE WHO GAVE YOU A NAME, DON'T YOU?
HUH?

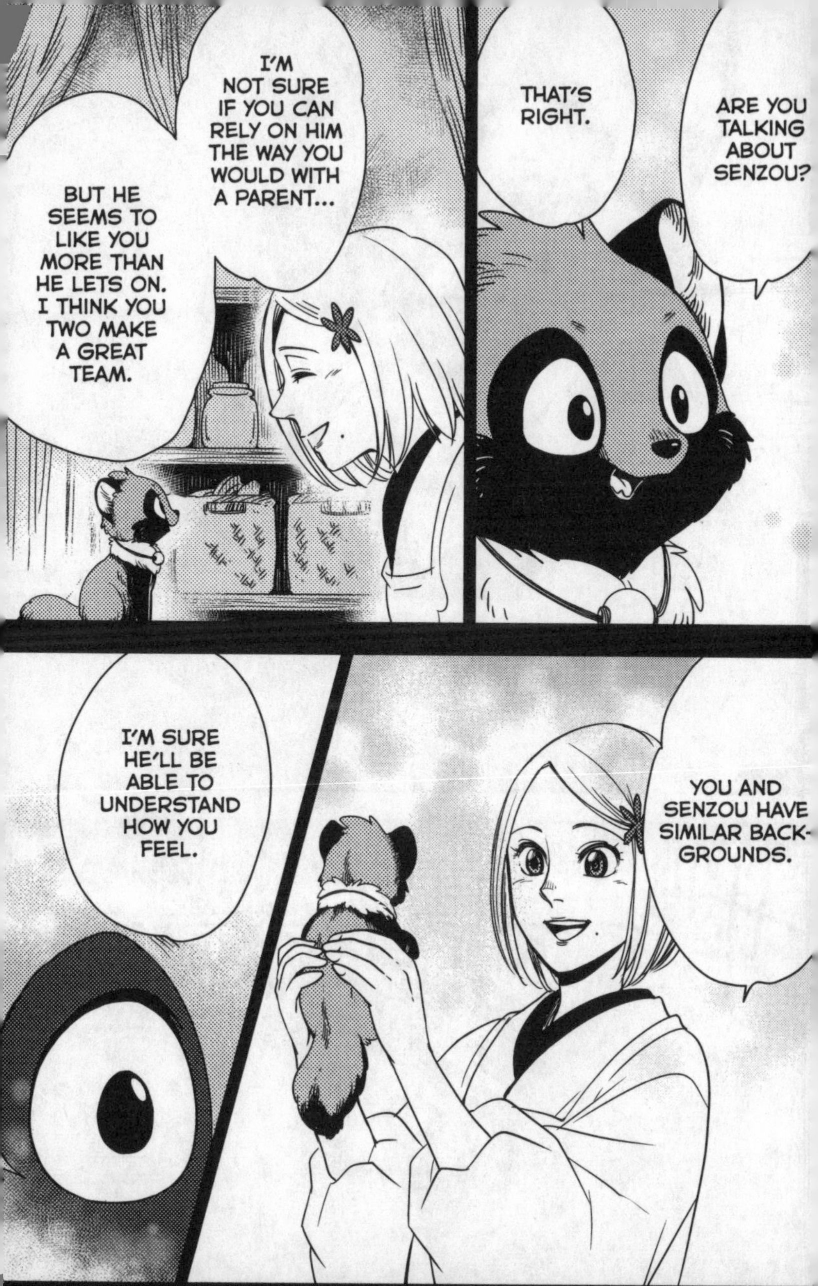
ARE YOU TALKING ABOUT SENZOU?
THAT'S RIGHT.
I'M NOT SURE IF YOU CAN RELY ON HIM THE WAY YOU WOULD WITH A PARENT...
BUT HE SEEMS TO LIKE YOU MORE THAN HE LETS ON. I THINK YOU TWO MAKE A GREAT TEAM.
YOU AND SENZOU HAVE SIMILAR BACK-GROUNDS.
I'M SURE HE'LL BE ABLE TO UNDERSTAND HOW YOU FEEL.

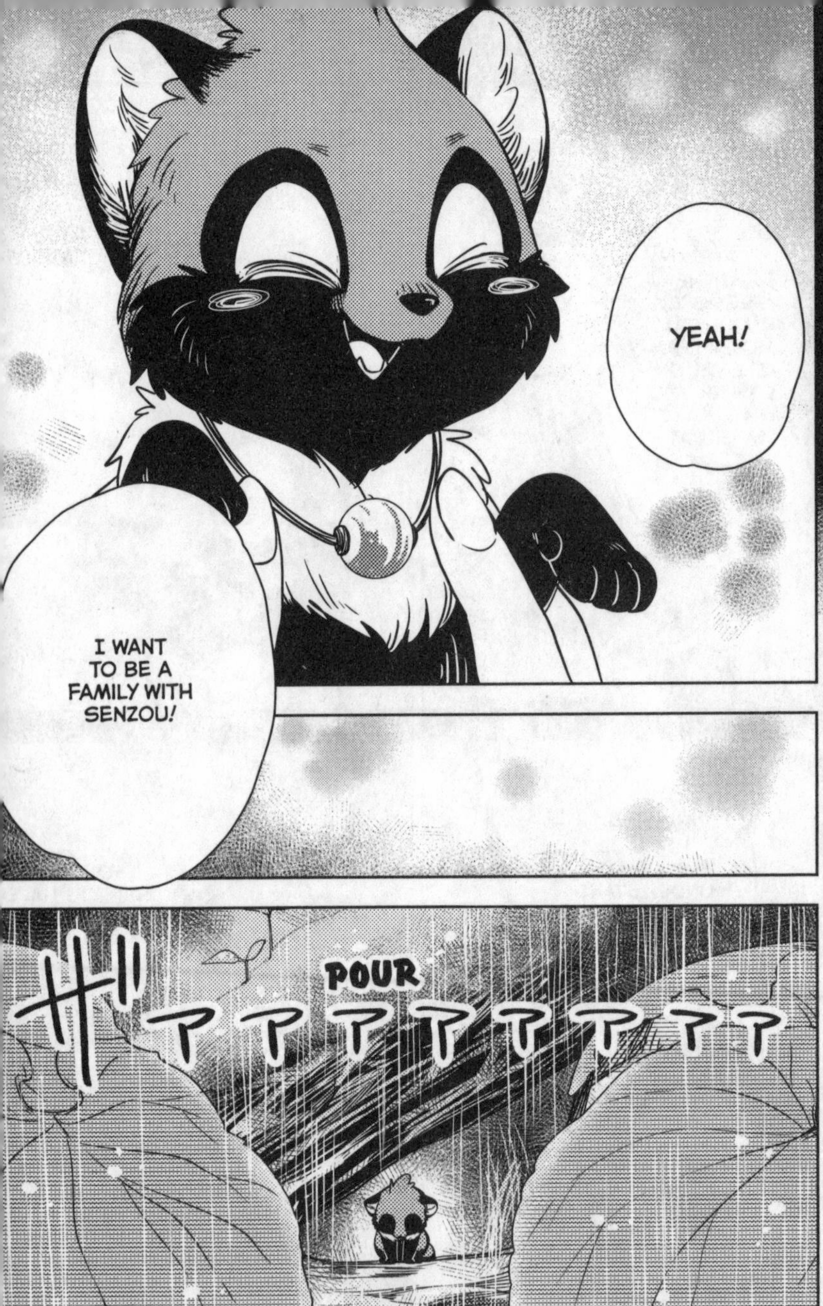
YEAH!
I WANT TO BE A FAMILY WITH SENZOU!
POUR

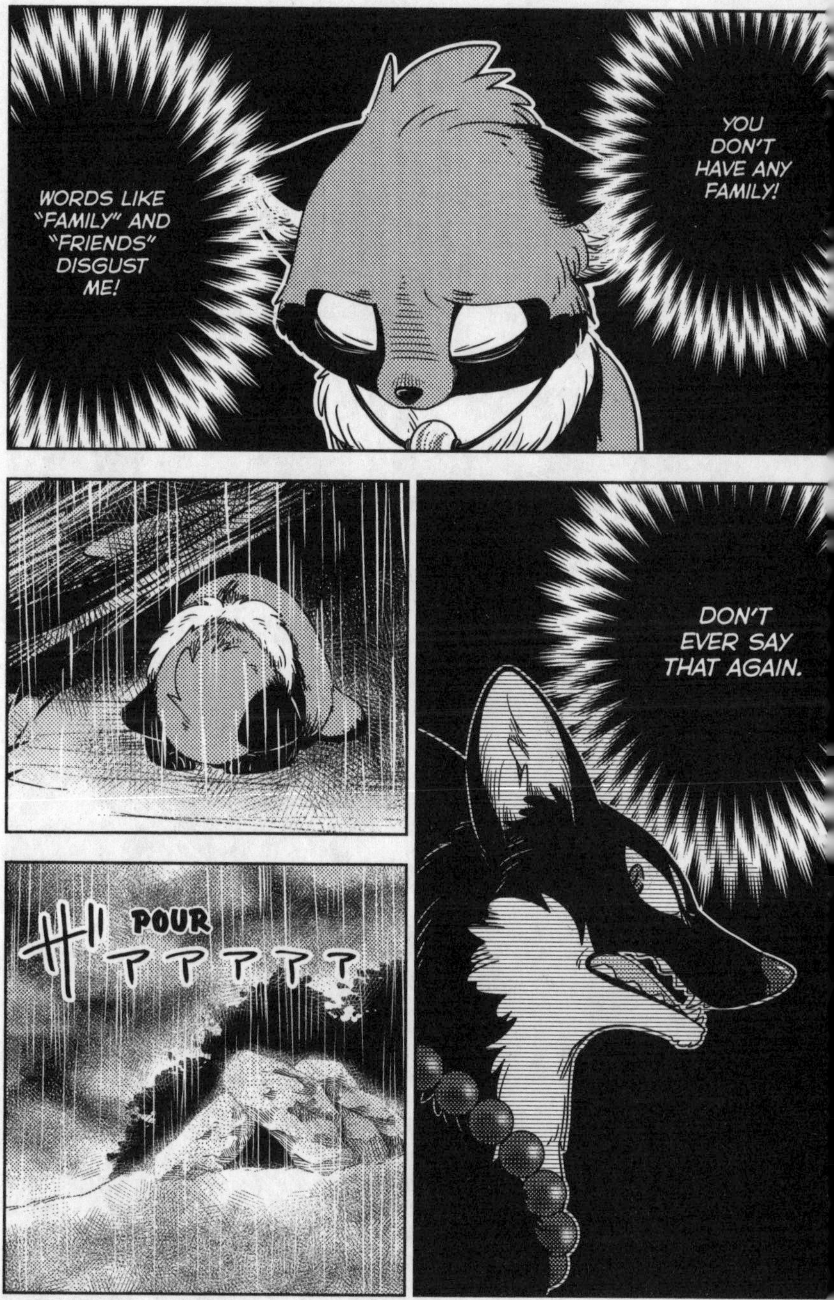
YOU DON'T HAVE ANY FAMILY!
WORDS LIKE "FAMILY" AND "FRIENDS" DISGUST ME!
DON'T EVER SAY THAT AGAIN.
ザァァァァァァ
POUR

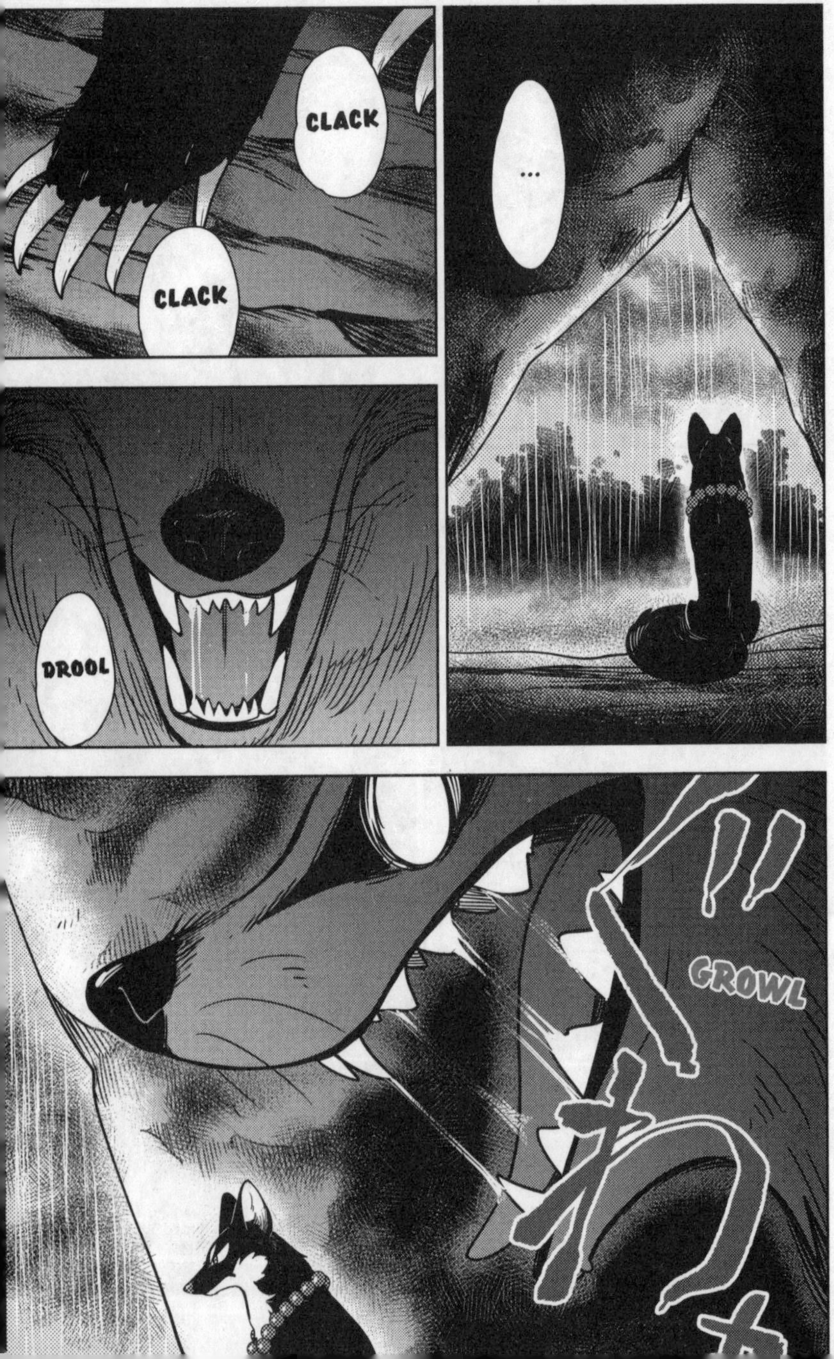
...
CLACK
CLACK
DROOL
!!
GROWL

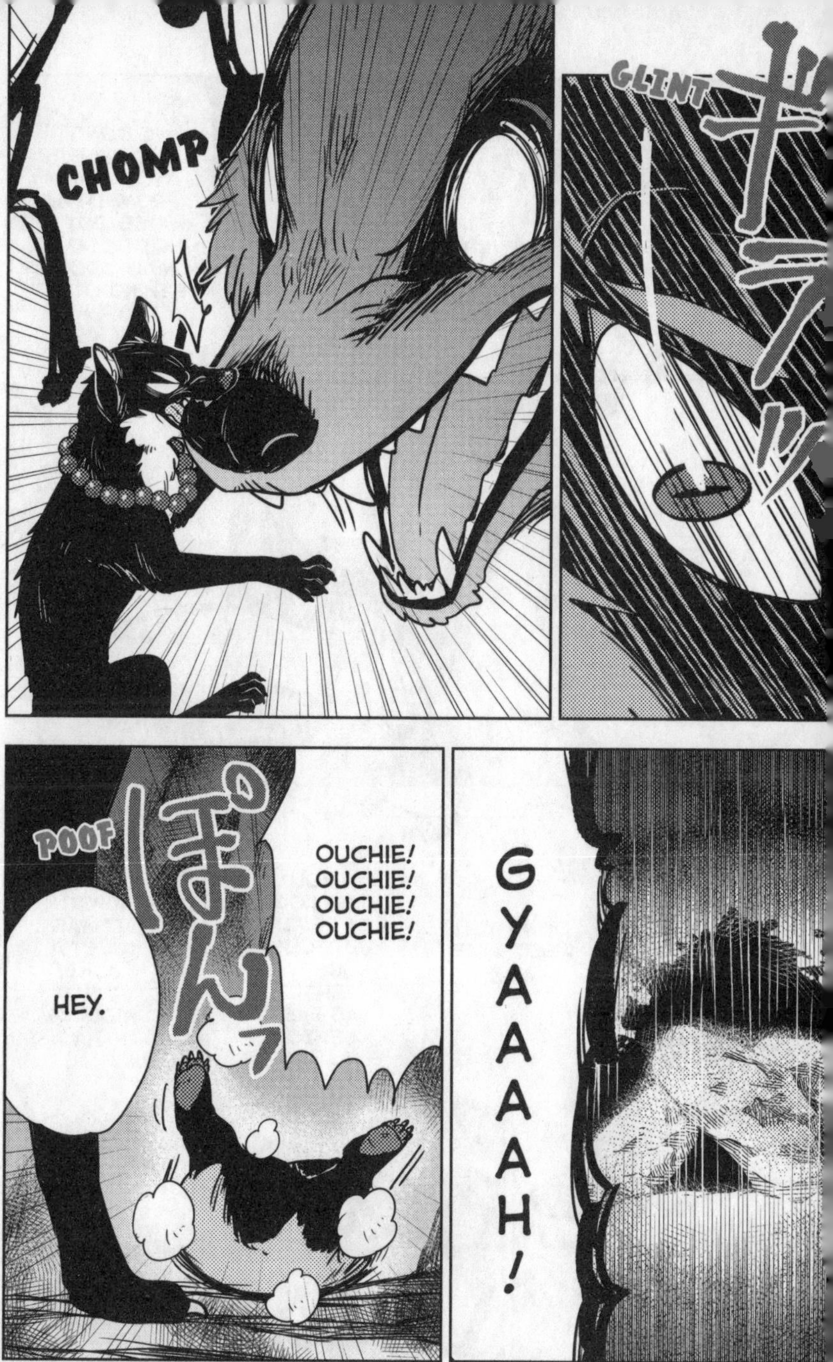
GLINT
ギラッ
CHOMP
GYAAAAH!
OUCHIE! OUCHIE! OUCHIE! OUCHIE!
POOF
ぽんっ
HEY.

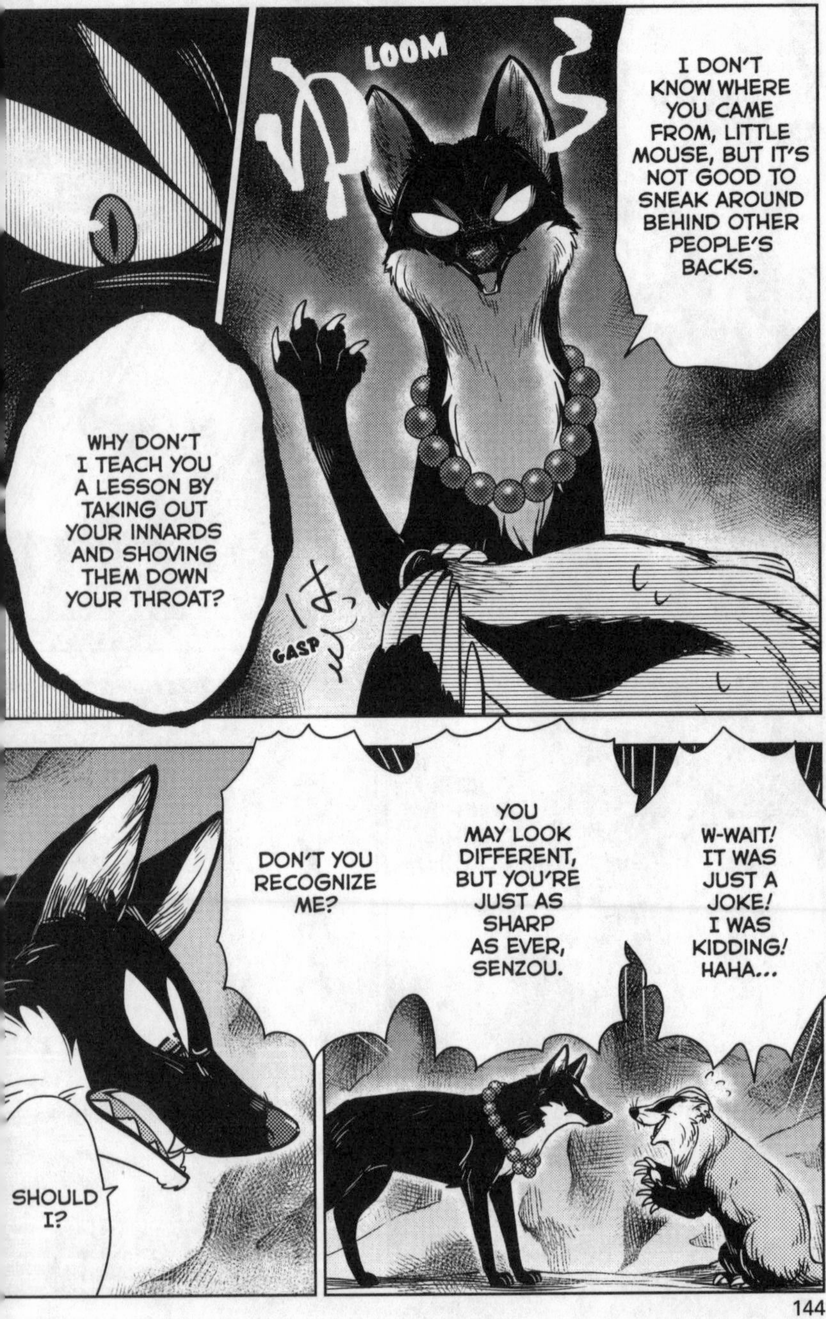
LOOM
I DON'T KNOW WHERE YOU CAME FROM, LITTLE MOUSE, BUT IT'S NOT GOOD TO SNEAK AROUND BEHIND OTHER PEOPLE'S BACKS.
GASP
WHY DON'T I TEACH YOU A LESSON BY TAKING OUT YOUR INNARDS AND SHOVING THEM DOWN YOUR THROAT?
W-WAIT! IT WAS JUST A JOKE! I WAS KIDDING! HAHA...
YOU MAY LOOK DIFFERENT, BUT YOU'RE JUST AS SHARP AS EVER, SENZOU.
DON'T YOU RECOGNIZE ME?
SHOULD I?

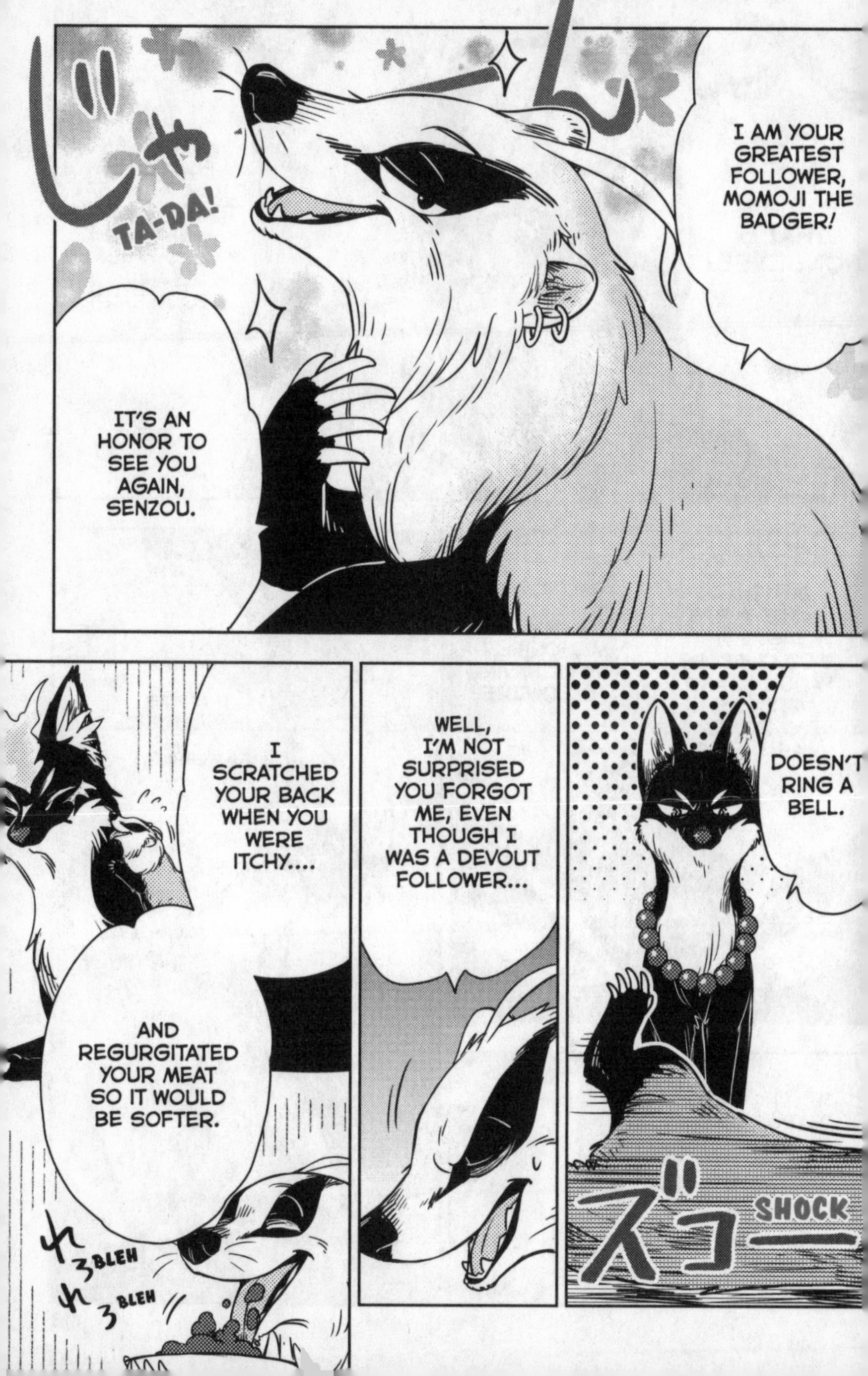

I AM YOUR GREATEST FOLLOWER, MOMOJI THE BADGER!
じゃーん
TA-DA!
IT'S AN HONOR TO SEE YOU AGAIN, SENZOU.
DOESN'T RING A BELL.
ズコー
SHOCK
WELL, I'M NOT SURPRISED YOU FORGOT ME, EVEN THOUGH I WAS A DEVOUT FOLLOWER...
I SCRATCHED YOUR BACK WHEN YOU WERE ITCHY....
AND REGURGITATED YOUR MEAT SO IT WOULD BE SOFTER.
れろ BLEH
れろ BLEH

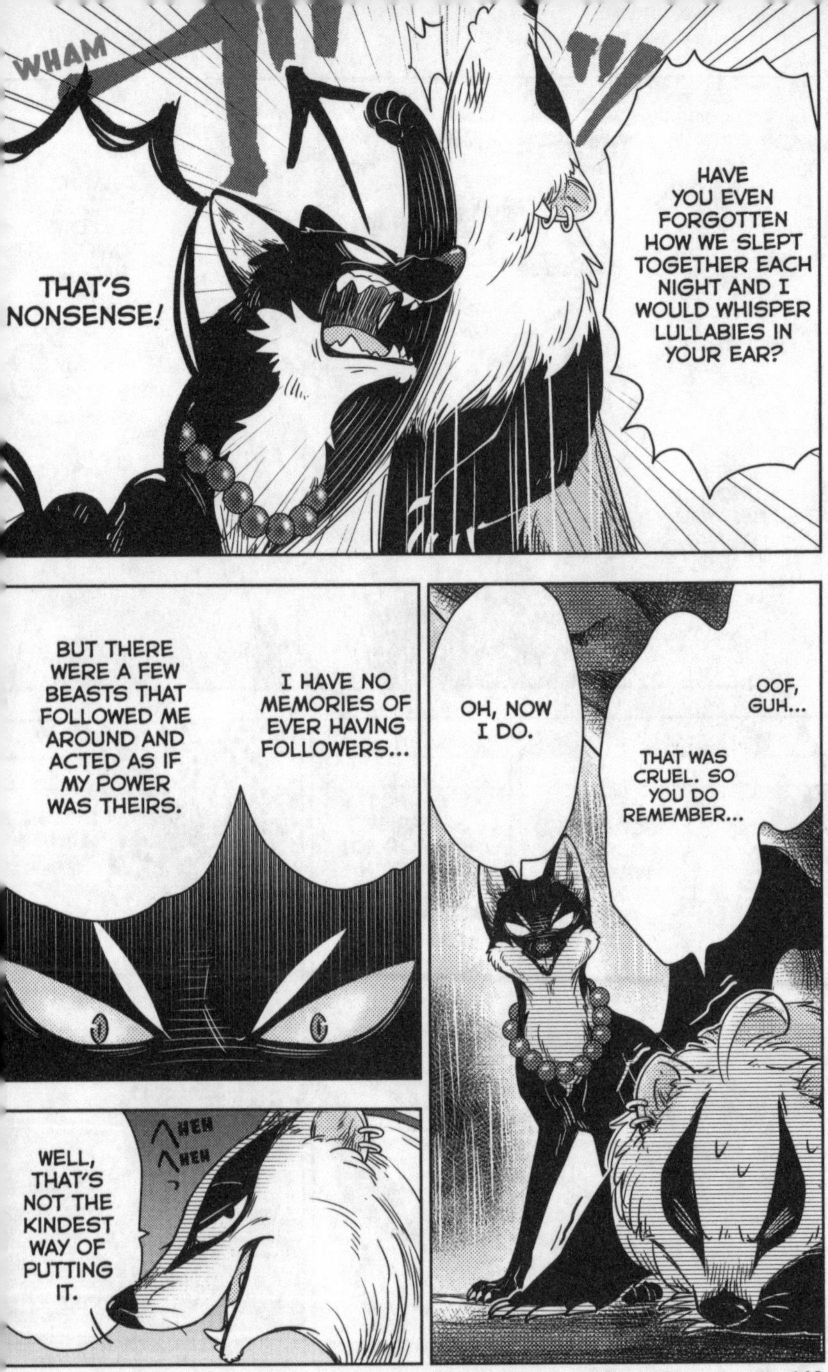
WHAM
HAVE YOU EVEN FORGOTTEN HOW WE SLEPT TOGETHER EACH NIGHT AND I WOULD WHISPER LULLABIES IN YOUR EAR?
THAT'S NONSENSE!
OOF, GUH...
THAT WAS CRUEL. SO YOU DO REMEMBER...
OH, NOW I DO.
I HAVE NO MEMORIES OF EVER HAVING FOLLOWERS...
BUT THERE WERE A FEW BEASTS THAT FOLLOWED ME AROUND AND ACTED AS IF MY POWER WAS THEIRS.
HEH
HEH
WELL, THAT'S NOT THE KINDEST WAY OF PUTTING IT.

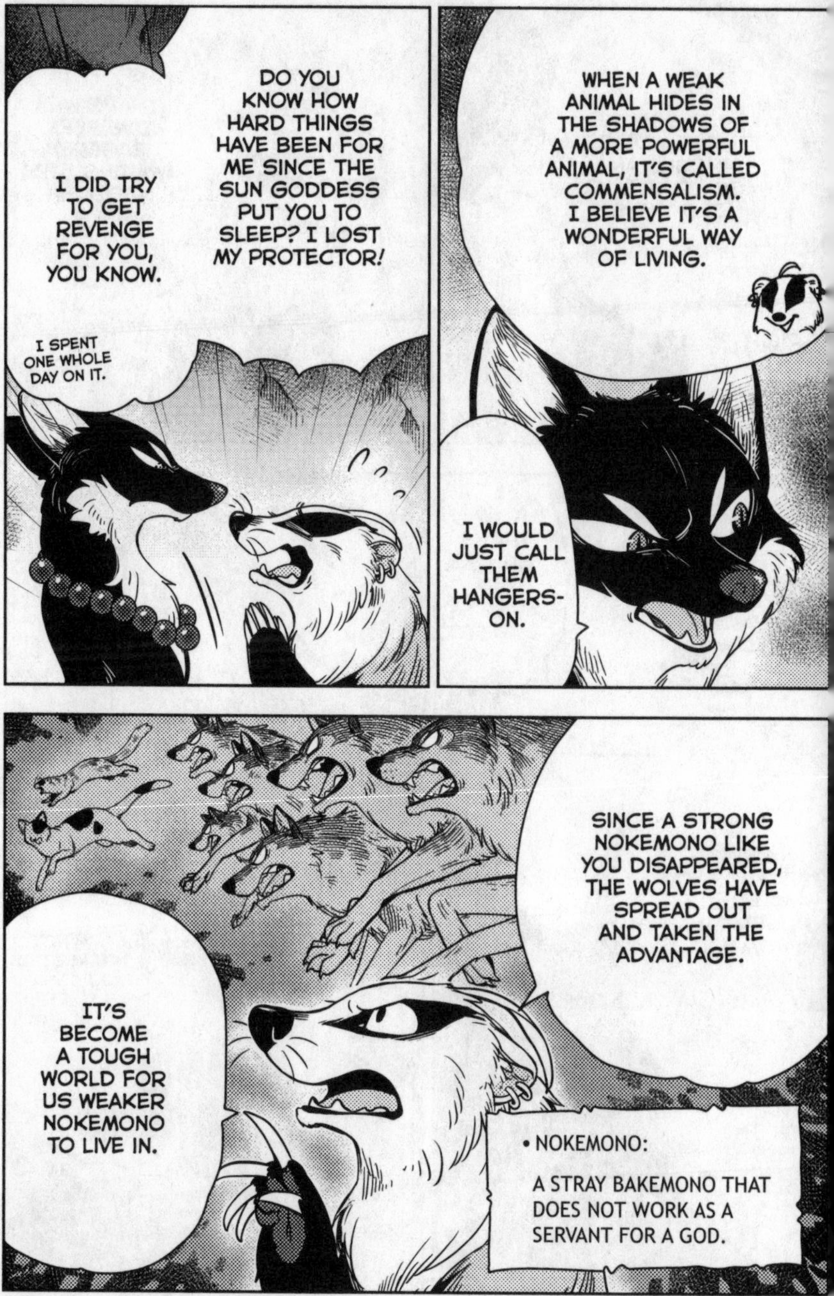
WHEN A WEAK ANIMAL HIDES IN THE SHADOWS OF A MORE POWERFUL ANIMAL, IT'S CALLED COMMENSALISM. I BELIEVE IT'S A WONDERFUL WAY OF LIVING.
I WOULD JUST CALL THEM HANGERS-ON.
DO YOU KNOW HOW HARD THINGS HAVE BEEN FOR ME SINCE THE SUN GODDESS PUT YOU TO SLEEP? I LOST MY PROTECTOR!
I DID TRY TO GET REVENGE FOR YOU, YOU KNOW.
I SPENT ONE WHOLE DAY ON IT.
SINCE A STRONG NOKEMONO LIKE YOU DISAPPEARED, THE WOLVES HAVE SPREAD OUT AND TAKEN THE ADVANTAGE.
IT'S BECOME A TOUGH WORLD FOR US WEAKER NOKEMONO TO LIVE IN.
• NOKEMONO:
A STRAY BAKEMONO THAT DOES NOT WORK AS A SERVANT FOR A GOD.

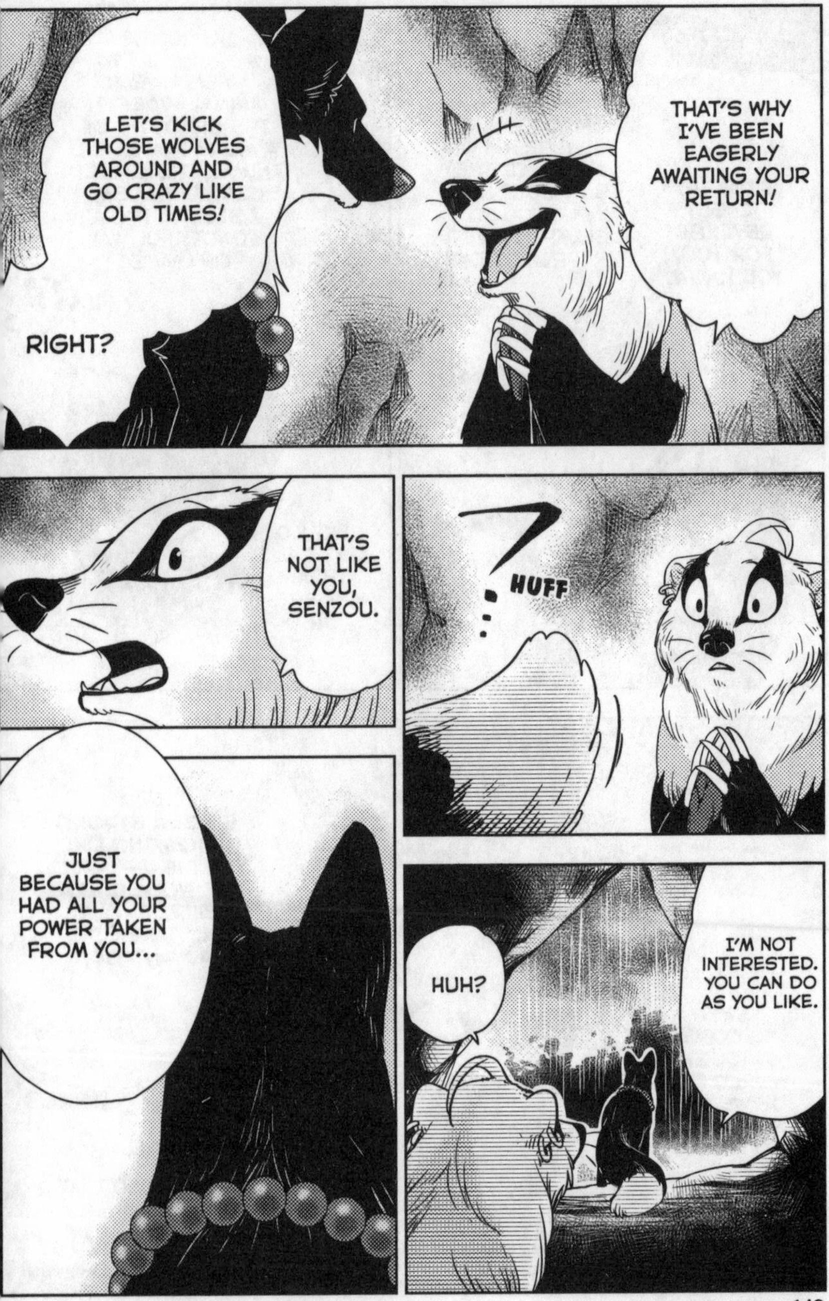
THAT'S WHY I'VE BEEN EAGERLY AWAITING YOUR RETURN!
LET'S KICK THOSE WOLVES AROUND AND GO CRAZY LIKE OLD TIMES!
RIGHT?
HUFF
I'M NOT INTERESTED. YOU CAN DO AS YOU LIKE.
HUH?
THAT'S NOT LIKE YOU, SENZOU.
JUST BECAUSE YOU HAD ALL YOUR POWER TAKEN FROM YOU...

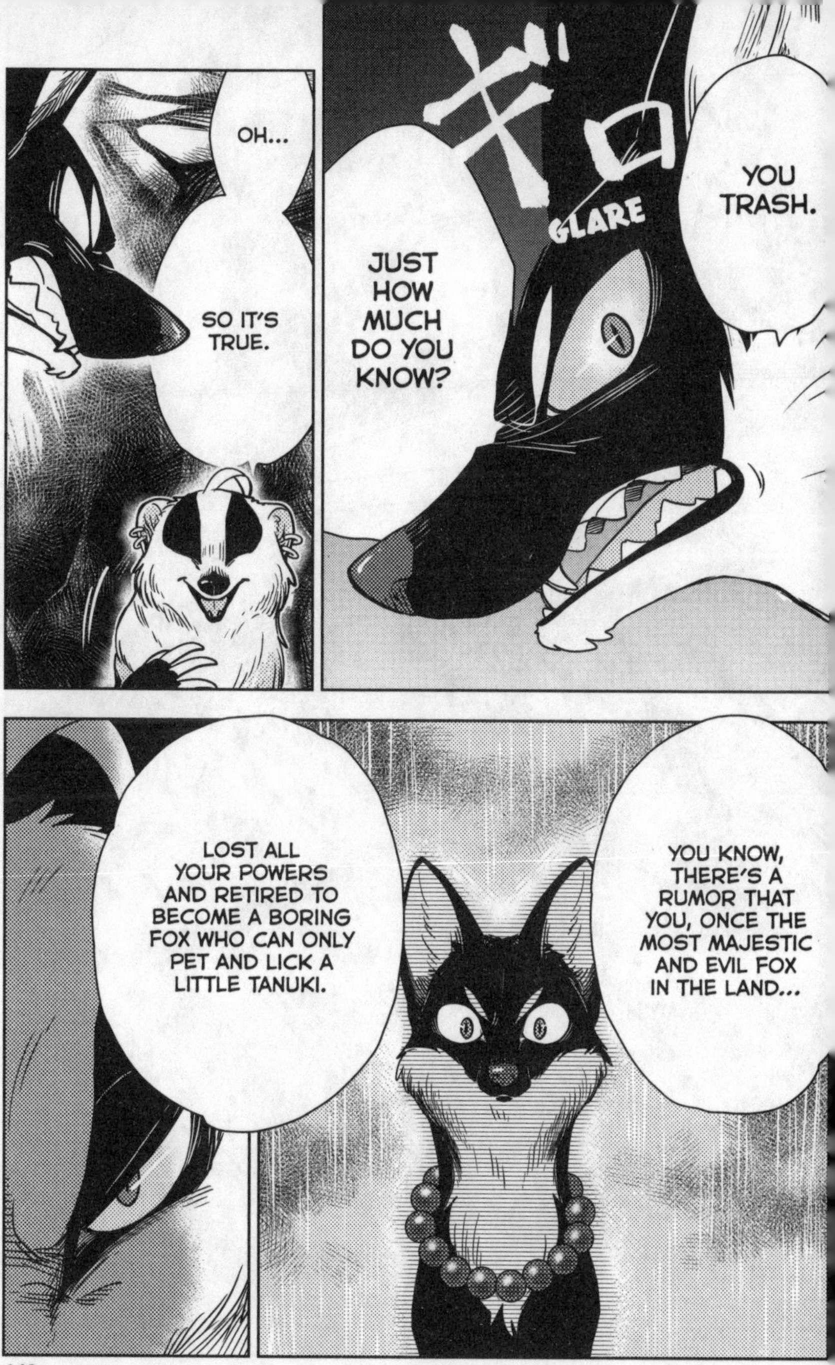
YOU TRASH.
ギロ
GLARE
JUST HOW MUCH DO YOU KNOW?
OH...
SO IT'S TRUE.
YOU KNOW, THERE'S A RUMOR THAT YOU, ONCE THE MOST MAJESTIC AND EVIL FOX IN THE LAND...
LOST ALL YOUR POWERS AND RETIRED TO BECOME A BORING FOX WHO CAN ONLY PET AND LICK A LITTLE TANUKI.

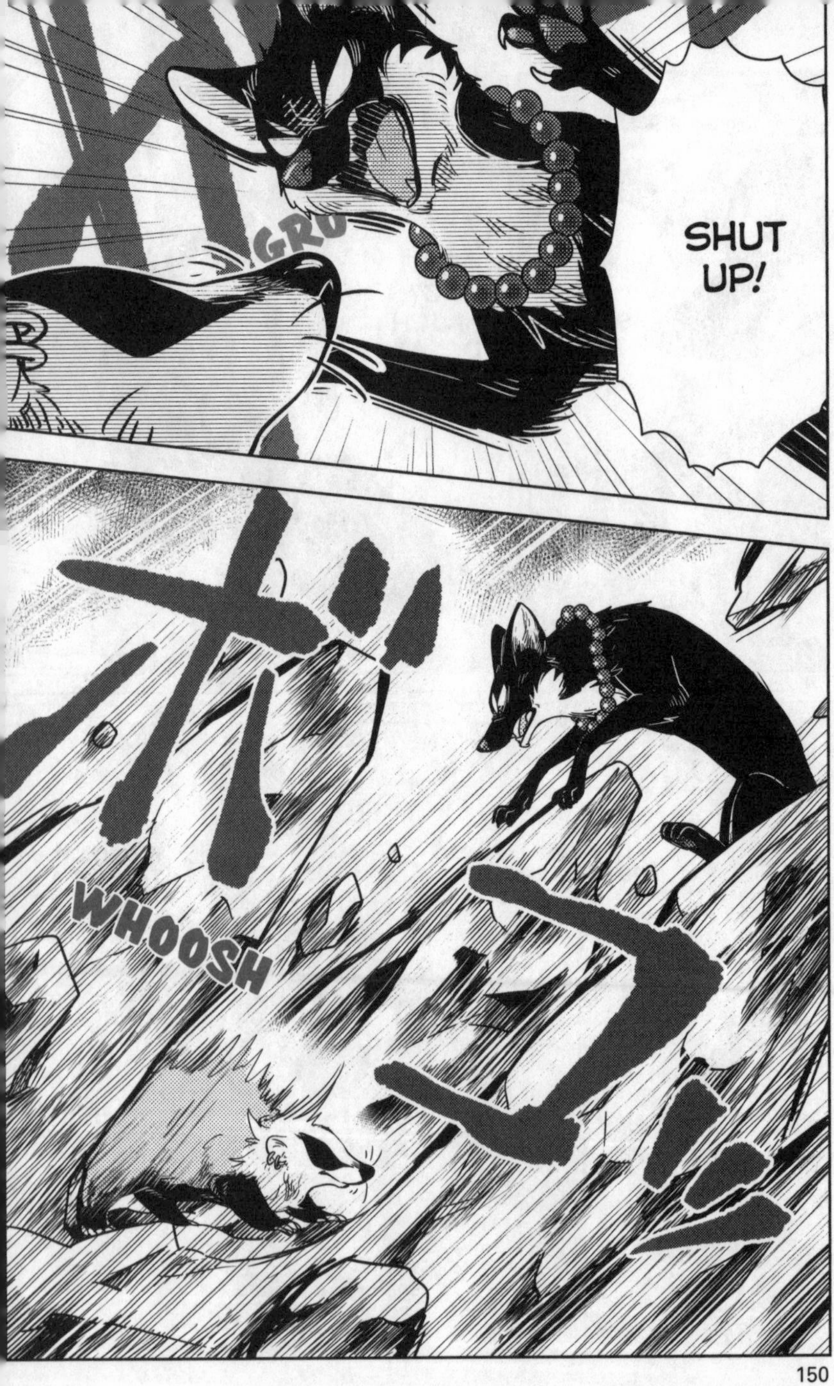
SHUT UP!
GRU
WHOOSH

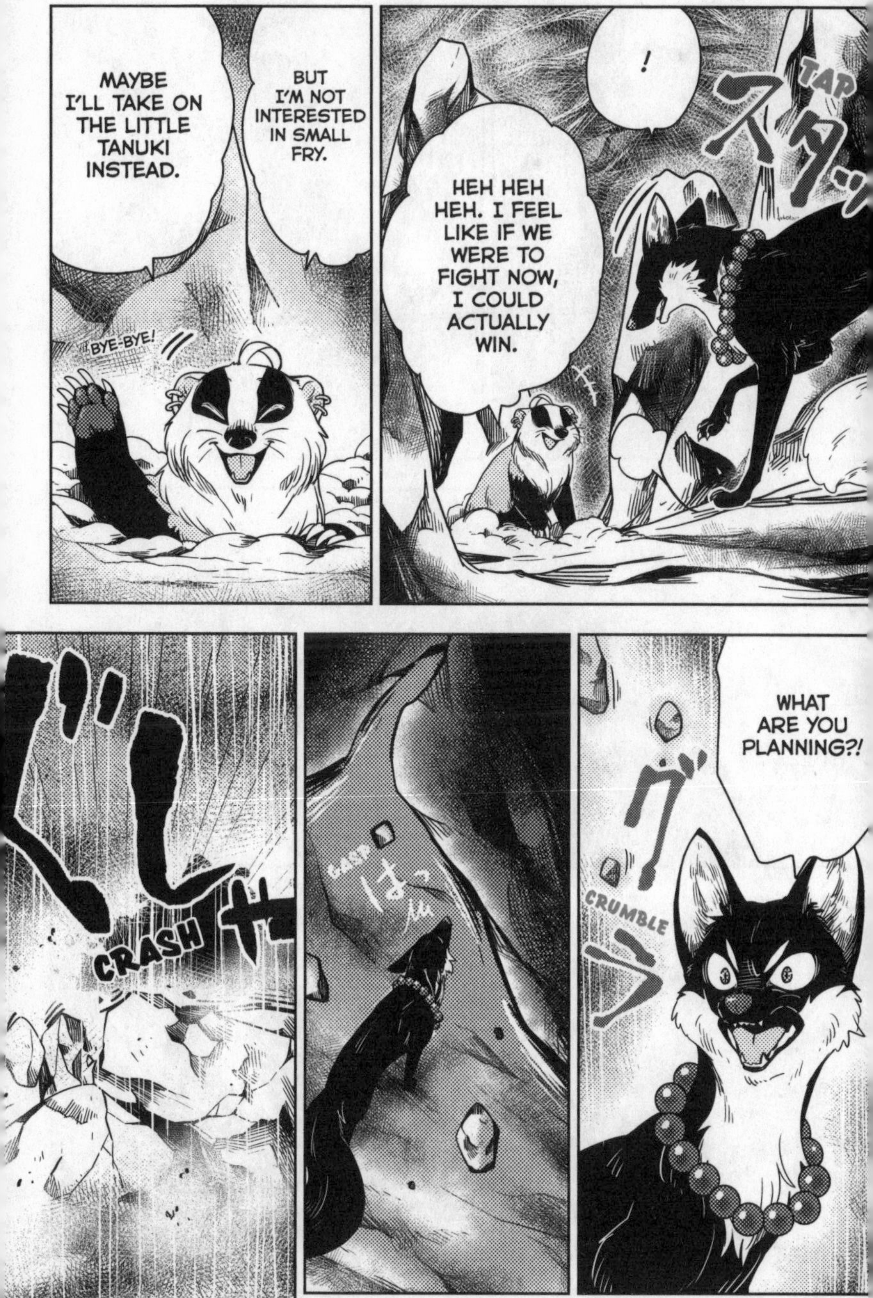
!
TAP
HEH HEH HEH. I FEEL LIKE IF WE WERE TO FIGHT NOW, I COULD ACTUALLY WIN.
BUT I'M NOT INTERESTED IN SMALL FRY.
MAYBE I'LL TAKE ON THE LITTLE TANUKI INSTEAD.
BYE-BYE!
WHAT ARE YOU PLANNING?!
CRUMBLE
GASP
CRASH

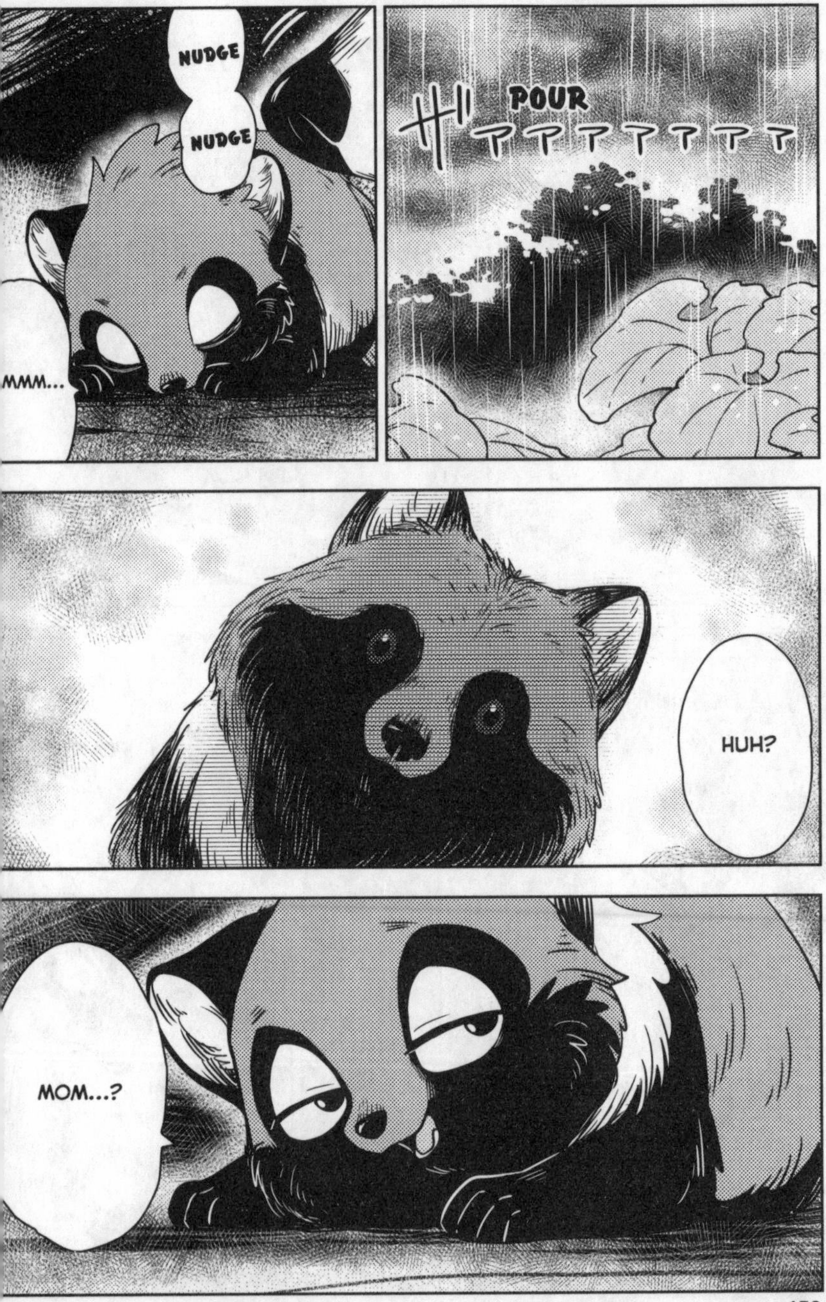
ザアアアアアアア
POUR
NUDGE
NUDGE
MMM...
HUH?
MOM...?

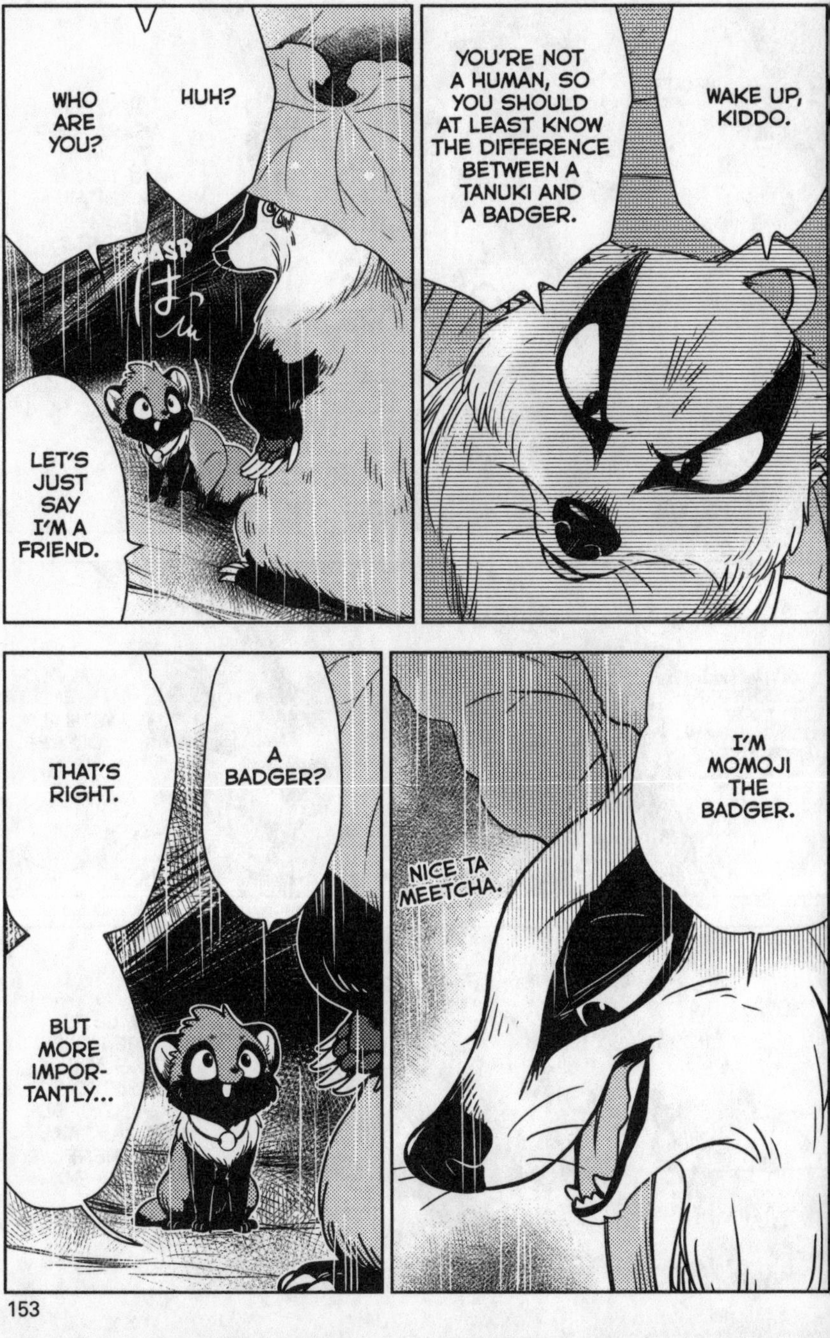
WAKE UP, KIDDO.
YOU'RE NOT A HUMAN, SO YOU SHOULD AT LEAST KNOW THE DIFFERENCE BETWEEN A TANUKI AND A BADGER.
HUH?
WHO ARE YOU?
GASP
はっ
LET'S JUST SAY I'M A FRIEND.
I'M MOMOJI THE BADGER.
NICE TA MEETCHA.
A BADGER?
THAT'S RIGHT.
BUT MORE IMPOR-TANTLY...

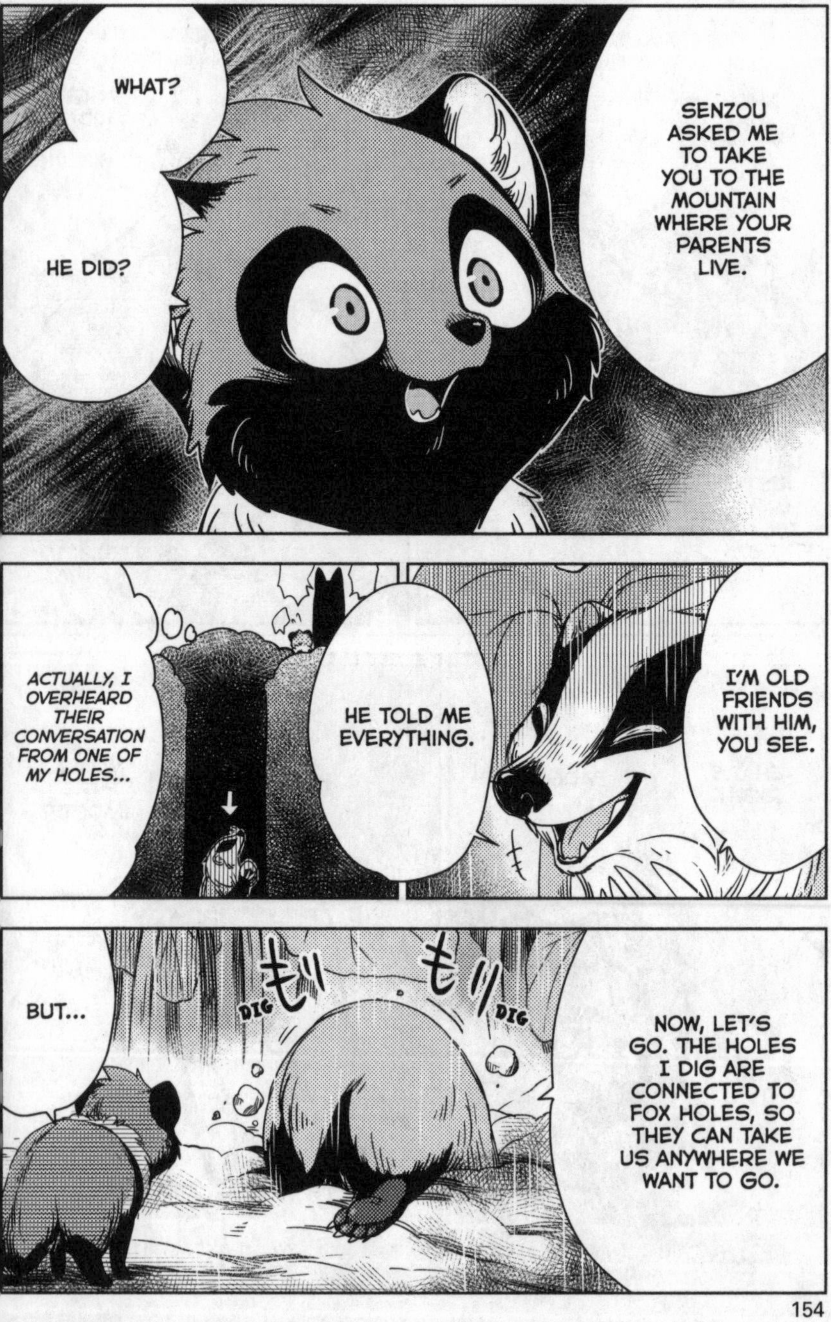
SENZOU ASKED ME TO TAKE YOU TO THE MOUNTAIN WHERE YOUR PARENTS LIVE.
WHAT?
HE DID?
I'M OLD FRIENDS WITH HIM, YOU SEE.
HE TOLD ME EVERYTHING.
ACTUALLY, I OVERHEARD THEIR CONVERSATION FROM ONE OF MY HOLES...
NOW, LET'S GO. THE HOLES I DIG ARE CONNECTED TO FOX HOLES, SO THEY CAN TAKE US ANYWHERE WE WANT TO GO.
もり DIG
もり DIG
BUT...

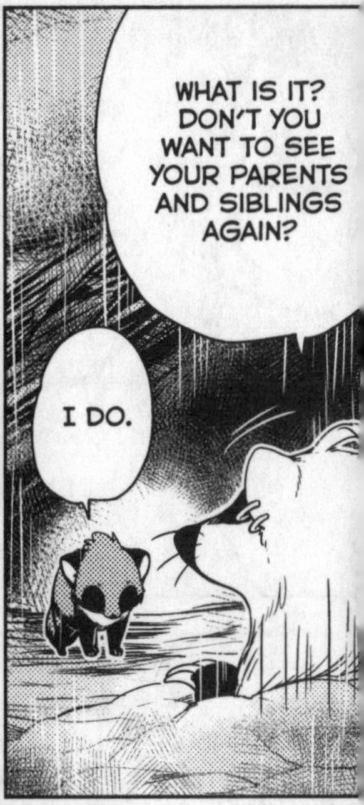
WHAT IS IT? DON'T YOU WANT TO SEE YOUR PARENTS AND SIBLINGS AGAIN?
I DO.

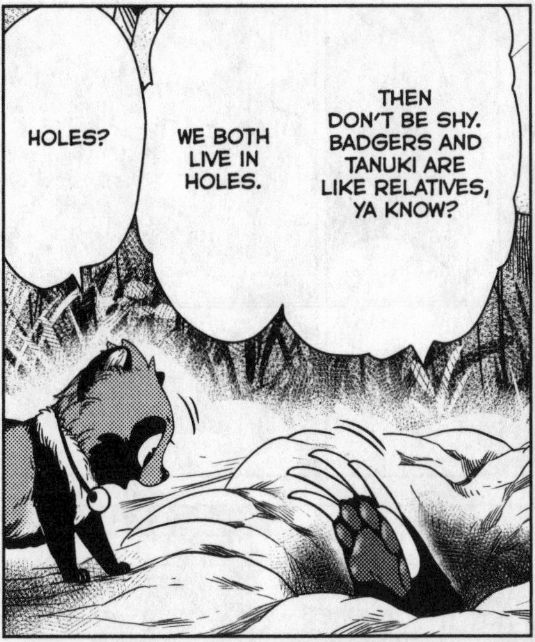
THEN DON'T BE SHY. BADGERS AND TANUKI ARE LIKE RELATIVES, YA KNOW?
WE BOTH LIVE IN HOLES.
HOLES?

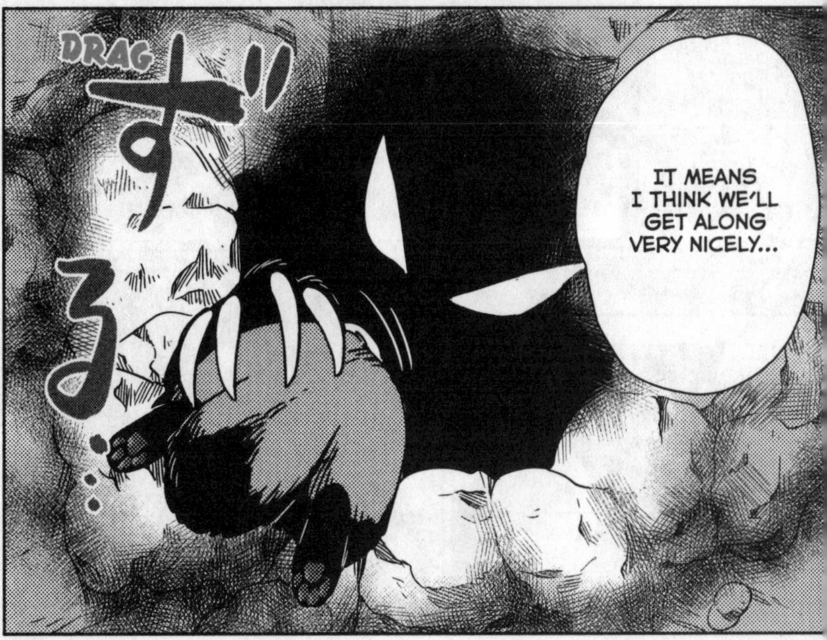
IT MEANS I THINK WE'LL GET ALONG VERY NICELY...
DRAG
ずる

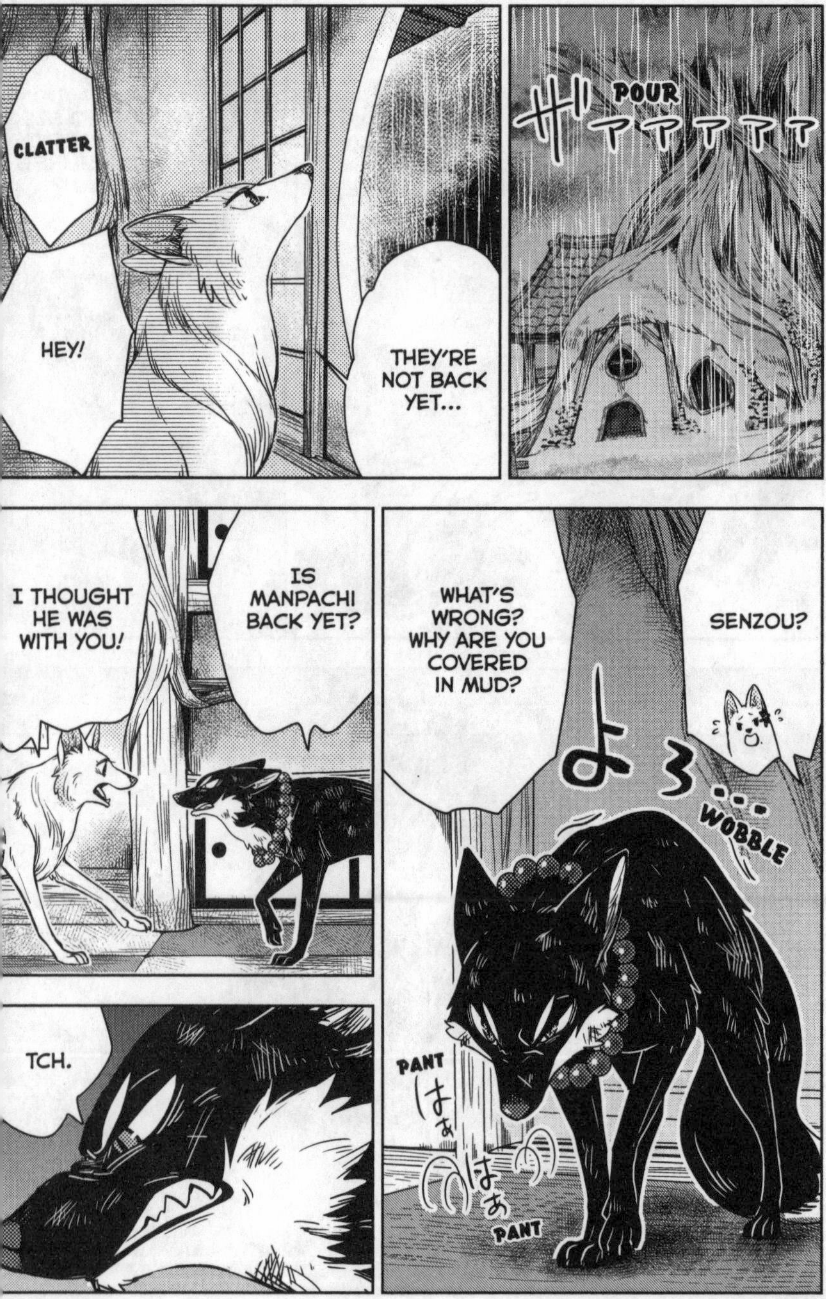
ザァァァァァァ
POUR
THEY'RE NOT BACK YET...
CLATTER
HEY!
SENZOU?
WHAT'S WRONG? WHY ARE YOU COVERED IN MUD?
よろ...
WOBBLE
PANT
はぁ
はぁ
PANT
IS MANPACHI BACK YET?
I THOUGHT HE WAS WITH YOU!
TCH.

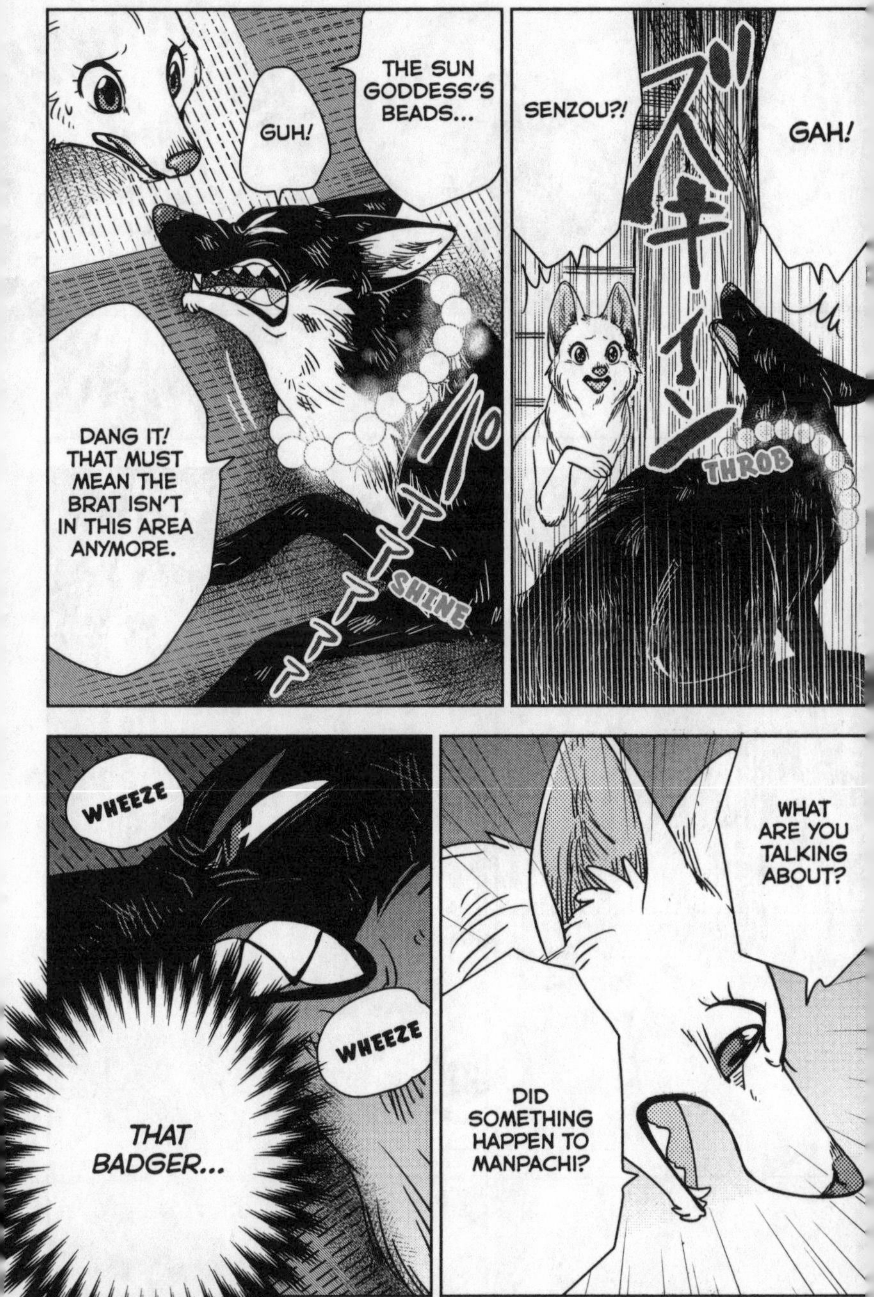
GAH!
SENZOU?!
THROB
THE SUN GODDESS'S BEADS...
GUH!
DANG IT! THAT MUST MEAN THE BRAT ISN'T IN THIS AREA ANYMORE.
SHINE
WHAT ARE YOU TALKING ABOUT?
DID SOMETHING HAPPEN TO MANPACHI?
WHEEZE
WHEEZE
THAT BADGER...

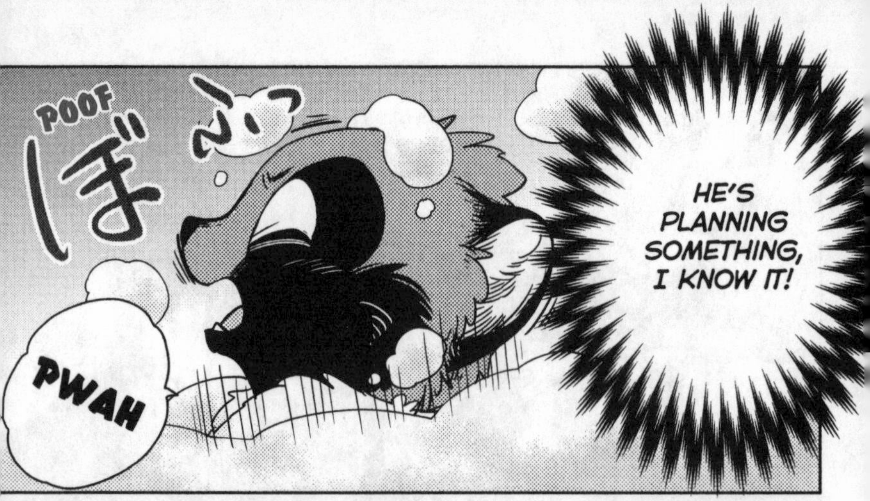
HE'S PLANNING SOMETHING, I KNOW IT!
POOF
ぼふっ
PWAH

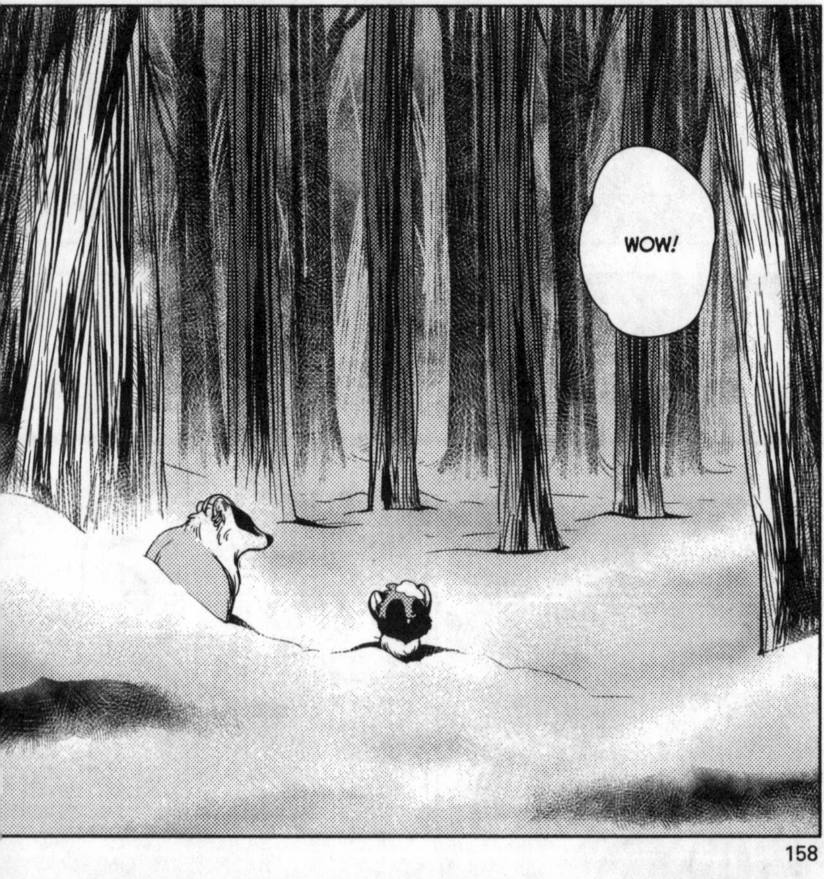
WOW!

The Bakemono Field Guide

Bakemujina
(Badger)

They are not as famous as kitsune or tanuki, but they're just as good at transforming. Apparently in the past, they were often confused for tanuki and a distinction was rarely made. Scientifically, tanuki are classified as canidae and badgers are classified as mustelids.

#6

The Fox & Little Tanuki

KORISENMAN

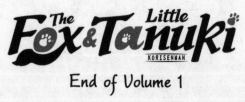

End of Volume 1

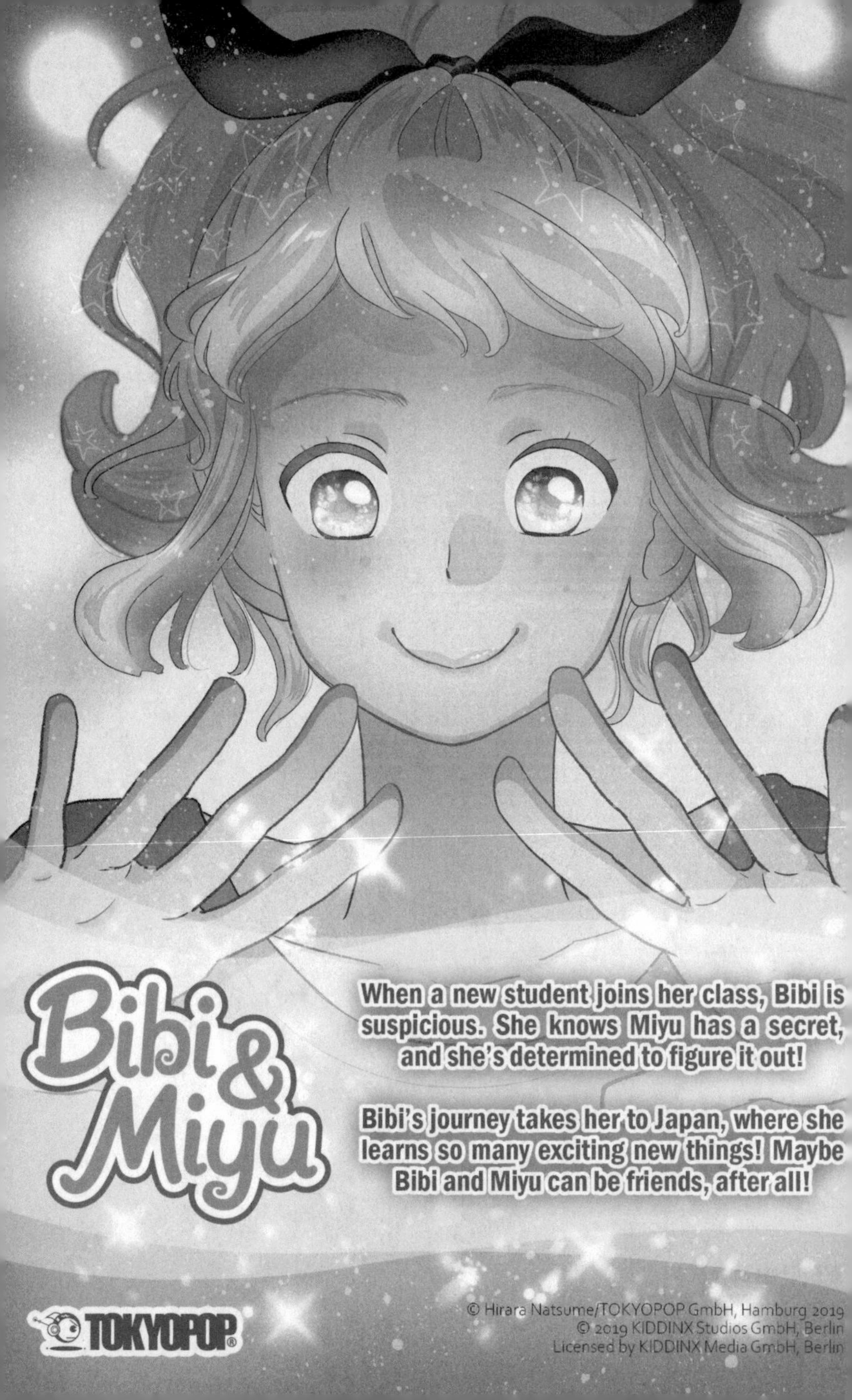

Bibi & Miyu

When a new student joins her class, Bibi is suspicious. She knows Miyu has a secret, and she's determined to figure it out!

Bibi's journey takes her to Japan, where she learns so many exciting new things! Maybe Bibi and Miyu can be friends, after all!

TOKYOPOP®

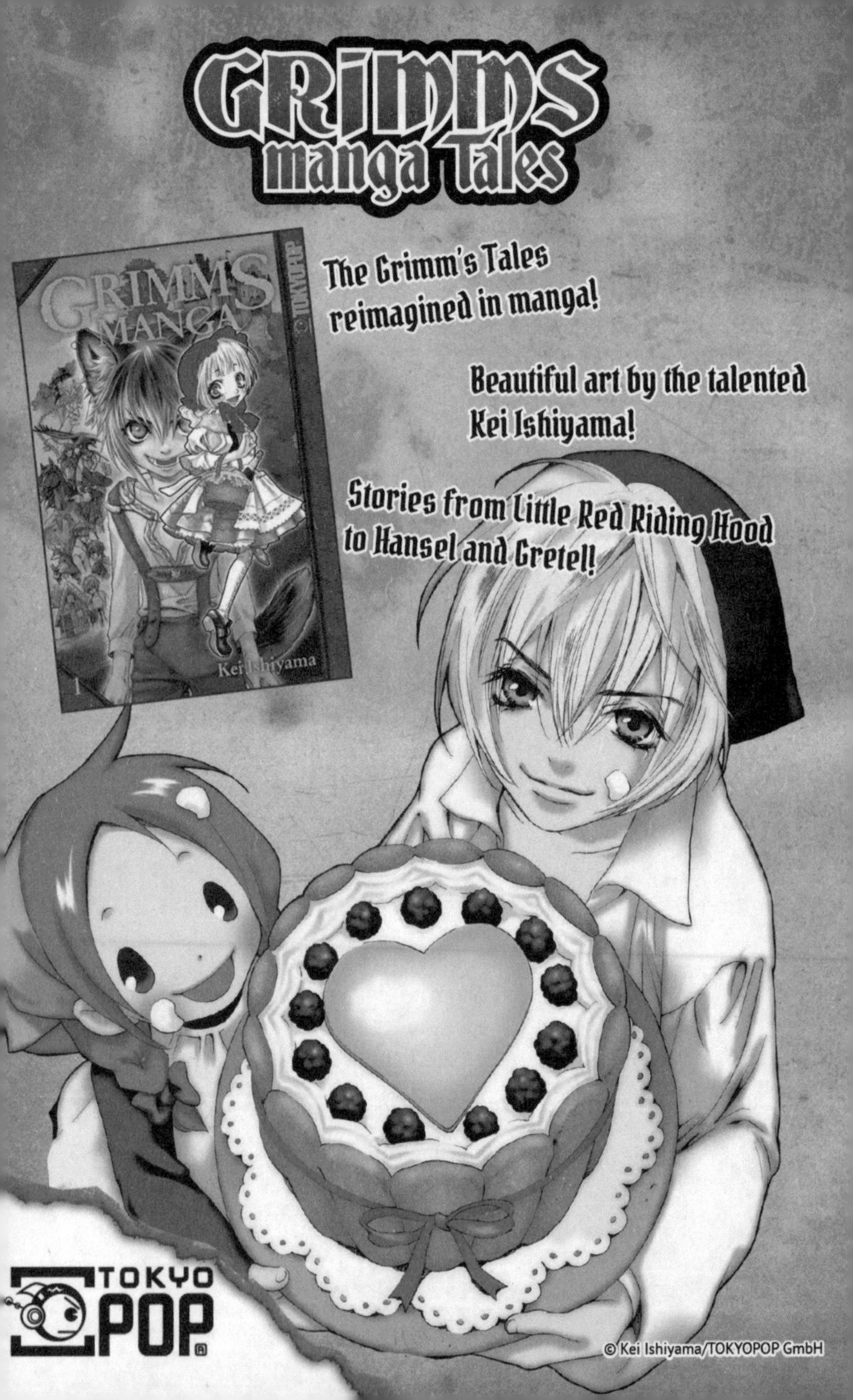
GRIMMS manga Tales
GRIMMS MANGA
TOKYOPOP
Kei Ishiyama
1
The Grimm's Tales reimagined in manga!
Beautiful art by the talented Kei Ishiyama!
Stories from Little Red Riding Hood to Hansel and Gretel!
TOKYO POP
© Kei Ishiyama/TOKYOPOP GmbH

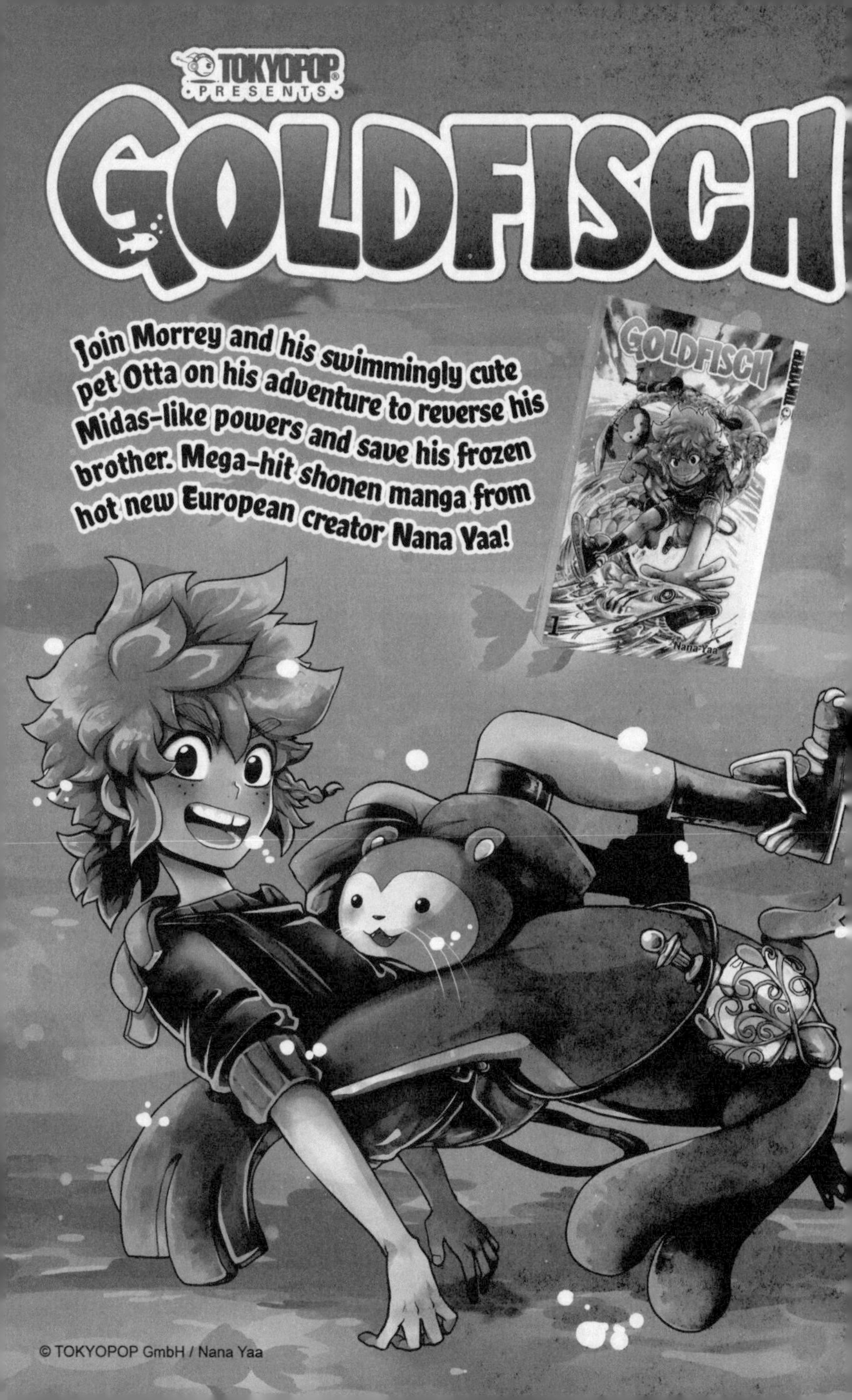
TOKYOPOP PRESENTS
GOLDFISCH
Join Morrey and his swimmingly cute pet Otta on his adventure to reverse his Midas-like powers and save his frozen brother. Mega-hit shonen manga from hot new European creator Nana Yaa!
GOLDFISCH
TOKYOPOP
1
Nana Yaa
© TOKYOPOP GmbH / Nana Yaa

Disney Marie — MIRIYA & MARIE

- ★ **Inspired by the characters from Disney's The Aristocats**
- ★ **Learn facts about Paris and Japan!**
- ★ **Adorable original shojo story**
- ★ **Full color manga**

Even though the wealthy young girl Miriya has almost everything she could ever need, what she really wants is the one thing money can't buy: her missing parents. But this year, she gets an extra special birthday gift when Marie, a magical white kitten, appears and whisks her away to Paris! Learning the art of magic is one thing, but getting to eat the tastiest French pastries and wear the most beautiful fashion takes Miriya and Marie's journey to a whole new level!

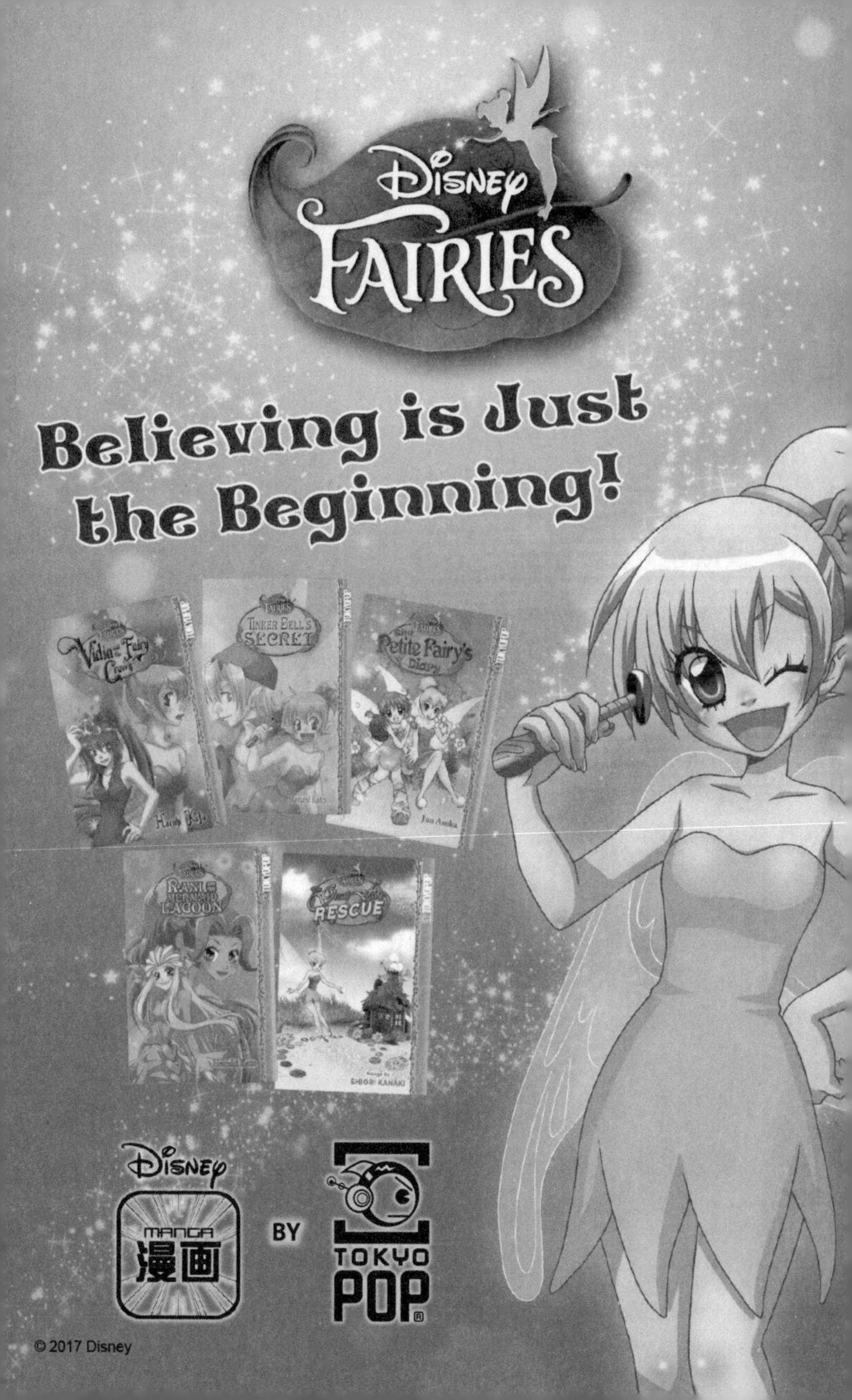
Disney Fairies
Believing is Just the Beginning!
Tinker Bell's Secret
Petite Fairy's
Rescue
Shiori Kanaki
Disney
MANGA
漫画
BY
TOKYO POP
© 2017 Disney

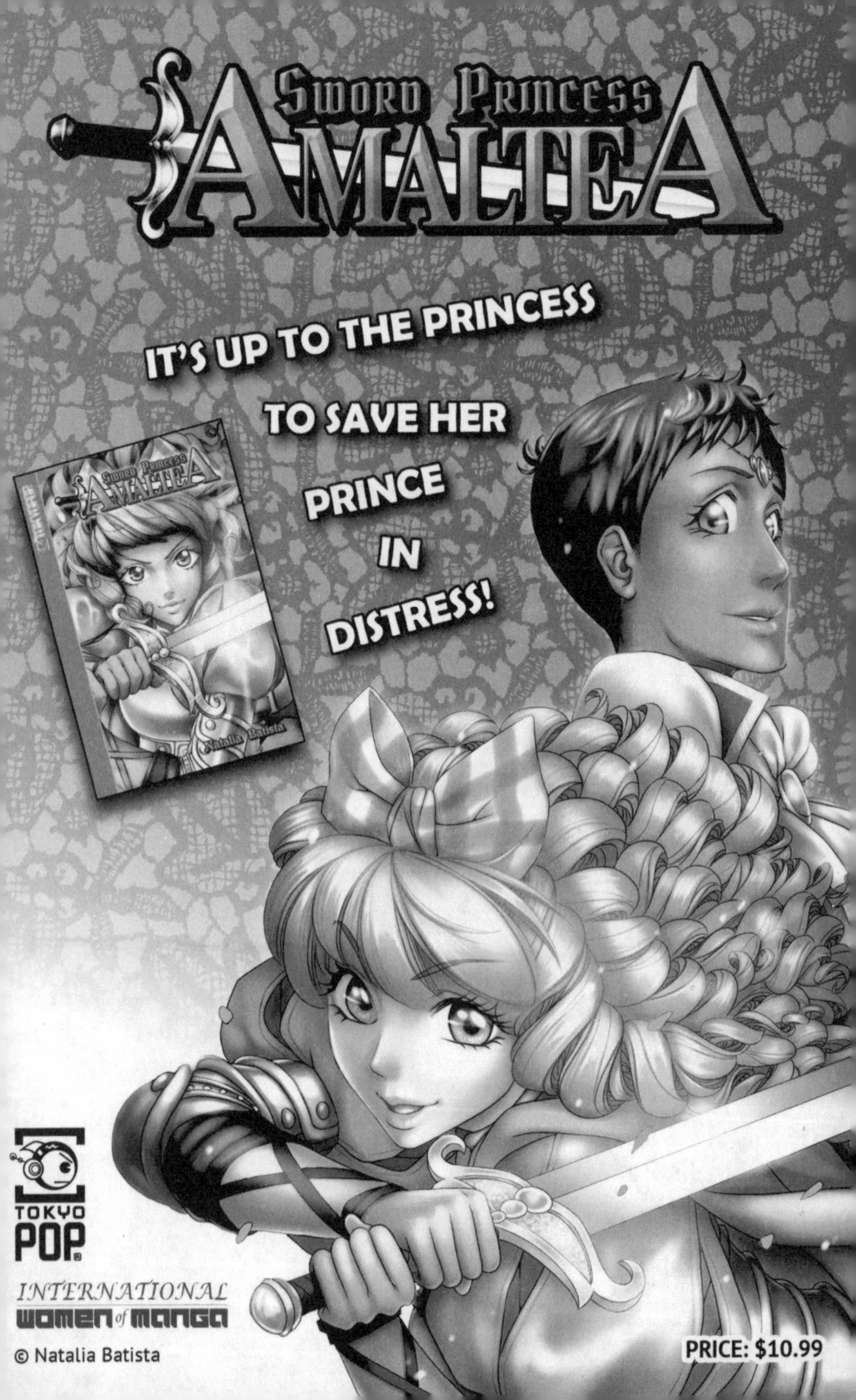

SWORD PRINCESS AMALTEA
IT'S UP TO THE PRINCESS TO SAVE HER PRINCE IN DISTRESS!
SWORD PRINCESS AMALTEA
Natalia Batista
TOKYO POP
INTERNATIONAL women of manga
© Natalia Batista
PRICE: $10.99

DISNEY DESCENDANTS

Full color manga trilogy based on the hit Disney Channel original movie

Adapted By Jason Muell

THE ROTTEN TO THE CORE TRILOGY
THE COMPLETE COLLECTION

Art By Natsuki Minami

Based on the beloved Disney Channel movie, *Descendants*. The children of the most frightening Disney villains (VKs) are invited to attend the elite academy of Auradon Prep to learn to be good. But the VKs have ulterior motives to steal the fairy godmother's wand and free their parents. Join Mal, Evie, Carlos, and Jay on this epic Disney adventure. The Complete Edition combines all THREE volumes of the original trilogy in an extra large size!

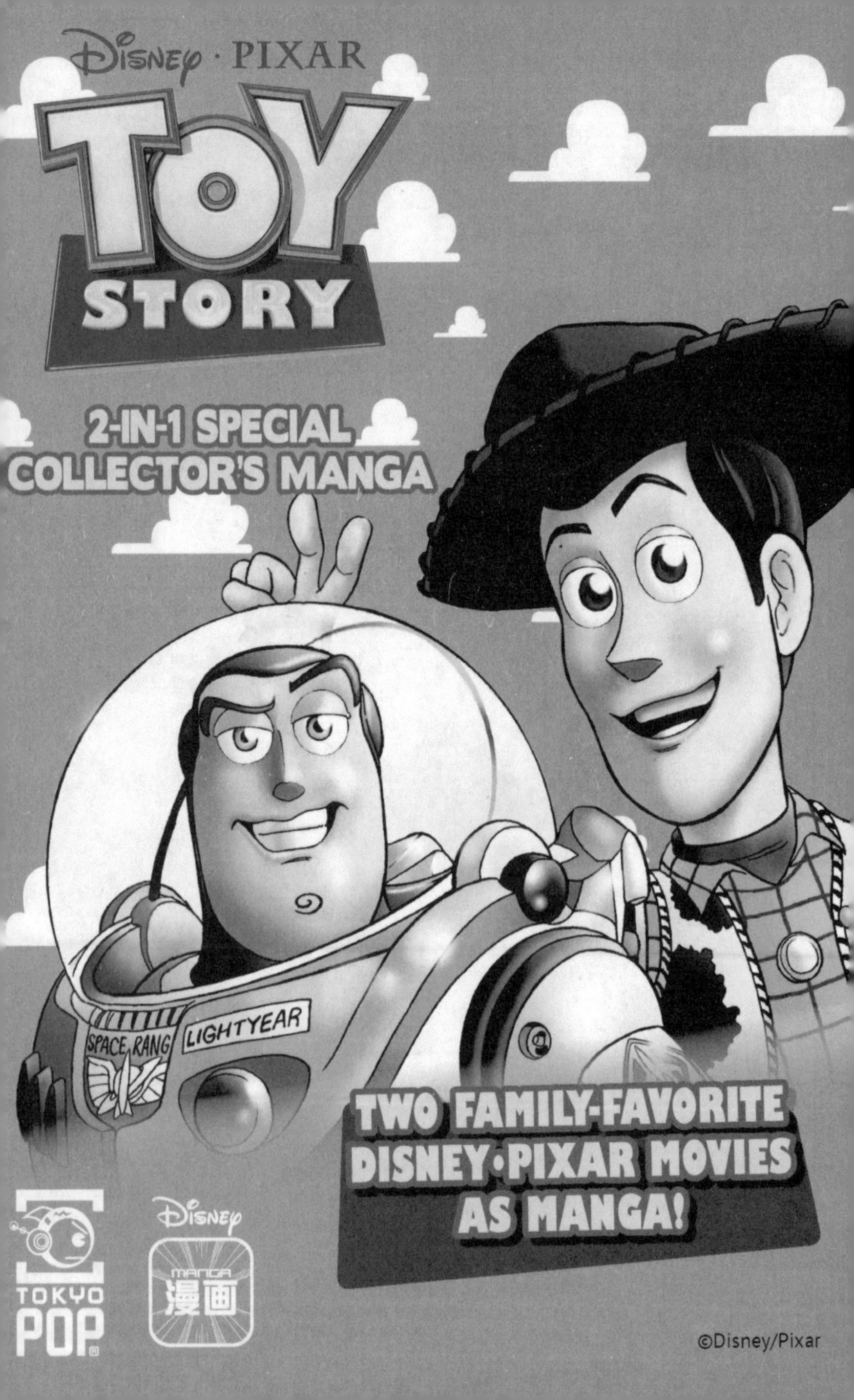
Disney · PIXAR
TOY STORY
2-IN-1 SPECIAL COLLECTOR'S MANGA
SPACE RANG
LIGHTYEAR
TWO FAMILY-FAVORITE DISNEY·PIXAR MOVIES AS MANGA!
TOKYO POP
Disney
MANGA 漫画
©Disney/Pixar

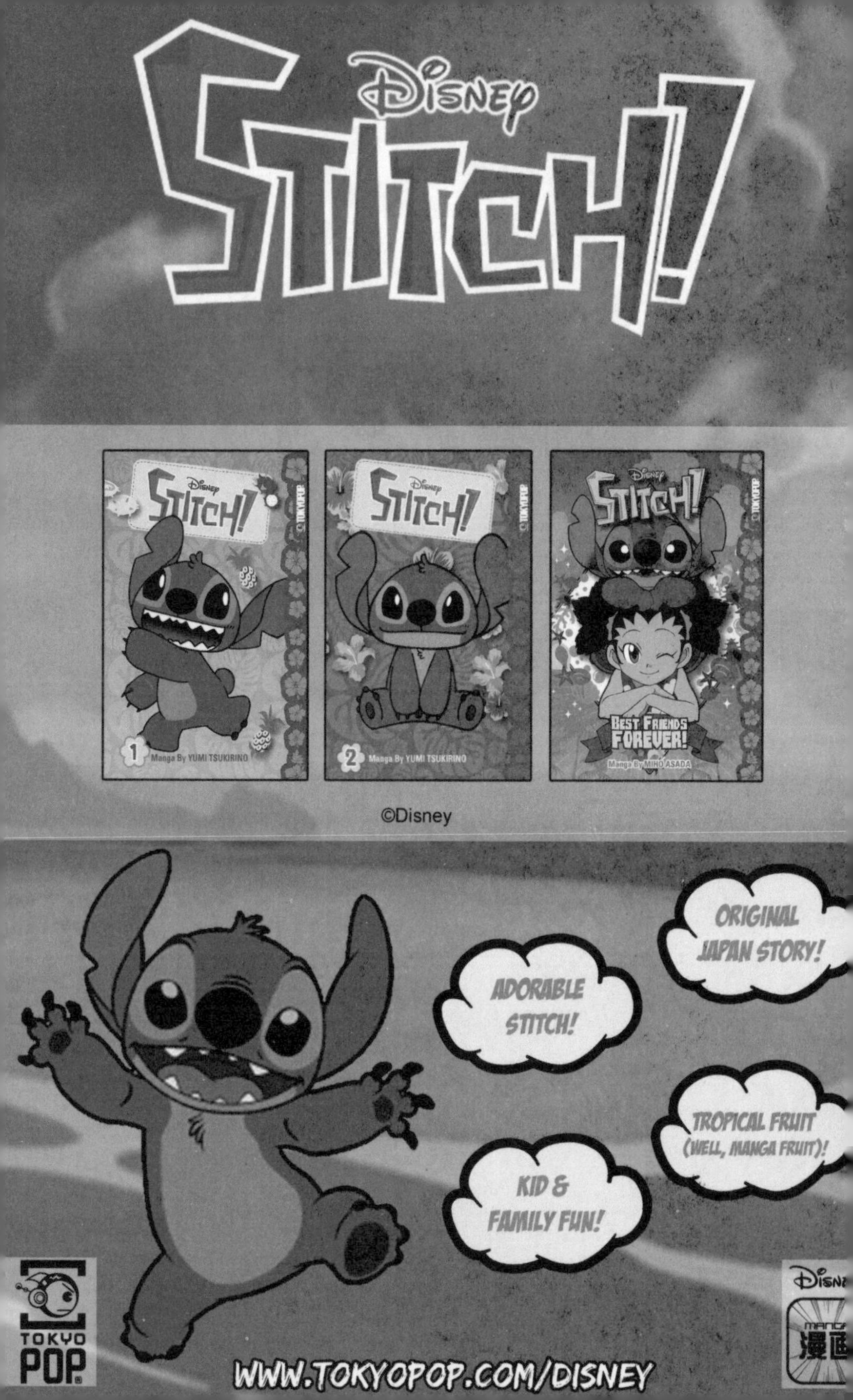

Disney
STITCH!
Disney STITCH!
1 Manga By YUMI TSUKIRINO
Disney STITCH!
2 Manga By YUMI TSUKIRINO
Disney STITCH!
BEST FRIENDS FOREVER!
Manga By MIHO ASADA
©Disney
ORIGINAL JAPAN STORY!
ADORABLE STITCH!
TROPICAL FRUIT (WELL, MANGA FRUIT)!
KID & FAMILY FUN!
TOKYO POP
WWW.TOKYOPOP.COM/DISNEY

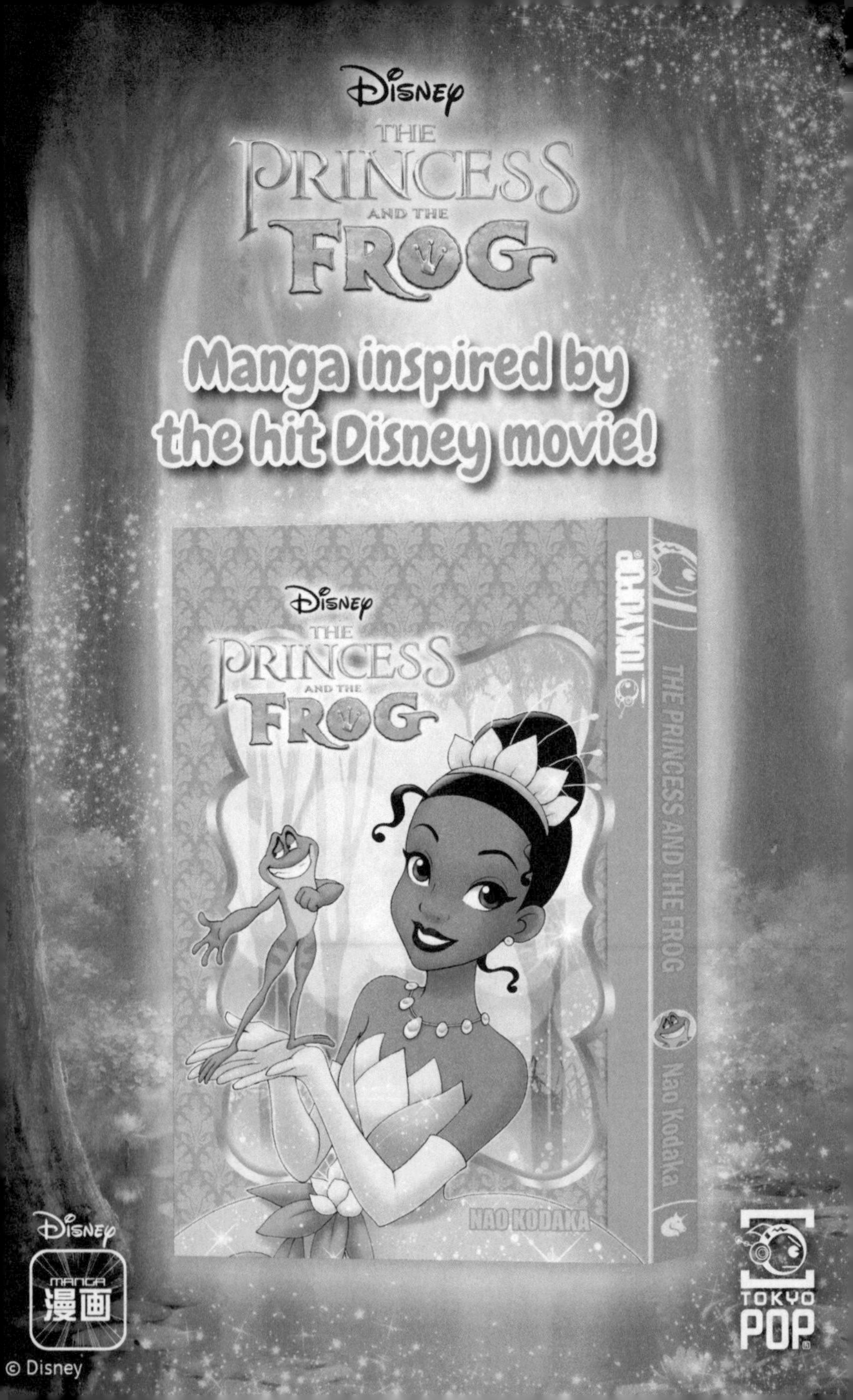
Disney
THE PRINCESS AND THE FROG
Manga inspired by the hit Disney movie!
Disney
THE PRINCESS AND THE FROG
TOKYOPOP
THE PRINCESS AND THE FROG
Nao Kodaka
NAO KODAKA
Disney
MANGA
漫画
TOKYO POP
© Disney

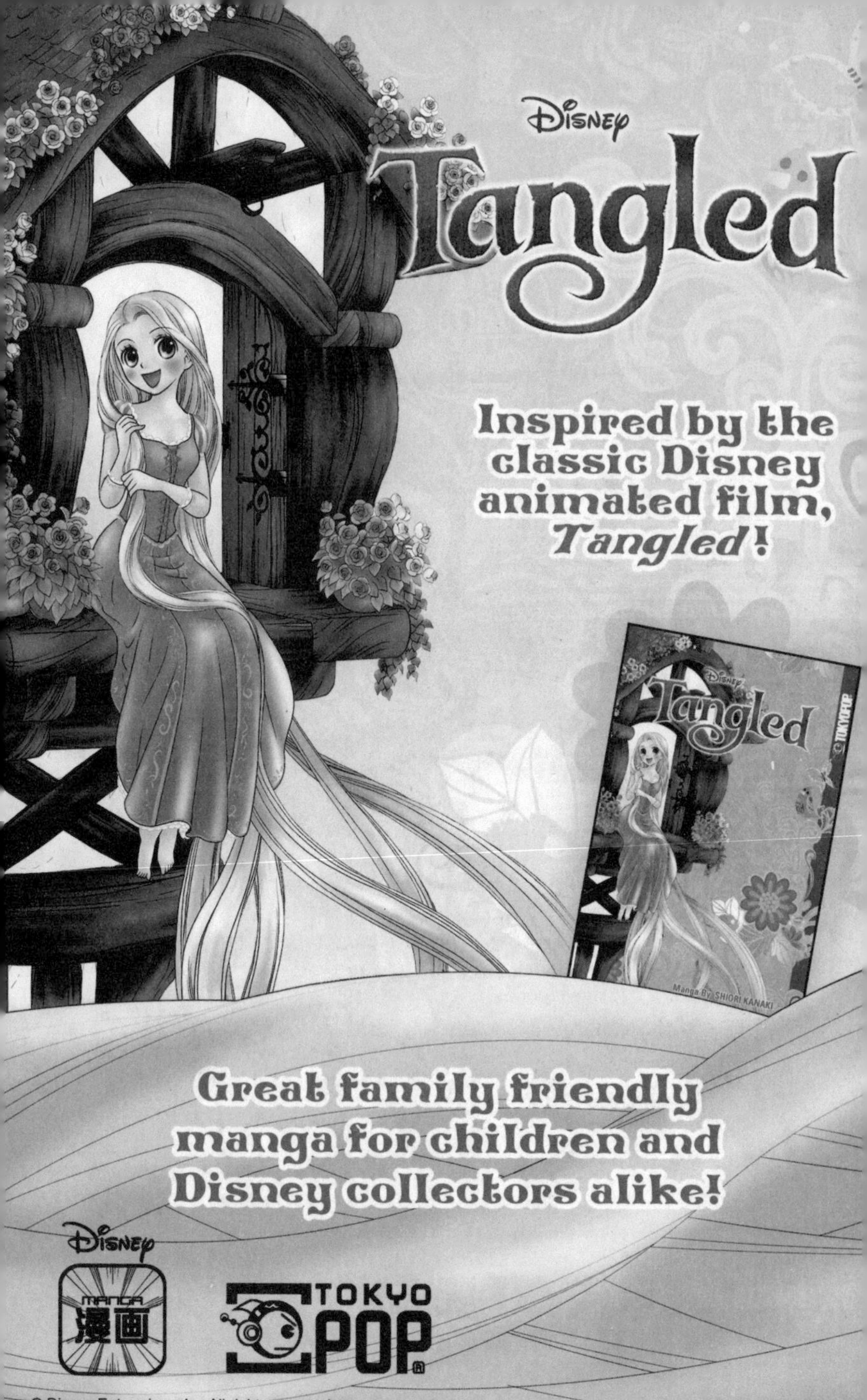
Disney
Tangled
Inspired by the classic Disney animated film, *Tangled*!
Disney
Tangled
TOKYOPOP
Manga By: SHIORI KANAKI
Great family friendly manga for children and Disney collectors alike!
Disney
MANGA
漫画
TOKYO POP

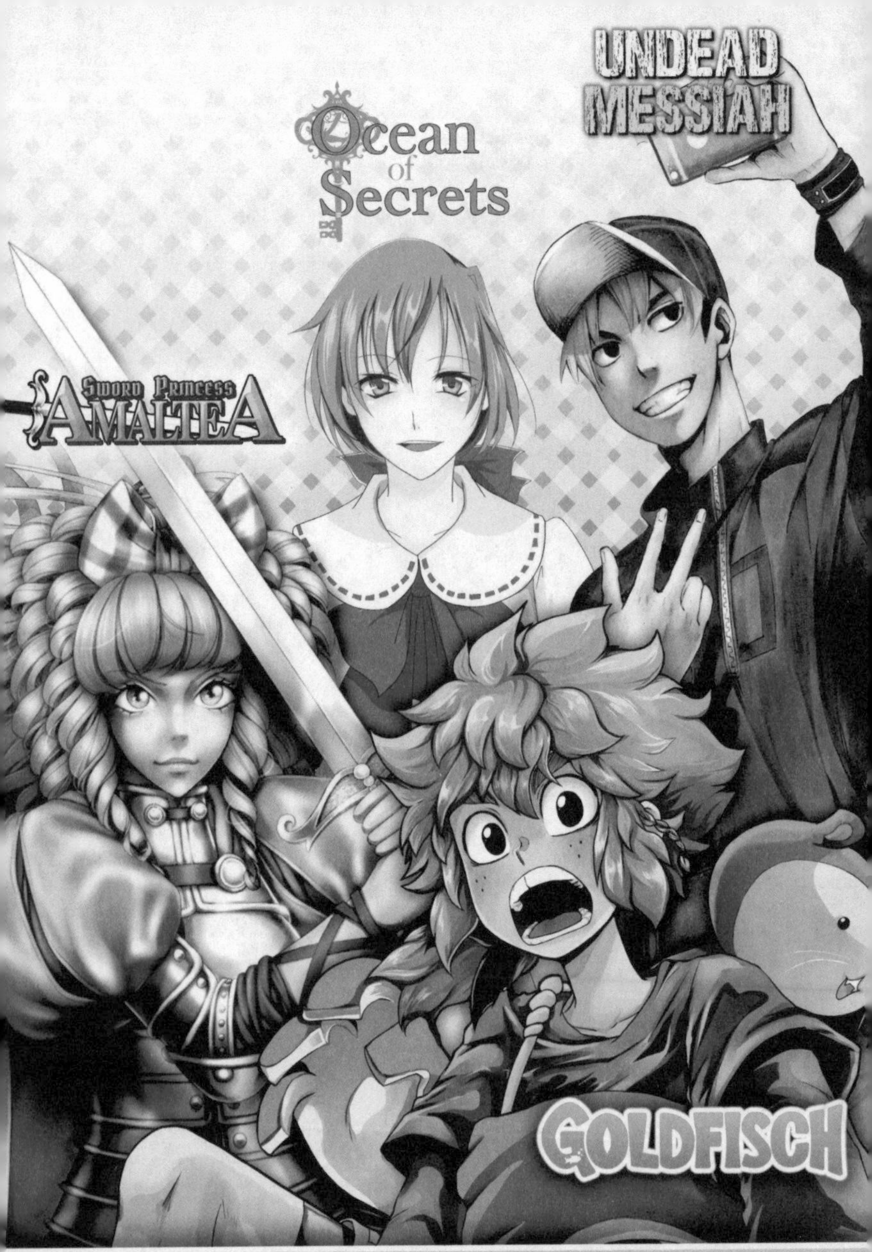
UNDEAD MESSIAH
Ocean of Secrets
SWORD PRINCESS AMALTEA
GOLDFISCH

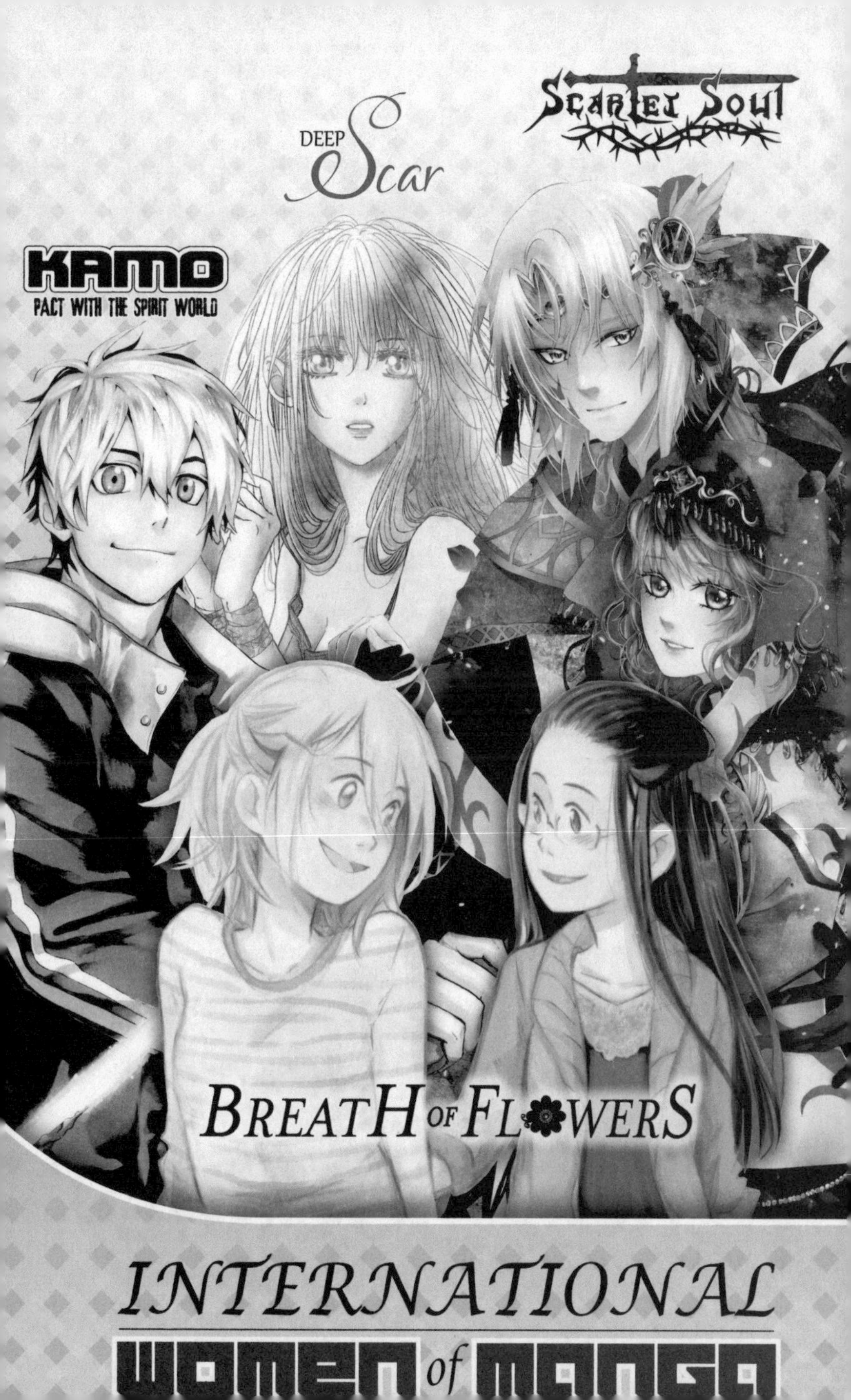

DEEP Scar
Scarlet Soul
KAMO
PACT WITH THE SPIRIT WORLD
BREATH OF FLOWERS
INTERNATIONAL
WOMEN of MANGA

ZERO IS LOST...
CAN HE FIND HIS
WAY HOME?

Disney

TIM BURTON'S
THE
NIGHTMARE
BEFORE
CHRISTMAS

The Fox & Little Tanuki
Manga by Mi Tagawa

Editor	-	Lena Atanassova
Marketing Associate	-	Kae Winters
Technology and Digital Media Assistant	-	Phillip Hong
Translator	-	Katie Kimura
Copy Editors	-	Massiel Gutierrez
QC	-	Akiko Furuta
Licensing Specialist	-	Arika Yanaka
Graphic Design	-	Phillip Hong
Retouching and Lettering	-	Vibrraant Publishing Studio
Editor-in-Chief & Publisher	-	Stu Levy

A  Manga

TOKYOPOP and 🔘 are trademarks or registered trademarks of TOKYOPOP Inc.

TOKYOPOP Inc.
5200 W. Century Blvd. Suite 705
Los Angeles, 90045

E-mail: info@TOKYOPOP.com
Come visit us online at www.TOKYOPOP.com

f www.facebook.com/TOKYOPOP
🐦 www.twitter.com/TOKYOPOP
📌 www.pinterest.com/TOKYOPOP
📷 www.instagram.com/TOKYOPOP

KORISENMAN   First published in Japan in 2019 by MAG Garden
© 2019 Mi Tagawa   Corporation English translation rights arranged with
MAG Garden Corporation through Tuttle-Mori Agency,
Inc, Tokyo
Original cover design © Hajime Tokushige +
Bay Bridge Studios

ISBN: 978-1-4278-6318-8
First TOKYOPOP Printing: March 2020
10 9 8 7 6 5 4 3 2 1
Printed in CANADA

STOP

THIS IS THE BACK OF THE BOOK!

How do you read manga-style? It's simple! To learn, just start in the top right panel and follow the numbers:

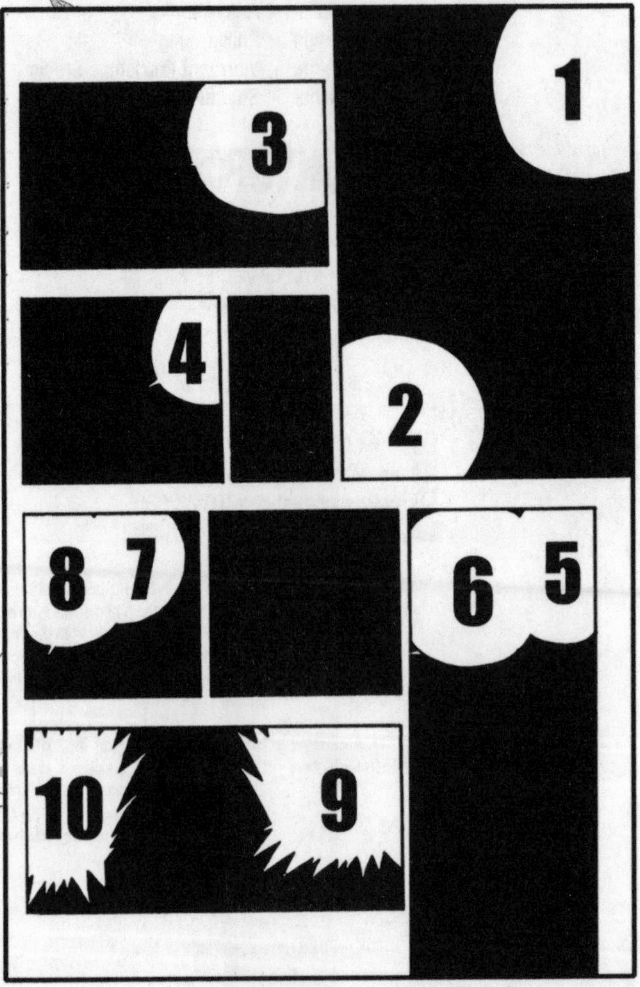
1
2
3
4
5
6
7
8
9
10